THE CALIPHATE

André Le Gallo

MOUNTAIN LAKE PRESS
Mountain Lake Park, Maryland

Also by André Le Gallo

Satan's Spy

The Red Cell

The Caliphate
Copyright 2020 André Le Gallo
Original Copyright © 2012
All Rights Reserved

Published in the United States of America
by Mountain Lake Press

Cover design by Jutta Medina

ISBN 979-8-6291036-5-3

No part of this book may be reproduced in any form or by any electronic or mechanical means, including information storage and retrieval systems, without permission in writing from the publisher. The only exception is by a reviewer, who may quote brief excerpts in a review.

For Christopher

Contents

INTRODUCTION by Porter Goss 6
PART I 9
   1. Paris: Neuilly-sur Seine 10
   2. Neuilly-sur Seine—the next day 15
   3. Tel Aviv 40
   4. Rue du Bac Metro 52
   5. Basilique de Saint-Denis 67
   6. Neuilly-sur Seine 73
   7. Blida, Algeria 82
   8. Rabat, Morocco 94
   9. Casablanca, Morocco 99
  10. Rabat: Tour Hassan Hotel 107
  11. Marin County, California 118
  12. Tour Hassan Hotel 124
  13. Timbuktu, Mali 142
  14. Langley, Virginia: CIA Headquarters 148
  15. CIA Safe House, Virginia 157
  16. Paris: Kella's Apartment 163
  17. Mali: Aéroport de Tombouctou 175
  18. Timbuktu: Hendrina Khan Hotel 182
  19. Al Khalil's Office 192
  20. Aéroport de Tombouctou 199
  21. Al Khalil's Office 204
  22. Hôtel Bouctou 206
  23. Timbuktu 216
  24. Gao, Mali 218
  25. Aéroport de Tombouctou 227

26. Gao: A Mosque 241
27. Langley 244
28. Paris: DGSE Headquarters 247
PART II 249
29. Outside Al Khalil's Office 250
30. Paris 252
31. DGSE Headquarters 258
32. Timbuktu: IMRA Building 266
33. McLean, Virginia 271
34. Paris 278
35. Gaza 280
36. McLean 289
37. Brussels: Salim's Apartment 311
38. DGSE Headquarters 312
39. On the Road toward Taba, Egypt 316
40. Herzlia, Israel 321
41. Church of the Holy Sepulcher 326
42. Brussels: Mossad Safe House 332
43. Jerusalem: El Wad Street 334
44. On the Road to Ashqelon, Israel 337
45. Gaza 351
PART III 355
06:25 HOURS 356
06:40 360
07:20 364
08:30 369
09:15 373
09:30 390
10:30 394
13:15 398

14:38 412
15:45 419
15:49 424
16:03 425
EPILOGUE 432
ACKNOWLEDGEMENTS 438

INTRODUCTION by Porter Goss

André Le Gallo's *The Caliphate* pours out a tale of exciting intrigue too frightening to believe—and too believable to ignore. But you had better believe it, because Le Gallo is the real thing. I went to spy school with him years ago. He's a natural as well as a gifted storyteller. As a long-time, top-ranked CIA operations officer, Le Gallo shares with us both what goes on in the convoluted and treacherous world of foreign intelligence and what might happen if we let our guard down.

Set in the volatile evolving areas of North Africa's Maghreb, a dangerous trail of violence and malevolence takes protagonists Steve and Kella through the sophistication and romance of Paris to the treachery of the Mid-East, areas well known to Le Gallo through his days "in the trade." At every turn, the increasingly deranged fanatic Tariq Al Khalil escalates the stakes at risk to restore the former glory and power of the ancient Islamic Caliphate—no matter the cost. Le Gallo's portrayal of Al Khalil reflects convincingly the vicious fanaticism of the radical Islamic fundamentalists we have uncovered since 9/11—and portends eerily those future terrorists who will continue to rally to the bastardization of the Quran by delusional radical leaders with their own agenda.

Le Gallo makes the case why these misguided monsters of inhumanity must be stopped and gives us professional glimpses of just what it takes in the intelligence world to get the job done. Even though *The Caliphate* is fiction, it captures faithfully many of today's real-world obstacles confronting the protagonists from all quarters. Intelligence officers in our services will relate to wind-shifting bureaucrats and politicians inside the Beltway, too timid to reward anything deemed risky; hesitant cooperation from supposedly friendly intelligence organizations, which often confounds success; shifting allegiances and devious betrayal by "trustworthy" agents; leaks to the media and sell-outs to enemies of important, sensitive information by confederates; desperate decision-making that must be done on the sketchiest of information; and terrible miscalculations by principal players that can cost innocent lives if not bring us to the brink of destruction.

These are not small matters. Le Gallo does not have to invent these aspects of intelligence work in today's global struggle for a peaceful world future. He is able from firsthand experience to arm his attractive protagonists with natural resources, life experience, and acquired skill to meet the unexpected twists and turns in a path that takes them ever deeper into danger. Even so, they are not larger than life. They are credible human beings living out a relationship with each other and against a malevolent force that seeks to destroy them. The excitement is palpable; the outcome is uncertain.

It is a fortunate truth that André Le Gallo's *The Caliphate* is fiction, but the quest for "the new Caliphate" by radical fundamentalists is not. Their vision of "Restoration" includes full control of much of the geography from the Pacific to the Atlantic, roughly in the Tropic of Cancer: the Philippines and Indonesia through Southern Asia, the "'stans" of Central Asia, the Levant of the eastern Mediterranean, the Horn of Africa, the Maghreb of Northern Africa, and the Sahel of sub-Saharan Africa. It is a vast area with millions of people, many barely surviving in substandard conditions.

While birth rates are generally declining for Western European nations, they are growing in the lands of the envisioned Caliphate. Radical Islamic fundamentalists advertise an intolerant, merciless view toward those not totally submitting to their "pure" interpretation of the Quran, the Hadith—the sayings of Muhammad—or all of the rules and regulations that have been passed down as Sharia law since approximately A.D. 650.

Even though the radicals represent a minority of the world's Muslims, they are a powerful voice and they have found a growing, receptive audience for their corrupted version of Allah's will. There is no room for sanctity of life, equal rights, or civil liberty; women are as chattel—or less; Islam is Submission, with a capital "S," and they decide who must submit to what. A loving, compassionate father god is not included. These people exist. They have struck the innocent countless times already, brutally and with increasingly sophisticated weapons and tactics. And they will strike again! Beware the Caliphate!

Porter Goss lives in southwest Florida, now retired from many years of activity in America's intelligence community. He was the last Director of Central Intelligence (DCI) and the first Director of the Central Intelligence Agency under the changes enacted by Congress in intelligence reform legislation after 9/11. Prior to that, he served eight terms in the U.S. House of Representatives, including several years as chairman of the Intelligence Committee. His earlier days as a clandestine services officer in the CIA triggered a keen interest in our national security and an unshakable awareness of how critical good intelligence is for our national well-being.

PART I

Allah Is Our Objective, the Quran Is Our Law, the Prophet is Our Leader, Jihad Is Our Way, and Dying for the Sake of Allah Is Our Highest Hope.
—Credo of the Muslim Brotherhood

Fight and Slay the Unbelievers Wherever Ye Find Them.
—Quran, Sura 9:5

1. Paris: Neuilly-sur Seine

In the darkness, on the city's outskirts, Farid stood on the ladder leaning against the wall separating the Saudi ambassador's and the American's back gardens. Wearing designer glasses and dark silk slacks, he seemed more like an aging poster-boy for the business-casual look than the typical second-storey man. In fact, Farid bin Abdullah was one of the thousands who depended on the patronage of the five-thousand royals of Saudi Arabia. A distant cousin had obtained this choice Paris assignment for him. The American's powerful security lights provided an excellent view of his garden and of the double stairway that led from the gravel walkway to each side of the patio on the first floor. On the patio, a French window was slightly ajar, as he had been told it was on warm nights. He lifted one leg up and, for a moment, stayed prone on the wall. He was conscious that he was about to leave the diplomatic immunity of the Saudi ambassador's residence to enter the infidel's space. He felt as though he was crossing the border between the land of Peace, the Dar al Islam, and the land of War, the Dar al Gharb. More accustomed to diplomatic cocktails than to surreptitious entries, he had never been a risk-taker. But he was confident in his ability to recognize a low-risk, high-reward mission; just as he was confident that the warmth of the night was the cause of his perspiration.

Before letting himself down, he pulled the aluminum ladder up. His sweating hands and the unexpected weight caused the ladder to hit the wall. The noise resounded into the quiet night of the residential suburb and was answered by a filthy dog yelping several houses away. He froze for a second, looking at the back of both residences, but he noticed no movement. Straining, he brought the ladder down on the American side of the wall. He descended the ladder and kept to the narrow grass and dirt strip at the foot of the wall to avoid the noisy gravel as he approached the stairs.

Farid knew that the house was empty. The American's cook, Benjamin, obviously a Jew, had told the Saudi maid that Dr. Coogan was going away for a couple of days and that he, Benjamin, was going to stay with a friend during that time. That was when Farid decided this would be the perfect time to carry out Tariq al Khalil's order. He corrected himself, al Khalil, a Salafist, didn't give orders to an officer of the Kingdom's Al Mahabharata Al A' amah (General Intelligence Directorate). However, both the international Salafists and the Saudi Wahhabists, who basically agreed on the need for a pure Islam based on the earliest writings, were outraged at Dr. Coogan's public statement that newly surfaced Quranic documents were causing the academic community to question the uniqueness of the Quran, a blasphemous concept. The word of God was incomparable and unchanging. There was only one Quran, unlike the gospels, which allowed the Christians to choose one they liked best. His mission tonight was to find the Quranic forgeries that Coogan certainly kept in his house.

When he reached the French windows, he took off his Gucci belt and folded it into a loop, which he then introduced through the slightly open doors and above the handle. He placed the loop around one side of the horizontal handle and pulled up, disengaging the iron rods secured into the bottom and top of the door frame. He pushed and both windows opened.

His flashlight scanned the room—a large dining room table was the centerpiece. China and crystal-ware glass-front cabinets lined one wall and paintings the other. Documents could be hidden almost anywhere. Luckily, there was no one home, and he felt unhurried. He moved to the next room, an office. The walls were covered with photographs of a person he assumed was Coogan with European and Middle Eastern personalities. He first emptied desk drawers filled with business cards, files on investments and newspaper and magazine articles on the Middle East. His heart skipped a beat when he saw one file neatly named "Quran Project." He opened it but there was only one letter from the German Knights of St. John (Hospitaller) informing Dr. Coogan that documents pertaining to the Quran had been donated to a research institute in Berlin. Nothing new about that. The original information had come from Germany. He guessed al Khalil had a source in the institute but had been unable to find the documents, the forgeries, in Germany. He dropped the file onto the floor.

He was moving toward a file cabinet when he heard a door open downstairs. The click of a light switch followed by the squeaking of the stairs leading up to the office and dining room level broke the silence. The stairway light intruded onto the file cabinet. His surprise and alarm doubled his pulse. He stepped back into the dining room away from the stairs. Shocked and angry, his first instinct was revenge and punishment. Bad information was turning an easy mission, for which he stood to be rewarded, into a possible confrontation, for which he had not planned and was not prepared. The stupid maid would suffer consequences. He felt sweat from his armpits and his back start to soak his shirt.

The rustle of soft clothing and of quick breathing forced him back into the moment. He began to move toward the French windows, his escape route. However, this might be his only chance. The forgeries must be found. He cared less about al Khalil than of the favors the Mukhabarat's director was sure to bestow on him if he succeeded. After tonight, Coogan would certainly either hire professional security or bring the documents elsewhere, perhaps to a bank vault. He peered carefully through the doorless entrance of the office toward the stairs. The light outlined a man in sweats and a tee-shirt with long unruly blond hair, probably an American, a domestic whom he could overwhelm easily. It must be Benjamin, the cook, who had lied and was thus responsible for this crisis. The cook's appearance turned Farid's anxiety into pent-up anger waiting to be released.

The American stepped into the office and switched the light on. "Holy shit," he said. He stood in the middle of the room uncertainly looking at the wreckage on the floor. He scanned elsewhere, his mouth half-open and his eyes searching into the darkness of the dining room. He took two steps forward and paused then turned around and stage-whispered to himself, "The police."

Benjamin moved toward the phone on the desk. Farid knew he had to decide: flee or attack. He stepped into the office, raised his flashlight and brought it down as hard as he could on the blond head. The plastic lens of the light flew off, and the battery compartment broke. Benjamin fell to his knees. Farid looked around for a better weapon, grabbed a desk lamp, and again struck. This time his victim fell face-forward. Farid leaned down and felt the man's pulse. He was alive but unconscious. A rivulet of blood seeped from his scalp down onto his face. As it approached his mouth, Farid, captivated, watched the red line reach Benjamin's chin, his throat, and his tee-shirt.

Farid stood with a slight grin, listened carefully and, leaving the lights on, went to the filing cabinet. Drawer by drawer, he quickly examined all the files, dropping them onto the floor afterward. He looked at the photos on the wall, took the biggest one and tore the back off. He did the same to several others with no better results. He went through all of the books on the shelves, shaking them with the binding up, and dropping them on the floor. He then went up one flight of stairs and found the main bedroom. He ransacked it but found nothing of interest. He returned to the dining room and examined the backs of the paintings by cutting them out of their frames. Al Khalil's information had been wrong. In frustration, Farid tried to topple one of the china cabinets, but it proved too heavy, even in his excited state, to do easily. Before leaving, he took a candlestick holder from the dining room table and smashed it into the one of the cabinet glass doors.

2. Neuilly-sur Seine—the next day

Steve Church stepped out of the taxi, relieved that the first leg of his trip was finally over. He stretched, feeling all the vertebrae along his six-foot-one spine release and ran his hand through his short brown hair. He paid the driver and looked at his watch, about ten hours door-to-door from his apartment in McLean, Virginia, to his temporary abode in Neuilly. Waist-high crowd-control barriers had prevented the driver from pulling up next to the curb. His temporary address turned out to be between the Saudi Arabian and Moroccan ambassadors' residences. On his left was the Saudi flag, green with an Arabic inscription in white. Steve didn't speak Arabic but knew what it was, the *Shahada*, the declaration of faith:

La ilaha illa la hu muhammadun rasulu llah.

"There is no God but Allah and Muhammad is his messenger."

A horizontal sword underlined the *Shahada*. To his right was the Moroccan flag, red, symbol of the Prophet's descendants, with a green five-pointed star. Two heavily armed French policemen walked within fifteen feet of the taxi, their eyes cold and their faces like poker players trying to decipher their opponents' cards. A van with blackened windows was parked twenty yards away; two helmeted paramilitary policemen were talking to the squad sitting inside.

One of the policemen asked him, "Your identity papers, *Monsieur*."

Steve produced his passport and the policeman waved him on. Steve walked up to the door and rang the bell, looking for the key that Dr. Coogan had sent him. No one opened the door and Steve let himself in. He found himself in a small entrance way with stairs in front of him and a door to the right that apparently connected to the garage.

He closed the door, picked up his suitcase and hand carry and started up the stairs when the front door opened in back of him.

A stocky young man came in. He wore a beret slanted to the right that partially covered a bandage around his head. On the left, his blond hair reached below his ears. They took stock of each other and the newcomer said, "Are you Steve Church? Dr. Coogan told me to expect you. So I came back as soon as I could. From the hospital."

He touched the bandage lightly.

"You have a key? He didn't tell me."

"Yes, I'm Steve. And you are...?"

"Oh, I'm Benjamin. I'm the cook. I'm actually a student at the Cordon Bleu school. In return for doing the cooking, I get room and board. It's a win-win for everybody, isn't it? Well, it was until last night. Look what they did to me."

He took off his beret to reveal a white pad being held in place by the bandage over the shaved right side of his head.

"They? What happened to you? Where is Dr. Coogan?"

Benjamin went up the stairs past Steve, who followed him to an archway that led to office.

"Look."

A tornado seemed to have hit. There were papers, books and files all over the floor.

"Look at this mess. Somebody came in during the night. I had just come back. My apartment is downstairs next to the garage. I was at my girlfriend's apartment since Dr. Coogan left but we had an argument."

He shrugged, raised his hands palm up and rolled his eyes.

"Anyway, I woke up, came upstairs and they knocked me out, but not before I saw this holy mess."

"Are you okay? What did they steal?"

"I bet Achoura let them in. She's the Moroccan maid—comes in at least once a week. We have cops out front twenty-four/seven. Only someone with a key could have come in. And she had a key. I called the police but they haven't shown up. The cops outside said it wasn't their job," he rambled. He blinked rapidly; he licked his lips.

"And where is Dr. Coogan?" Steve tried again.

"Didn't I tell you? He's on a business trip. He left pretty suddenly. Hard to remember now. Two days ago?"

Steve tried to calm Benjamin but decided that only time could help. He wanted to go for a run and take a shower. Benjamin was too agitated to answer questions, but Benjamin kept talking.

"What did they take? I wouldn't know about missing stuff. Achoura is the one who has the run of the house. We won't see her again, I'm sure. Look at this."

He led Steve from the office into the dining room. Destroyed paintings and broken glass on the floor.

"Well, with the police outside, nothing big could have been stolen." Steve grinned. "I just hope the beds are still here. I'll be ready to crash pretty soon. If they didn't steal anything, why did they come? Do you think they could come back?"

"Come back? The hell you say!"

Benjamin's eyes suddenly got bigger.

"I guess you can take any bedroom on the top floor."

He left Steve to fend for himself and went downstairs.

The house had a narrow front on the street and was designed vertically. The garage and servants' quarters at street level; kitchen, living, dining room and a den up one flight; the master bedroom and a sitting room on the next level; and several bedrooms on the top floor.

As soon as he could, Steve changed and went out for a run, leaving Benjamin to deal with the police, if and when they came. After being strapped in a flying box across the Atlantic, he needed to get out and breathe, to clear his mind. He was mystified by the break-in. If no valuables were stolen, what was the purpose of the intrusion? Had they found whatever they were looking for?

Steve wondered what his absent host was involved in, and where he was. Steve was on a business trip to Morocco. Success in Morocco would give him a step up on the promotion ladder. And, hopefully, Morocco would open the door to other projects in the Arab world. He would show his father that there were careers outside of the CIA. He wanted to carve his own path. More practically, he needed to pay off longstanding student and credit card debts and he feared that a government salary guaranteed that he would be in debt forever.

But he had gone along with his father's suggestion to stop in Paris and meet his former CIA colleague Ted Coogan, who had left the Agency and, based on his fluent Arabic and Ph.D. in Middle Eastern studies, had gained respectability in European academic circles. He would be an excellent resource on the Arab world and on Morocco in particular, Marshall had told Steve who had grudgingly admitted that it couldn't hurt. His father has suggestions for everything.

Coogan and Church had served together in Morocco under diplomatic cover. Steve wondered if Coogan was still with the CIA.

The Bois de Boulogne was less than fifty yards south of the Coogan house and his legs were soon propelling him on a path that took him past the Jardin d'Acclimatation and to the Allée de Longchamps, where he turned right. A mile and a quarter farther he made another right to complete a triangle. He looked at his watch: twenty-five minutes, or about three miles, he calculated. It was still fairly early but not too early for other runners and equestrians. On the way from the airport, Steve's taxi had driven by butchers and fish markets raising their metal shutters. Delivery trucks monopolized the streets. The city was waking up—a great time to run. It made him excited to be in Paris.

Steve stopped in the kitchen on his way upstairs and found a note from Ted Coogan that he hadn't seen before.

Welcome Steve, make yourself at home. Sorry I wasn't able to meet you at the airport. I had to go out of town but will be back before you leave. Feel free to use anything in the house. The cook's name is Benjamin, and the maid is Achoura. Also, I attach an invitation to the American Ambassador's residence if you're interested. Enjoy.

Next to the note was a key that he put in his pocket.

His body was still on East Coast time where it was the middle of the night. He took a quick shower and laid down for a nap after which he would be "good-to-go," an expression he had picked up from his Air Force buddies in Korea where he had obtained his pilot's license. But, before he could go to sleep, he heard the police come in.

After a few minutes, Benjamin called him, "Steve? Steve? Can you come down? The *gendarmes* want to speak with you."

Benjamin was sitting at the large dining room table across from a police detective dressed in *mufti*. The mahogany table was easily large enough for a dinner party of twenty-four.

"Steve, the inspector here wants to talk to you," Benjamin said then left the room.

The detective extended his hand.

"I am Detective Beauvais, *Monsieur*."

Except for his ample girth, testifying that he had not been a street cop for a long time, Beauvais's broom-like mustache and bald head reminded Steve of the Dupont and Dupont twins, inspectors from the *Tintin* cartoons he had loved while living with his family in Francophone countries.

After inspecting his passport and flight tickets, the detective asked, "Why are you in Paris, *Monsieur*? Business? Tourism?"

"Vacation. Dr. Coogan is a friend of my father's. He was supposed to pick me up at Charles de Gaulle airport this morning but he didn't show."

Steve remembered his surprise that Coogan might even be late. If he had learned anything from growing up with a CIA father it was that there was no alternative to operational punctuality; lives depended on it. It was one of Marshall's unbending, and unending, rules.

"And who is your employer?"

At this point, Steve sensed that the detective was well aware of Coogan's prior incarnation. Beauvais might have looked like a cartoon character but Steve realized that it would be a mistake to underestimate him.

"West Gate Scientific International. We provide consultants, experts, in the area of national defense and crisis management to state and federal agencies in the United States."

"Very interesting. And what is your specialty *Monsieur* Church?"

Steve guessed from the line of questioning and the conspiratorial smile that the detective thought he had an American intelligence officer on his hands.

"I'm just an analyst. Have you tried to reach Dr. Coogan? He should be informed."

Steve surprised himself that he did not tell Beauvais that he was on his way to Morocco on business. There was no secret about it. With annoyance, he recalled another of his father's saying, "Don't answer questions that have not been asked, especially when speaking to cops."

Another rule, but probably not bad advice.

"Yes. We are trying to reach him. The cook gave me his number."

Two *gendarmes* appeared on a patio off the dining room and called the detective who joined them outside. Steve followed. Stone stairs led down from the patio to a rectangular gravel garden demarcated by three walls at the base of which were shrubs and flowers growing in a three foot wide ribbon of earth. One of the policemen pointed toward the left. There were footsteps in the dirt around flowers that had not survived a trampling. Steve assumed that the Saudi Ambassador had a similar garden on the other side of the wall.

Steve asked the detective, "What happens next? Do you go next door and ask questions?"

"No, *Monsieur*. We don't deal with the diplomatic corps. That's not in our jurisdiction. But, if nothing is missing..."

His voice trailed off.

Steve guessed that, since the evidence involved the Saudis, the investigation was over. He went upstairs. A half-hour later, he knocked at Benjamin's door dressed in a dark suit, blue shirt and a tie decorated with a multitude of national flags.

"I'm leaving. I'll be back after dinner."

Not certain that he would get to talk with Ted Coogan, Steve decided to pay a visit to the Institut du Monde Arabe. In the Metro, the French President's memorable statement, "We are all Americans!" made immediately following al Qaeda's attack against New York and Washington, came to his mind. *How long ago that seems*, he thought. Since then, al Qaeda had inspired and directed attacks in several countries, to include Morocco.

The Arab Institute building seemed to be of recent vintage. His guide book informed him that the southern façade was a geometric pattern of metallic rectangles at the center of which was a camera-like aperture that opened and closed according to the available light. He noticed, however, that some were wide open and others closed.

One of the guards explained, "They haven't worked for several years now."

The exhibits were disappointingly sterile and bare as if the funding had run out.

Before leaving, he went up to the ninth floor terrace for a view of Notre Dame across the river but was turned away. It was closed for a special event. Steve looked past him where a group of men dressed in suits were being served drinks and finger food. A cluster of VIP's had their backs to him and seemed to be listening to someone hidden by their bodies. The signs to the cafeteria reminded him that he hadn't had anything to eat since landing.

As he sat enjoying his *tabouli* at a plastic-topped table, a light rain drove the VIP's into the cafeteria. The well-dressed group was men-only and seemed a bit out of place in the low-ceilinged, self-help, cafeteria. Steve noticed that the center of attention was on one man, short but with good shoulders. When he sat down, the group pulled tables and chairs around him. He spoke Arabic, a language everyone seemed to understand. When Steve got up to leave, he saw that the man had a full black beard, an intense gaze and a sharp nose.

This guy is on a mission, Steve thought.

Then he recognized him. Tariq al Khalil had attended the Unversité Libre de Bruxelles at the time Steve had obtained his Master's in International Relations there. Steve left without making any sign of recognitions. He and his classmates had always thought al Khalil to be from another world. He was obviously more comfortable here then he had been in a strictly European setting.

He looked at is watch and decided he could still make the ambassador's reception. The ambassador's residence near Place de la Concorde was well guarded and he had to produce Coogan's invitation to get through the French security gauntlet and then the Marines on duty at the door. He knew from the invitation that the reception was in honor of the American Deputy Chief of Mission Jack Hastings, who was being reassigned to Tel Aviv as the new ambassador.

Here we go, he thought, as he waited his turn to go through the reception line. He was familiar with the ritual of the diplomatic reception. He understood that the cocktail reception was the professional vehicle of choice for the members of the diplomatic community. As wandering waiters in their impeccable white jackets circulated with flutes of American sparkling wine they referred to as "champagne" and trays of caviar, the several hundred guests in suits and cocktail dresses were busy playing their roles as diplomats, as spies pretending to be diplomats, or as reporters hoping to get a story. In the ecology of these affairs of state, Steve thought, members of the media were as remora to a shark. For the French officials, showing up was truly the most important part of their jobs—they enjoyed being courted. He was sure of one ground truth: the successful players never underestimated the size of the egos in the room.

Out of the corner of his eye, Steve spotted an attractive woman striding across his field of vision apparently toward a bar set up in one corner of the large reception area. She appeared to be in her late twenties and was wearing a black halter dress that showed off her wide, coppery shoulders. He hesitated a second, his fingers lightly touching wooden beads he wore around his neck through his shirt, and then directed his steps to intercept her and took inventory of her model's height and poised gait. Unlike many models, however, she was not anorexic; he let his eyes savor the outline of her body. As he got closer he saw that her face was oval with pronounced cheekbones and full lips, framed by tumbles of thick, black, wavy hair. Her almond shaped eyes and tawny skin color suggested Caucasian ancestors wedded to diversity before diversity became *de rigueur*.

Still on course, Steve swept two glasses from the tray of a passing waiter and, a second later, handed one to the focus of his attention.

"Hi. I'm Steve Church. I'm a guest of the American Embassy passing through Paris. Which embassy are you with?"

The woman took an instant before replying, looking at him with a frank and bemused smile.

"I'm Kella Hastings, Jack Hastings' step-daughter. I don't remember you coming through the reception line. Don't you know about protocol?"

She's smiling encouragingly, Steve thought, glad to have passed muster.

"I came late. I did go through the line but I didn't see you either. You must have been on a break. Does protocol allow breaks? Are diplomats unionized? I'm in Paris for a few days, sort of on vacation. I gather that your father is being assigned to Tel Aviv. Are you going with him?"

"No, no. I'm going to graduate school here in Paris. I'm at the Ecole Nationale d'Administration, better known as ENA. It's like Harvard in reputation."

She grinned.

"It's also a great way to become prime minister. Over half of France's prime ministers have graduated from ENA. Well, okay, Sarkozy is not an ENA graduate. Paris on vacation? By yourself?"

"I'm actually on my way to Morocco—business trip. Do I detect an accent? What is your first language?"

"I was born in Mali. My birth parents were Tuareg. Have you heard of the Blue People—the Tuaregs?"

"A little. They're desert nomads, right? So this means that your first language was...?"

Afraid he was being too direct, he changed course.

"You know, this is turning into more than idle cocktail chatter. What does the future prime minister say to moving the venue of this meeting to a more private location, away from the old folks?"

In response to Kella's raised eyebrows, Steve added, "Such as the bar at the Crillon Hotel. If I recall correctly, it's within walking distance, right? OK if I check with you later?"

"Well, maybe. I'm not sure what else is planned tonight," she said, with controlled enthusiasm.

Kella turned back to the reception line. The traffic of arriving guests had stopped and reversed. People with other diplomatic functions to attend were saying their goodbyes.

While Kella played her role in the line, smiling and shaking hands, Steve quickly worked the room. He liked the give and take and circulated from one group to another. His social skills had caused him to be elected president of his fraternity at Lehigh University.

Eventually, the American ambassador, as host, gave Jack a quick thanks, goodbye, and good luck speech, and Jack Hastings responded in kind to American, French, and other colleagues. The French foreign minister added his own thanks and best wishes to end the official part of the reception.

After the speeches, Steve found Kella in the crowd.

"Well, what do you think? There are some important issues to discuss."

"You didn't give up; I'm glad," Kella said with a laugh.

Steve and Kella left together through the security barriers, and walked to the Crillon Hotel nearby on the Place de la Concorde.

"We'll be lucky to get in," Kella said. "This is a favorite hangout for movie stars, kings, presidents and their coteries, as well as the paparazzi they love to attract."

More parasites, Steve thought.

A waiter stopped them at the entrance to the bar. "Do you have reservations?"

Steve looked over his head and could see that the room was crowded.

"Yes, Ambassador Hastings' office called ... from the American Embassy," he added. "That must be our table there."

He pointed to a small table in the back being cleared by another waiter. The waiter delayed until Steve slipped him a Euro note and they sat at a table for two in the wood-paneled bar.

Kella smiled and asked, "Do you always get what you want? What are you going to do in Morocco?"

"I had a bright idea, trying to capture part of the Moroccan market. Be careful what you wish for. Now I'm a one-man posse to bring back a contract. But what about you? You have a fascinating background."

"I lived in Northern Mali as a little girl, around Timbuktu. Our people rebelled. Tuaregs have never gotten used to the restrictions of borders. Maybe it was like when fences went up in the American West."

"You've come a long way, from Timbuktu to receptions at the Ambassador's Residence in Paris! How did you do that?"

"During the fighting, the Malian Army killed many civilians, including my parents. The Hastings adopted me from an orphanage run by Catholic nuns in Timbuktu. Jack was posted to Mali during the rebellion."

"I'm sorry about your parents. Are you legally French, American or Malian?"

"My adoptive mother is French, her maiden name was Joulet. Her father is..." she hesitated, "with the French Government. I'm a dual national. Actually I'm probably a triple national," she laughed. "I spent a couple of years in the States. My stepfather insists that I am an American and that my English should be as good as my French."

After another hour, Kella sat back in her chair and said, "You're on vacation but I have an eight o'clock seminar on the administration of the DOM-TOMs. In French that's the Departements d'Outre Mer-Territoires d'Outre Mer. In English, the Overseas Departments and Territories. I think I had better go."

She paused and added, "But only if you've finished all your questions."

Steve acted as if he hadn't caught the slight sarcasm in Kella's tone.

"Just the name of that seminar is giving me a headache. Wait, I do have one last question. What about the markings on the back of your hand?"

He gestured to four small black dots arranged in a diamond pattern on the back of Kella's right hand.

"Okay, but this is the end of the interrogation. It's the Southern Cross, a small constellation between Centaurus and Musca. In the Southern Hemisphere, it will help you locate the South Pole. I've had this tattoo since I was very young. My mother had the same one. It also has something to do with high authority and status in the tribe and a symbol of the Tuaregs' mastery of navigation in the desert."

"In my tribe, we have the same thing."

Pointing to the watch on his right wrist, he said, "It's called a Suunto X-Lander. I got it at the PX in South Korea."

Kella giggled. "It has so many dials and buttons—can you actually use it to tell time? I don't think I've ever seen one like it."

"It has an altimeter, a thermometer, and a compass. Now you could get one with a GPS."

He raised his right wrist and glanced at his watch.

"Directly north of you there is a tall American named Steve with whom you're going to have lunch tomorrow."

Kella's laugh was brief.

"Well, I'm not sure. I have a lot to do tomorrow."

"Oh-oh, a boyfriend on the horizon," he said in mock alarm, surprised at his own words. He hadn't had that concern about anyone for a long time.

"Nothing like that," she smiled at his concern. "I have classes in the morning and I promised to meet a friend in the afternoon. She lives in St. Denis. Troubles with her father. I'm not sure that I'm doing the right thing but I want to try to help her. Her father is super-conservative, super-Islamist. He sounds like he wants to go back to another century. Although Faridah lives in Paris in the twenty-first century, he expects her to behave as if she lived in eighth century Mecca. In Algeria, where female genital mutilation is not widely practiced, her father had her cut before she was five years old."

Female genital mutilation was the last thing Steve wanted, or could, talk about.

"St. Denis, the Basilica, where all of the French kings were buried. It's on my list of things to do in Paris. We could meet there after you visit your friend. But first, we'll have lunch. You have to eat lunch somewhere, right?"

"I don't think that's going to work. If you want, we could go to St. Denis together. Then, while you go to the Basilica, I'll go with Faridah. And we can meet at the Basilica later."

Before she got in a cab and disappeared into the swirling night traffic of the Place de la Concorde, they had agreed to take the Metro to St. Denis together the next day and see if their schedules meshed on the way.

On her way home, Kella thought about Steve. She was intrigued but wary. She guessed that he was several years older than her twenty-seven years. He had mentioned having lived in Korea, Hawaii, Morocco, and West Africa, which appealed to her. He had more than held his own with the diplomats at the reception. At first, she had been a bit put off by his directness. She smiled; he was so American, so different from the French students at ENA, many of whom came from families that would gladly have a monarch rather than a republic. She felt that they had made a connection. He would leave Paris soon. But he was fun and pleasant to be with. She herself felt more confident when she was with him.

Her last thought about Steve that night—and she knew he would get a good laugh if he knew—compared him to a World War II figure whom she had recently studied, General George Patton, forceful, often did the opposite of what was expected, and who didn't mind the limelight.

Steve's thoughts about Kella were conflicted. He had almost been engaged a year before but he hadn't dated since the sudden death of his fiancée. Vera also had been tall and intelligent. He had loved her spontaneity, something he didn't detect much of in

Kella. He often wondered whether Vera might still be alive—he knew she would be—if he hadn't been so selfishly focused on high-altitude skiing during their few days in Canada. She had gone off with another group that day and he had not seen her again. An avalanche had killed them all.

The evening with Kella had started to unshackle his emotions. His hand went up to his neck and he felt the necklace Vera had found at the hotel gift shop the day before she died. He had worn it ever since.

As he neared the Coogan house, his mind went back to the robbery. Where was Coogan and what were the thieves looking for?

Two policemen approached Steve as soon as he got out of the taxi. They recognized him after shining their lights on his face and, politely but firmly, asked him to hold his arms up. They frisked him before they allowed him to go in the house.

The phone rang as he walked upstairs. He took the call in the kitchen. It was Ted Coogan.

"Steve, I'm calling from Berlin. I had an accident. Well, not exactly an accident. I'm calling from the Benjamin Franklin Hospital. Someone attacked me with a knife. But he found out that I'm not entirely defenseless," Coogan chuckled. "Anyway, I have to ask you a favor. Take my car, it's in the garage, and pick me up at the airport tomorrow morning. I'll be on Lufthansa flight 4212, landing at 10 a.m."

"Wait a minute. Do you know about the break-in at your house?"

"Yes. I got a call from the French police. Benjamin must have given them my number. But I'm not surprised. It's all related to my trip to Berlin, I'm sure. I'll tell you more tomorrow. Thanks for doing this. I appreciate it. By the way, I'm five-eleven with white hair, and glasses. Oh, and I'll be the guy with the cane."

He was barely off the phone when Benjamin came running up the stairs.

"I didn't hear you come in. The phone woke me up."

He wore sweats and a t-shirt. He frowned and spoke in a loud voice.

"A couple of hours ago a policeman came to the door. He said not to worry. Ha!"

He looked up and threw his arms open as if imploring God to be his witness.

"*Ne vous en faites pas, Monsieur*," Benjamin said in a deep voice mimicking the policeman. "We have an unconfirmed report that a terrorist group is planning something soon. Something soon! Are you kidding? What the hell does that mean? He thought we should know because of the break-in. As if that explained everything!"

"Well, did you ask him what it meant?"

"Yes, of course. I asked him several times and he finally said that the terrorists might use a suicide bomber!"

His voice had become shrill.

"What else?"

"That it was almost certainly a false report, that it had nothing to do with us and that we should not worry because there had never been a suicide bomber in Paris. But he was just following orders. In the meantime, they would reinforce the police in the front."

Steve was weary from the long day but his mind was racing. The knowledge that the break-in and the attack on Coogan in

Berlin were related was interesting, but it didn't suggest a line of action.

Now, a suicide bomber threat the police don't believe because there has never been a suicide bomber in Paris?

Then there was Tariq al Khalil's appearance at the museum. He remembered that al Khalil had also gone to school in Cairo and that he came from an Egyptian family, although born in Belgium. So al Khalil's presence at the museum should not have surprised him. He recalled that al Khalil was supposed to be an expert on Islam. Maybe he should talk to him. But he immediately dismissed that thought. Coogan should be able to connect the dots. And then there was Kella. The next day promised to be just as full.

* * *

The next morning, after relishing Benjamin's Eggs Benedict, he drove to the airport. It took Steve a few minutes to get comfortable in Coogan's blue MINI Cooper S. The top of his head was only an inch from the small vehicle's roof. He reached Charles de Gaulle, parked, and made his way through what once had been Europe's most modern airport but now was beginning to show wear. As the crowds walked out toward public transportation, Steve felt he was swimming upstream.

He realized why Coogan had asked to be met at the airport—he walked with a cane to alleviate his limp when he came out of the customs check point. Steve waved and made his way through the crowd.

Coogan grinned and said, "Those thugs sent a boy to do a man's job."

His grin was replaced by a grimace of pain and a sudden intake of breath as they started to walk toward the covered parking lot. Steve carried Coogan's overnight bag and laptop.

"I was leaving my hotel and he came at me in broad daylight. I was lucky because he showed his knife too early. He gave me a chance to…"

A light flashed on their left. A news photographer said, "Thank you Dr. Coogan. Mind if I take another?"

Without waiting for an answer, he took two more shots. The reporter who was with the photographer stepped forward, put a microphone in front of Coogan's face and asked, "How did you feel when you were attacked in Berlin?"

Coogan tried to walk past but his limp, the gathering crowd and the large reporter planted in front of him made a civilized escape impossible.

Steve wedged himself in front of Coogan.

"This is not a good time," he said "Please excuse us."

The reporter scowled and leaned forward aggressively.

"Who are you? Don't interfere with the press."

His face inches from the public's right to know, Steve stepped forcefully on the reporter's foot.

"Sorry," he said.

With the reporter now slightly off-balance, Steve lowered a shoulder and walked straight through him with Coogan in his wake.

The reporter called out, "*Crétin!* Dr. Coogan, is it true that the attack in Berlin was related to your work on the Quran?"

Coogan kept walking behind Steve and said over his shoulder, "Thank you. Contact Berlin."

Once in the passenger seat of his MINI Cooper, Coogan sighed and rubbed his leg.

"Thanks for picking me up. That thug did stick me in the leg," he pointed to his right leg. "No big deal. The hospital bandaged it and let me go. But the effect of the painkiller has worn out. Could you reach my bag for me? There's an envelope in the side pocket."

Steve gave him the envelope and Coogan took two pills that he immediately swallowed. As Steve drove out of the airport, he asked, "What was that reporter talking about? The Quran project?"

"Right, but first things first. Tell me how I can help you. I understand you're on your way to Morocco. Great country! It was anyway. Things are changing. What do you hope to do there?"

"My company, West Gate Scientific International, does a lot of consulting for the Pentagon. You know, almost everything is outsourced these days. I've been involved in counter proliferation in Korea and in helping the new North American Command for its first Congressional hearings. Now I'll be trying to sell our services to the Moroccan defense establishment."

Coogan shifted in his seat, winced, and grabbed his leg as he tried to get in a more comfortable position.

"It's okay, I'm fine. The painkiller should kick in soon. Go on. Sounds like your company hired the Renaissance Man."

"You sure you don't want to stop? After the 2004 terrorist attack on Madrid that had killed one hundred ninety-one people, I learned that the Army's European command was starting to provide counterterrorist training and equipment to North African countries. Anyway, I put the two together and made a pitch to my boss that this was a business opportunity to win contracts either with EUCOM or with the countries receiving the assistance. Long story short, the idea found traction. Before I knew it, I was packing. Anyway, my father said you were the expert I needed to talk to before I went to Morocco. But this Quran project sounds interesting."

"It's certainly bringing out the nut cases, isn't it? The German Order of the Knights Hospitallers recovered very old, and very different," he looked at Steve for emphasis, "versions of the Quran. They might have had them since the Crusades. These pre-date the official version started under the third caliph, Othman. They were lost during the Second World War, or hidden. The Hospitallers donated the manuscripts to a German research institute. I have been invited to join the research team."

"And why would anyone try to kill you for that? And you said that the break-in was related? How?"

"The Quran is supposed to be the word of God, immutable, eternal, unique—in other words, unchallengeable. A group of infidels claiming that they have different versions of God's word is upsetting to certain Muslim groups, to say the least. And the most extreme, the Salafists, are more than ready to eliminate those other versions as well as anyone who claims they exist. As for the break-in, they must have assumed that I had copies of the manuscripts at home. In fact, I had received one page by email to allow me to decide whether I could handle the skeletal Arabic. But, I brought my laptop with me."

He pointed in back of him toward his computer.

"Speaking of which," Steve asked, "have you ever heard of a Tariq al Khalil? I went to graduate school with him in Brussels.

We weren't exactly close friends but I saw him today, at the Institut Arabe."

Coogan nodded thoughtfully.

"Al Khalil lectures and writes extensively. From a Muslim Brotherhood family as I recall. His pitch depends on his audience. He tries to be moderate with European audiences but, in front of a Muslim audience, he's a take-no-prisoners kind of guy. Gaining in influence, too. I hope my former employers are keeping an eye on him. He has become a leader in Salafist circles."

Coogan smiled, looked at Steve and added, "Your father thought I could give you some useful background before you go to Morocco, so let me fast-forward for you. We are witnessing the renaissance of a religion, no, of an authoritarian ideology. Its proponents—jihadists, Salafists, whatever you choose to call them—honestly believe everyone must fall in line, that it is God's will that we all submit. In the short term they are skillful at perception management, using the internet, killings, whatever works. In the long term, the only constituency they care about is God, Allah. Those who liked the Taliban will love the new Caliphate, the idea that they're going to recreate the Middle East as a borderless Muslim empire, but only as a first step. My generation struggled against one global 'ism.' Your generation is faced with another. That can be your first lesson on contemporary Islam."

"Are you saying that I'm going to have to deal with these guys in Morocco?"

"Depends. Just keep in mind that the true believers are deadly. They are a small minority of the Muslim world to be sure. Some say, what, only one-to-five percent are extremists? That's between fifteen-million and seventy-five-million people. Some of them are in Morocco. That's where the terrorists who bombed the Spanish trains came from."

When they reached Coogan's house, Benjamin met them in the hallway.

"Welcome back boss. What do you think of your Arab neighbors?"

Seeing Coogan's expression he continued, "Oh, you don't know? I thought the police called you. Well, it turns out that the robbers came over the wall in the back, from the Saudi residence. Their footsteps are still there. The gang that couldn't shoot straight," he said, with more bravado than Steve had seen yet.

Coogan and Benjamin went to go have a look. Steve was anxious to leave to go meet Kella.

"I'm off to the Metro. I promised to meet someone. But could the thief have come from the Saudi residence? What do you think?"

"We'll talk about the theft later," Coogan told him. "You look in a hurry. Forget the Metro. Take my car if you want. I won't need it for the rest of the day. I'm going to be busy right here." He turned to Benjamin and said, "I'll be here tonight for dinner but not tomorrow. So just prepare your usual fine cuisine tonight, and Steve can tell you what he would like tomorrow."

"Thanks. The car will be useful since I'm late."

As Steve turned to go, Benjamin said, "By the way, a reporter called you this morning Steve. But he didn't leave a message."

"A reporter?" He looked at Coogan. "What did he want?"

"He asked for the person who met Mr. Coogan at the airport. He said that you had given him your name but that he hadn't had a chance to get the spelling right for the article. So I gave it to him."

Steve and Ted looked at each other. Steve smiled at the reporter's ingenuity but Coogan frowned. Steve hurried to the MINI Cooper to go meet Kella wondering what Coogan looked worried about.

3. Tel Aviv

On consultation from his assignment in Brussels at Mossad's European headquarters, David Ben Tov had been summoned by Mossad Director Nahum Ben Gal to his top floor office. Mindful that Mossad's American desk chief often lunched with the CIA chief of station at the Asia House near the Mossad building, David Ben Tov parked two blocks away from the Hadar Dafna Building on King Saul Boulevard in Tel Aviv. Seemingly a business office building, the Hadar Dafna was the headquarters of the Ha Mossad, le Modiyn ve le Takfidim Mayuhadim, the Institute for Intelligence and Special Operations, Israel's external Israeli intelligence service.

Ben Tov was in his late forties, with blondish receding hair, light skin, in reasonable shape for his age, and dressed in loafers, cargo pants, a sport jacket and white shirt. He wore no tie, a style established early by the David Ben Gurion tie-less generation of pioneers.

The sky was cloudy, threatening rain. Ben Tov quickened his step.

In the elevator on his way to the director's top floor office, Ben Tov reviewed his operations in Europe to be ready for whatever Ben Gal wanted to take up with him. He ran several agents: a Libyan and an Ethiopian diplomat, a Belgian businessman who did business in Saudi Arabia. The Turkish Ambassador was his very good friend, although not yet an agent.

He was cultivating the manager of a five star hotel in Brussels where many Arab plenipotentiaries stayed when visiting Brussels to lobby the European Union.

Ben Tov hoped to be able to plant microphones and cameras in several of the suites. He also had a number of other lesser contacts including a promising young Palestinian with intriguing family connections. By the time he stepped out of the elevator, he hadn't dredged up any problems that would reach Ben Gal's level.

Ben Gal, tall, still dark-haired although ten years older than David, was dressed in slacks and a shirt with sleeves rolled up. He walked to greet him from behind his desk and extended his hand. *Good signs*, thought Ben Tov. He had been in Ben Gal's modest office only once before, when Ben Gal's predecessor had told him that Mossad would pay for his last two years of university studies at the University of California, Berkeley, assuming he was accepted. He had met his future wife Rachel there, also a Sabra, and picked up American-accented English and expressions.

Ben Gal moved back to his chair. "I understand that we sent you to Berkeley a few years ago. It's time to amortize our investment, to use your American background for the country. Here is a file I want you to read." He handed him a thick green colored file. David held it sideways to read the title, "Muslim Brotherhood. Western Europe."

David, wanting to show he was knowledgeable, said, "I believe that the *Ikhwan* moved to Europe from Egypt, first to Germany to take advantage of the Muslim émigrés from Russia left over from the war."

"Your target is Salim Salaheldin, the brotherhood's senior official in Europe. He lives in Brussels. Actually, the real focus of the operation will be Tariq al Khalil. Salaheldin is his uncle and mentor. He has a great deal of influence on al Khalil. And it's al Khalil I'm concerned about. He's young, charismatic, has a following through his academic activities, lecturing and so on, but he's also an activist. Both Salim Salaheldin and al Khalil are related to the Brotherhood's founder. That gives them automatic credentials.

"The radical Muslims right now are leaderless. Al Khalil badly wants the job. We're going to help him. I think that we can control him, well at least influence him, if we can recruit Salim. Nature and politics abhor a vacuum. If al Khalil doesn't take over the movement, someone else will. At least, if we, that is if you, can recruit Salim, we're in the game. Al Khalil wants to recreate the old Caliphate. I want you to keep him as far away from Israel as possible. Have him recreate his Caliphate in the Sahara. Let him get a tan while he's doing Allah's work."

Ben Gal smiled sardonically.

Recalling Ben Gal's reference to Berkeley, David said, "Are you saying you want me to put my American hat on to do this? To pretend I'm CIA?"

Ben Gal smiled again.

"Exactly, this will be a false-flag recruitment. I will establish a 'bigot' list of the people who will be cleared for this operation. Until then, you are to discuss it with no one other than me."

"And do we have reason to believe that Salim can be recruited?"

"It's all in the file."

Ben Gal's tone turned abrupt. He looked out his window at the dark clouds for a second and, in a more measured tone, continued, "We have reason to believe that Salim's predecessor, also with family connections to the Brotherhood, met with a CIA officer, Joe DiPietro from New Jersey."

"What did they have in common, I wonder?"

"Well, it was the Cold War. The CIA wanted access to the Muslim émigrés from Russia to send them back as sources. The Brotherhood needed cash and approved the contact. The Brotherhood also established sympathy in the CIA by providing occasional snippets of counterterrorist information through their own penetrations of Fatah, Force 17 and other groups."

"Was Salim aware that his predecessor was in touch with the CIA?"

"That's not clear. You'll have to read the file for yourself."

Ben Gal looked at his watch and Ben Tov took the hint.

"One more thing," Ben Gal said as Ben Tov got up, "Al Khalil has a wife and daughter in Brussels. Find out where and establish their living patterns, school, shopping, friends, you know. Could be useful later."

Ben Tov gathered the green file. He glanced out the window before going out the door. The dark clouds were no longer threatening, they had burst and the wind was whipping the water against Ben Gal's window.

* * *

The Boeing 767-300 descended over the Mediterranean as it neared the coast of North Africa toward Algiers. Tariq al Khalil looked out his window and could understand why the French traditionally referred to the city as Alger la Blanche. On the northern edge of the green coastal plain, the whitewashed buildings of the Casbah nestled in an arc overlooking the port and the bay, reflected the morning sun. Several container ships were unloading and two were leaving. Al Khalil noted the absence of cruise ships with satisfaction.

During the flight, al Khalil had been thinking of his last conversation with his wife Malika. He wanted their daughter Jamila to grow up in a Muslim environment. Malika did not, could not, oppose him. But he still seethed at the deception in her comment, "She will be better off here. She can grow up Muslim, attend the madrasa right here in Brussels."

In his absence, she had been invited to a meeting of the International Women's Club by the wife of the Egyptian ambassador, a woman who liked to play bridge with her international friends. Al Khalil suspected that Malika was telling him what he wanted to hear but secretly pined for the life of her Egyptian friend. He decided that he would send them to live in Cairo or Riyadh as soon as he had time to plan the move.

His thoughts wandered when he found a map of North Africa in an Air France brochure in the pocket in front of him. The outlined borders reminded him of the interference of the Christian powers and his frustration stayed high. He took a deep breath. In North Africa, it had been France. In other regions of the former Caliphate, it had been Great Britain. The Christians had created the borders to divide the Caliphate into separate countries to divide and conquer. But, knowing that he soon would be able to reclaim the populations on the ground below for Islam, he felt empowered. He knew that he could harness the humiliation and the anger of the people to his advantage and fill the current power vacuum in the leadership of the radical Muslim movement. He felt energized.

Al Khalil turned to his Syrian deputy and chief of operations Hussein al Kaylani.

"Petrol and alcohol in those ships. During bad years, the difference between the production and the export of Bordeaux wines from France comes from Algerian wines. Hypocrisy and corruption are the West's capstone principles. A Muslim country in the alcohol business is unacceptable, an insult to Allah, May he favor our actions."

"Yes, that will come, Hussein replied. "There are more important things ... I mean, you're right. But don't you think that petrol is where the power is?"

Al Khalil didn't reply. He thought Hussein's common sense sometimes made up for his lack of true religious fervor.

* * *

They landed at Houari Boumedienne International Airport. Mediterranean sunlight flowed through large and high windows. Architecturally clean lines offered uncluttered and expansive spaces. Large posters from the Ministry of Tourism greeted tourists in several languages. However, al Khalil immediately felt the embattled atmosphere. The presence of countless military patrols—soldiers walking in pairs with leveled semi-automatic machine guns hanging from their shoulders—sent a clear warning not to abuse the welcome.

Al Khalil chuckled. He turned to Hussein and said, "Our Salafist friends obviously have convinced these apostate rulers that their days are limited."

Hussein took his cell phone out of pocket.

"Yes. When the Algerian Salafists became al Qaeda in the Maghreb, they became more aggressive, more deadly. It was a good idea to plan a meeting with them on our way south."

Following a two-hour wait, the Land Rover representative met them on the street side of the airport explaining the delay as the will of God, *Insha'llah*. Hussein took title to the car after another hour of haggling over the final price and a sizable bribe, or *bakchich*.

Al Khalil saw the boxy-looking green car with outsize Michelin desert tires but was only interested in the brand name. As he got in the car, he asked, "Why a British car, Hussein? The British have troops in Iraq; their damn SAS commandos are fighting the Taliban in Afghanistan."

Hussein's shrewd eyes didn't move from his maps as he replied flippantly, "I'm more concerned about being able to traverse the Sahara than who made the car." He looked up at al Khali. "It's a good car."

Al Khalil gave his deputy a sharp look but said nothing.

They followed signs to Avenue Franklin Roosevelt, which became National Road #1 and proceeded south. The sign informed them that the distance to Blida was twenty-eight miles. As they neared the entrance to the town, they were stopped at a roadblock. They were let though after a check of their passports. However, off to the side, two soldiers had ordered the driver and passenger of the previous car to get out. There was yelling and one soldier, holding his weapon parallel to the ground, hit the passenger with the stock of his rifle, stepping forward with one foot for more force.

Just like in training, al Khalil thought.

The passenger fell, his head bleeding.

Hussein, who drove, asked, "How well do you know the AQIM chief, El Maghrebi?"

"Ibrahim El Maghrebi is more of a survivor than a fox. He was a sergeant in the Algerian army when he tried to enlist fellow officers to his Salafist beliefs. He was jailed, later released in an amnesty, and went underground. I agree with him on many things. The execution of uncooperative village officials, as the North Vietnamese practiced, is an effective path to control the population. Since 1991 when they started to fight, they have killed over two-hundred thousand. No wonder they convinced al Qaeda central to incorporate them."

"But will he help us?" Hussein asked. "And does he have the purity of spirit that you seek?"

Al Khalil glanced at Hussein; his only response was a thoughtful nod. He knew that Hussein was still trying to convince him of his Muslim motivation.

They found the small grocery store with the safety signal—a Coca-Cola sign in Arabic in its window, which signified to al Khalil and Hussein that the site was secure, and that the Algerian police was neither in control of the location nor surveilling it. Immediately inside the door, a bearded guard holding his AK-47 casually let them into the smoky and narrow room where a young boy swept the floor.

After an exchange of greetings, the guard said, "He's up there," and looked toward the ceiling. He shouted, "They're here!" toward stairs in the back of the store. Between coughs, a voice replied, "Bring them up." They walked past shelves lined with bottles of Evian and cans of *Petits Pois de Clamart* to reach the stairs.

Ibrahim el-Maghrebi sported an unruly mustache hiding his upper lip but not his tobacco-stained teeth. His dusty brown *jellaba*, the hooded garment that covered the body from the head to the ankles, couldn't completely hide a sturdy physique. Al Khalil could feel El Maghrebi's familiarity with command and easily imagined him in uniform.

"*Salaam Alaikum.* We are honored by your visit. Your reputation precedes you. Your family is the royalty of our Muslim Brotherhood. We honor your grandfather, a man with the Quran in one hand and a gun in the other. He promoted the renaissance of a pure brand of Islam to reverse the perversions of Western ideology: Christianity, imperialism and nationalism."

Al Khalil waved a fly away from his face. "You are kind."

El Maghrebi continued, "I'm sorry I have to receive you in this unworthy place. Please understand that we are at war. The next time we meet will be in my palace in Algiers."

They both chuckled.

Asked to sit next to his host on a banquette against the wall, Al Khalil accepted. A blade of sun cut through half-closed curtains and lit part of the room.

El Maghrebi reached for a pack of cigarettes from a pocket in the folds of his *jellaba* and held it in his hand.

"AQIM is on the verge of victory," he said. "A few days ago, we attacked a Coast Guard installation a hundred kilometers east of Algiers. We killed almost a hundred soldiers. We act in the name of Allah. The time for talk is past. But what can we do for you?"

He opened the pack of cigarettes and offered it to al Khalil, who declined, and then to Hussein, who took one. The ashtray next to El Maghrebi was full.

Hussein mentioned the roadblock they had encountered in Boufarik, but El Maghrebi didn't seem worried.

* * *

After the required tea and courtesies demanded by Muslim hospitality, al Khalil was soon up and pacing in the small room, his shadow appearing on the far wall when he crossed the narrow beam of sunlight. Al Khalil was not physically imposing but his coal black beard, aquiline nose and penetrating gray eyes gave him the air of a prophet.

Stroking his beard, he said, "We are conscious of your actions. With the help of Allah, the Merciful, the Omnipotent, my Salafist brothers and I will reconquer all the lands of the ancient Caliphate. AQIM will play a key role in North Africa. We will work together. I will bring all of the countries bordering on the Sahara to our cause. You will help us. Acting and preaching must go together."

An hour into the meeting, Al Khalil said, "You have been right in not destroying the country's oil industry. We will need it when we take over. But you must do something about the wine…"

The phone rang downstairs and the tone of the guard's short imperative questions cut him off. The guard ran up the stairs.

"A mobile patrol is heading this way—one squad with a sergeant. They are now searching the house where Abdullah stayed last month. We must move."

As though anticipating the warning, El Maghrebi said, "Come, my brothers. Follow us. We will go to another safe house."

Out in the street, El Maghrebi, two guards and the boy got into a brown pick-up truck. Hussein and al Khalil followed in a Land Rover. A third vehicle followed with four other men. Using back streets, the small convoy circled around the patrol to the northern edge of town and parked on a side street. They walked at a brisk pace for two blocks until they reached a three-storey building with a café downstairs where they went in by a side door and found themselves in an apartment behind the café.

El Maghrebi pulled curtains shut.

"I apologize but this is the life we lead. The military has been searching for us with more vigor since our raid on the coast. Abdullah, the man they are looking for, hasn't been here for a while. They've working from dated intelligence."

El Maghrebi gave his men orders and they started to file out again with purpose but not before checking the weapons they carried under their *jellabas*. Al Khalil felt El Maghrebi's eyes on him as men pulled the bolts of their AK-47s back and let them slide forward to chamber a round. Al Khalil knew that El Maghrebi respected his intellect and passion and wanted to project his composure under stress.

"We are safe here," El Maghrebi said, "but these patrols never come in single squads. We may have to move again. You will be safer if you get on the road. No need to rush but today is better than tomorrow. I will send another car with you. My men know the desert. And it's always safer to travel with two cars. But first, I have something for you in honor of your visit."

El Maghrebi gave his two guests, who had arrived from Paris wearing rumpled European suits and tie-less white shirts, two *jellabas* for desert travel. They both changed immediately. He then gave each al Khalil and al Kaylani a highly polished teak box.

"You did us the honor of asking for our hospitality and help. We are blessed by Allah to join you. Please accept these gifts as symbols of AQIM's unalloyed allegiance. We are as true to Islam as the blades of these two knives."

Al Khalil opened his box and pulled out a Damascus Amourette knife with a contoured gunstock handle. Al Kaylani received a Combat Trident Gerber knife with a double serrated blade. Al Khalil's five-inch blade closed into the light horn handle but Hussein's gift, with a blade slightly over six inches and a hilt, was clearly a hunting or fighting knife. Each was nestled in a gift box with the same care as an expensive watch.

As they left, Al Khalil said, "I'm happy to have had this discussion. We will work well together. Your gifts will be put to the service of the Prophet, the All Powerful, the Compassionate."

El Maghrebi's men led the way out of town and into the desert evening. On the left of the small convoy, the lengthening shadows of the vehicles brushed against the buildings of the town before caressing the sands of the Sahara. Al Khalil soon appreciated that only experienced drivers wary of the perpetual attempts of the sand to cover the road could have driven them safely in the dark. He thought ahead to their next stop on their way to Timbuktu, the oasis town of Ghardaia, the center of the first fundamentalists, the Kharijites.

4. Rue du Bac Metro

Kella turned her back on a driver obviously trying to attract her attention. She was at the entrance of the station where she and Steve had agreed to meet. Dressed in loose clothing down to her ankles, she was surprised that she would attract any male attention. Then she heard her name and turned back toward the car parked at the curb, to the great annoyance of the cars behind.

"Kella, come on before I get run over," Steve shouted.

She recognized him and ran toward to the car.

Steve explained the car and, glancing at her clothes, said, "Very chic. Is that the latest Paris fashion?"

"The Saint-Denis suburb is very North African. Faridah told me to dress like this to fit the role of a friend her father would want her to have. The idea is to reassure her father that Faridah hasn't gone to the dark side, that she hasn't rejected her Muslim roots."

Steve nodded and said, "You better give me directions to St. Denis."

Kella navigated and continued talking about her friend. She was conscious that she was trying to justify to herself the wisdom of her idea.

It sounded better yesterday, she thought.

"Faridah's father is very strict, very fundamental. Now, he suspects that she is not being chaste. She does have a French boyfriend, and her father is assuming the worst. He is talking about moving the family back to Algeria."

"So what do you hope to accomplish? Make a moderate of the father?"

A bit annoyed at Steve's negative tone, she said, "I'm just trying to help her, show her father that she has decent, well, non-threatening, friends, like me. Faridah said that her father often beats her mother, on the smallest pretext. He probably hits Faridah also, although she didn't say so."

"You think that going to their apartment is a good idea? If I understood you last night, you aren't Muslim, well not any more, right?"

Kella took out a scarf from her shoulder bag and refolded it before putting it back inside.

"That's why I told Faridah to convince her parents to come and have coffee in a public place."

As planned, Steve and Kella met Faridah at the exit of the St. Denis Metro. Kella made the introductions while Faridah appraised Kella's outfit.

"Perfect, except you do need to cover your head."

Kella put on her scarf.

"What if I came with you?" Steve asked. "Are you sure you know what you're doing?"

As Kella seemed about to agree, Faridah spoke up turning toward Steve.

"Absolutely not. Unless your name is Ahmed and you are a Muslim. I'm not even sure if bringing Kella is a good idea. Bringing an American male? That'll burn my father's short fuse in an instant. And, by the way, we're going to my apartment rather than to a café as you suggested. I talked to my mother about your idea and she said that my father wouldn't do it. So this way is simpler. It's also the only way."

Kella turned to Steve.

"Why don't you go to the Basilica and I'll meet you there in, say, an hour?" Pointing, she said, "There's a sign for the Basilica, it's about five minutes from here."

Kella and Faridah walked from the Metro, past the Hotel de Ville, toward a row of drab buildings much like those put up in Eastern Europe's socialist heavens after World War II. A car full of young men passed. Faridah looked down instinctively and Kella followed suit. They walked quickly to an intersection and crossed catty-corner to a faceless apartment building. Faridah held the front door open.

"*Le Grand Palais*," she said sarcastically. "The security buzzer and combination pad have not worked for as long as I can remember," she added.

Inside, the small lobby's walls and mailboxes were nicked. A graffito in Arabic, *ISLAM IS THE ANSWER*, was spray-painted on the far wall.

We're on the third floor," Faridah said with a slightly encouraging smile.

She and Kella went through the small hallway, which reeked with a perceptible odor of urine, and started up the stairs. On the way up, a family passed them on its way down, the mother dressed in loose clothing that hid her shape and shooing three handsome children ahead of her. The youngsters looked up at Kella with curiosity.

Once they reached the third floor Faridah said, "Wait out here a minute, just in case my mother hasn't mentioned your visit yet."

She rolled her eyes and smiled. She walked up to her apartment door taking keys out of her pocket. The hallway's only light seeped in from a small window at the end of the hall, although Kella noticed a light bulb hanging from a wire over the stairwell. Faridah turned her key in the first door lock, but before she could find the key for the second lock, the door flew open.

"I was just asking about you!"

A dark-skinned, full-bearded, bulky man in his early fifties grabbed Faridah's left wrist and pulled her into the apartment before Faridah had time to say anything. Kella presumed the man to be Hamad, Faridah's father. The door began to shut, but Kella rushed forward and braced her foot at the bottom of the door to keep it from closing completely. At first, she leaned toward the slight opening and listened. She was prepared to walk in when the angry tone of Hamad's voice stopped her inside the dark hallway.

"You are not the daughter I knew when we lived in Algiers. You have become someone else, someone who shows no respect, a girl who is anxious to show her body. You no longer attend the Mosque."

Hamad's voice was rising in tone and in volume. Kella felt that he was on the verge of physical violence. Kella stayed in the hallway, out of sight.

"Stop" Faridah cried. "You're hurting me. Please! Let go!"

Kella could see Hamad standing in front of Faridah in the kitchen. There was a stove on the left, a square table with metal legs and four folding chairs. A woman that Kella assumed was Faridah's mother sat at the table. She wore a loose gray house dress. Along the wall on the right was a narrow but lengthy shelf on top of which she could see dishes and glasses. Under the shelf was a small refrigerator with silverware scattered on it as if Faridah's mother had been interrupted in the act of putting them away. Kella assumed there was a sink next to the refrigerator but she couldn't see it.

Hamad shouted, "I know that as soon as you got on the Metro, you took off your scarf. You went to the Ile de la Cité and met your Christian devil. You touched and kissed in public. I know you've done more. And with an infidel! The neighbors know and talk about it. It shames us!" Kella had originally assumed that Hamad simply wanted to protect a daughter for whom he cared. Instead, Hamad's rantings reflected more concern about what others thought about him. Should she step forward and make her presence known? She was undecided.

In a weak, pleading voice, the woman said, "She is your daughter. For the love of Allah, have pity on your flesh and blood."

She sounded upset, but not surprised. Kella wasn't catching every word of the woman's high pitched and rapid appeal. Kella guessed that much of the woman's speech was in a Berber dialect, from the Kabyle Mountains of Algeria.

Still holding Faridah's wrist, Hamad turned toward his wife now on her feet and approaching him. Fearfully, she brought her arms up to protect her head.

"Fatima, our daughter, may she be forever damned, has soiled our flesh and blood. You know what I must do. It is Allah's will."

"Allah would have pity," Fatima replied in a weak voice.

Kella drew closer. She noticed that Faridah's mother was looking at the top of the refrigerator and Kella now could see a large knife lying apart from the silverware.

Hamad's voice grew louder. "You whore! You've disgraced us, dishonored me and the whole family!"

He pulled Faridah's arm hard toward him and she lost her balance as Hamad let go of her wrist.

"Filth!" he shouted as she sprawled on the discolored linoleum floor of the kitchen.

Kella's thoughts raced. What could she do? She looked for something she might use as a weapon, something to hit him with, but she saw nothing. She wished that Steve were here. She didn't move, paralyzed by the fear that she might make things worse for Faridah. She looked at Fatima, trying to judge whether the two of them together could help Faridah. But, at that moment, Hamad, his eyes fixed on his wife, turned away from her. He then quickly rotated his muscular shoulders back toward her and, clenching his fist, whipped his right elbow like a piston into her chest. The blow knocked Fatima to the floor.

He returned his focus to Faridah and kicked her in the stomach as she tried to get up. She fell again and brought her legs up and wrapped her arms around her body trying to make herself as small as possible. Hamad aimed his next kick to her head, which started a slow trickle of blood down her cheek. His strength increased by his wrath, he stood her up and pushed Faridah back until she was wedged against the waist-high refrigerator. She leaned away from him and to the side to avoid the shelf in back of her. For an instant she uncovered her face to look at her mother. Kella felt guilty. Was Faridah looking for her? The blood from her scalp continued to flow down her face mixing with the tears, and onto her clothes. There was blood on the floor.

"You're insane! Stop it!" Faridah shrieked.

"You're going back to Algeria, tomorrow!" Hamad said, his voice viciously calm. "You'll spend the rest of your days atoning." Thrusting her hands out, Faridah tried to keep Hamad at bay.

"Never! I'll never go back there!"

Hamad froze, struck by his daughter's statement. Like a boxer in training, he struck her head and arms with his fists as she tried to protect herself. Faridah let out a piteous wail and, unable to move away in any direction, leaned her upper body back until her head touched the wall behind the refrigerator. Then, pressing her back with his left forearm, Hamad reached behind Faridah for the knife on the refrigerator. Kella saw his rage subside and another quieter but more menacing emotion took over.

As Hamad raised the knife, Kella sprang forward, no longer able to stand by. She seized his arm from the side with both hands. Surprised, Hamad lifted his foot and tried to kick Kella's knee. But she was too close. With his knife hand still up over Faridah, he swung his left fist into Kella's stomach, hitting the nerve center of the solar plexus. She dropped her hands to her stomach, unable to breathe. Aware that she was now extremely vulnerable, she backed off, still doubled over and breathing in short gasps. Still bent over, she looked up at Hamad terrified that he would attack her but he refocused on Faridah. With a violent swing of the knife, he slashed Faridah's shoulder. Her blood sprayed his shirt.

"*Allahu Akbar*," he said in a loud voice.

Again, he raised the knife, but Fatima sprang up and hit him with her fists. He shoved her aside. Then, Hamad brought the knife slowly and deliberately over his head with both hands, chanting, "*Allahu Akbar*," a sacrifice to his God, and plunged the blade into

Faridah's chest, again and again, each powerful thrust accompanied by its own "God is Great!"

Kella forced out a scream of horror. To her ears it sounded like a weak squeal. Taking as deep a breath as she could, she managed a louder, "Murderer!"

Hamad pushed Fatima away and turned toward Kella, the knife still in his hand, blood on his shirt. Their eyes met. She felt the hatred and rage burn into her soul. Acting instinctively, she turned and ran from the kitchen, through the dark hallway and out the door of the apartment.

She pushed past neighbors who had assembled on the landing and took the steps down several at a time despite her bulky clothing, aware that her life depended upon getting to the street before Hamad caught up with her.

Kella reached the street-level hallway, still breathing with difficulty. She ran toward the entrance but was stopped by four hefty men bringing large boxes into the building. The entrance was blocked from side to side by heavy looking cardboard containers. One was more than halfway inside and two men were struggling with another. Kella briefly wondered if she could get over the container but was instantly convinced that she could not. She looked around and saw a wood and glass door in the back of the lobby. She ran to it but could not see through the greenish opaque glass. She feared another dead end, but she nevertheless turned the white porcelain handle and found herself in a narrow corridor that led out to a small courtyard. She jogged past garbage cans and entered a corridor similar to the one she had just left and reached the front hallway of the building next door. She kept moving and reached the sidewalk.

She nearly lost her balance when she saw the movers who had blocked her exit in front of Faridah's building and barely managed to turn course and run the other way. After a few steps, she realized she had no idea how to get back to the Metro. On the way to the apartment, she had been talking and had paid little attention to direction, expecting that Faridah would guide her back.

But Faridah was dead—dead!

The thought and the word shocked her. She looked back for Hamad but did not see him, just a crowded sidewalk with working people going about their daily routine. Kella's scarf came undone and she first tried to put it back on, but decided after a few steps that the effort was slowing her down so she crumpled it into her left hand as she ran. The images she had just witnessed were seared in her mind—Hamad's face a nightmarish demon's mask; Faridah bleeding and screaming; the knife plunging into Faridah's body. She was now only fifty yards away from Faridah's building and already breathing hard.

She ran around a corner, slowed to a walk and put her scarf back on. No one seemed to be paying any particular attention to her. She scanned the street for a taxi and tried to get her bearings. No taxis in sight. She glanced at her watch wondering if Steve would still be at the Basilica and was surprised that less than twenty minutes had elapsed since she and Steve had separated at the Metro station. She glanced at the Tuareg tattoo on the back of her right hand wistfully and looked up hoping to spot the Basilica's spires but the street was too narrow and its buildings, while not particularly high, were still too tall to enable her to see anything beyond them.

What she did notice for the first time was the number of young Arab men on the streets, in small groups. Most had a cigarette protruding defiantly from the corner of their mouths as if each was an Ali La Pointe, the small-time thief who had become the psychopathic hero of the movie *The Battle of Algiers*, and all with no particular place to go. Every Arab male on the street seemed like another Hamad, full of anger ready to erupt if provoked. She saw a sign for the Basilica and she hastened her steps in that direction, consciously avoiding eye contact with any of the loiterers.

She came to an intersection that broadened her line-of-sight, and saw the market she had passed after leaving the Metro. As she crossed the street she noticed a man walking quickly, half running, in her direction. He seemed to be searching over and around the people in front of him. She did not get a close enough look to determine if it was Hamad. Instead she stayed close to the other pedestrians crossing the street, using them as concealment.

At the open-air market, she stopped briefly at a stall and bought a long dark-gray scarf, to change her appearance a bit from the beacon of a bright white scarf she had worn earlier. As she completed her purchase, she spotted Hamad. He was scanning the market. Kella moved behind a display of Damascene tablecloths. With the intention of appearing to be just another shopper, she examined the material. She could no longer see Hamad and she directed her steps toward the Metro beyond the Hotel de Ville.

As she detached herself from the crowd at the market, Hamad reappeared, now running toward her. Spurred by energy born of desperation, Kella also started running. She looked for a policeman, but the police were wherever the absent cab drivers had gone. Kella, who had considered going straight for the Metro, veered to the right toward the Basilica.

She realized that she would have no protection from Hamad's violence in the Metro unless a *gendarme* showed up or unless she could hop on a departing metro with quickly closing doors, both unlikely to happen. The Basilica had Steve and Catholic priests who, in her mind, stood for safety and sanctuary. Further, there would be tourists, Westerners, visiting the necropolis of the French Kings. All in all, the environment would be more protective. She raced to the front doors of the church and went in.

She took a breath and got her bearings. She was in the middle of a thin crowd that was starting to disperse. A mass must have just ended. Two priests stood in the back of the church, not far from the main entrance, talking with parishioners. Kella looked for Steve but did not see him.

The area in which she stood was partially occupied by rows of chairs in the middle flanked by wide columns rising up about thirty meters toward the vaulted ceilings. Statues and mausoleums took up the far half of the Basilica. Not far from her in the public area and on the right was a small souvenir shop. Further away from her in the center of the mausoleum area a guide was leading a tour group. Kella started walking toward the tour, in the hope that Steve was with the tourists. But a railing about a foot and half high that divided the public area from the tombs stopped her. Kella saw a side door that the tourists must have used to enter and guessed that the ticket booth to pay for the tour was outside that door.

Not seeing any authority that might object, Kella quickly stepped over the railing and headed toward the tour now behind a large monument with four arches on one side and two on the other. She noticed two effigies inside the monument, and with great relief, saw Steve listening to the guide and reading an inscription beneath the figures of Anne de Bretagne and her husband Louis XII.

Steve saw her, moved closer and, with a false intellectual air, said, "I've always wanted to know more about Anne de Bretagne. Did you know that her marriage made Brittany a part of France?"

Kella was not listening. She tried to peer through the openings of the arches but could not see over the effigies inside.

She looked around the monument and was terrified to see Hamad inside the Basilica. Kella grabbed Steve's arm and pulled him away from the tour group but still behind the monument. In a low, breathless voice she said, "Steve, something terrible has happened. That's Hamad, Faridah's father. He just killed her. I saw it."

A sob escaped, and she put a hand to her mouth.

"Killed her? Is that what you said? No!"

He put his arms around her for an instant until she stepped back, having regained control.

Hamad had stopped very close to the spot where Kella first paused to look at her surroundings. He seemed hesitant to go further into what to him must have seemed a strange but sacred place.

"I was there. It was awful. I ran. Now, he's after me," Kella said.

"That guy over there?" he said looking in Hamad's direction, "Show me."

She pointed from behind the monument. Hamad was moving forward, getting closer to the railing. Kella and Steve stayed with the tourists and their guide as they moved. The tour guide was speaking about Anne de Bretagne's marriage.

Then Hamad, with stains on his clothes, stepped over the railing and came toward them. Steve stepped in front of Kella. A woman who came out of the souvenir shop said in a raspy, vernacular accent that told Kella volumes about the owner's view of Arab immigrants, "*Alors*, look at you! Where are we going—and without a ticket?"

Hamad looked back and spotted the source of the voice, a red-faced female walking toward him, an infidel not fit to clean up behind him. But he felt intimidated.

The woman continued, the superior acoustics of the church lending her words additional authority.

"Have you no respect for the house of God?"

Kella watched Hamad's anger turn first to puzzlement then fear as he looked to the far end of the church toward the altar and the cross. Then Kella's and Hamad's eyes locked for an instant. She saw him turn away in extreme frustration. With fists tightly clenched and the muscles of his jaw bulging he strode out of the church.

Steve whispered, "You stay with the tour, I'm going to take a breath of fresh air."

Before Kella could reply, he left the group, walked past the woman in the souvenir shop telling her, "You're right, *Madame*. I'm going to make sure he doesn't hang around the front."

When Steve stepped outside, he saw Hamad standing on the steps that led to the Basilica's main entrance, motioning to another man coming in their direction about fifty yards away on the sidewalk. He went up to Hamad, who appeared surprised.

"I don't ever want to see you again," he said, "and neither does the woman you followed here. If either you or your friend..." he pointed toward Hamad's friend who was now running toward them, "are still here when we come out of the church, your days in sunny France are over, unless you want to spend them in a prison cell."

Hamad reacted instantly with a wild swinging right fist. Expecting it, Steve stepped forward under Hamad fist and he caught him under the chin with an open palm. The force of the blow was multiplied by Hamad's forward motion. His head jerked back and he fell backward on the stone surface of the parvis. When the other man reached them, Hamad seemed unconscious. Hamad's friend looked down at Hamad, undecided, but reached in his pocket and produced a knife.

"Don't make it any worse," Steve said. "Take care of your friend. Maybe he'll live."

He turned around and went back into the church.

When he rejoined the tour, Steve whispered, "Let's stay with the tour to give Hamad a bit longer."

They went downstairs to the crypt. Kella was in a daze. She stayed close to Steve, trying to keep out images of Hamad's knife thrusts into Faridah's body. When the guide explained that Saint Denis had been beheaded in Montmartre in the third century and had carried his head in his hands for several kilometers to this spot, where the church had been built to honor him two centuries later, Kella gasped at the grisly image that reinforced her painful memory.

She asked Steve, "What about her body? What is he going to do with Faridah's body? Steve, I ran away. Instead of helping her, I ran away."

Quiet tears ran down her face.

"I want to get out of here."

Steve took her back up to street level and toward the exit. Kella stopped him.

"Wait. Before leaving, I want a couple of minutes to myself."

She glanced around and walked to a side chapel, knelt, and prayed for Faridah. After a few minutes, she stood up. She looked up at a statue of the Virgin Mary in whites and blues with arms out in a welcoming gesture and murmured, "Please care for the soul of my friend who meant no harm."

Kella met Steve by the front entrance.

"You have to tell the police. Let's go to the local police station," he said.

She hesitated a second, wiped her tears, blew her nose and regained her composure.

"No. I just want to get away from here. I'll call my father and he'll make arrangements for me to talk to the police later."

Seeing the surprise on Steve's face, she added, "As the dependent of an American Foreign Service officer with diplomatic status, I'm not supposed to be in touch with the French police without either a consular officer or the regional security officer. My double nationality status makes things more complicated. It's better if someone from the embassy is with me when I talk to the police."

They went out, looking left and right for any signs that Hamad was near. With Kella clutching Steve's arm tightly, they walked quickly to the parking lot, climbed into the MINI Cooper and left St. Denis behind.

5. Basilique de Saint-Denis

"Steve, I don't want to go home. Let's go somewhere else. Or let's just drive," Kella said.

It was evening, but the French capital's northern latitude provided natural light late in the day. At first they drove in silence. Then little by little, at times sobbing, at times almost incoherent, Kella relived the horrible memory of her friend's murder. She imitated Hamad's killing motion with her hand, repeating as he had, "*Allahu Akbar.*" The retelling was at once traumatic and cathartic for her.

"Steve," she said, "you know that I was initially raised Muslim. But I'm confused. The God to whom Hamad sacrificed Faridah is not the same God I thought I knew."

The intensity of his glance surprised her as he said, "Radical Islamists pray to a different Allah. I should have gone with you—I should have gone. Your friend might still be alive."

Kella shook her head.

"He stabbed her again and again. There was so much blood. There was a point when Faridah looked for me, I think. She expected me to help her. I tried..."

She sobbed again.

Stopping at a light, Steve said, "Killing your daughter in the name of Allah! What kind of religion is that?"

"I had heard stories, but I didn't really pay much attention before," Kella said, shaking her head. "I thought these 'honor killings,' as they're called, only took place in the uncontrolled areas, in the mountains of Afghanistan."

They had reached the Place Charles de Gaulle and Steve turned onto the Avenue des Champs Élysées. Taking his cue from the bright lights and lively rhythm of the wide boulevard, he tried to change the mood.

"Listen, you know that I have to leave for Morocco in a couple days. I'm going to drive you home now. But, before I get on a plane, I'm going to try to help you forget today's nightmare. I'm going to treat you to the greatest meal you've ever had. Tomorrow night, come to my house in Neuilly and I'll surprise you."

Kella forced a smile.

He continued, "It's a difficult time. I'm sorry about your friend. This is the kind of thing one never forgets. But I want to put you on a good path before I leave."

"I know, and I'm grateful. But I don't know if..."

She looked over at him and put her hand on his.

"I want you to hold me."

Steve turned onto a lateral street and stopped. They held each other for a moment.

"Thanks. That was good. Until you lose someone, it's impossible to know, to understand, how it feels."

"I know that. I know exactly how you feel. And that's why I'm driving you home right now."

Later, they parked in front of her apartment building off the Rue de la Tour.

"A year ago," Steve told her, "I took my girlfriend Vera skiing in Canada, in British Colombia's Purcell Mountains. On the last day, she joined a small ski-mobiling group so I could go heli-skiing for the day."

He gestured with his right arm, palm out, and looked in the middle distance.

"'Ski on the Untouched Powder of the Backcountry Slopes,' the ad said. My plan was to propose that evening. An avalanche ... I never saw her again. There was an investigation ... the guide was inexperienced, according to the report. He should never have taken the group to that area."

After a few seconds of silence, he added, "There was someone on the flight the other night who looked like her."

"I'm sorry," Kella said. "What you're saying, I think, is that grief strikes many people. But they go on, like you. And I will too."

Neither said anything for a few minutes.

"But what can be done about the Hamads of the world? Is your country doing anything? Is France? To stop these barbarian acts?"

"Good question. People like Hamad don't feel controlled by the laws of the state. He gets his justification from Allah. The only interested organizations are the intelligence agencies. But, in the U.S. anyway, their main responsibility is to gather information."

Kella got out in front of an apartment building in the sixteenth *arrondissement* off the Rue de la Tour. Before getting out of the car, she kissed Steve on the cheek.

"Thanks. Food is the last thing on my mind, but I'll probably change my mind. See you tomorrow night."

She buzzed herself in and disappeared behind a wrought-iron and glass door.

*   *   *

Steve savored driving back to Neuilly. He loved the surprising turbocharged power of the small engine—a kiddy car on steroids. He was glad that Coogan had chosen manual transmission and the six-gear system was smooth, quick, and responsive. Although left-handed, he had long ago adjusted to a right-handed world and the center console mounted shifting lever offered no problems for him. Feeling the machine respond to his commands restored a good measure of the control he felt he had lost during the day's events—a good antidote to the high emotions of the previous hours.

*   *   *

In the morning, Steve and his host had breakfast together. French *café au lait*, croissants, toasted buttered slices of crusty French bread, juice, and a jar of peanut butter.

"Peanut butter? In France?"

"It's the only thing I miss about American food," Coogan laughed. "It looks like I need to buy another jar. It's only available at Fauchon's, an exclusive shop near the Madeleine. It's right next to the caviar, and almost as expensive."

After Steve described Kella's experience, Coogan said, "Honor killings are not all that rare. They just don't get reported. So if there is a hint or a rumor that a female is promiscuous, it becomes the duty, the obligation, of the senior male to either kill her himself or assign one of his sons to do it."

Steve's voice went up a notch.

"You don't sound surprised. It's incredible to me that these killings, these dishonor killings, are accepted as part of the landscape. I've even read that in a rape case, the female is usually the one who is punished. I assume, I hope, that the French police will hunt this guy down."

He could see that Coogan was letting him blow off steam. He took a breath, had a sip of the strong French coffee and changed the subject.

"What about the break-in? Anything new?"

"The advice from the police and from the U.S. Embassy is to wait for the investigation to take place. As far as I know, the police haven't even contacted the Saudis yet. So I'm going to raise the wall or make it somehow more difficult to get over."

"I don't think you can make that wall high enough."

"You're right. Then I'll just have to mine the flower beds."

He chuckled at the idea." Actually, I'm going to pay call on my neighbor."

"Why would a Saudi want to break in here?" Steve asked.

Coogan studied his toast before replying.

"It's not surprising that the intruder came from the Saudi residence, assuming that the reason for it was to find the Quranic documents. I can't believe that this was an officially sanctioned attempt; it was pretty sloppy. It was probably an overzealous servant. The House of Saud tries to keep everyone happy through hand-outs. They need the American military but are also dependent on the fundamentalist Wahhabi clerics with whom they have had a Faustian agreement since the 1800s. The Saudis finance the spread of Wahhabism globally, to include madrasas in the United States. But they're also attacked by al Qaeda for being apostates, for being too close to the American 'Jews and crusaders.'"

Steve reached for the coffee pot and said, "Looks as if, by trying to please everyone, they please no one."

"By the way, you probably haven't seen this yet."

Coogan handed him a French newspaper that was folded to a story about the discovery of the documents, complete with pictures of Coogan and Steve at the airport.

"They spelled your name right."

"Yes, thanks to Benjamin. With everything that's going on, I don't like having my picture in the paper."

"You're right, and I'm sorry I got you involved."

6. Neuilly-sur Seine

That evening, after the police frisked her, Kella rang the bell of the Coogan house under the unwavering gaze of the French policemen.

Steve opened the door and, in answer to her curious nod toward the armed security guards, explained, "The Saudi ambassador lives next door. And the Moroccan ambassador is on the other side. I don't know if I should feel safe or if I'm in the middle of a shooting gallery."

"I can't believe it. They actually searched me."

"Yes. Me, too. I'm sorry; I should have warned you."

He led her up the stairs to the den. Coogan had stacked the books and photos in piles since his return.

"There was a break-in the other day. Nothing is missing but they took the place apart."

She sat on one of two leather sofas as Steve opened a bottle of Veuve-Cliquot champagne that had been chilling in a silver ice bucket.

"A break-in?" she asked. "I saw your picture in the paper this morning. You're famous. Is the break-in connected?"

He handed her a glass of champagne.

"That article is trouble. But, there is no *fatwa* on me yet," he grinned. "But I'm starting to believe that these people are serious. Now they're going to associate me with this Quran research."

"Plus, Hamad, Faridah's father, saw you. I doubt that he reads the French newspapers, but if he does, he now knows who you are. I don't know if he has my name."

They moved to the dining room carrying their champagne glasses. The table was set for two with baccarat wine glasses, a formal setting of silverware and dishes in rich gold and red design. She sat down puzzled by the absence of food smells. Steve went to the kitchen and soon Kella heard the noise of a dumbwaiter. Steve came in carrying two plates, each with six oysters on the half shell set on shaved ice. He put them down and plates and took a paper from his pocket, which he folded in half and placed in front of Kella. It was the menu: *Belons Mignonettes*, Duck *a la Bigarade* with potatoes *Parisiennes*, *Salade Frisee*, *Plateau de Fromage*, and *Mousse au Chocolat*.

Kella looked at Steve, dumbfounded.

"Okay, okay," he said. "I have a confession to make. No, I'm not a world-class chef. A student at the Cordon Bleu school works here in return for a place to stay. I'm doing my best to give him some practice."

He smiled at his own humor. He poured the *Vouvray* to accompany the *belons*, and later there would be a six-year-old Gevrey-Chambertin for the duck course, and a twelve-year-old Chateau Potensac with the cheese. He knew he would have to dig deep into his pocket to replace the wines he was borrowing from his host's wine cellar.

Steve had a sip of his wine and said, "You don't have to talk about yesterday if you don't want to, okay? You look worried. We're surrounded by Paris's finest. You met them at the door. Let's just enjoy the dinner. This is the best wine I've ever tasted."

"Okay, but I just want to tell you one thing."

She got up from the table to get her purse on the sofa and came back, digging around in her purse.

"This afternoon I found my notes from a seminar I attended a couple of months ago on Sharia Law in the twenty-first century. I read them over because I want to make sense of Faridah's murder, I guess. I know I'll never really understand, or accept it, but maybe I can get some insight into the thinking that provoked it. The speaker was a Salafist born and raised in Belgium."

Steve was surprised.

"Belgium? I bet I know him, Tariq al Khalil, right?"

"You're right! Wow, that's an amazing coincidence."

She fiddled around in her purse, as though distracted.

"But go ahead. I didn't mean to interrupt. Later, I also have an al Khalil story."

At last she retrieved a notebook.

"Let's see. Al Khalil, al Azar University in Cairo and the Université Libre de Bruxelles, where you must have known him. He was, in my memory, supremely self-confident to the point of arrogance—not a hint of uncertainty about him."

She looked up.

"I remember the way he looked at his audience; it was almost mesmerizing—like a snake hypnotizing its prey."

"Well then, it's definitely the same man I knew!"

"He stressed a couple of key points."

She tapped her page where words were dramatically underlined.

First, regardless of time and place, Islam is Islam, given to the Prophet by Allah and immutable. Any changes are treasonous and constitute apostasy, or takfir.

"So, I guess that all interpretations over the last thirteen centuries are out the window. And the last thing they want is a discussion over the reliability of this particular version of the Quran as the word of God."

"Exactly! Then, if being a good French citizen leads to being a bad Muslim, being a good French citizen is unacceptable. Here is a quote: 'We are under constant pressure to reform, to modernize, and I can understand this impulse. But the answer is not the modernization of Islam, but rather the Islamization of modern life. Islam is the answer.'"

Steve was actually paying little attention to the duck with orange trimmings Benjamin had spent hours preparing.

"Since Islam can't change, it's up to us to change? So we should all accept Islam, just like that? Not a lot of flexibility. By the way, 'Islam is the answer;' that's a Muslim Brotherhood slogan."

Kella nodded and shifted in her seat.

"Someone asked about the oppression of women in Islam. His answer was that Islam has actually been in the vanguard of equality for women, that the Quran has raised them to full status. He quoted from a Sura, 33:35. I meant to look it up. Then, and this is why I had to find my notes today, someone else asked 'If women and men are equal under Islam, would it be all right for women to kill their husbands or fathers if they commit adultery the way that men can commit honor killings upon women suspected of having been unchaste?'"

"That must have hit home."

She had an oyster before continuing.

"He almost lost it. He was trying to see who had asked the question. He said, 'you should look at your own society, which debases women by using their bodies to sell cars, to sell anything.' Frankly, he was scary. Finally, he said that what Westerners call democracy is insulting to Allah and to all Muslims. And then he turned and left the room."

"I don't think I understand why. Do you?"

"Well, since our laws are man-made and not straight from God, our laws aren't worth the paper they're written on. Any law other than God's is an insult to God. Right? I'm glad that I don't have to live in his world."

Steve took their dinner plates to the kitchen and returned with their desserts.

"So, how do you like my going away dinner so far?" he asked. "How was the duck?"

"Memorable. I'll tell my grandchildren."

Between bites of *mousse au chocolat*, Kella said, "Okay, your turn. What's your al Khalil story?"

"Somehow, fine food and wine don't go together with al Khalil. I'll make it short."

He had another taste of the *mousse au chocolat*. In spite of the topic, the bitterness of the chocolate and the aftertaste of Cointreau liquor that complemented the duck sauce of the last dish satisfied his taste buds. He put his spoon down.

"I was a student in Brussels when my father was assigned there at the embassy. He captained the American team in the annual diplomatic tennis tournament and recruited me to be his doubles partner. It turned out that al Khalil was playing for the European team and I played against him. When a point went against him, he almost brained the referee with his racquet. His partner was barely able to stop him."

"Same deal I guess," Kella said. "Western rules, rules that have not come from God, don't have to be honored. In that setting, Mr. al Khalil was a misfit."

"You said it. After the match, trophies were awarded and we had dinner. Al Khalil's intense stare caused one of the female guests sitting across from him to move to another table. Al Khalil doesn't know how to behave in the presence of free-range western women. Oh, by the way, our team won."

Kella took a sip of her Chateau-Potensac.

"There's something I've been thinking about all day," she said.

Steve gestured with his spoon that she go on.

"I want to take a break from school and go to Timbuktu to see my relatives. On the other hand, I can't just pick up and leave ENA. I may have to wait for a vacation or a holiday period when the school is closed. Frankly, I'm having a difficult time making decisions right now."

"A change of scenery might do you good. Why don't you come and visit me in Virginia? I'll be back there in a week or two after my Moroccan trip. I have an apartment, with a guest room."

"Thanks for the offer; it sounds lovely. But I do want to spend some time around Timbuktu where I grew up. My stepparents are off to Tel Aviv and they're busy settling in. They don't need me underfoot. Anyway, we're not going to lose sight of each other, right?"

They got up from the dining room table and went back to the den where they sat on the sofa. Steve put his glass down on the coffee table, and took Kella's and put it down next to his. Pushing Vera to the back of his mind, he cupped her chin in his left hand and drew closer. They kissed softly.

She smiled and said, "I see that free-range Western women don't scare you."

Gradually, they slipped lower on the sofa, but then the doorbell rang. They looked at each other and laughed at the timing of the interruption. Like a software program that is open but not currently in charge of the computer's operations, part of Steve's mind had been thinking of Vera the whole evening. The doorbell was a welcome distraction. Was he betraying her? It had been just over a year. Was he being callous by being attracted to Kella? The bell rang again and someone pounded on the door with a hard object. He went downstairs and opened it.

Two policemen held a woman by each arm. She wore a *hijab*. Steve thought she looked like many of the women he had seen in St. Denis the day before. The older policeman asked Steve, "Do you know this woman. She said she works here."

"You better ask Benjamin. He's the cook. I'll get him. One second."

Steve turned and knocked on Benjamin's door.

"Yes, what is it? How was the dinner?" he smiled proudly.

"Great, but the police want to talk to you."

"Again? Tell them I'm not here."

"No, you'd better come," said Steve, gently pulling him by the arm into the hallway. Benjamin looked toward the open door and exclaimed, "*Achoura!* That's her!"

The police asked Benjamin to come outside and Steve joined them. He noticed several police vehicles with their lights on and engines running in the street. He looked to his left, toward the Bois, and saw that the street was closed off. He assumed it was closed at the other end as well.

"We arrested this woman before she rang your doorbell. She was acting suspiciously. My men had to restrain her. Here is what she was wearing under her clothes."

He led them to one of the vehicles and pointed to the open cargo space of one where one of his men was taking photos of an explosive belt.

Steve went back upstairs and left Benjamin to the tender mercies of the *gendarmes*. He explained what was going on to Kella.

"Like you said," she replied, "these people are serious. I hope your friend Mr. Coogan is all right. Well, I think better go home. I'll call a taxi."

She made the call, and as she gathered her coat and purse she said, "Ever since my father's reception, ever since I met you, I've been on a roller coaster. Going back to school and normal life in Paris is going to be a relief, and a bore."

She smiled.

"I don't know if I can return to normal. Faridah's death has changed everything. I'm now anxious to get into the real world. I want to get involved in something more meaningful than studying. I think I'll actually miss you. Who's going to listen to me and get me out of trouble?"

"You're strong. You'll be fine. Think about coming to Virginia. But I admit that I'm not being totally altruistic here."

Now he smiled.

"Thanks. First I'm going to go to Timbuktu as soon as I can. I think that spending some time with my cousin Thiyya, who helped raise me, will be a good thing. I will visit you in the States. I'll work it out, I promise. And I want to take you to the airport tomorrow."

The doorbell rang again, and Steve knew that Kella's taxi had somehow made its way through the security gauntlet.

7. Blida, Algeria

Tariq al Khalil and Hussein al Kaylani followed El Maghrebi's men out of the city and headed south toward Ghardaia, where al Khalil hoped to meet with a local leader. They expected to get to Timbuktu in about ten or twelve days, struggling through heat and the occasional sand storm during the day and stopping in oasis towns at night.

So far, the road to Ghardaia was broad and paved. Both cars were equipped for desert travel with special sand filters for the air intakes, an extra jerry can of water and another of gasoline in retaining holders on each side, an additional spare tire, and tools that neither Al Khalil nor Hussein knew how to use.

Hussein, normally physically unimposing, now was even less so in his oversized *jellaba*. His eyes, slits in his dark face, reflected an alertness and cleverness that some had under-appreciated at their expense. Keeping his eyes on the road and the watery-looking mirages that shimmered in the distance, he asked, "What did you think of El Maghrebi?"

Al Khalil replied, "El Maghrebi said he was a Salafist, committed to pushing the borders of the Land of Peace back to their former boundaries and to impose Sharia law. I think that he just wants to rearrange Algerian furniture. We will rebuild Allah's house."

"We need activists, doers, more than we need ideologues," Hussein said. "Your vision is our guide. I wish we had somebody like El Maghrebi in Morocco."

"You're right. In forging a pure faith, in the heat of fire if need be, to the glory of Allah, the Beneficent, the Merciful, we need no more interpreters of the faith. But we can use all of the El Maghrebis we can find."

He paused for a second then continued.

"You're right about Morocco. It's been very quiet. The leader of the cell, Lahlou, is neither a thinker nor an activist. Maybe you should pay them a visit, soon."

The men lapsed into silence. The world was losing its color; everything was becoming a sun-worn brown collage of sand and rock.

Al Khalil dozed off but Hussein's voice woke him. Hussein gestured at the desert and said, "I hope that you have thought about this strategy very carefully. Is governing this sandbox really the way to recreate the Caliphate that you want?"

Al Khalil looked out the window at the arid, monotonous ground with the occasional group of nomads riding, or walking alongside their camels. He woke from his reverie and looked at Hussein.

"The Prophet, may Allah bless him, started from Medina and conquered Arabia. His companions and successors then conquered most of the known world. They started from the desert. We, too, can start from the desert."

The thought provoked a vivid memory of Al Khalil's uncle Said, and of his protégé Salim Salheldin, who were the reasons he was now driving through what Hussein called the "sand box." The decision point for al Khalil had occurred after Said's death.

Drinking dark coffee in a Brussels apartment on Avenue Albert 1er, he had listened to Salim, his uncle's protégé and replacement.

Salim was tall and spare. Although dressed in a double-breasted suit, he could have spent the last forty days and nights in the desert. He had a hawkish profile and his hairline had receded to the top of his head. Al Khalil had always thought he dressed like a banker.

"What the movement needs you to do in the countries bordering on the Sahara is what your uncle and I did in Europe. Already, we either control or can control entire towns in France, in Holland and Belgium through Sharia law."

Al Khalil knew that immigration combined with a high birth rate made Islam the fastest growing religion in Europe. He also knew that alienation was driving many immigrants to the mosque. Some immigrants were more Muslim in Europe than they ever were at home in Algeria or in Pakistan. One only had to look at the growing number of the faithful, especially the young, dressed in Levi jeans, Harvard sweatshirts and Yankee baseball caps, crowding around the mosques of Europe. It was easy to screen and recruit the more zealous.

Tariq hadn't replied right away, thoughtfully taking Salim's cup and his own and refilling them. When he came back with the small, steaming cups with their scent of cardamom, he stood by the window and looked down at the traffic on the broad avenue below.

"Isn't putting my efforts in the Sahel a waste of my time when the countries of the Middle East, especially Egypt and Saudi Arabia, are ruled by apostates? Our future, the Caliphate, needs those countries as the pillars of our empire."

Salim leaned back in his chair.

"If you go to Cairo and speak out you'll be killed just like your grandfather and what will we have gained except another martyr? Martyrs are plentiful. Besides, playing the Americans' game of democracy is helping us make inroads through elections."

Tariq savored the irony of taking over through democracy for the purpose of later imposing the dictatorship of the mosque through Sharia.

Salim went on, "Others are focusing on the Far Enemy, the United States and the other Western countries supporting the apostate leaders in the Middle East. If you can bring the populations of North Africa home, the tide will be irreversible; the Near Enemy, the corrupt leaders in Egypt, Syria and other countries will fall like ripe dates."

He paused. Tariq felt Salim's eyes fixing on him over his Sèvres porcelain cup.

"You will realize our dream of recreating the time of unqualified glory when Islam ruled. Your mission must be to politicize minorities living on the edges of the Sahara. The way to attract them is to provide what they don't have, starting with pharmaceutical goods. Your key to success may start with the lowly aspirin," Salim laughed.

Relenting a bit, Salim added, "Of course, your work in the Sahel can't take all of your time. It will not help us for you to become forgotten in the sands of the Sahara. You must also continue your speaking and intellectual discourse in Europe. It's what your uncle would have wanted."

Tariq furrowed his brow as he paced.

"Islam is submission. Those who will not become Muslims must still submit—they will acknowledge the dominance, the superiority, of Allah, Lord of the World, the Merciful. Or they will die."

Tariq liked Napoleon's characterization of his foreign minister, Talleyrand, as an 'iron fist in a velvet glove.' Talleyrand had begun his political career in the Church and al Khalil knew he could also use his religion as the path to power.

* * *

Until they neared the *wilaya* of Ghardaia, the view from the car was made up of rocky, sometimes gravelly, ground punctuated by tufts of brownish grass, bizarre black rock formations and leafless shrubs. At the initiative of El Maghrebi's men, they had stopped once, seemingly in the middle of nowhere. However, they had almost immediately been surrounded by a dozen curious nomads. For a few *dinars*, they had gone about collecting enough twigs for a fire over which the driver of the lead car had made tea. The nomads had displayed a few items for sale, including "desert roses," petrified sand shaped in the form of roses by the wind.

The scenery changed as they entered the stony M'Zab Valley, a conglomeration of five walled towns each built on a hill and dominated by its own minaret. They drove into Ghardaia, the largest of the five and followed the lead car driven by El Maghrebi's men. As they passed by the mosque, its height and location symbolic of its importance, it reminded al Khalil of medieval Europe when the church dominated society and its cathedrals commanded the skyline. Later, government buildings had grown higher, and today, all over the world, the highest structures were those of businesses. It was fitting, he thought, that the most horrendous blow against the West in modern times was the attack on the Twin Towers in New York City.

Tariq noticed the different dress of people in the street. Men wore baggy trousers, beige was a favorite, and flat round hats. There were few women in the street, most totally covered in white cloaks, only one eye visible.

That night, he and Hussein walked back from the house of a religious leader they were hoping would join them when Tariq said, "I've been thinking about Morocco. What's going on there? I think you made a mistake in appointing this fellow Lahlou to run our operations there."

Before Hussein could reply, they heard singing and shouting. They turned the corner and saw two tipsy Europeans, probably French oil workers from the Total operation in Hassi-Messaoud about two-hundred-fifty miles to the East. Hassi-Messaoud was Algeria's main petroleum center, operated by French, American, and Italian oil companies. These foreign expats did not normally come to Ghardaia for their R&R. Their companies paid their trips back home for a month before they returned to their oil camps in the middle of the Algerian desert for another month.

In Brussels, when confronted with repulsive behavior, he had not been able to act. Here, he had no doubt as to what he must do.

"Hussein, let's go," Tariq urged.

They quickened their step to catch up. It was dusk and very few people were out. As the Frenchmen became aware of the approaching men, one turned to the other and said, nodding toward Tariq and Hussein, "Look, Arab *indigenes*—locals."

Addressing them, he said, "We thought your town was deserted. I am so glad to see a human, even an Arab."

He winked at his friend.

"We came all the way from Hassi, you know, Hassi-Messaoud—we're making Algeria rich! What is there to do here?"

To al Khalil, the tone of their voices was insulting. Here were infidel outsiders, exploiters of Arab resources and defilers of Islamic law. Tariq glanced at Hussein. Each understood the other.

In French, Tariq said, "It looks like you're having fun. You deserve it. Hassi must be hard work."

The drunker one said, "Yes." Tariq noticed that the other's eyes were well focused and that he was evaluating the situation.

"You won't find any restaurants open now," Tariq said, "None that serve liquor anyway."

The French spokesman said, "That's right. That's why we're going back to the hotel. My room is the only bar in this damn town. Do you know of any place that's open where we can have some fun? If you know what I mean?"

Al Khalil smiled conspiratorially at the Frenchmen, and nodded at Hussein, who couldn't understand French. "We know of a place where you'll have the best time of your lives."

"Well, tell us. I guess you want money," the drunker one grumbled. He reached for his back pocket.

Tariq held up his hand. "Keep your money. We'll take you there because otherwise you won't get in. Besides, that's where we're going."

Once off the main street and into an alley, Hussein and Tariq looked around, and seeing no one, on cue, drew the knives Ibrahim El Maghrebi had given them in Blida. Hussein quickly took advantage of the element of surprise. Holding his knife with the point up, he stepped forward and immediately used a killing thrust just below the rib cage and to his right, hoping to drive the knife up under the ribs to the heart. Tariq slashed at his opponent.

The two Frenchmen stumbled back, looking for a way to escape. Hussein drew blood but wasn't close enough for the decisive blow. The Frenchmen turned to run but Tariq and Hussein were quicker and soon had them on the ground. To defend themselves, the Frenchmen turned over to try to grab their attackers' hands or arms or knives. The Frenchmen were strong and they put up a fight. They yelled for help, but if anyone heard or saw them, they didn't come to their aid. They were, however at a disadvantage, being drunk and without weapons.

Soon enough their loss of blood weakened them. Tariq's fury made him relentless. The drunker Frenchman was on the ground trying to stop Tariq's knife thrusts and was able to get both hands on Tariq's knife hand. With strength born of desperation he began to push the knife away. But suddenly Hussein kneeled over both and, with one swift and muscular motion he slit the Frenchman's throat. Blood spurted on Tariq hands and face. They dragged the bodies behind steps that led up to a front door so that the bodies would be hidden at least from one side. Then, quickly, they retreated.

Afterward, Tariq felt immensely satisfied and exhilarated. This was the first time he had felt relieved of the straitjacket he had been forced to wear while living and working in a non-Muslim environment. He was thinking, for the first time, that the advice of his uncle Said was more than just logically sound. He felt purified.

Al Khalil had a mixed reaction to Hussein's performance. He had dispatched his Frenchman in a very workmanlike way. But the lack of emotion puzzled Tariq. The killing of an infidel was one of the greatest acts one could perform in the service of Allah. It had greatly aroused him while at the same time released the pent-up desire for revenge against the infidels and anger at the European world.

Al Khalil ran his fingers lightly over his cheek and saw blood on his hand. He took a handkerchief and wiped his face and his hands. Their hotel, The Rostemides, although small, was the best hotel in Ghardaia. Built in the M'zab style with arches, columns and minarets, it nevertheless had air conditioning, a pool and a TV.

Back in his room, Tariq put on the TV news on while he undressed to wash. Right after the soccer news—Oran 2, Annaba 1—a photo from a French paper appeared as the announcer read, "In Paris, an American working for the CIA died in a hit-and-run accident as he was crossing the street in front of the restaurant that he had just left. This photo of Dr. Coogan and of his assistant Steve Church appeared in the French paper *L'Humanité* two days ago when they came back from Germany where they participated in a slander against the holy Quran. We take you live to our Paris correspondent Lachine al Masri."

The image changed to a middle-aged man in front of a restaurant named Chez André.

"Dr. Coogan and his dinner companion Sandrine Légier had just left Chez André, a favorite of writers, and were crossing the street right here..."

The camera panned to a crosswalk.

"When a car came out of nowhere and hit both at considerable speed. The car, described as either a dark blue Renault or a black Peugeot, did not stop. They were both taken to the hospital but Dr. Coogan died on the way. Wait..."

The correspondent pressed his left hand to the earphone from which he was apparently receiving information.

"I have just learned that this may not have been an accident. A message from the Global Islamic Front Against Jews and Crusaders now claims responsibility, in revenge for Dr. Coogan's role."

He pressed a finger against the earphone.

"Sorry, *alleged* role, in the forged CIA documents claiming to be original versions of the Quran. Dr. Coogan's maid was arrested yesterday for attempting to kill him by exploding a bomb tied to her waist. Coogan's assistant Mr. Church has apparently fled the country."

Al Khalil watched in rapt attention. He had ordered Coogan's execution. However, he had had to leave before the operation was carried out. He was startled by the second person in the photograph identified as Steve Church. He had a vague recollection of the American but couldn't place him. He made a mental note that Church had to be found and sent to join Coogan.

Al Khalil wanted to stay another day in Ghardaia to meet with other potential backers for his vision. However, El Maghrebi's men were on a schedule and explained that they needed to get back to Blida as soon as they got al Khalil to Timbuktu. And, with the killing of the Frenchmen, they needed to move on.

★   ★   ★

The next morning, Tariq, Hussein and the two men on loan from the AQIM had breakfast at the hotel. The dining room was bright with the morning light from large windows facing south. The air conditioning was on full blast causing Hussein to sneeze repeatedly. He got up to ask the reception to shut it off and came back to the table. The four men sat at a table on which were dates, oranges, flat bread, jam, a pot of coffee, and a can of Nestlé's condensed milk with two holes punched in the top.

They were alone in the small dining room until an elderly French couple came in and occupied another table, to Tariq's great annoyance. It seemed to Tariq from the Frenchman's conversation that he had been a young officer in the French Army fighting the Algerian rebels before Algerian independence. In a lowered voice Tariq announced, "I've decided that I have to stop to meet with potential backers in Adrar…"

One of the AQIM men interrupted to say, "That's almost a thousand kilometers south, on the edge of the Erg of Chech."

Tariq continued, "In Adrar, I want you, Hussein, to take the Land Rover with one of you," and he pointed at the two AQIM men, "to go on to Timbuktu as fast as you can. You're right, Hussein, nothing is happening in Morocco. Fly there as soon as you can. We need action. I'll continue on with the other car on schedule. I need to gather supporters along the way."

Hussein sneezed. The air conditioning was still on.

On their way to the cars, Tariq pulled Hussein aside.

"Coogan, the American involved in the Quran documents, is dead, *al hamdu Allah*. It was on TV last night. And I recognized the guy working with him from a newspaper photo. I remember him from the university—from Brussels—another American. He was the son of a diplomat. I assume that our friends will have enough initiative to take care of him also."

8. Rabat, Morocco

Steve was having lunch at the Marine House, home for the small Marine detachment assigned to guard the American Embassy. The U.S. Defense Attaché had chosen the venue. Air Force Colonel Dan Spaceck was in his late forties, tall and tanned, carefully groomed, although without a military haircut, and with remarkably white teeth. His double handshake—left hand on his opponent's right elbow—was firm. Spaceck gave off a cloying scent that Steve guessed must be cologne—it was too late in the day for after-shave. Spaceck's elegant appearance, Steve thought, was in contrast to the rather Spartan surroundings. A dour Moroccan cook had prepared and served their hamburgers and French fries from a menu geared to the taste of the young Marines who lived there. Steve detected the smell of stale grease when the door to the kitchen opened. He wondered why Spaceck had wanted to meet at the Marine House when there were so many more attractive restaurants in Rabat.

Spaceck took a French fry in his fingers, looked at Steve, and said, "Tell me a little bit about yourself—how did you wind up in Morocco? If you don't mind my saying so, you seem a little young to be talking to the Moroccans about such a major project."

Spaceck smiled to show no implied criticism.

Steve hesitated a moment and said, also with a smile, "I guess West Gate thought I was right for the job. And the project is my idea. It seems to me that the Moroccans have a problem here with the radical Muslims. West Gate has considerable experience in counter-insurgency and counterterrorism. How long have you been in Morocco?"

"Two years. I have another year, probably. I applied to the National War College at Fort McNair in D.C., and I'm waiting for a decision. Where else have you worked for West Gate?" Spaceck asked.

"You'll like the War College. My father did. I worked for West Gate in South Korea, Osan Air Force Base…"

"Osan! Did you know General Adams? Bruce Adams? He was in my class at the Air Force Academy," Spaceck said, animated.

Steve nodded vigorously.

"I worked for him! West Gate ran a major counter-proliferation exercise for him. I worked on it for six months just to get it set up and organized and, afterward, another month to analyze outcomes and make recommendations."

Steve didn't mention that what probably had won him the job offer from West Gate was that he had opened a NATO office in Moldova and run it for eighteen months. Nor did he mention the reason for his sudden departure.

Two young Americans walked in, wearing shorts. With their heads shaved on the sides, they could only be off-duty marines. They nodded to Spaceck.

"Hi Colonel. We ran twelve miles this morning, on the road toward Kenitra. When are you going to join us?"

They looked at each other and grinned in a way that told Steve that Spaceck was the last man on earth they expected to take the offer seriously.

Spaceck waved a greeting, "Hi Mike," without replying to what was obviously a rhetorical question. Turning back to Steve, he said, "Well, I'm impressed. Adams told me the exercise was a big success. What did you do after Korea?"

"I was assigned to Hickam Air Force Base in Hawaii, working for Pacific Command. And now I'm working out of the Tysons Corner office in Virginia."

Steve guessed from Spaceck's questions that the man wanted to befriend him. Spaceck was of the age and rank when he would naturally be thinking of retirement, and West Gate employed a good number of retired military. Steve wondered if Spaceck was trying to use him as a conduit toward a retirement job, which gave him pause.

"What can you tell me about the Moroccan brass I'll be meeting?"

"The first thing you need to understand is that, to the extent the Moroccans think about the type of management consultants you're talking about, those guys come from France. Except for the senior staff, the officer corps is now more oriented toward Arab countries. They speak less French and more English. And speaking of the younger officers, some are much more fundamentalist in their religious beliefs than the generals. But don't worry about it. They're more interested in stuffing their pockets than in the five pillars of Islam," Spaceck said with a grin.

Steve wondered at that analysis. He doubted that true Muslim radicals, young or old, could be bought. Besides, bribes were out of the question. Spaceck was becoming less solid by the second.

"Trust me; I know how this place works. Since I know all of these people, I can go to your meetings with you and help you establish that essential personal trust that is so important here. I can open doors for you, and, after you leave, I can carry the ball for your company."

Steve didn't want or need the colonel to carry the ball but he did want to avoid a confrontation.

"Thanks. Let me see how the initial meetings go first."

They both finished their coffee and Spaceck pressed two of his business cards into Steve hands.

"Call me anytime. And how about giving my card to your boss back in the States? Maybe I'll give your company a call next time I'm in Washington."

They got up to leave. On their way toward the door, Colonel Spaceck asked, "So your father is in the military? You said he was at the National War College."

"Yes, but he was a civilian. He was with the Agency, the CIA, but he's semi-retired and no longer under cover. Rabat was one of his assignments. I was very young. In fact, he's writing about radical Islam and terrorism, and he wants me to scoop up anything I can find in the book stores on the topic."

"It's still dangerous for people in this country to be writing about the terrorist side of Islam," Spaceck said. "There are Salafists here for sure, but I can't tell you more than that."

"Well, thanks for spending the time with me. Appreciated it."

Spaceck favored him with another patented handshake then, seeming like an afterthought, he said, "If you hear anything at all about a Tariq al Khalil while you're here, please let me know. He's a Salafist leader with North African aspirations."

"Tariq al Khalil a terrorist?"

He had no desire to prolong the conversation any longer and he restrained himself from sharing what he knew about al Khalil.

"Why do you think he's here?"

"I don't know if he is or not. We know that there are Salafists around who look to him for leadership. We just don't know where they're going to strike next."

Steve stepped outside and was half blinded by the sun's glare. He put on his sunglasses. As he left, he noticed a small pick-up truck park in front of the Marine House next to a brash American car with "arrest-me" red metallic paint and a mean-looking grill. Steve guessed that the only person he had seen in the Marine House who could afford the car was Spaceck. He found the choice of car strange for an intelligence collector.

The driver of the truck hoisted a gas cylinder on his shoulder and walked around the side of the building toward the kitchen. The sight reminded Steve that, in Morocco, all gas stoves worked off individual butane tanks, For safety reasons, the tanks were normally outside and grounded to prevent an explosion of the pressurized gas through a buildup of electrostatic charges.

He walked away feeling that Spaceck didn't fit into a complex North African environment that required cultural awareness and sensitivity. The man was as out of place in Morocco as al Khalil had been in Brussels. His thoughts turned to al Khalil and he wondered how successful he was at grafting his radical views onto a society with a fairly relaxed view of Islam. And, if he was indeed active in the region, what he was doing.

The red car, with Spaceck at the wheel, pulled up as Steve walked back toward his hotel.

"Can I drop you somewhere? I should have offered earlier."

"No thanks," Steve answered. "It's not far, and I need the walk."

9. Casablanca, Morocco

Following the evening prayers at the Hassan II Mosque, Hussein followed Mohammed Lahlou, the Salafist cell leader, from the blue, white, and yellow geometric tile designs of the mosque through an archway that led to several study rooms. Lahlou was a grizzled and sad-looking man who'd spent eighteen years in Moroccan prisons. He looked older than his forty-eight years, the toll of a terrorist life without the inner flame of a fanatic. For both Hussein and Lahlou, their individual trials and lives in the field, in prison, or on the run, were taking their toll.

Lahlou knew Hussein as a tough fighter, as ruthless in combat as with those in the movement who failed out of personal weakness or commitment.

"Hussein my brother, your visit honors us. Thanks to Allah for sending you. You are not Moroccan. Do I detect a Syrian accent?"

"Yes, I was born in Aleppo but my family moved to Hama. My father was with the Brotherhood. Hama was an important political center for the *Ikhwan*."

"Were you in Hama during the massacre?"

"I was young, but yes, I was there. Those Syrian dogs felt threatened by the Brothers."

"And for cause, as I recall."

"Old man Assad was so scared for his life that he sent his brother Rifaat to kill us all—first with artillery, then with tanks.

After the fighting stopped, they killed all of our fighters and their families hiding in the damaged buildings with cyanide gas. And only then did Rifaat's Mukhabarat butchers arrive to eliminate those who were still alive."

"How many brothers were lost?"

Hussein felt patronized. But he also never missed an opportunity to contribute to the Assad family dishonor.

"Thirty-eight thousand! May Allah receive them in his house."

"But you survived, *Al Hamdu 'llah.*"

"The soldiers caught me. I was fourteen. They put me to work with other prisoners to clean the streets of rubble and corpses. That's how I found my father's body, May Allah favor him. That's when I made a covenant with Allah to revenge my father's execution."

Lahlou shook his head.

"May you achieve your revenge," he said softly.

Hussein stopped walking and held Lahlou by the arm.

"Al Khalil is not happy with you. You have put me in a bad situation. I would be sorry to lose you."

In giving Lahlou his performance review, Hussein's voice was sad, as if killing Lahlou was an undesirable but unavoidable event. Hussein knew his reputation.

"Al Khalil doesn't understand what's going on here," Lahlou said. "The Moroccan police are all over. Security has spies everywhere. But I have not been asleep. I have my own spies and we are getting ready. You will see."

They resumed walking and entered the back room of the mosque, normally used by pre-teen students to memorize the Quran. Light green tiles with arabesques covered the lower half of the otherwise white-washed walls. Worn rugs were strewn across the floors. The only furniture was a small desk and a chair in one corner. Two men in their twenties sat cross-legged on the rugs, waiting for Lahlou and Hussein. They got up when the two older men came in. They exchanged the traditional greeting, "S*alaam alaikum*," and bowed slightly, their right hands brushing their foreheads and ending on their hearts.

One of the young men wore a faded *jellaba*. He had the typical round Moroccan face and wore tinted glasses that made him look both studious and closed. Hussein thought he looked like an accountant, but Lahlou had told him that he was a law student and an explosives specialist. The other wore stained dark slacks and a gray shirt that once had been white. He seemed to be from Southern Morocco, a Berber from the Anti-Atlas Mountains.

"This is Ribb, from the Ministry of Defense—the one I told you about," Lahlou said to Hussein, gesturing toward the man in the stained western garb. "Ribb sometimes works in the kitchen, often as a messenger, and he unloads trucks. He knows the drivers at the Ministry and heard them say they had picked up an American who flew in from Paris, but the American told his driver he had started his trip from Washington."

Lahlou seemed pleased and nervous at the same time that he could report on a target of opportunity.

"Repeat what you told me about the American," Lahlou told Ribb.

"I know that one of our drivers picked him up at the airport and took him to the Tour Hassan Hotel in Rabat. The drivers think that he's here to set up a secret project," Ribb said.

"Is he CIA?" asked Hussein.

Ribb smiled. "Of course."

"If he's CIA, why didn't the American Embassy send a car for him?" Hussein demanded.

"The very fact that an Embassy car didn't pick him up proves he's CIA," Lahlou said. "He's hiding his American government connection," he added, giving Hussein a knowing look to emphasize that he understood CIA methods. Lahlou felt he was playing at the top of his game. He was also nervous because he might be asked to mount an operation against this American. Taking on a dangerous mission had never been Lahlou's strong point.

"Well, I don't know. He could be a nobody. Why focus on him? We would do better to go after the CIA chief in Morocco, or the American Ambassador." Hussein said.

He suddenly remembered al Khalil's comments about the young American in Paris who was Coogan's helper. He also started putting this information together with a conversation he'd had in Paris with a Moroccan diplomat who had met a young American at a cocktail party. The American was on his way to Morocco on business, allegedly.

He asked the student with the tinted glasses, "Are you any good with computers, the Internet?" The law student nodded and Hussein told him, "A couple of days ago, there was a news report in a Paris newspaper about a Dr. Coogan who was killed by the *Ikhwan*. The reporter was close; the execution was ordered by al Khalil. Coogan was involved in the forgeries of the Quranic documents. I assume you know about it. There was a photo with the article. I want you to get the photograph through the internet. I want to know if Allah is smiling on us and answering our prayer."

The student took his glasses of and wiped one lens with his finger, "I'll make a copy of the photograph."

Ribb, the Berber, said, "I can find out from the drivers when they're supposed to take the American back to the airport."

"I'll get in touch with Tariq and see what he wants to do," Hussein said. "Maybe we can kidnap him and get some of our militants out of jail in an exchange."

"A kidnapping will wake up the whole security establishment against us," Lahlou said. "We would have to take him to Marrakesh and have our men hide him. Killing him is simpler and easier. We do it and it's done."

Lahlou surprised Hussein by his boldness.

"I didn't ask what would be easier," Hussein said dismissively. "Get more information on him and I'll see what Tariq has to say."

"Take me to my hotel," he instructed Lahlou.

On the way, Hussein was surprised at the high number of Europeans, both men and women, in the street shopping or otherwise going about their business. He noticed that most women wore the usual loose *jellabas* down to their ankles, but that many were without veils. Some walked with long strides that revealed their high heeled shoes. In fact, it seemed to him that they wanted their European fashion to show. He was startled, to say the least, that one woman's high heeled shoes were bright red. *Al Khalil will go ballistic*, he thought.

* * *

The next morning, Hussein and Lahlou met at the mosque and Lahlou suggested they go to a café he often frequented.

"More comfortable," he said.

They walked out of the mosque into the maze of old passageways and stingy streets without sidewalks. Here, Hussein noticed, the occasional European stood out, unlike in the more modern part of the city. On a broader street, they went past a theater playing an Egyptian movie. The women were all veiled. None dared to wear western garments, least of all red high-heels.

"I sent an email to al Khalil about the American," Hussein said. "No answer yet. But I know what he'll say. Do it, with greatest impact. So start planning."

Hussein didn't know Casablanca, but he knew the culture of the Arab world's rabbit warrens, be they called *casbahs* or *medinas*. Each political party and labor union had its public fronts and its underground factions. The ruling families, many claiming to be descended from the Prophet, the Arab equivalent of Mayflower ancestry, had its alliances based on strategic marriages and grievances going back generations. Each group kept an eye on the others through paid informants, ambitious men aspiring to become members of the organization or family, and others seeking favors. Watching them all was the king's security service. The pecuniary opportunities for clever informants, who frequently were able to sell their information to several paymasters, were abundant. But establishing and violating trusts, the essence of the game, was a high-risk enterprise. Those who did not grasp this ground-truth either disappeared or survived as maimed warnings.

Hussein looked about him with the surface interest of a visitor but with the educated eyes of a master of the game. He assumed that their walk was not unobserved. He also assumed that Lahlou had a reason for taking him on this walk through the labyrinths of the old city. Hussein wondered if Lahlou was cleverer than he appeared, if perhaps in this warren, he, Hussein, was not the rabbit rather than the ferret.

They reached a café whose owner welcomed Lahlou. Hussein assumed he was part of Lahlou's network. Lahlou led the way inside and they sat at a small table in the back by the wall. The air was heavy with smoke. No women or tourists had ever crossed the threshold. The owner came over immediately with a pot of sweet mint tea and two glasses decorated in imitation gold leaf.

"What is your source for your information on the American, besides Ribb I mean?" Hussein asked.

Lahlou hesitated a second and replied, "Our informant knows a colonel at the American Embassy. He wants to retire in Morocco after he leaves the Air Force next year."

"What about the visiting American?"

"Spaceck, that's the colonel, said that the visitor really is a nobody and that he, Spaceck, could get them a better deal on anything they want."

"But is the visitor CIA?" Hussein insisted.

"Oh, here is what my lawyer got from the Internet," and he handed the photo and the article about Coogan and Steve to Hussein.

"So, is this the same person?"

"I don't know yet. Ribb will show it to the driver and get back to me."

"Let me know as soon as possible," Hussein said with a slight smile of anticipation.

"All right, I'll call you at the hotel. In any case, Spaceck said that the American's business story doesn't make sense, and that he is too young to have the job he claims to have."

Hussein smiled.

This Spaceck character could be useful, he thought. But he also wondered if Spaceck wasn't trying too hard. Perhaps his reasons went beyond money. Maybe Spaceck was the spy. Hussein had survived in an environment rife with duplicity, betrayals, and obscure motivations.

That night, Lahlou called Hussein at his four-room hotel in the depths of the *medina*.

"My brother, you were inspired by Allah. You were right."

Hussein answered, "*Al hamdu 'llah*. You know what to do."

Before al Khalil answered his first message, Hussein sent him a second one.

"The merchandise is genuine. I will consummate the transaction, which will terminate the Berlin-Paris activity. There is only one God, only one Quran."

As an afterthought, he added, "May Allah bless this enterprise."

10. Rabat: Tour Hassan Hotel

In his room, Steve checked his email. He and his father, Marshall, used a still-experimental encryption system developed by the Los Alamos National Laboratory to secure their email communications. Based on his CIA experience, Marshall had said don't write anything that would get sources killed, cause catastrophic consequences, or embarrass you or your employer if it appeared in The New York Times. He had long ago concluded his father and the CIA had too many rules.

Marshall's last message to Steve said, "Just a reminder to get in touch with my friend Abdelhaq in Morocco. He hasn't seen you since Iran in 1978 or '79. You'll enjoy his hospitality, as well as the best Moroccan meal in the country."

When preparing for his trip from Virginia, Steve had not done enough to set up his schedule in Rabat. But other than the car sent to pick him up at the airport by the Ministry of Defense, the few appointments he had made seemed to have been written in disappearing ink. He spent a day showing up for appointments in Rabat only to be told by smiling secretaries that either her boss was busy or out of town, or that the very important person for whom she worked would deign to see him very soon, *Inshallah*—if God willed. "Very soon" invariably turned into a wait of hours, and Steve was muttering to himself, "Welcome to the Third World."

He had PowerPoint presentations on the three main topics that he hoped would interest the Moroccans. First, he'd present the accumulated experiences and lessons learned of the U.S. Army special ops warriors. What they had to say about Iraq and Afghanistan should be of interest to the Forces Armées Royales, the FAR, which was still fighting the Polisario in Mauritania.

Second, he would present the use of technology in keeping track of insurgents and terrorists through ground sensors and Unmanned Air Vehicles. And third, Steve had learned that the FAR were planning major relocations of their bases away from the cities to the less developed areas of the country. West Gate had a track record of helping establish new bases in Iraq and of moving old ones in the United States. West Gate could offer people with hands on experience in all of these areas. Steve was convinced that West Gate could add value to Morocco's military capability and that Morocco's 1.3-billion-dollar defense budget could add value to West Gate's bottom line. Steve could already see himself into a new corner office.

* * *

Steve went out to see the city before leaving for his first appointment. The taxi took him by his old house, his school, and eventually left him off at the Salé *medina*. Salé had been a homeport to Barbary Coast pirates in the eighteenth century and now offered the best shopping in Rabat.

A water-seller with bare legs, sandals, a short tunic with red and gold fringes but no sleeves and a large flat hat in several colors from which small bells hung, was trying to attract customers at the entrance to the *medina* by ringing a bell he held in his hand.

Steve went by this Moroccan Harlequin as someone made a purchase. Harlequin unhooked a brass cup from several hanging from a bandolier across his chest and filled it with water from a water skin hanging from one shoulder. Steve entered a narrow alley lined with stalls.

He wandered through the alleyways of the small Salé *medina*. He stopped to watch an artisan chiseling intricate geometric designs on a round brass tray. He could see several finished products hanging in the shop and bought one, after a bout of rigorous and expected bargaining. Farther on he started to bid for a handmade Rabat rug, blue designs in the center on a field of red that would have to be shipped. But it was getting late. He suspended the negotiations and went back to his hotel.

Once in his room, he wanted to check his PowerPoint one more time and went to his laptop. It had been turned off for the last two hours but was surprisingly warm to the touch. Concerned, he quickly went through the password and thumbprint identification procedure and satisfied himself that his presentations were still there. It seemed unlikely that the hotel maid had been surfing the Internet or that she could even get through his biometric security software.

He returned to his dresser and wished that he had paid more attention when taking fresh clothes from the drawers. He couldn't be sure but, on closer inspection, he thought his clothes were not as he had arranged when taking them out of the suitcase. He had brought brochures to leave behind after his meetings and, on checking them, was sure someone had been through them; they were definitely out of order.

He found no other suspicious indications but wondered whether he should have "trapped" drawers and doors as he had seen in the movies. Nothing had been stolen, as far as he could tell. He was annoyed that one of his father's stories forced itself on him. From his service in Romania, he had concluded that if a surreptitious visitor has taken nothing, it is most likely that he has left something behind. He started looking for microphones, half-heartedly and self-consciously, a bit embarrassed. Wasn't this just another of his father's rules? Still, he felt uneasy.

* * *

The next day, Steve walked out of his hotel toward the center of town and went into a shop. Several singletons came in after he did—two men and a woman. None paid attention to him. He went out, walked two blocks to another shop and again observed people who came in shortly after he did while ostensibly looking at the merchandise. None was a repeat. He figured the people he was looking for were probably young men, which allowed him to eliminate seventy-five percent of his possible surveillants thus far.

He went to one more shop and he had a repeat, a young Moroccan in sunglasses, a New York Yankees t-shirt and Nikes, easy to remember. He then took a cab to the Mausoleum of Mohammed V, the monarch in power when Morocco became independent in 1956. There he told the driver to wait, and went up the marble steps of the white crenellated mausoleum, past a guard in red with a white cape, black boots, and a green fez.

The guard's rifle looked very much like an M-1, the U.S. Army's primary infantry weapon in World War II and Korea. As a member of Lehigh's rifle team, he had seen but never fired the weapon. He wondered if that was the vintage of the average FAR weaponry. At the top of the steps, he looked back at the surrounding ruins of the old mosque on which the mausoleum was built and noticed New York getting out of a cab in back of the one he was still using. New York had a friend, same age, about twenty-five, also slight of build but at least five-feet, ten.

Steve concluded that the unwanted attention was not a mugging in the making. They didn't seem threatening; they apparently just wanted to keep him in sight. He cut short his surveillance-detection, went back to the hotel to pick up his briefing materials, and headed for the Ministry positioning himself in the back seat so as to keep his eyes on the cab's rear and side view mirrors. A white Fiat shepherded him from the hotel to the Ministry.

He arrived early for his meetings and drank more sweet tea than he really wanted while he waited. He sensed a changing attitude for the better from the outer offices. The Moroccan officers liked that he had been in Morocco as a young boy and that he was familiar with their country. His presentations were also creating interest.

The colonel with whom he had met walked him out of his office and gave him a promising handshake as he left, further bolstering Steve's confidence. His next appointment was at a training camp, not far from Rabat, he had been told, whose commandant was interested in West Gate's interactive software, Urban Warfare Tactics for Small Unit Leaders 2.0.—not at the top of Steve's priority list. Nevertheless, it was a useful entrée to the training side of the FAR.

The ministry car assigned to him was waiting. They left at 10:25. As they headed out of town, Steve heard something loose in the trunk clanging against one side then the other on the turns and over bumps, as if the spare tire was not well secured. They were not quite beyond Rabat's city limits when the driver received a call.

"Mr. Church, General Labibi has asked me to bring you back to the ministry," the driver said. It was 10:38.

General Labibi was one of the heretofore unavailable principals. Steve hoped Labibi's sudden interest meant his project was picking up traction with Labibi's superiors. Steve decided to go back.

"I'll be right back," he told the driver, who parked in the street outside the Ministry entrance. "Keep that air conditioner on. I think something's banging around in the trunk—can you hear it? Is it the spare?".

The driver merely shrugged.

Steve was inside General Labibi's outer office for no more than five minutes when he, and most likely everyone else in Rabat, heard a thunderous explosion.

Shards of glass from the window flew across the room like arrows seeking their targets. A uniformed officer fell to the ground with a glass shard in his neck. The building rocked. Inside the offices of the Ministry, the blast was followed by several seconds of total silence.

Steve, the secretary to whom he was speaking, and the dozen officers and secretaries either sitting or walking through the office, froze as if the projector depicting their lives had stopped. They looked at each other questioningly for another second. Then the choreography broke down. The slow learners rushed to the windows, others attacked the telephones, and a few ran out. Steve heard a secretary stage-whisper, "It's a coup!" The room reeked of fear born of confusion and uncertainty.

Since everyone was ignoring him, Steve extracted the glass from the fallen officer's neck, grabbed a Moroccan flag from the wall, gave it to him to stop the bleeding, and walked out, suspecting damage but uncertain just how bad it would be.

Despite his expectation, the sight of the wreckage stopped him in his tracks. A half dozen people had reached the site of the explosion. Some had started to help the wounded. He walked the spot where his car had been, through still-falling small debris and dirt.

He put his handkerchief to his nose. It was abnormally quiet, as if the noise from the blast had stopped everything and everyone in the city. The only sound came from the several people on the sidewalk; the injured were moaning. He could see a deep hole in the street where the car had been parked. The twisted metal remains of the car were scattered over the street and the sidewalk. The chassis, on its side about twenty feet from the hole, burned fiercely at the base of a tall plume of black smoke.

He turned away from the heat of the burning fuel. His eyes scanned the bodies of the victims to try to find the driver. Drawn by dark trousers at the bottom of a garden wall adjacent to the ministry building, he walked around the bodies of the victims. He reached the dark trousers. The lower half of his driver's body was at his feet. A white hip bone contrasted with the intestines partially spilled on the ground in a widening pool of blood. The blast had pulverized the driver's head and upper body. One shoe was missing. Steve's insides tightened. He doubled over and vomited violently.

The constriction of his abdomen closed his eyes but he still saw the legs with the missing shoe. Suddenly it overlaid with a memory from Moldova several years before. He was looking at the body of his friend and Russian translator Misha, his head oozing blood from two small holes, his legs outstretched, one shoe missing.

★ ★ ★

Assigned by NATO to open an office in Chisinau, capital of Moldova, Steve had been driving with Misha to go meet with leaders of the breakaway Transnistria Republic on the Eastern side of the Dniester River. At Misha's initiative, after driving for two hours they had stopped at a village for coffee. A waiter came to take their order.

Misha had said, "You need to taste *mamaliga*. It's a local dish. I ordered it for you."

After the waiter left, Misha picked up the menu and laughed. Reading from the back, he said, "Romanians have odd proverbs. Listen to this one. *Muncat bine, baut bine, dimineatsa sculat mort.* It means, 'He ate well, he drank well, in the morning he was found dead.'"

He laughed and shrugged his shoulders.

The waiter brought their coffee and their orders. Steve tasted his *mamaliga* and said, "This tastes no better than it looks. It's cornmeal mush, right?"

Misha finished his coffee first and said, "I'll meet you by the car. Take your time. Have the last *gogosh*."

He got up and headed for the men's room, and Steve reached for the donut that Misha had put on his plate. The waiter was not in sight and Steve waited for the bill. Eventually, he went to a heavy-set and heavily made up woman sitting behind a small counter near the door and paid. As he turned toward the door, he heard two popping noises followed by the sound of a car accelerating out of the dirt and gravel parking lot. When Steve reached his car, Misha was dead.

The next few hours had been a blur. The police had questioned him extensively about Misha: his background, his friends. Steve knew Misha had been in Afghanistan serving with a Soviet Spetsnatz unit, the Soviet Special Forces. Misha had talked about it openly. He had even given Steve his former uniform, at the time a souvenir of the Cold War.

A police inspector had said, "Your translator was a KGB officer. How could you not know that?" Another had said, "This Misha was just another Russian trying to get rich by running guns to the secessionists."

His NATO boss had brought him back to Brussels twenty-four hours after the killing. Steve had forever been sorry that he had not stayed and seen the investigation through. He felt strongly Misha would not have betrayed him. But Steve would not have been surprised if Misha had been involved in the arms trade.

Steve came to believe that the Moldovan Government had killed Misha and had orchestrated the subsequent character assassination campaign. He was convinced he could have done something for his friend had he stayed.

* * *

He shook off the memory and stood up. People continued to spill out of the ministry. Sirens wailed in the distance. With all the resolve in his body, he pledged to avenge this mindless act of terror. At the same time, he looked around with new apprehension. Who were these people? Why was he of such interest? He busied himself trying to help the wounded until ambulances arrived.

* * *

Hussein had driven from Casablanca to Rabat in record time and was soon in Lahlou's apartment in Rabat's New Medina. He was halfway up the stairs when the scratchy recorded voice of the *muezzin* called the faithful to prayer from overstressed loudspeakers at the top of the nearby mosque. He joined Lahlou in prayer as soon as he entered the one room apartment.

Hussein held his anger in check until the end of prayers.

"You are an incompetent idiot! You told me you had it planned to the minute. Now, not only is this American still alive, you've made us look like fools."

Lahlou, shoulders sagging, said, "It was fate. The American returned to Rabat. He got out of the car."

"All you did was kill a Moroccan government employee, wound a few others, and demolish one of the king's cars. May Allah have mercy on you!" Hussein said, unable to keep his voice and anger down.

"We used a timed charge. It was set with a ten-hour delay at one o'clock this morning. Ribb knew that the American had an appointment and would be in the car for about forty-five minutes on the way to the military camp where he had an appointment at 11:15—very precise timing. Not my fault. It was Allah's will."

Lahlou was sweating.

"A timed charge? Are you crazy? A timed charge robs you of control over the time of the explosion. Why didn't you set off the explosion remotely? Further, why did you involve the Ministry? You could have killed the American in his room, on the street, anywhere. Why in a government car? Now Military Security is going to take this as an attack on them and put all of our people under great pressure!"

Lahlou shook his head. "Security doesn't know anything about the identity of our militants. We're underground." He wiped his face with a handkerchief. The pitch of Lahlou's voice went up as he continued his bluster. "They'll huff and puff for a couple of weeks and then everything will be back to normal. Besides, we have our own informants in Military Security."

"I want you, Ribb, and your so-called explosives expert, and anyone else who knows about me, to get out of town and go into hiding. I'm leaving the country first thing tomorrow, while I still can," Hussein said.

11. Marin County, California

Steve's father, Marshall Church, just back from the gym, prepared for a TV interview. He looked at his red-walled office and didn't even try to organize the papers and books on and around his desk. What might appear as confusion to an outsider made perfect sense to him.

Since the CIA had approved Marshall's request to drop his cover, the San Francisco media had discovered him and regularly contacted him any time there was terrorist-related news. Marshall initially found the sudden attention gratifying. But he became less available when he saw how the media cherry-picked sound bites to fit the anchor's agenda.

The phone rang. "Marshall, how are you?"

It was Abdelhaq al Fassi. Marshall had recruited Abdelhaq for the CIA during the 1978-79 Islamic revolution that overthrew the Shah when both Marshall and Abdelhaq, a Moroccan intelligence officer, were posted to Tehran. They had contacted each other following their respective retirements, and their friendship had grown, transcending the typical case officer-agent relationship.

"Abdelhaq, we're all fine. In fact, my son Steve is in Morocco on business. I was going to call you myself to tell you."

"Well, it's Steve I'm calling about. I haven't spoken to him yet. But something has happened. Military Security is talking to him and that's why he hasn't had a chance to call you himself."

"What in the world does security want with Steve?"

"An IED blew up a Ministry of Defense car he was using. Steve wasn't in it at the time. He's okay. We think it was a Salafist operation. It just happened so we don't know much more than what I've just told you."

Marshall's grip tightened around the phone.

"Don't keep anything from me."

"Well, I've been away and just came back to town. But security heard from one source that there was Islamist interest in an American who was supposed to be a recent arrival and a CIA officer. I'm not connecting this with Steve right now, but who knows?"

"I assume you'll see him soon?"

"Consider it done. His company must think well of him to send him on such an important business-mission by himself."

"To tell you the truth, Abdelhaq, I sometimes don't recognize him. He always tested and interviewed very well but school bored him. Too many rules, he said. He was stronger on the people side."

A few minutes later, the doorbell rang. Through the window Marshall saw the TV crew. He first straightened a small frame. It read:

> WE FACE A HOSTILE IDEOLOGY, GLOBAL IN SCOPE RUTHLESS IN PURPOSE AND INSIDIOUS IN METHOD. UNHAPPILY THE DANGER IT POSES PROMISES TO BE OF INDEFINITE DURATION.
>
> —Farewell Radio and Television Address to the American People by President Dwight D. Eisenhower, January 17, 1961.

Marshall put on his blazer before realizing it was the one with the Knights of Malta crest on the pocket. He quickly changed his jacket and then put his tennis racquet in a closet out of sight next to a German Heckler and Koch G3 rifle that had hung in his office until recently. His wife had finally persuaded him that it made their home look too martial. He opened the door.

Bruce, the Channel 32 producer, and his cameraman came in. Their white van with the dish antennae was parked in his driveway. Marshall brought them upstairs to his office. He knew they preferred his office for these interviews because of the large framed 1676 map of the world, decorated with likenesses of the rulers of the time, and a large globe on a wooden stand.

"Thanks for letting us come out," Bruce said.

He was in his early forties, with short dark hair, just under six feet and fairly trim. With the long sleeves of his checkered blue and white shirt rolled up, Bruce was all business but in a smooth, non-confrontational style.

"We'd like to talk to you today about the latest terrorist video that Al Jazeera aired last night."

The cameraman set up his equipment and aimed his lens on the globe with a close-up of the Middle East. Marshall sat with his back to his desk and to the map.

Bruce asked, "Last night, Zawahiri again mentioned their goal to recapture Andalusia. That's been a theme in al Qaeda's public statements over the years and one that we have not explored. What is that all about?"

Looking into the camera, Marshall said, "Until a Frankish army stopped it in the eighth century, Islam expanded by force of arms into the vacuum left by the virtual disappearance of the Roman Empire. For several hundred years afterward it continued to rule over Spain, which they called Andalusia. The Islamists now claim all of the countries in their former Caliphate—from Spain to Bokhara, Tashkent, the Philippines and Burma."

"Of course, they can't be serious," Bruce said. "The world has changed."

"In his last statement," Marshall replied, "the Prophet Muhammad declared that Allah had ordered him to spread the faith to all corners of the earth, to bring Islam to all unbelievers. This is taken literally by the radical Muslims."

Marshall pointed to the portraits on the map.

"This fellow on horseback, Muhammad the Fourth, between Louis XIV of France and Pope Innocent XI here at the top, was the Ottoman Caliph. After conquering Baghdad in the thirteenth century, the Turks established the Muslim capital in Istanbul and, until Kemal Ataturk shut down the concept of the caliphate in 1924, the Arab lands were basically Turkish provinces. Then, in World War I, the Turks were on the wrong side, after which the British carved up the Ottoman Empire into new countries. The fundamentalists have never accepted the partitions. But that's a topic for another time."

After the interview, Marshall called Steve, who picked up on the second ring.

"Steve, what's going on?"

"Hi Dad. Moroccan Security wanted to know anything I could tell them about the explosion, which was nothing. I did tell them that I thought I might have been followed."

He recounted details of the men who'd followed him.

"Keep in mind that there are a lot of criminals out there looking for rich Americans," Marshall said. "They're usually focused on tourist sites. But if they meet the time and distance test—if you see the same people in separate locations over time—then they're probably professionals and have interests other than just stealing your wallet."

"One of the security guys debriefing me, Driss Benjelloun, looked uncomfortable. He squirmed when I told them about the surveillance. I got the feeling that he knew more than he was letting on. Security offered to give me a bodyguard if I wanted one. I said no. But I have the feeling that they'll keep an eye on me anyway."

"You should just get the hell out of Morocco," Marshall told him. "In the meantime, get in touch with Abdelhaq right away. I just spoke with him by telephone. With his background and his contacts, he should be able to help you out and find out what's really going on."

"What should I do if I'm under surveillance again? Tell me how to lose them."

"In your case, go to the nearest authority—the police or the embassy. Usually, if the surveillance is official, it's best to ignore them and lull them to sleep—convince them you're not a threat. If the surveillance is official, you really can't escape them except for brief periods. They'll simply bring more resources to bear. But these guys tried to kill you, Steve. This is serious. I want you to get on an early plane."

He said he would think about it.

After hanging up, Marshall reflected on what he knew from both Abdelhaq and Steve. Should he go to Morocco? Was Steve safe by himself? There was no hard indication that the attack was against Steve. The car could have been a target of opportunity based on the hope it would kill an important general. If the Salafists were targeting Steve, what was the reason? It didn't make sense that it was just because he was an American. There were plenty of Americans in Morocco. Maybe they thought he was selling weapons.

Could Steve, untrained in basic intelligence tradecraft, handle this situation? He knew his son was not averse to physical risk. But this was clearly different. Marshall recalled that Steve's Myers Briggs test results had painted him as extraverted, sensing, thinking, perceiving, and the "ultimate realist." He was also objective and analytic, yet spontaneous and action-oriented—a good formula to assess the danger and act accordingly. Marshall understood the frailty of psychological assessments but, in this case, he felt confident Steve would make the right decisions.

Morocco was Abdelhaq's turf. He and Abdelhaq had faced danger together and he knew the man to be cool and decisive when necessary. Marshall figured he would probably get an ulcer worrying, but he decided to stay put.

12. Tour Hassan Hotel

When Steve opened his room door, he was face-to-face with a smiling man about his own height. A tonsure of gray-white hair circled the bald top of the man's head. He had a bushy gray mustache, and wore tan slacks, a lightweight dark blue jacket and a loose checkered tie that exposed the open top button of his dark-blue shirt.

Steve took some clothes from the easy chair and motioned for Abdelhaq to sit down while he sat on the bed.

Abdelhaq glanced around the room and his eyes came to rest on Steve.

"It's a pleasure to meet you as a young man. I first met you about thirty years ago in Tehran. I spoke to your father yesterday."

"My father told me to be sure and get in touch with you while I'm here. Although he wants me to leave on the next plane," Steve smiled. "He spoke highly of you. You know about the explosion?"

"That's why I'm here. I'm in charge of the investigation. I need your help. Please tell me everything you told security. This is looking more and more like the work of the Salafists."

Steve gave him every detail he could remember, and then said, "Salafists, Salafists! That's become a mantra. A couple of weeks ago, I had barely heard the term."

"Do you know about this article? Do you know that Doctor Coogan is dead?" Abdelhaq asked as he handed Steve a copy of the article naming him Dr. Coogan's assistant.

"Dead?" Steve exclaimed. "What happened? He was slightly wounded by some nut who attacked him with a knife in Berlin but I didn't think it was serious."

"This was a hit-and-run later claimed as an execution by a Salafist cell. Since you're identified as Coogan's assistant, you were probably the target yesterday. What's your role in this Quranic document affair?"

Steve recounted what Coogan had told him and added, "But I was never his assistant. I was just visiting him for a couple of days."

He took a deep breath and stood up. He went to the window and looked outside with a slight frown. He turned around and said, "I want to help catch whoever did this. The IED killed people, innocent people, just people walking by. These were senseless murders. I want to help send those guys away for a long time."

Steve looked Abdelhaq in the eyes to make certain he understood his commitment.

"What you can do is to stay here and finish your business. Right now you're our only connection to those who blew up the car—until the interrogations that are going on now shed some light on all this."

Steve mulled that for a moment.

"Like a tethered goat to attract the lion. Can you protect me?"

"I'll have you covered. The minute you leave the hotel, I'll have discreet protection on you."

"Isn't this ironic? I came to sell expertise on counterterrorism, and now I'm in the middle of a counterterrorist operation."

"Don't worry; we have our own counterterrorist experts."

"Are your Salafists home grown?"

"In a way. You can compare them to the old Communist parties. Like them, they have local activists, and they have a unifying ideology that comes from outside. This time, instead of Marxism and Leninism, the dogma is subverted from the Quran, written for seventh century Bedouins. The radicals claim it has all the rules that humankind needs. In American terms, it's the Constitution, the Bible, the Bill of Rights and the rules of the Securities and Exchange Commission all rolled into one. But they regard man-made laws to be sacrilegious, to be an affront to Allah."

Steve nodded. "A constituency of one: Allah. Well, I assume that you have a plan, other than dangling me out there to draw their fire, right?"

Abdelhaq smiled. "You remind me of your father. He's more concerned with the practical than with philosophical. As a matter of fact I do have a plan, and it should allow you to leave when your business is concluded, whether we have arrested the terrorists or not. You stay in Morocco for a while, go about your business normally. Your continued presence should bring the bad guys out. You'll be protected, don't worry."

"My father trusts you, so I do as well. Plus, I still have work to do with the Ministry of Defense."

"There is a Moroccan proverb that tells us, 'If you know his father, you may trust his son.' I know you will do the right thing in a crisis. The minister knows about the threats against you. Go to your meetings. You'll be protected. And don't worry—you won't lose your contract."

"And?" Steve said. Despite Abdelhaq's reassurances, he felt unsure.

"First thing in the morning, I want you to go see a friend of mine, a photographer, in Fes. He'll fit you with a disguise and an alias, including a passport that will allow you to leave the country 'black;' that is, in a way that will hide the fact that you've left. We don't want to drag this out too long. Marshall would not allow it," he smiled. "If we don't catch them soon, you can still leave the country in a few days. I assume the Salafists have their sources and will know as soon as you go through airport controls if you go under your true name. Their searching will make them more visible to me."

★ ★ ★

Steve was off to Fes in a rental car the next morning. He frequently glanced into the rearview mirror but could see no car behind him. On one hand, if there was a friendly tail on him, he was happy they were so invisible, so professional. But, was there really a friendly team keeping an eye on him?

Once in Fes, he parked near the Palais Jamai and headed for the photographer's shop. He was thirty seconds away from the car when he abruptly turned around—he had forgotten to lock the car. When he reached it, a man in his mid-twenties wearing a black, long sleeve Nike sports shirt, sun glasses and with long curly black hair was peering inside. He turned away as soon as Steve came into view. Steve watched him get into the back of a black BMW. Steve concluded the car must have just reached the large parking lot; its engine was running and he could see two people in the front. Steve almost gave a friendly wave to the occupants of the car but restrained himself—it might not be professional to wave to your guardian angels.

He directed his steps toward the city's *medina* in search of Daud, Abdelhaq's friend, and his shop. The air was heavy with the scent of jasmine. Cascading bougainvilleas lit up the whitewashed walls with brilliant shades of crimson, orange, yellow, and purple.

The alleys of the *medina* were crowded with merchants and tourists. Young children wove in and out on their way to the bakeries balancing wooden boards on which rested round loaves of unbaked bread. A donkey carrying cases of Coca-Cola in wicker baskets strapped to his sides rocked and rolled down the alley forcing Steve to step into a shop that sold brass and copper trays. Since the donkey effectively blocked traffic, Steve had time to look at an artisan etching geometric designs on a tray with a hammer and a center punch. He resumed his walk steering clear of the leather tanning area because of its smell of urine and noxious chemicals. But he did like the smell of finished leather in an alley specializing in belts, saddles and *babouche* slippers.

Steve walked into the photographer's shop where a young man in western slacks and long sleeve shirt approached him. He asked for Daud, the owner. With a knowing smile, the salesman went to the back of the store and disappeared behind a dark curtain. Daud came out quickly. His gray hair and gold-rimmed glasses gave him the air of a professor.

In a low conspiratorial voice that made Steve feel more nervous than secure, he said, "We cannot meet here. Maybe someone has followed you."

Looking toward the front of the shop carefully, Daud guided Steve beyond the curtain with great respect. Steve followed him into a long and narrow room, past boxes and files that overflowed the narrow shelves. Daud managed to squeeze in between the wall and a large wooden desk. He sat behind it and invited Steve to take a plastic chair in front. Steve noticed "HMS Invincible" inscribed on the front of the desk.

Peering from behind a twenty-four-inch, cutting edge, flat-screen iMac computer, Daud spoke in French.

"Yes, the desk comes from a sunken British ship. My father, may Allah keep him, bought it in Tangiers many years ago. His Excellency, Mr. al Fassi, has of course told me you would come. We need to go to my house where I will outfit you with all you need. To avoid bringing troublemakers with you, you will follow my directions exactly. There is one long street with nothing but brass plates, lamps, and decorations of all kinds. Do you know where it is?"

"Yes, I was just there," Steve said, remembering the Coca-Cola donkey.

At that moment, the young man from the front of the shop joined them and stood by the curtain keeping an eye on the shop.

"Start from the east and walk west. My son Youssef," he pointed to him, "will be at the far end of that alley. If Youssef detects no surveillance behind you, he will run his hand through his hair. That means you're okay, no one is behind you, and he will lead you to my house."

Youssef stepped closer to Steve and said, in good American-accented English, "If I do not signal, that means you are being followed. You should then enter the last brass shop on the left side of the alley, and quickly walk to a door in the back before any surveillants draw abreast of the shop. The door will lock when you close it behind you. A guide will be there to take you to my father's house."

Daud gave Steve precise instructions on how to get to the alley. He said it would take him about twenty minutes.

Youssef added, "Don't deviate from that route. There will be friendly eyes on you at key locations until the final checkpoint when you will see me."

Steve had not gone farther than the first hundred yards of his choreographed walk when he sensed rather than felt something in back of him. He instinctively put his hand on his wallet and closed his fingers around a small wrist. He turned to find a young boy at the other end of the wrist. The boy began yelling in Arabic, "American, American, money for my mother, in *hôpital*."

Steve retrieved his wallet and was about to focus on the little Moroccan thief, but his attention was diverted by a millisecond sighting of Curly, whom he had seen hovering around his car. Steve thought he had seen him behind a group of Japanese tourists—not a wise concealment choice for a full size Moroccan. But he had disappeared. Likewise, the boy had taken advantage of Steve's distraction to make his get-away. Remembering Abdelhaq's assurances, he was tempted to believe that Curly's presence was a positive sign. However, he was getting confused.

When Steve arrived at the end of the surveillance detection route he was relieved to see Youssef run his fingers through his hair. Youssef walked Steve quickly into the heart of the old quarter. As they went by the historic Karaouine mosque, Steve wondered if this was the smartest route. If Salafists or their sympathizers were around, they'd most likely use the mosque as their Fes headquarters. He put his head down and kept walking—

it was too late to change routes and he had no choice but to trust Youssef.

They walked down an alley flanked by windowless walls about three stories high and came to a nail-studded wooden door with a large iron lock and handle. The door opened instantly when Youssef tapped the palm of his hand against its surface. They stepped into a world out of *A Thousand and One Nights*, a lush garden, a riot of greens and yellows and pinks, surrounding a bubbling fountain. Several dark-skinned servants hurried about. Daud welcomed him and ushered him inside a room bordering on the garden.

Daud was the perfect traditional Moroccan host. He placed loose tea, lumps of sugar, and sprigs of mint in a silver teapot. At his signal, a servant brought boiling water that Daud poured in the pot. After pleasant conversation concerning the history of Fes, Daud took the teapot and poured, first with the spout close to the glass and gradually extended his arm to produce a long stream of steaming tea between pot and glass, never spilling a drop. They each drank the traditional three cups.

Then Daud introduced Steve to what he called his *atelier*, his workshop—an office-sized room with dozens of wall-mounted wooden drawers and cabinets, square work table on one side, running water and a waist-level counter on the other. Out of one cabinet, inside of which were smaller pull-out drawers, he selected several pairs of glasses. He tried several on Steve and finally selected a highly noticeable black-rimmed pair. He then looked at Steve hair and opened another cabinet inside of which were rows of wigs on wire wig-stands.

"The idea is to make you look older and give the observer something to fix his attention away from your basic, unchangeable *physionomie*," he explained, "your height and bone structure for example. We could change those also but not in a couple of hours as Mr. al Fassi wants, and not on such short notice."

He outfitted Steve with salt-and-pepper hair and a severely receding hairline. Steve looked in the mirror and saw himself aged fifteen-to-twenty years—*an expert job*, he thought. Daud took his picture with the disguise on for Steve's new Canadian passport, then removed the disguise, explained to Steve how to put it on and slipped it into a small cloth bag. He went into an adjoining room for a half-hour and came back with the passport.

"You are a Canadian tourist, Ian Ross. You came from Paris five days ago. You're on your way to Dakar, Senegal. The passport has the French, Moroccan, and Senegalese stamps and visas that you need. You were born in Toronto. That will explain your accent when you speak French. I cannot help you with your Canadian past. You will have to create that yourself based on what you can convincingly talk about. You must memorize all this information. It has to come out instantaneously if needed."

"Abdelhaq is lucky to have you as his friend. How can I thank you?"

Daud held up his left palm toward Steve and said, "Not your worry."

Steve thanked him again, shook his hand, and Youssef walked with him back to his car. Steve was now extremely aware of his physical environment but he didn't spot Curly.

* * *

On his way back to Rabat, Steve noticed a black BMW 740 that stayed doggedly behind him. Whether he sped up or slowed down, the car stayed within sight. Since this tail didn't seem to be hiding, Steve assumed it was the friendly, protective team sent by Abdelhaq, probably the same BMW he had seen in the parking lot when he arrived in Fes.

On a straight stretch of road, the BMW sped up and was quickly behind him. There were no other cars on the road. The black car swerved to the left to pass. In his driver's side mirror, Steve noticed that the black car's windows on the right, on his side, were open—the hair of the man in the back was blowing around. His mind quickly processed the information and concluded that the face and hair belonged to Curly.

He checked his mirror again and saw movement. A hand appeared from the front passenger side window, but it was not waving in friendly gesture. Steve caught sight of the barrel of a gun. Instinct powered by fear made him pull on the handbrake hard.

The BMW shot past him. He heard the popping of the shots. Most of the bullets flew over his car, except for one that scored a long gash across the hood. As the shots punched past him, he pulled the hand brake and whipped the steering wheel to the left triggering his car to skid into a one-hundred-eighty-degree turn, even as it continued down the road.

He kept his hand on the brake, ready to release it when the car went off the road onto the dirt and grass strip punctuated by poplars every fifty yards. He regained control, released the brake, drove the car back on the asphalt and accelerated toward Fes at full throttle.

Steve knew that heading in the opposite direction was the only way to put more space between him and the BMW. Without a weapon, surprise had given him perhaps a minute advantage. He was around the first turn and the black car had disappeared from sight. He had a good head start.

He saw a sign, KHEMISETT 3 KILOMETRES, and reaching Khemisett before the BMW became the most important goal in his life. He urged more speed from his car. There was no one else on the road except for the occasional *jellaba*-clad peasant walking alongside with his donkey carrying farm produce. He stayed in the middle of the narrow road and took the turns as fast as he could. The BMW had more horsepower and soon appeared in his mirror. But he reached Khemisett with about a quarter-mile lead.

He hit the brakes and turned onto a side street, passed a restaurant-hotel sign, and furiously jammed the car into the parking lot in back. He grabbed the keys and the bag with his disguise and went into the building through the back door. He entered the kitchen where he saw only one person, the cook. He put his hand on his heart, smiled and said *"labess-alik,"* a Moroccan greeting he had picked up, and kept moving. The cook barely paid attention to him. Steve went through the only other door and saw the letters WC on a green door on the left.

He hadn't anticipated he'd ever have to use his disguise, but now he was glad to have it. In a few minutes, a middle-aged man with a receding hairline came out of the bathroom, walked through the dining room and out the front door. Steve reasoned that, with his car in the back, this restaurant would soon be the object of the search.

With his eyes out for his pursuers, he walked down the street and soon found a taxi with the driver asleep in the front seat. The driver demanded an absurd sum to drive him to Rabat. Steve, not in the mood to bargain, got in the back seat of the yellow Simca and cut the sum in half.

He told the driver, "I'll give you the entire amount if you can break the world's speed record on the way to the Tour Hassan Hotel in Rabat."

Only a few minutes later, Steve knew he had made a mistake. The driver had already used two of their lives passing trucks around blind curves.

But the Simca was no match for the BMW. Fifteen minutes later, the black car appeared. The hit team drew abreast of the Simca and two faces peered out of the open windows, hands held out of sight. Steve knew what they would see: a sleeping passenger in black-rimmed glasses, the back of whose graying head was leaning against the far window. The BMW dropped back. Steve glanced at the side view mirror and saw the BMW pull off the road, turn around, and head back toward Khemisett to conduct a more thorough search. He breathed a sigh of relief, though his body was still wired with adrenaline.

* * *

As he neared the Tour Hassan, Steve wondered about the wisdom of returning to his hotel. Had the guys in the black BMW called ahead? Would he have a bad surprise waiting in his room? What did he have there that he couldn't live without? He had left most of his cash and American passport in an envelope in the hotel safe, for one thing. But he had his credit card and alias passport with him. He decided to go in, retrieve his stuff, and check out that evening. He didn't think this group was seeking martyrdom. If and when they tried again, there would be an escape route in their plan, which probably meant no attack in a public place.

In order to gain entrance to the hotel without being challenged at the reception, he had put Daud's disguise back in its cloth bag and out of sight by the time he walked through the lobby.

He tried to record everything he could see without obviously moving his head. A thousand thoughts and possibilities were going through his mind. Everything and everyone was suspicious. What about the guy in the white *jellaba* just sitting in the lobby not even pretending to read a newspaper like they did in the movies? On an impulse, he went to the reception desk and told the clerk that he would like to stay a week beyond his original reservation. Steve thought that would allow his adversaries to think they had plenty of time to plan their operation. He didn't want them to do anything hasty. With an officious smile, the clerk said that would be no problem and he made a notation.

He went up to his room, gathered some essentials in a small bag, and left his suitcases, most of his clothes, and his toilet articles. He would go to another hotel—that should buy him more time. He knew there was a Rabat Hilton. There would undoubtedly be shops there where he could get what he needed.

He called Abdelhaq. A woman answered in Moroccan Arabic then in French. Abdelhaq was not home and Steve left a message: "Steve will be at the Hilton." He hung up and cursed himself. Someone might have been listening. He wondered about the hotel receptionist. Steve took a deep breath.

Think clearly, he told himself. You cannot afford even one mistake.

He went back downstairs and asked for access to the safe, explaining apologetically that he wanted to place other personal documents in the care of the hotel. In the privacy of the small closet-like room provided for this purpose, he extracted all of his cash and passport from the manila envelope, replaced it with hotel stationary and a thick leaflet from the Moroccan Office of Tourism to give the envelope some weight, sealed it, and gave it back to the clerk.

Steve went out through the ornate lobby. He looked across the street before making a right turn up the slight incline of Rue Chellah and noticed another BMW with three men inside. This car was dark blue. The one in the back was hard to see. They seemed to be looking at him. He made his way around the corner to find a taxi before the blue car made its way around the block. He tried to remember what his father had said about surveillance. Where was Abdelhaq? Whatever happened to his vaunted protective team?

He went into a bookstore to plan his next move where he picked up a guidebook. He should not have left the hotel without a firm plan to get to the Hilton. He was deep in thought when someone whispered his name, making him jump. It was a smiling Abdelhaq who wordlessly guided him to the blue BMW waiting outside.

They drove past the palace, and past the Zawa Theatre. Abdelhaq pointed out the small airport behind the Rabat Hilton where King Hassan II had always kept a plane and crew for a fast get-away in case of a coup. Abdelhaq's house was in the Pinede section of Souissi, named for its evergreens.

Abdelhaq pointed to an inscription by the front gate: VILLA LEILA.

"That's my wife's name," he said, smiling. "We bought the house just before I was assigned to Tehran."

They walked through a spacious marbled entrance and Abdelhaq led Steve to a wood-paneled living room that looked out on a rock garden. They sat on banquettes against the wall.

Steve brought him up to date about the events on the road back to Rabat and asked, "What happened to the protection you promised?"

"It's been a full day for me too, Steve. We interrogated all the drivers and mechanics that had access to the ministry cars. All but one, that is. And we pretty much concluded that he was the one who placed the bomb in the car. Anyway we're looking for him. He'll lead us to the rest of his group. The bottom line, as you Americans like to say, is that the protective team assigned to you was led by Benjelloun, the Salafist penetration of our service."

Abdelhaq stood up.

"How about some dinner?"

He opened the sliding glass doors to the dining room. A maid, head covered and with fading hennaed designs on her hands and feet, soon came in with a *tagine*. The couscous was already on the table. The maid removed the onion-domed top of the earthenware dish to reveal steaming chunks of lamb mixed with prunes, sprinkled with sesame seeds and almonds.

Abdelhaq poured from a bottle of Gris de Boulaouane, a Moroccan rosé with an alcoholic content that matched the strong tastes of the dish. The aromas of saffron and cinnamon caused Steve's stomach to signal that it had been a long eventful day with little food. They both helped themselves directly with their fingers. Abdelhaq took the couscous with his fingers, rolling it into a ball, a feat that Steve didn't even attempt.

"Tell me about Benjelloun and his gang. Is he now under arrest?"

"We're still looking for them. I suggest that you stay here tonight. Now that we know who to look for, you should leave Morocco. Since you told us he was in Khemisett a couple of hours ago, my people are looking for him right now. It shouldn't take long. We'll get you on a plane out tomorrow. But it would help my investigation if the Salafists think you're still here. Some might do something else to reveal themselves. You can leave as a Canadian tourist in your disguise and with a Canadian passport."

"That guy Benjelloun was part of the security team that I met with. He seemed very uncomfortable when I told them I knew I was under surveillance."

"Your antennae are obviously better than Benjelloun's boss in security. He should have pegged Benjelloun as a problem. That cretin comes from a politically connected family, so he may have gotten into security through the back door. He's a problem we will deal with," Abdelhaq said, with a scowl.

After the meal, Steve and Abdelhaq returned to the banquettes, low to the floor and with an abundance of backrest pillows. Steve was beginning to feel safe and relaxed for the first time all day.

"I know you and my father met in Iran but I was too young to know you then. How did you meet? What were you two doing?"

"If your father hasn't told you himself, it's probably not my role to talk about it. I only will tell you that I probably owe him my life. At a roadblock, he wrested a rifle. I remember it was a German Heckler and Koch G3 rifle—standard issue for the Iranian army at the time, from the hands of the leader of the thugs who wanted to take us prisoners. You can ask him for the details."

"Well, I can tell you also that my father has the greatest respect for you."

* * *

The next day Abdelhaq took Steve to the airport at five a.m. for his Air France flight to Paris. Abdelhaq's people, in plainclothes, were on both the public and the passengers-only sides of the passport check-in booth and security control area. Steve was wearing his disguise. Steve went through police and customs control with his fake passport with no problems.

Abdelhaq took Steve to the VIP lounge and took his Canadian passport.

"It will be easier for you now to travel under your true name. Ian Ross is registered on our airport records as having left Morocco today. That fills our need. If anyone is looking, you are still here. By the way, did I tell you that we arrested Benjelloun and his crew, the team that tried to shoot you? After we knew from you that they had been in Khemisett, it was easy to find them."

"Was that the whole cell? Is everyone under lock and key?" Steve asked.

"Unfortunately, the leaders, one named Hussein, a Syrian, and Lahlou, a Moroccan, were able to leave the country. We're dealing with the most dangerous and the most ambitious Salafist group. Their leader is Tariq al Khalil. He sometimes masquerades as a moderate intellectual, as you know."

"Al Khalil again!" Steve cried out.

He told Abdelhaq how al Khalil's name had come up during his lunch with Colonel Spaceck.

"Today, we asked your embassy to send their defense attaché home. That was your friend Spaceck. He was part of the problem. It seems that he fingered you to Benjelloun as a CIA officer."

Steve, eyebrows raised in surprise, said "Why the hell would he say that? I never had a good feeling about that guy. He seemed out for the main chance. I wouldn't be surprised if this was just the tip of the iceberg."

Steve's flight number was called out over the loudspeaker as boarding. Abdelhaq briefly gripped his upper arm and said, "I want to thank you for the part you played in getting rid of this Salafist cell. It's not over but we've a got on line on the others. We've gotten you a seat in first class, by the way."

He gave him a fatherly hug and told him to convey his greetings to Marshall.

* * *

Steve sat back in the Air Bus that would take him to Paris on the first leg of his trip back to the United States. As the two Pratt & Whitney 6122 engines lifted the aircraft up to its cruising altitude of thirty-thousand feet, Steve became aware of his heartbeat—it was normal for the first time in several days. He felt good he had been able to draw the Salafists out of their holes, even if it was only by playing the role of the tethered goat Abdelhaq had chosen for him. He had taken a measured risk, which he now realized had been based on false information, that Abdelhaq's men would protect him. But he had made his own luck.

Later, on his connecting flight to Washington Dulles Airport from Charles de Gaulle, he realized he had learned something else about himself. Being a successful businessman would never be enough. He needed to be a part of something bigger.

13. Timbuktu, Mali

Al Khalil entered the impoverished town of mud and sand and likened its decay to the decay of Islam. He knew that twenty-first-century Timbuktu was a far cry from its days as a center of trade and scholarship. A visitor needed to bring the history of Timbuktu with him or be disappointed.

The Malian Office of Tourism claimed that the oldest Islamic law library in the world was in Timbuktu. Although the United Nations and private foundations were providing resources to keep this institution from disappearing completely, it was only a dusty shadow of its former self.

Al Khalil found it hard to imagine that the town had once been fabulously wealthy and that pirogues loaded with gold from the Malinke Empire of Sundiata Keita had once come up the Niger River to meet the caravans from Libya and Egypt carrying spices and other goods.

His cover, his front organization, was the International Muslim Relief Agency. His office occupied a mud-walled building distinguished from similar buildings only by a green banner with the initials IMRA. Warm breezes pulled on the banner's loose ties.

The day after al Khalil's return to Timbuktu, Mamadou Diallo, his moneyman in Mali, came to report. The year before, Diallo had brought the director of the Morila goldmine on board. The mine had an output of eight-hundred-million dollars that year, and Diallo made sure that a ten-percent "tithe" was embezzled and placed in Tariq's Swiss bank account. There were gold mines on the other side of the Guinean border to the south and west of Timbuktu as well, and he hoped to be able to work similar arrangements there.

He stepped around people waiting outside in the shade of the building and went into the IMRA offices past a guard sitting in the in the open doorway. The IMRA offices were surprisingly well furnished, a step up from the bare Malian Government offices. Several Afghan rugs were on the floor, Arabic posters of Cairo's Al Azhar Mosque and Jerusalem's Dome of the Rock hung on the walls and, instead of the usual photograph of the current Malian president on the highest place on the wall, green Islamic calligraphy spelled out the word "Allah."

Diallo walked by the case handlers talking to their applicants and knocked on the door to an internal office. He wiped the sweat from his face on the sleeve of his mud-cloth bubu before walking in. He exchanged greetings with al Khalil and went to an open case of water bottles in the corner of the room, grabbed one and took several swallows.

Al Khalil sat behind a table rather than an office desk. In the corner was a locked metal cabinet. Because graven images were too close to *Jahhiliya* image worship, his secret was locked in the file cabinet. It held two prints, one an inexpensive engraving of Sheikh Abdelkader al Khalil, who had fought and died at the Battle of the Highway of the Martyrs in A.D. 732, when the Muslim armies had been beaten back by Charles Martel, who would become Charlemagne's grandfather, and the other of Sheik Tariq Ibn Ziad, the Berber warrior who had led the Arab armies across the Straits of Gibraltar into Europe in 711, both in the style of Jacques Louis David's painting of Napoleon crossing the Alps, a victorious warrior on a white horse. The hill, or *jebel*, overlooking the straits crossed by Tariq Ibn Ziad and his men had been named *Jebel Tariq*, later corrupted to Gibraltar.

Out in plain sight on his desk was a sign in Arabic, quoting his grandfather, the founder of the Muslim Brotherhood.

It is in the nature of Islam to dominate, not to be dominated, to impose its laws on all nations and to extend its power to the entire planet.

Al Khalil looked up and said, "Amadou, what's going on at the mines? The gold you're getting for us is helpful. But you know that's not why we're here. The gold is only a means to an end."

Tariq looked down at papers in front of him, but before Diallo could say anything, he stood up with his hands on the table. "We need more recruits among the miners, not only the gold mines but the salt mines in Taoudenni. We need to organize special indoctrination for the more susceptible and transform them into dedicated warriors. We need to identify individuals from these groups for special training. They're perfect recruits for our army. We must go faster."

His tone was commanding.

"I know that and I'm working on it," Diallo said defensively. "But these people are not like us, they're Sufis. They even drink beer. They would rather play soccer than go to the mosque."

"At this rate, it's going to take a hundred years. I'm taking the recruitment function away from you and giving it to Mohammed Lahlou. Maybe Moroccans are better at talking than at operations. You keep your focus on the money."

★ ★ ★

Four days later, Lahlou walked into the IMRA building and went directly into Tariq's office. Tariq closed the top drawer of his metal file cabinet and turned around to witness an agitated and sweating Lahlou.

"I spent the last couple of days at Taoudenni, like you told me. I think we're wasting our time there. The workers are the scum, the rejects, of every other possible employment possibility. Taoudenni used to be for political prisoners working off their sentences. I'm sure some stayed, if they didn't die first, because that's the only thing they could do."

"All right, let's forget about Taoudenni. But I wouldn't bring up Morocco if I were you,"

"Going after that American so quickly, with no information and no planning, was not my idea. I could have done it very well by myself, and our best penetration of Security, Benjelloun, would still be alive today and working for us," Lahlou said.

"If you're such a smart operator, how is it that you spent eighteen years in prison?"

At that point Hussein came in and sat down. Tariq could see Hussein had better news than Lahlou, whom he waved out of his office.

"I'm making arrangements for the Gao meeting next month," Hussein said.

Tariq tapped a finger on his desk.
"I was just going to ask you about that. It's going to be the first meeting of all of my key Salafist leaders from the Atlantic to the Indian Ocean. I want to give them my orders for the next twelve months. Is everything ready?"

"Remember the Tuareg rebellion a few years ago?" Hussein asked. "One of the concessions given to the Tuaregs was that the

145

Malian Army would decrease its presence in the Northern region of the country. One of the forts they closed down was the one in Gao. That's where we'll meet. It used to be a French Foreign Legion Fort. I told the Malian colonel in charge of the Gao military district that IMRA needed it for its annual Saharan Conference. He'll take five thousand to make it happen and clean the place up for us, but you know he's going to pocket most of it."

Hussein went to get himself a bottle of water.

"Good Hussein, I want you and Lahlou to make all the arrangements."

Tariq paused and looked down toward this desk on which several papers were lying.

Frowning thoughtfully, he said, "Now, I keep hearing about the crusaders, the Western missionaries, and what they call NGO's. How many are there in this area? What organizations do they belong to? Are they having any success turning our people away from Islam? Getting the Western influence out of our lands is our first priority. We need to eliminate these proselytizers. These infidel missionaries think that their blessings increase with their difficulties? I want to heap such blessings on them that they go straight to their heavens!"

Tariq got up from his desk and walked toward the door. Hussein followed as Tariq said, "Hussein, work on it. Give me a plan. It shouldn't be that hard. How many of these foreign preachers could there be? They need to be encouraged to go home."

Tariq opened the door and Hussein left the office.

"You're right. Eliminating the competition, priests and other do-gooders, should not be a difficult challenge."

Using more force than necessary, Tariq closed the door hard behind him.

* * *

Later that day, Tariq took a plane to Paris via Bamako for a speaking engagement. Hussein knew that he also would stop in Brussels to see his wife Malika and daughter Jamila. Tariq had confided that he would probably send them to live in Cairo.

In his absence, Hussein had time to reflect on his role in Tariq's grand design. His objective had never been religious. He wanted to take revenge on the Syrian Baathist leadership. He would have been perfectly happy, and fulfilled, to shoot the entire Assad family, starting with Rifaat al-Assad who led the attack that killed his father, and now Bashir, the former president's son who had taken over the country on old man Hafez al-Assad's death. Creating a new Caliphate was much bigger, too grand an idea to hope for, and probably too vast to even begin to contemplate.

When recruited by Tariq, Hussein's mind had focused on only one thing: Tariq's promise to overthrow the Syrian regime and install a leader who would be loyal to the new Caliph.

But the Assads still ruled Syria. No country had yet been folded into Tariq's grand scheme, although potent groups within each of the Sahel countries professed an allegiance to the Salafist banner. The meeting in Gao would be critical for the continued success of Tariq's movement. He decided he would stay with Tariq. His was the only game in town, for now.

14. Langley, Virginia: CIA Headquarters

Steve and Marshall were about to enter the Old Headquarters Building. Marshall had mentioned Steve's brushes with radical Islamists in Morocco to his colleagues at the agency, who wanted to hear about it firsthand. They passed a statue of Nathan Hale.

"Why Nathan Hale?" Steve asked. "Wasn't he captured and hanged by the British? There must have been more successful American spies."

"Yes of course. But, as the first spy to be executed for the United States, he stands for the patriotism and bravery of clandestine operators over the years."

In Steve's absence, to-do's from other projects had accumulated in his Tysons Corner office. The catch-up work weighed like a millstone. Steve already suffered from the boredom of too many hours spent writing overdue periodic progress reports and attending staff meetings; the routine was almost numbing. He was also frustrated over the lack of news concerning Coogan's death. The good news was that, to everyone's surprise, the Moroccan Ministry of Defense had already asked that West Gate send a team to Rabat to begin the next phase of the negotiations. But Steve's job as the initial developer of the project was over for the moment.

As they walked over the CIA seal in the marble lobby, Steve saw on his left the bronze statue of General William Donovan, an Irish Catholic from Boston who had become the most decorated soldier of WWI and then founded the OSS, predecessor to the CIA. To his right was the Memorial Wall with eighty-eight stars symbolizing the CIA officers who had died in the line of duty and whose names could not be revealed.

"I have friends among those stars," Marshall said. "I've been lucky." He paused and added, "And so have you."

A dozen men and women approached the security turnstiles on the far end of the lobby in front of steps leading up to a large corridor backlit by windows on an interior courtyard. As Steve and Marshall turned left in front of the turnstiles, Steve saw a woman in a *hijab* go through the turnstiles. Steve stopped Marshall.

"Did you see her? A Muslim woman? In here?"

"I know. The CIA is an equal opportunity employer. And the Agency can use people who understand Islam. Besides, she passed the screening and the polygraph. Getting a job offer here is not easy."

"Okay, okay, but what happens when she decides that she's more Muslim than American?"

Steve shook his head.

They went up several steps and turned into a small room where a guard was waiting for them. He checked Marshall's badge, gave an ESCORT REQUIRED badge to Steve, and led them to an open elevator being held for them. They exited on the fifth floor directly into a conference room, thus avoiding the need to share corridors with under cover intelligence officers of the National Clandestine Service who might be leaving on secret missions the next day.

"Hello everyone, I'm Isabel," said a black-haired woman with lively dark eyes and a broad smile seated at the large conference table. "I'd like you to sign several forms Mr. Church," she said, pointing to Steve.

Marshall interceded, "If that's a secrecy agreement, Steve is here not to acquire information but to share it."

"He still has to sign them."

She pushed them forward and, hesitating just a second, Steve signed them—rules and regulations. He shook his head slightly. Isabel then led them to a windowless conference room where four people waited for them. On one wall was a row of portraits that reminded Steve of the photos of Bogart and Bacall in movie theater lobbies. Certainly less glamorous but he assumed these people were stars in the world of clandestine operations.

As they sat around the table, one of their hosts, a woman who seemed a bit younger than Steve, greeted them.

"Hi. My name is Nicole. I'm with the Maghreb section of the Directorate of Intelligence."

She looked to her right.

"And this is Jason. He's with the National Counterterrorism Center. He focuses on radical Muslim terrorism. I don't know if you realize it, but you're one of the few survivors of a Salafist attack. In fact, you're the only one I know of who lived through two attempts—two in less than a week, a record. We're interested in anything you can share with us. For example, in hindsight, were there any indications of surveillance or any other interest in you beforehand?"

After recounting his story, Steve said, "So, in a nutshell, yes there were signs. Somebody went through my stuff in the hotel, I had company for sure when I went to the mausoleum, but I thought Curly and his friends in Fes were on my side. The Moroccan police must have all those guys in jail by now."

"This definitely sounds like Tariq al Khalil's style. We knew they had a cell in Morocco but it hasn't been very active," said Jason, his dark hair lightly spiked.

At that point a slim woman in her late thirties entered the room.

"Steve, this is Thérèse LaFont, the Chief of the Africa Division of the National Clandestine Service," Marshall said.

Steve recognized her from the last photograph on the wall. She had short blonde hair and was elegantly dressed in dark tailored slacks and jacket with a white silk blouse. She gave him a firm handshake.

"I only heard part of your story, but that was some driving. The only thing that's going to keep your father from going to jail for sharing our methods with an unauthorized and uncleared individual is for you to come to work for us."

She laughed. Steve managed a laugh, too.

"My father showed me how to do that maneuver on a vacant lot in an old Ford. It stuck with me, luckily."

They spent the next few minutes focusing on the respective roles of Benjelloun as the Salafist penetration of the Moroccan security service, Spaceck's over-the-top-zeal in trying to gain favor with the Moroccans to build himself a retirement sinecure, and Abdelhaq al Fassi's continuing value to the king.

"I understand, Steve, that you know Tariq al Khalil?" said LaFont, abruptly.

"I met him a couple of times when I was in school in Brussels," he replied, noticing the meeting was moving beyond his Moroccan experience.

Nicole and Jason left the room and the two officers who had been sitting against the wall moved to the table. LaFont introduced them.

"This is Philip, branch chief for the Maghreb and Mel, West African branch chief."

Philip, average height, average weight, dark hair with specks of gray. *Could be any age,* Steve thought. He was the original gray man who would be undistinguishable in a crowd. Mel was a heavy-set woman in her fifties with white hair. She was draped in an abundance of striped fabric.

"According to our information, al Khalil has a front in Timbuktu called the International Muslim Relief Agency," Philip said. "From there he is trying to establish a base for radical Islam in the entire Sahel, across North Africa, especially in countries with weak governance. His tools are his academic reputation, his Muslim Brotherhood ties, plenty of money, and the willingness to use physical violence. He is starting to make an impact. His goal is to establish a new Caliphate in the Sahel and grow it to include all of the Middle East."

He turned to Mel, who asked, "Steve, at West Gate International, do you need medical clearances before you travel?"

Steve, puzzled by the non sequitur, nodded.

"Why do you ask?"

Philip shot a frown in Mel's direction and took the conversational lead back.

"Al Khalil recently traveled through Algeria with his operations chief. While he was in Ghardaia, a major town in the Northern Sahara, two French oil workers were killed for no known reason. We suspect that his presence in the area was not a coincidence."

LaFont leaned forward.

"We have no one who can give us an "eyes-on-target" view of his set up in Timbuktu. Islam, radical or not, is not a topic the

Malian Government wants to talk about with us. You know, I assume that Mali is a Muslim country. I'll be up front with you, since you're family," she glanced and smiled at Marshall. "Our eventual goal, of course, is to have a source in al Khalil's office, in his group. So what we need to get started is a general overview—who these people are and what they do. Of course names, identifying data, and assessments would be great."

Steve glanced at his father, leaned back, and said, "I definitely want to help. What I've seen and learned in the last month has convinced me that the Salafists are a threat." He hesitated and added, "But if you're thinking I can get this information for you, you've got the wrong guy. I have no idea how I would go about it."

"Well, you could do more than you think just by visiting him in Timbuktu. It's just to give us context. The biggest thing we'd like you to do, that we would appreciate your doing, is to meet with al Khalil once or twice under some pretext. Hopefully you could go to his IMRA office and take a look around. We'll take it from there."

"What do I tell my boss at West Gate? I do have a day job." Marshall, who had let the conversation take its course, now jumped in.

"Your people just told us that the cell that attacked Steve in Morocco came under al Khalil. Now you want him to walk into al Khalil's office? Why does that make sense to you?"

He looked at LaFont and at the two other CIA officers.

"Yes, we talked about that and we reviewed the communications between al Khalil and the Moroccan cell," Philip answered. "They never mentioned Steve's name per se. The cell leader in Casablanca and al Khalil's operations chief, who was in

Morocco at the time, only mention a young American who worked for Ted Coogan."

Marshall looked a bit surprised.

"That's new. When did you have those messages? Why weren't they available while Steve was in Morocco? If you knew that he was in danger, why didn't you take action to warn him and get him out?"

He slapped his hand on the conference table with restrained anger.

"We didn't have those messages until after the fact, unfortunately," LaFont said, shaking her hear. "Sorting and translating and then figuring out where the information should be sent took the National Security Agency a bit too long to make it actionable. Further, we didn't know who the messages were about either, until you told us what was going on Marshall."

"When will the NSA understand that its information is not just for the historical record?" he asked.

LaFont nodded in sympathy and turned to Steve.

"I hope you don't mind, we've already talked to your boss at West Gate. He said that he would reluctantly lend you to us, but he wants you back. Sounds like he's got you on the fast track."

Mel, who had been silenced earlier, came back to the charge.

"Before we let you go overseas on our behalf, you need to be medically cleared. We'll sign you up for a full physical next week. Secondly, I don't know what it's like in the private sector, Steve, but here you'll have to keep a tight record of all the expenses you expect to get reimbursed. And we'll need receipts. We'll buy your flight tickets, of course. We'll get cheaper government fares."

Steve thought he was in the presence of a frustrated accountant.

"Mel—it is Mel isn't it? I admit that I'm new at this, but right now I think it's more important that I ... that we ... focus on the actual mission."

Marshall looked at Steve then at LaFont and said, "Welcome to the government, Steve. For the privilege of taking risks on behalf of your country, you get to spend more time filling in forms than you do on actual operations."

Turning to LaFont, Marshall continued, "But since Mel brings up the issue of money, keep in mind that Steve, if he agrees to do this, will continue to be paid by West Gate since you've already made the arrangement. He won't be paid by the Agency. In other words, you're getting a freebie, so..."

LaFont frowned at Mel.

"Of course, and we appreciate it. I agree. We'll minimize the paperwork."

Mel frowned back and said, "I only thought that since Steve's new to the government he should know the rules."

LaFont looked at her watch and got up to leave.

"Steve, thank you for your willingness to help us. I suggest that the next step is to train you on basic tradecraft, especially agent assessment, reporting, and show you what we've got on your new best friend al Khalil."

She left the room and they laid out a training program for Steve. As they were leaving the CIA's Langley campus, Steve asked his father, "What's with this Mel? I've met a lot of your CIA friends. She's not like them."

"No, she's not. The Agency is so thin that it's taking people like her with no overseas experience in order to staff the desks. I heard she comes from HR and spent some time with the Recruitment Center. She's obviously big on process."

Steve laughed.

"If people like Mel are the face of the CIA with new applicants, the Agency has more problems than I thought." Left unsaid were internal warning signals that he was entering a situation with more rules and oversight than he wanted.

15. CIA Safe House, Virginia

That evening, Marshall drove Steve to the safe house out in the countryside where he would live during his brief training period. They soon got off the highway and drove across familiar rolling hills. Although it was dusk, Steve could make out the large estates and forested properties.

The training safe house turned out to be a comfortable six-bedroom structure on twenty wooded acres. An unobtrusive fence surrounded the property. In the front, the white cross-buck fence was the same type used by the horse farms in the area. The front gate was a simple white wooden pole with a counterweight dropped across the entrance road to bar vehicular access. It was controlled remotely by the authorized visitor or by security from inside the grounds.

"The periphery of the property is guarded by concealed sensors and cameras monitored from a separate building recessed just inside the tree line," Marshall said. "The office of security normally keeps a unit of guard dogs on the grounds. I want to remind you of a couple of things that you already know, which may come up early in the training. First, remember that the CIA is not part of law enforcement. It doesn't have the power to arrest and doesn't fall under the Department of Justice. Also, an 'agent' in CIA parlance is a foreign national recruited to steal secrets for an intelligence officer. The media still uses the FBI meaning of the word to describe the FBI staff officer who investigates and makes the arrests."

They turned into the driveway as Steve said, "Don't worry Dad, I won't embarrass you."

Inside, Steve resented his father's assumption that the talk was necessary.

★   ★   ★

After a week during which Steve had been introduced to basic tradecraft topics such as the spotting, assessing and developing of potential agents, Marshall dropped by after dinner as Steve was going through French language cards, French on one side, English on the other.

"Sorry to interrupt you. I thought I'd come over and see how you're doing, whether you need anything since you're not allowed to leave."

"I guess these French irregular verbs will just have to wait," Steve said, putting his cards aside.

Marshall moved some books off a chair and sat down.

"I have something to ask you. You know that two years ago I was initiated into the Knights of Malta, an organization created in Jerusalem in A.D. 1099. I think you would make a great addition to the Order and I would be proud to sponsor you. The investiture is scheduled to take place at the Church of the Holy Sepulcher in Jerusalem. The ceremony itself dates back centuries; a lot of tradition there."

Steve had avoided following in his father's wake, but he was intrigued by the offer.

"What is the purpose of the Order, exactly? What do you do?"

"Exactly?" Marshall grinned. "We raise money for wounded veterans from Afghanistan and Iraq. That's what my chapter does anyway. Each chapter has its favorite cause."

"Sounds like a good cause. Let me think about it. You think I qualify to be a member?"

"Well, there's no test, if that's what you mean. It is a Christian organization—it started in the Holy Land during the Crusades. We look for professional people who have attained a high level of accomplishment in their field. And the usual qualities, you know, trustworthiness, integrity, the usual personal values."

Steve looked serious.

"I'm just getting started. I don't have accomplishments."

"You're wrong about that. But it's also for people who we think have all of the personal attributes and who we judge will become successful. And that's you. Am I wrong?"

He grinned again.

Steve didn't want a confrontation with Marshall at this point. In fact, the offer actually sounded interesting. It sounded even better when Marshall added, "While we're in Israel we can visit some of the Crusader castles—all part of the Order's history."

* * *

The next day, he met his new instructor Juan, dressed in boots and cammies. Juan had black hair and a squat build. Steve learned over the next forty-eight hours that Juan was a former Special Forces master sergeant who had trained counter-narcotics forces in Colombia and Mexico.

"I'm going to introduce you to weapons and explosives," Juan told him. "We don't expect you to use them but you need some knowledge for defensive reasons."

That day, Steve fired the Glock and other personal weapons. He was shown the various improvised explosive devices used by international terrorists and how these groups built and used car bombs, a weapon of choice in the Middle East.

On the way back from the range in the old Ford Fairlane assigned for his training by the Base's administration, Steve asked, "What about butane bombs?"

"Yes, I heard about your experience in Morocco. Using the pressure inside the butane cylinder multiplies the force of the blast several fold—more bang for the buck. I understand they used Semtex to set it off. I'm not surprised. Remember Vaclav Havel, who became President of Czechoslovakia? He said that during the Cold War, his country had sold or given enough Semtex for the worlds' terrorists to have an ample supply for the next one-hundred-fifty years."

* * *

When Juan picked up Steve the next day, he told him over coffee at a table in the kitchen, "Today, you make an IED and set it off. Like yesterday, the purpose is defensive. The rule of the range is that the student picks up his own duds—that means that if your device doesn't explode, it's your job to go pick it up. Nothing new about that; sort of like packing your own parachute."

They drove out to the range and, following Juan's directions, Steve timed a six-inch piece of fuse, which allowed him to then cut a length that would burn for forty-five seconds. Steve held the cap up to his eyes and crimped the metal around the fuse.

He pushed the cap into the C-4 and walked it out about fifty feet. Then he lit the fuse, turned around and walked back with a determined but unhurried step. Juan had taught him that, when dealing with explosives, one needed to be calm and measured.

They both got into the bunker and watched through a quartz bomb-blast window and waited. Juan looked at his watch and said, "It's been two minutes. Wait another minute and then go get it." Juan watched him closely, Steve assumed, for any signs of fear or nervousness, but Steve was determined to show none.

A long minute went by. They were waiting and watching through the window. Juan looked at his watch and said, "Time." Steve started out of the bunker.

"Don't worry," Juan said, "we've only lost a few students. Besides it would look bad on my record. Seriously, I'll go with you, Steve."

"No. I don't need any special favors. If the SOP is for me to get it, I'll get it."

As he walked out of the bunker, the instructor followed and quickly caught up with him. Having Juan beside him made Steve feel that the danger was acceptable—here was someone whose expertise was explosives; he wouldn't be with him if he thought the risk was high.

They walked toward the IED, both watching closely for telltale smoke. Steve and Juan stood for another second by the device before the instructor picked it up and pulled the fuse out of the detonating cap.

He gave the whole package to Steve and told him, "The problem was that you didn't push the fuse into the cap firmly enough. Also, we normally use two fuses and two caps for insurance, but I didn't tell you to do that this time. The problem was in part mine. That's why I came with you."

He had Steve do it again, with two detonator caps, and this time the device exploded, sending a cloud of dirt and rocks up into the sky.

As they left the range, Juan said, "Now that I gave you instructions on what headquarters thought you should know, tomorrow morning I'll show you what headquarters should have told me to show you. Ever hear of non-lethal weapons? Sounds like an oxymoron but the military has been doing a lot of work in this area and so have we. We've adapted the technology that the military needs to stop a crowd at a distance without shooting and reduced it to something you can carry in your pocket with a range of thirty feet. It's called Pulsed Energy Projectile, or PEP. I'll show you after breakfast tomorrow."

Steve left the next day at 10 a.m. after two hours of instruction on the new personal weapon.

16. Paris: Kella's Apartment

Kella ran down the stairs as fast as she could. The fear of Hamad behind her coursed through her veins. To get away from him, she thought of jumping down from landing to landing.

Was it possible?

She jumped and came down lightly, but Hamad jumped after her.

He reached for her.

She felt the touch of steel on her back.

Was the knife in her back?

Somehow she knew that her blouse had been cut open.

She kept running down the stairs—for her life!

How many flights of stairs so far? How long would it take to reach the street?

She lifted up her robe with one hand to go faster.

Hamad yelled, "Whore! Whore!"

She tripped and Hamad suddenly was on top of her.

He straddled her.

She was terrified.

Was he going to rape her?

She couldn't move her arms or legs.

He raised the knife and shouted, *"Allah hu Akbar,"* his face a demon's mask.

The knife came down slowly but inexorably toward her heart.

His face was closer, grimacing with anger, with the effort.

Was she dead now? Bells were ringing. She must be in the Basilica of Saint-Denis.

* * *

The ringing woke her. She was in a sweat, her head turning from one side to the other. Her heart pounding, pounding, told her she was alive. Her phone was ringing. She put her light on. It was 6:30 in the morning. It was Steve.

"Hey, I was hoping to catch you at home before you left for the day so I stayed up late. I'm in Virginia, at home. I've been thinking about you. How are you?"

"I'm okay. Wait a minute, I'll be right back."

She went to the bathroom and washed her face.

"It's early here you know. But I'm glad you called. I'm okay, but to tell you the truth I have problems concentrating, in my studies I mean."

"I have the remedy: a trip. I've just accepted a temporary freelance assignment as a photojournalist. I'm going to do the definitive piece on the Tuaregs. Come with me."

"What? The Tuaregs? It's been done already," she told him, laughing.

"Maybe, but it's not like I'm going to do it because you're going to be my secret weapon. How about going with me? What better guide could I have? You even speak Tuareg, don't you? Have you already taken your trip to Timbuktu? I hope not."

"It's Tamasheq—the language, I mean."

She was glad to be distracted from her nightmare of Hamad, but Steve's call was doubly welcome. She was attracted to the prospects of traveling with him in her native land. Yet she felt she had to put up a little resistance.

"Steve, it's a wonderful offer, but I can't just pick up and leave my studies at a moment's notice. I was planning a visit to my relatives in Timbuktu but not this afternoon. Are you going through an early mid-life crisis? I thought you liked your job."

"Trust me, Kella. I know this is sudden and you've got a ton of questions. I'll answer them all when I see you in Timbuktu. Think of it as Fate. Think Lady Luck and the spirit of adventure. Think *Baraka*."

Without too much effort, he persuaded her to join him and they agreed to make their own separate ways to Timbuktu and meet there a week later.

* * *

In coordination with the central cover staff, Marshall, Phillip, and Mel had settled on Steve's cover. Sitting in the staff's conference room, Yukio, the cover officer explained.

"Your photojournalism cover will give you a reason to be in Mali and to make contacts with just about anyone in the Timbuktu area. And it will provide a pretext to contact al Khalil and IMRA, which presumably provides assistance to Tuaregs."

"What about sending Steve into the lion's den in true name?" Marshall asked. "The Salafists targeted him in Morocco. They know his name. Everybody has his name it was in the newspaper."

Mel interjected, "I'll get the forms from State for Steve to fill out."

"I can't very well contact al Khalil in alias since we've already met," Steve spoke up.

"An alias passport at this late date is out of the question," Yukio said. "Passports are controlled by the State Department with an iron grip—you wouldn't believe the red tape."

"Listen, since I have to travel in true name, and since I have to meet al Khalil in true name, I'll use my middle name, Christopher, when making contacts in Mali just to keep a lower profile," Steve said decisively. "I have a hard time believing that al Khalil has anyone actively screening the names of everyone arriving and leaving Mali; the risk must be minuscule. As far as Tariq himself, I'm sure I can convince him that I have no involvement with the Quran documents."

If I can actually reach him, he thought.

When the meeting was over, Marshall pulled Steve aside in the hallway. His father's face was drawn and serious.

"As usual, the real cover will not be what the CIA provides, but what you can do with it and how you conduct yourself."

With Marshall's interference, Mel was forced to let Steve plan and buy his own flight tickets. Mel was only looking at the cost to the government, but Marshall had pointed out that all tickets bought at government fares are so labeled and would give Steve away.

★ ★ ★

Steve left Dulles on a five-and-a-half-hour night flight to Paris, had breakfast at Charles De Gaulle airport during the four-hour layover, and read and dozed during the eight-and-a-half-hour leg to Bamako.

As they flew over the hundred-mile-long ergs and then the massive dark and rocky plateaus of the Anti-Atlas range, Steve was struck by the vast desolate space and wondered how anyone could survive down there.

The moment he stepped out of the plane at Bamako Airport the acrid smell of smoke filled his nostrils. He had expected the heat and the poverty. He knew that, with few paved roads, it would be dusty. But he knew he would always associate the burning smell with Bamako.

Upon arrival at l'Amitié Hôtel, he made arrangements to rent a Toyota Land Cruiser for pick-up in Timbuktu.

In answer to his question, the desk clerk told him, "The smell, *Monsieur*? Ah, you mean you smell smoke! That's from the fields, *Monsieur*. They burn the old crop."

He looked at Steve like a kind teacher at a student with limited intellectual ability.

As pre-arranged, he met the CIA's chief of station, Rod Descouteaux, at his home on the banks of the Niger the evening he arrived. The purpose of the meeting was simply to give Steve a local contact in case of problems.

Rod was in his thirties, tall and thin, with sandy hair combed straight back. They sat outside on a patio lit by the dining room lights. Outlined against the moonlit sky were hundreds of fruit bats flying over the river.

Sipping a dirty martini, Rod said, "I appreciate your help. IMRA is an information target but I have had problems just getting access, let alone recruiting anyone in al Khalil's group. Since you already know al Khalil, it should be simple. You meet him once or twice, take his temperature, take a look at his operation, and you're done."

"I don't guarantee anything but I'll do my best."

Before Steve took his leave, Rod told him, "You should call on the cultural attaché at the embassy tomorrow. It will reinforce your cover. He's in charge of contacts with the media for the embassy and might know some people who could open doors for you in Timbuktu for your photo shoots."

* * *

Before getting on an Air Mali flight to Timbuktu the next day, Steve stopped by the American embassy, a whitewashed building that had once been a bank. He told the cultural attaché, a bearded, rather short and rotund Afro-American, about his photographic assignment. In return, he received the names of a couple of Malian officials in Timbuktu who might be helpful. The attaché, a friendly and outgoing *bon-vivant* walked him out to the street and, laughing, he said, "Thank God that my great-grandfather was a slow runner."

"What do you mean?"

"Nothing really." Seeing Steve puzzled face, he added, "Only that I'm here today as an American diplomat rather than in the ranks of the local unemployed getting picked up by government trucks for unpaid labor only because one of my ancestors got caught and sold to the slave traders on the coast."

As his Antonov-24 landed in Timbuktu, he noticed the rusted wreck of his plane's twin that had been pushed to the side of the runway. After checking in at the Hôtel Bouctou, he followed Rod's advice and hired a local driver. By any measure, anyone born and raised in Mali was not half as expert behind the wheel as the average Westerner. He hired a Tuareg named Atrar who had driven a truck in Marseilles for five years and spoke decent French. He soon realized that, along with Atrar, he inherited the driver's wife, young son, and brother.

When Atrar showed up to take Steve to a Tuareg camp outside of Timbuktu, he came with his brother, Izem. On the way out, Atrar proudly told Izem, who sat in the front passenger seat like a security guard, "Tell Monsieur Christophe; go on."

Izem appeared initially reluctant but said, "I am a soldier. Ever since I was a young boy. When we fought the Malian Army, maybe fifteen years ago, I rode with my brothers. It is our history to fight. At the beginning we won. We knew the desert. But too many Malians—they took over the wells."

"And what did you do after the fighting?" Steve asked. "Were you a prisoner?"

"No, never. Many of us made our way to the military camps on the other side of the Libyan border. At first, the Libyans didn't know what to do with us. But, they saw that we were good soldiers. They trained us, gave us guns, and we became part of the Libyan Army. We patrolled the Libyan Desert, and then we fought in Chad."

Again prompted by Atrar, Izem said, "My name means 'lion' in Tamasheq."

Steve realized Izem could be useful to him, although he didn't yet know how.

Later that day, he began to establish his cover credentials as a photojournalist. Back in his room, he sent his first message to CIA headquarters in Langley. Using steganography, Steve was able to hide his message in the photographs he took that day. His email, sent to an ostensibly commercial URL, summarized his visit to the Tuareg camp and the attached photographs hid his real message.

Steganography is the modern version of microdots. Steve had the option of hiding his messages in graphic images, Web sites, or recorded music. In view of the questionable reliability of the Malian telephone system, he communicated to the outside world through his handheld Iridium 9505A satellite phone.

He first called Kella from his hotel room phone. The phone made clicking noises for so long that Steve assumed the call was being relayed through Paris. Eventually, after finding stairs that led to the flat roof of the small hotel, he called her on the satellite phone, which could not be used inside. He reached her quickly and they made plans for dinner that night at the Poulet d'Or, not far from the Petit Marché, an open market.

When he found the restaurant and sat at a table for two, Steve learned the Poulet d'Or, or Golden Chicken, took its name seriously. Fried and boiled chicken dishes accompanied by couscous monopolized the menu. He was ordering Gazelle beer from Senegal when Kella entered.

He took in her harmonious curves as she approached. She was conservatively dressed in jeans, sandals, and a military-style long sleeve shirt with épaulettes. He had looked forward to this moment and he was not disappointed. He hoped he'd read the same conclusion in Kella's smile when she seated herself at the table.

Suspecting Steve's apparent change in career was a result of the events in Morocco, she asked, "Did you leave West Gate?"

"No," he replied. "I'm just taking unpaid leave. The Moroccan project is moving along nicely. My part is done. I ran into a magazine publisher and we just clicked. He said he was looking for a freelance photographer who could write and had overseas experience for a project that would last a month or so. When he said the focus of the article was going to be the Tuaregs, I told him that he had found his man."

"You're full of surprises. I can't stay here a month, though. I've got ten days."

"Well, let's make the most of them. By the way, the name I'm using here whenever I don't need documentation is Christopher—my middle name."

Reacting to Kella's questioning glance he added, "Well, okay, I'm a little nervous that the same guys who tried to get me in Morocco might somehow learn I'm now here. If you don't mind, I'd like you to call me Christopher in public—in fact all the time here."

"Sounds mysterious. I never thought of it before, but are there Salafists here too?"

She glanced around the restaurant.

"Are you ready for this? I learned that Tariq al Khalil is here, running a social welfare group."

"You're kidding. What happens if he learns you're here? What about the publicity surrounding you and the Quran documents?"

"For now, I'm just going to get material for the magazine. It may turn out that going to see him with my cameras may be the best defense. What about the relatives you want to find?"

Kella looked at him with one eyebrow raised like a question mark. Steve didn't respond and she said, "Thiyya is my birth mother's cousin. Her husband is Azrur. Other Tuaregs will know them. It's a small tribal community. I've been thinking about spending time here with them ever since that day when Faridah died. They're my closest birth relatives. Besides, I'm sure that they'll be able to help with your article, and I hope to write a paper for school out of this time in Timbuktu."

"Okay, I'm good to go. How do we start looking for them? There's a lot of desert out there. Your *Imazighen* relatives could be anywhere."

"I'm impressed. You've been doing some reading. Did you also know that *Imazighen* means 'free and noble people?' You must have read some of Timbuktu's history. Do you know about Mansa Musa? He was a fourteenth-century Malian emperor who made a pilgrimage to Mecca with sixty-thousand men and twelve-thousand slave girls. His baggage train included eighty camels each carrying three-hundred pounds of gold. He spread so much gold in Egypt that the price fell and didn't recover for years."

"Sounds like something out of a movie."

Steve drove her back to her hotel, the Hendrina Khan. On the way, Kella related a a bit of trivia.

"Remember A.Q. Khan, the father of the 'Islamic Bomb?' This is his hotel. He named it after his Dutch wife."

He stopped in front of the hotel.

"Fascinating!"

Under the gaze of a guard and the doorman, he kissed her goodnight. As he drove away, it occurred to him he was now thinking of Vera *after* rather than before the kiss.

* * *

The next day, Kella went to the Catholic orphanage from which the Hastings had adopted her. The building was fairly large including a dormitory for fifty children, two classrooms and an office. A sandy courtyard surrounded by a seven-foot wall was full of running and laughing children. Next to the courtyard was a church. Mother Superior Catherine was still there, surprised and pleased to see her.

"Oh my dear!" she exclaimed. "I still remember how the Hastings fell in love with you the moment they saw you, especially Madame Alexandra. Your stepfather held a very important position at the American Embassy in Bamako, you know. He came to Timbuktu to take care of any American citizens affected by the Tuareg rebellion. And when Madame came with him, I made sure that she saw you. Somehow I just knew that she would want to adopt you."

"My stepmother said that you had warned her that Tuaregs are very independent people."

Mother Catherine laughed and said, "That is true. I didn't want her to be surprised. I also told her that your DNA was quite a mixture of European, Berber, Arab, and Negro, and she said that explained why you were such a beautiful child. She promised to bring you up in the church. Has she?"

"Yes, Mother Catherine. I would like to get in touch with my birth relatives while I'm here. How do you think I can find them? I suppose they're still nomads and moving around quite a bit."

"Start with the marabout, a Muslim holy man very close to the Tuaregs. He knows everything."

Then Mother Catherine told her how to find him.

* * *

Steve made calls to the office of tourism in order to establish his official presence in Timbuktu and try to avoid the high degree of red tape he had been warned about by the cultural attaché. Then, wanting to begin both his cover and his CIA assignments, as well as try to get a fix on Kella's relatives, he went to the airport to rent a plane.

The airport was deserted, other than a few Malians who seemed to call it home. He headed for the control tower. It was an incongruously elegant piece of architecture consisting of a long neck rising out of an administrative building at a sixty-degree angle to support the control room forward of the tower.

Overdone, Steve thought. Like having an army to protect a bank with no funds.

He reached the control room but found himself alone. He eventually went back to his car. Just as Atrar was putting the car in gear, a pick-up truck pulled. He told Atrar to wait while he got out and went up to the other car as the driver stepped out. The man was in his late twenties and sported a stubbly beard. Steve determined immediately from his speech that he was Australian.

"No, mate, there are no Hertz-rent-a-plane outfits here. The only private aircraft at the airport is shared by several NGOs. That's non-governmental-organizations to you, mate, if you're new. It's a Cherokee Six, a Piper. You're talking to the owner and pilot.

"I'm Campbell," he added. "What is it exactly you want, Yank?"

Steve explained his photojournalist status and said he wanted to use the aircraft for half a day or so for a reconnaissance of the area around Timbuktu, looking especially for Tuareg camps he could visit by car later.

"I've got a pilot's license and could fly your plane but, for the first time, I could use a pilot who knows the neighborhood."

"You've got a deal, mate. How about tomorrow morning?"

They settled on the price.

"Great. There'll be one other passenger."

Campbell walked toward the field while Steve told Atrar to drive back to town.

17. Mali: Aéroport de Tombouctou

Steve and Kella waited for Campbell. When he showed up, forty-five minutes late, Steve thought he smelled the sweet odor of marijuana from Campbell's clothes. He leaned in for a closer look. His eyes were indeed a bit bloodshot.

"Have a late night last night?" he asked, wondering if the Aussie was one-hundred-percent together.

Steve saw Kella's concerned look and squeezed her arm in reassurance. Campbell laughed.

"The biggest secret about Timbuktu is the party scene. I'm not staying here for the money."

They got settled in the Piper Cherokee, a six-seater, with Kella sitting behind the pilot.

"We're looking for a place just north of Lake Faguibine," she said. "Do you know where that is?"

"Yes, it's west of here about a hundred miles."

"Then I'd like to fly over any Tuareg camps within, say, a hundred-mile radius of Timbuktu."

"You got it," Campbell said, pushed on the throttle.

The plane picked up speed down the runway and Steve quickly sensed something was missing: He hadn't seen Campbell go through the take-off check-list. With the plane still on the ground but gaining speed, the engine sputtered for a couple of seconds but resumed its normal operation. Steve, on the pilot's right, looked at Campbell and asked, "What's that?"

Campbell didn't answer. He pulled back on the control and lifted the plane off the ground. At three-hundred-fifty feet altitude, the engine coughed again, alternating between no power and normal function for several seconds and then stopping completely.

Kella leaned forward to Steve.

"I don't like this. Christopher?"

At almost the same time, Steve said sharply, "We'd better land." He expected Campbell to keep going straight and land on the hard desert floor in front of the runway. Instead Campbell initiated a sharp turn to the right.

"No, we're not high enough!" Steve yelled, and wrestled the yoke from Campbell's control to get out of the turn before the plane stalled.

"Oh my God! What's going on?" Kella shouted from the back as she looked at the ground rushing toward her.

The plane swiftly lost lift and altitude as the wings became almost perpendicular to the ground.

Kella yelled, "No!"

Campbell, fighting back Steve's pull on the yoke, shouted, "Drongo Yankee!" But Steve was too strong, and Campbell relinquished his hold. The plane was only thirty feet from the ground before Steve managed to return the wings to a horizontal position. Their sharp descent became a glide toward the sand.

Steve glanced down at the fuel selector controls and noticed the setting was all the way to the left, on the off position. With his left hand, he quickly moved the setting to number 3 position, the left main tank, going right past the number 2 setting for the left wing-tip tank.

Barely ten feet off the ground, the engine came back to life. Steve moved the throttle forward, gently at first gently, but when the wheels touched the ground he forcefully pushed on the throttle and the Piper jumped up, the engine no longer coughing.

At a thousand feet, Steve turned the plane around and circled the airport but kept climbing. He reached two-thousand feet and the engine seemed to be functioning normally.

"What do you say? The engine sounds okay. I vote for going on. The sand looks pretty hard. If we have to, we could glide down. Your radio works, right?"

Campbell nodded but without enthusiasm and Steve added, "I'll do the piloting and you be the navigator."

"Look Yank, I'm still the captain," Campbell protested, his face white and sweaty.

"I know that, and you are in charge. But you have to agree you're not at your best this morning. Right? That must have been a helluva party last night. You don't put a plane in a tight turn like that at less than at least seven hundred or eight hundred feet. We were barely off the ground, with no power! You could have killed us. You're still under the effect of whatever you smoked."

Steve smiled at the Australian to keep the situation as calm as possible.

"Let's watch that fuel-selector switch. Did you gas up this morning? Are the tanks full?"

"The tanks are not full but we've got at least two hours of gas. Okay, okay, head directly west at two-seven-five degrees."

Steve was sure Campbell didn't want to lose the fee.

"How did the fuel selector get to the off position?"

"You must have hit it with your knee."

"I don't think so," Steve said firmly, convinced now that Campbell hadn't gone through his checklist.

He looked back at Kella and gave her a reassuring smile.

"You okay back there? Having fun yet?"

She did not smile.

"This is not a joke. We almost crashed. I think we should go back and forget about this."

"We can do that," Steve said. "But I think we fixed the problem. The fuel selector was set on an empty tank. We're okay now, right Campbell?"

He sulked and said nothing. Steve again looked at Kella.

"I'm for going ahead. We're okay, really. I've got things under control."

"I hope one of you knows what he's doing," she said.

* * *

Timbuktu was still visible to the north as they flew over a track that headed first to the west and then to the southwest, paralleling the Niger River. As far as the eye could see, the only traffic consisted of one truck heading west. However, there were scattered small groups, some with a camel or a donkey or two.

Soon Lake Faguibine was visible in the distance. Indeed, on the northern side was an outcropping of rocks rising a couple of hundred feet above the desert. Between the northwest side of the lake and the rocks were palm trees and bushes. Steve lowered his altitude and could see several camps among the trees. The black tents, the whites and blues of the men's clothing, and the blacks of the women's, together with the green of the vegetation starkly contrasted the otherwise monotonous color of the sand.

"They're Tuaregs," Kella said. "That's where the marabout told me I would find Azrur and Thiyya."

Steve came down to a hundred feet above the camp and waggled the plane's wings in a friendly gesture.

"Here, put an X on the map so we can find them again," he said, pointing the plane on an azimuth of forty-five degrees heading toward the oasis of Dayet en Naharat, to start a wide northern arc around Timbuktu. They soon reached the track that led to the oasis and followed it north until they overflew it. They then headed directly east and soon reached the oasis of I-n-Alei.

Off to the east about four miles sand and dust swirled into the sky. Curious, Steve headed for it, skirting the cloud on its southern side. A convoy of trucks and jeeps apparently coming from I-n-Alei was at the source of the disturbance. The trucks were loaded with barrels and with goats and cases of vegetables.

"Where do you think they're going?" Steve asked Campbell, who shrugged.

"I'm not sure I want to know. They look military, probably the Malian army resupplying its desert troops somewhere."

"Well, let's see," Steve said as he directed the plane to follow the desert track being used by the convoy. Thirty miles farther, flying at a thousand feet, they could see the outlines of a camp. There were vehicles, several large tents, and a group of men in single line getting food and water—a chow line. It was lunchtime. There was another group doing push-ups and calisthenics.

Steve could also see an obstacle course and a rifle range. The men in line had weapons and a few pointed them toward the plane, others waved their arms for the intruder to leave their space, and others appeared to be shouting. A black flag flew at the top of a pole in the middle of the camp.

"What's that?" asked Kella from the back of the aircraft.

She leaned forward and pointed to the far end of the camp where they could see an airstrip about a thousand feet long. As

Steve looked toward where she pointed, a small plane about half the size of theirs was taking flight from the airstrip. Steve banked the plane to circle the camp and headed higher.

"Looks like a UAV, an unmanned air vehicle. It's too small for a pilot. But big enough to carry other stuff, like cameras, machine guns, even missiles," Campbell said. "I'll take over here, I feel fine," he added with a new air of authority, and Steve reluctantly relinquished control of the plane to the Australian.

The UAV was also gaining height, and it soon was only about a half-mile away but clearly heading toward the Piper at an altitude of thirteen-hundred feet, only two-hundred feet below them. As it got closer, they noticed it had no identifying number, only a black rectangle on its tail.

Campbell climbed to keep some distance from the UAV until the ground controller made his intentions known, which he did quickly. Heading toward them at right angle, the UAV shot a hail of bullets their way. The bullets were high, Steve noted, because some of them were tracers, bullets modified with a pyrotechnic charge that burn brightly making the path of the bullet visible to the naked eye, giving the shooter a way to correct his aim.

Campbell headed higher while Steve got out his camera and shot photographs of the camp and of the UAV that continued to follow them, firing an occasional burst.

"Let's get out of here!" cried Kella.

This was advice Campbell took gladly and pointed the aircraft south gaining speed. After ten minutes, the UAV turned back.

"What the hell was that all about? I never saw that camp before," Campbell said. "What kind of flag was that?" he asked.

"It only needs a skull and cross-bones," said Steve, suspecting that they had just flown over a Salafist installation, an open secret the Malian Government was choosing to ignore.

* * *

On their way back to the airport, they flew over Timbuktu. It was clearer from the air that the city of legends was struggling to survive. The sands of the Sahara, with the patience of centuries and the power of the wind, were trying to smother the city. Houses on the outskirts of town acted as a barrier to the slow but irresistible juggernaut of rock ground by the elements into tons of minute granules and moved at the command of the wind. Heading north was a caravan of at least fifty camels, with two Tuaregs walking in front and a few others near the middle and the rear of the caravan. Steve wondered if they were going to Morocco.

After a surprisingly smooth landing Campbell said, "I went through a difficult patch back there but, hey, thanks mate, I don't know what happened. I couldn't think straight. I shouldn't charge you anything for this flight but you must understand, my bank account is a little low right now."

Kella got out of the plane as quickly as she could and, without another word, headed toward their car.

"Well, it was a memorable flight. I don't like getting shot at," Steve answered.

Boy, had his life changed. His CIA briefings had obviously been incomplete. He wondered what other surprises were out there.

18. Timbuktu: Hendrina Khan Hotel

The next day, Steve and Kella had breakfast together. They were planning on an early start, and the dining room was otherwise empty. They sat at a table against the wall.

Kella wore khakis and a white t-shirt, over which she had an open, light-blue shirt with long sleeves rolled up above the elbow where she buttoned them down. Her black hair was pulled back, and Steve noticed that her only make-up was a light trace of lipstick as protection against the sun. She looked rested and fresh faced.

She put her tan bush hat on one of the other chairs at their table and took a sip of her orange juice.

"I'm really excited about seeing my cousins again. This is going to be a good day. Do you think we'll get there today? I don't know about you, but I don't ever want to fly with that Aussie again. Yesterday was a miserable day. I thought we were going to die before we even left the airport."

"I'm sorry," Steve said, "but we did find the Tuareg camp. Your marabout knew what he was talking about. We should get to your relatives early tomorrow."

Atrar loaded their backpacks, two large plastic containers of water, and a cooler that Kella had found in the Timbuktu market in which she stocked flat bread, fruits, and a chicken she had persuaded the hotel to cook for them. At the time, Steve had said the cooler looked ideal for the beer, but he had lost the argument and sent Atrar to find another cooler. So they left with his-and-hers coolers.

The camp was about a hundred miles due west, as the crow flies. However, by land, it was more like one-hundred-fifty miles, since Atrar wanted to use tracks as long as he could before heading out across the desert. On the way, Kella talked about her early childhood as a nomad tending the goats, pounding millet into meal, seeing the world from the top of a camel when the clan changed grazing areas and desert wells and, when possible, attending school.

"As a kid," she said, "I did a lot walking when we changed grazing areas. Now, I'd rather ride, thank you very much. Although I do jog for exercise, I really hate it—so boring."

"What about women's role in the tribe?" Steve asked. "You hinted at it in Paris. It sounded very different from the Muslim tradition."

"You're right. In the Tuareg tradition, ancestry flows through the female line. My mother and her mother always had positions of leadership. That didn't mean necessarily that I would also have been a tribal leader. But, in a way, it was mine to lose."

* * *

They spent the night in Goundam, a town surrounded by several lakes created by the Niger's annual floods.

Before they left the next morning, they had coffee at the hotel on a deck overlooking a tributary flowing into the Niger where a family of hippopotami was bathing.

A young American couple joined them. The man wore a white shirt with a pouch slung across his chest bandoleer-style. The woman wore khakis and a long sleeve shirt, also white. It seemed big for her as if it belonged to her companion. The newcomers introduced themselves as John and Elise West, a brother and sister team of the Church of Jesus Christ of Latter Day Saints—Mormons—in the last few days of their two-year proselytizing mission.

Steve asked the waiter to set the table for two more people.

"All Mormons go on a twenty-four-month mission normally right after high school," John explained. "We took French at Highland High School in Salt Lake City. Then, before we left Utah, we picked up some Bambara, the dialect of the dominant Malian tribe, at the LDS language center. Elise has a knack for languages and she learned Tamasheq after we got here."

Kella and Elise exchanged a few words in Tamasheq, each surprised and delighted that the other spoke the language.

"We could have been sent to Poughkeepsie or to Vladivostok, just about anywhere," John said, as the waiter poured coffee for the four of them. "But we were sent to Mali and here we are, on the edge of the Sahara. We normally work out of Beautiful-Downtown-Timbuktu-on-the-Niger."

"I've dreamed about a mission like this since I was fifteen," Elise said. "It's important for all of us to spread Jesus's word."

Kella had been listening closely, leaning back in her chair. She took a sip of her orange juice and asked, "This is so interesting. Are there other Western organizations around Timbuktu?"

"There are at least a dozen NGOs in Mali with different goals, humanitarian, medical, religious, and sometimes, political. The United Nations has its groups. The United States has the Peace Corps; Medecins-Sans-Frontieres is here. Cuba has medical technicians; the International Red Cross also."

Steve looked at his watch and asked, "How about Muslims? Have you met anyone from IMRA?"

The Wests glanced at each other and John said, "Yes, Sunnis. They don't mix with the rest of us. Although their boss, Tariq al Khalil, claims Belgian nationality, I've heard that he has little use for Europeans. We've never met those people."

"But what do they do here?" Steve persisted.

"They're supposed to be helping the people in the region with health and social services," Elise answered, "and they use that as a springboard to urge their audiences toward a pure brand of Islam. Rumors are rampant that they have a dark side, that the Malian authorities don't dare interfere in their activities, and that they're forming a secret army."

"Are they successful?" Steve asked, looking at John.

"I'm not sure. The brand of Islam around here is more basically Sufi than strict Wahhabist, so there is natural resistance. The strict Muslims don't even believe the local Muslims are Muslim at all because their religion has marabouts, saints, and worship images. Some of the rumors about IMRA claim that they are responsible for the deaths of several of these holy men who were not interested in the IMRA version of Islam."

The Wests offered to introduce Steve and Kella to their world by inviting them to their going away party the following week in Timbuktu. Many NGO workers would be there as well as Malian employees and friends. They accepted the offer.

* * *

From Goundam, Atrar left the track and headed straight west in the desert and then found a path on the western side of Lake Kamango that took then north toward Lake Faguibine.

In mid-afternoon Atrar stopped the car and pointed toward the horizon. Steve took out binoculars and said, "It sure looks like the camp we saw from the air."

"Can I have the binoculars?" Kella asked.

In the far distance she saw dark rock outcroppings above the desert floor. After a few kilometers of rough, off-road driving, she saw a track heading up a long, sloping incline, and at the top, between the two lakes, a number of horizontal slashes in the landscape as the land rose again.

The Tuareg camp was at the bottom of the outcroppings. Atrar stopped the car beside a steep rock wall. A hundred and fifty feet away a dozen camels looked down at a herd of cattle drinking in clusters from metal drums almost completely buried in the ground.

A barefoot boy in a loose white garment that covered him to his elbows and knees used a stick with his left hand on a short-horned bull that, with the exception of his black nose, blended with the hard-packed brown sand. In his right hand, the boy held one end of a rope that curled almost down to the ground to a tight noose around the animal's horns. His long muscular neck held his head low but his eyes looked up to his left and his horns were at an angle that pointed the left horn directly at the boy's waist. Another rope tied to his horns trailed on the ground behind him toward several branches planted in the ground like tent poles the height of a man. A pulley hung under the apex of the branches over a well. Kella realized that it was the boy's job to draw water from the well.

The animal suddenly swung his horns toward the boy who nimbly jumped out of the way. A blue-clad adult shouted at the boy who stepped behind the bull and hit him several times with his stick. The bull's defiance flagged; he pulled and the rope tightened behind him.

Kella and Steve followed a path around the rock wall. A young boy about age seven or eight ran up to them and said, "Welcome" in Tamasheq. Kella replied with the normal courtesies of the desert and asked him about Azrur and Thiyya. "This way," he shouted as his bare feet took him running and bouncing like an élan up the path.

"Oh it is so familiar," said Kella as they followed the boy. "I can't help but remember my own childhood."

The boy had run ahead to the camp ground, a wide plateau with perhaps fifty tents made of black animal skins with open sides. As Steve and Kella entered the camp, a couple emerged from their tent. The man was tall and wore a beige robe. His head, his nose, mouth and neck were covered by a long indigo cloth. His eyes inspected them quickly but he did not put down the thin lance one end of which he rested on the ground. The woman wore a black turban and a loose sleeveless indigo overgarment with large openings for the arms.

Kella yelled, "Thiyya!" and ran toward her. They hugged closely, speaking in rapid and joyous exclamations.

Azrur was more reserved but his words welcomed Kella. Both were in their early fifties. Thiyya had an air of supreme self-confidence without the sharp edges of the dictator. Kella thought in another age she could have been an ambassador or led a salon in late seventeenth-century France—a Tuareg Germaine de Stael.

Kella smiled, her eyes moist. Thiyya's eyes were like dark brush strokes. When not speaking, her lips were pressed softly together. Her skin was the color of cinnamon batter. Kella wondered at the absence of wrinkles. Kella remembered Steve and introduced him as a group gathered around.

Thiyya announced to all, "Kella is my cousin's daughter. Her parents were killed by the army during the troubles. She is my blood."

Then she took Kella's right hand and raised it for everyone to see the four black dots arranged in a diamond on the back of her hand. The women called out happily to Kella, while the men crowded closer to have a better look at her hand and throw looks of suspicion in Steve's direction.

Thiyya made tea and served biscuits with goat cheese. Later Azrur took Steve and Kella to the well at the edge of camp.

"Azrur's great-great grandfather, by the way, led a Tuareg Army that fought the French army at the Battle of Goundam in the 1890s," Kella said. "I should have told you when we were there."

Knowing Kella was saying something about him, Azrur looked in their direction and his eyes were made narrower by what Kella knew to be a smile.

"Tell him it's an honor to be his guest," Steve said. "What about your name, and Thiyya's. Do they mean something in Tamasheq?"

"Thiyya means 'beauty,' and Kella was the daughter of Tin Hinnan, a Tuareg queen."

"I'm impressed. Both of you were well named."

Later that night, after small talk, Kella and her cousin drew aside while Azrur and Steve stayed by the fire.

Kella told her about the horrific scene she'd witnessed in Paris. Thiyya hung her head while the story unfolded. As Kella finished recounting the story and the reason she came to her cousin for comfort, Thiyya opened her arms and held them out to her. The young woman slid over to her and rested against her bosom as

Thiyya's arms folded around her and rocked her gently. Kella cried softly.

"We Tuareg women have never let ourselves be dominated by the men," Thiyya said. "When the Arabs came and imposed their religion, the Tuareg tribes fought them but there were too many. But we hang on to our culture. We Tuareg women are the equals of men, in some ways our situation is even better. We can decide whom to marry, and we can manage our own wealth. Our marriages are monogamous, unlike Muslim practice."

She guided Kella to a corner of the tent where some blankets were laid out.

* * *

On the evening of the next day, Kella's cousins organized a tribal feast in her honor. Goat and camel steaks cooked on a wood and dried dung fire to eat, and for drink, they offered goat and camel milk. Steve had Atrar bring Gazelle beer from the cooler he had left in the Land Cruiser.

The main event was the camel races. Steve seemed amused when Kella translated the good natured ribbing from her cousins.

"They recall that I grew up riding camels and have insisted I participate," she told him with an expression caught between amusement and dread.

"Well, I'll be cheering you on!"

"I'll wave to you so you can recognize me in my blue robe."

Steve pointed to his cameras, "You'll be the star of my article."

Kella watched Steve and Atrar drive their car close to the starting line. Steve opened the sunroof and readied his cameras. There were fifteen contestants. Most riders, men and women alike, had sticks for riding crops, but only the men were veiled. Kella's mount was easily the largest animal on the starting line.

She assumed that her cousins were being the perfect hosts, or perhaps Kella's noble lineage gave her certain rights.

Men, women and children had lined up on the side of the ad-hoc racecourse. Kella guessed there must be at least a hundred people waiting, talking, with occasional ululations of jubilance from the women. Both men and women were in colorful billowing robes.

Suddenly, the mounts were off. Both riders and watchers were in the moment. The excitement was palpable. Just about everyone was yelling and the riders encouraged their mounts by slapping their sticks against their sides.

Kella did not have a good start and she was in the middle of the pack for the first fifty yards. But the long white legs of her camel gobbled up the ground and gained yard after yard on the leaders. Finally, the race was between Kella and another woman on a sandy-brown camel who used her stick with vigor. In a nose-to-nose finish, it seemed to Kella that she finished a close second.

As the camel folded its ungainly legs and Kella dismounted, Steve hurried over to her.

"Wow, that was close! This is serious competition. You looked a mile high up there on that beast. The way it was rocking and rolling I don't know how you stayed on."

"This is not as easy as I remembered. Another fifty yards, though, and I would have won. Don't you think?"

Steve laughed and said, "I'm certain of it!"

* * *

Before they left the next morning, Thiyya took Kella to her tent, opened a wooden box and took a bracelet out. Thiyya's face, always reflecting control over herself and her immediate environment looked solemn. The unusually stern set of her eyes and mouth presaged something important. Kella wondered how she did that without gaining a wrinkle.

"This bracelet belonged to your mother. It has been passed on from generation to generation since before any of us were born. According to the legend, retold by our tribe's storytellers over the years, it belonged to an ancient Tuareg queen. Now, it belongs to you."

Kella remembered that her mother used to wear a gold bracelet during important occasions but she never knew the story behind it.

"Thank you, cousin. What else can you tell me?"

"There is another story that an American ship captain who was shipwrecked off the coast long ago and sold inland into slavery was also one of your ancestors. He was the first outsider to reach Timbuktu and leave alive. He was ransomed by a British official in Morocco and returned to the United States. And when the French soldiers were here a long time ago, one of them stayed and married into the family. You are Tuareg royalty, with an American, and a Frenchman, maybe more, in your family tree."

"Not too different from my current life. I have a French mother, an American father. Except, you're all the royalty I need!"

She hugged Thiyya.

19. Al Khalil's Office

A knock on the door interrupted al Khalil's thoughts. He had been analyzing IMRA finances and found them coming up short. Hussein walked in and he closed the computer.

Before Hussein could speak, al Khalil said, "We have to find ways to raise more funds. Our donors are going to sleep because they think we're going to sleep. I have to pay new recruits—fighters, martyrs, politicians, *imams*. Incoming funds are not sufficient. We have another year at the most."

Hussein tried to interrupt, "I understand..."

Al Khalil put his hand up.

"All of our income from private and public sources, from secret sources, and so on, is not enough on which to build the renaissance of Islam."

His eyes transferred to Hussein the burden of action.

"I do have good news," Hussein said. "One of my sources, a Malian who works for a Canadian NGO, told me that the missionaries are having a big party tomorrow. A lot of Western infidels are also going to be there. Is this the opportunity you've been looking for? It would be easier to hit them all at once than to kill them one by one. What do you think?"

"Yes, I've been urging you to do just that for some time. We need a highly visible operation, and a *successful* one, to attract funds. Attacking a few missionaries is thinking small. We need a bigger, much bigger, operation to regain our funding."

Hussein and all his other assistants were small people with small ideas. He resigned himself to this incremental action for now. He willed himself to be more positive. Perhaps Allah was smiling.

"What do you want to do? A bomb in the middle of the party? Who do you plan to use?"

"A bomb means finding someone with natural access to the location, or a martyr. We don't have time for a bomb operation. And I have better uses for my fighters than blowing them up. This is a soft target, the softest. I say keep it simple. Two men with AK-47s can walk in and mow them down. Direct and short, with immediate results."

He smiled at the picture Hussein was painting.

"Dahmane is well experienced in this type of work. I trust Dahmane. Although he's Malian, he's a Fulani. He claims ancestry from the Quraysh, the Prophet's tribe. He shares my vision. After this, we'll give him more responsibility. And give him another fighter."

"Yes, I want to give him Karim, the Algerian. It's time he got more directly involved and I think he's ready. He's still young but he has had combat experience in Algeria."

Tariq drew himself up and declared, "This will send a message to the infidels that they are not wanted here. They need to go home. They have to get out of Muslim lands. Make sure the operation is clean. We want no repercussions, although our friends in the police won't investigate very hard. It should be like target practice. AK-47s against unarmed missionaries at a party."

He chuckled and Hussein joined in. Then Hussein left and al Khalil went back to his EXCEL sheet.

The world had to pay attention or he would never replicate the work of the Prophet. People were apathetic, too inured by selfishness and the media's constant focus on irrelevant problems. Only a major action on the order of Hiroshima would wake them up.

He'd had several false starts in his efforts to acquire nuclear materials. He'd had lines out in several directions to obtain the means to make the nuclear splash that would bring the apostate rulers to his door. He thought of the underground storage at the training camp. He still didn't have the right people to help him use the large amount of yellowcake he had hidden. He couldn't do it all. His focus was in establishing a base in the Sahel states of Africa. Influencing the local authorities through bribes or coercion was working but too slowly. He leaned back in his chair and looked at the posters of Jerusalem and Cairo on his wall.

* * *

When Steve and Kella arrived at the NGO warehouse where the going away party was planned, tables and chairs had replaced. The cases of bottled water, blankets, medicine and tents had been restacked in the back. Each group had brought food and drink.

John and Elise were already there, as was Campbell. An old Charles Aznavour song was playing in the background. Tables along one wall were for the *mechoui*—lamb slow-cooked over a wood fire—and grilled capitaine, the huge freshwater fish from the Niger River. Along another wall was a table laden with fruit, chicken, dates, teas and soft drinks. Soon the room was full of laughter from several dozen people who were celebrating a job well done and wishing bon voyage to good friends. Each new arrival brought more food and drink. Steve heard at least a dozen languages being spoken, with English dominating.

"Quite the international group," he said to Kella.

Frank Sinatra replaced Aznavour until a live Tuareg musical group, called Tivaren, began to play and sing.

"My driver's brother Izem met the members of this band when he was in the Libyan Army," he said. "Many of the Tuareg rebels went to Libya after the rebellion. As a favor to him, they came to help the international workers celebrate."

"I like their music," she replied. "It's called *ishoumar*, a mixture of traditional Tuareg music, John Lee Hooker and reggae."

They soon served themselves and went to find seats. But almost as soon as they sat down, Kella said, "Oh, I'm going to go say hello to Elise. I'll be back."

Steve tasted the *mechoui* and looked around for something to drink. He saw a large white plastic cooler underneath a food table near the front wall and got up hoping that he would find a beer. The space was alive with music and conversation. He looked back to spot Kella as he walked toward the cooler. She was half kneeling by the Wests who sat at a center table in the back. He bent down to open the cooler and was reaching for a beer when a staccato sound of gunfire suddenly dominated the room. He dove to the floor and shouted, "Get down. Get down."

Steve could see that many had not immediately recognized the sound of gunfire. They seemed almost paralyzed. He looked up to see the legs of two men walking down the center of the warehouse. Looking up a bit more, he saw them firing AK-47s, one from the center to the right and the other to the left. The gunfire had plunged the party into total chaos. Most people were now on the floor. Steve could see that a few in the center had been hit by the steel jacketed bullets. A Malian waiter and a Canadian with Medecins-Sans-Frontieres were down and not moving. Few in the middle of the room were not wounded. He couldn't see Kella.

The sound of the guns punctuated the screams of pain and terror. Tables, chairs, and other furniture were knocked over. Dishes, glasses and bottles exploded and crashed to the floor, spraying their contents and shards of glass around the room.

He crawled closer to the entrance and noticed that he still had his bottle of beer in his hand. The gunmen were past him but still firing mostly to their front and side. He was in back of them and to their right. He again looked for Kella near John and Elise with mounting anxiety. He could easily run out the front door and try to get help. The gunfire continued in shorter bursts and he saw one assailant drop an empty magazine clip and reload. Unconsciously, Steve knew the gunman had sixty more shots and there was no time to look for help.

From the first bursts of AK-47 fire, even as he plunged to the floor, Steve remembered that his explosives and weapons instructor had given him a concealed self-defense weapon on the last night of training. He turned to one side on the floor in order to get his hand in the pocket where he had placed the device when getting dressed for the party. He took out what appeared to be a Mont Blanc pen that actually was a still-experimental, pulsed-energy-projectile gun.

He turned the top quickly to the left, felt it click, pointed the top of the pen toward the closest assailant but stopped when he realized his hand was shaking. He quickly got to his knees, steadied his left hand on the back of a chair and pushed the clasp firmly inward. The pulsed energy immediately superheated the air and moisture around the target with a flash of light and a loud bang.

The effect was not exactly what he had expected. In training, both light and sound had been twice as great. Nevertheless, the whole room instantly froze in time, its population temporarily deafened and paralyzed. The gunman that Steve had fired at appeared unsteady on his feet. He looked as if he was about to drop his weapon, holding it limply. For an instant, the only sound was from the Beatles singing "Help."

Steve recovered first. With adrenalin pumping, he sprang to his feet and rushed toward the second gunman who was starting to drop to one knee, his hands going up to his ears as if to protect them from another explosion. He still held his weapon. Steve's tackle took the gunman down.

Simultaneously, a shot rang out and the attacker immobilized by Steve's weapon fell over backward. As the man fell, his carotid artery, pierced by the bullet, began to pump blood from his body in cadenced spurts. Steve quickly got his adversary face down and seized his weapon. He looked up and saw Izem about to fire a second shot.

"Tie them up!" he yelled, and directed one of the waiters to help him. He then went to look for Kella at the Wests' table. He first saw Elise bending over John.

She looked at Steve and said, in shock, "He's dead. John is dead."

He bent down and felt for a pulse but could only hear and feel his own heart. He moved his hand from John's throat to his chest but felt nothing.

"How about you? Are you hit?" he asked her.

"My brother is dead," she said in a low monotone, eyes unfocused. "We were going home tomorrow."

Then Steve saw Kella under the table. Blood colored the loose white shirt she wore over her halter-top. "Don't move," he said. "How are you?"

"I don't know yet," she said. "I can't move my arm." Steve helped her up to one of the chairs. She was holding her left arm. Blood seeped onto her slacks. Steve took off his belt and used it as a tourniquet around her upper arm.

Izem had tied the surviving terrorist's hands behind him and was now tying him to a chair. The wounded moaned, a woman shrieked in shock, her friend joined her in sympathy, some cried over their dead friends, some were in a helpless daze. Steve saw two men, whom he knew to be part of the Medecins-Sans-Frontieres group, trying to help the wounded. The floor was covered with broken glass, food, dishes, and silverware, forming islands in the middle of a crimson-tinted mixture of blood and Orangina soda.

"Take this guy to my room and keep him there until I get there," Steve told Izem. "See what information you can get out of him in the meantime. Do not turn him over to the police. I'm going to take Kella to the hospital."

He found Atrar, assembled Kella and two others who had been wounded and hurried to the hospital. There were as yet no police sirens to be heard.

20. Aéroport de Tombouctou

Kella, with a crewman in a flight suit on one side, and the French Embassy nurse on the other, walked under the tail and up the loading ramp of the French Air Force cargo plane—a Transall C-160, according to the crewman who had met her and Steve inside the terminal.

It was dark but she could see the outline of the high-winged aircraft outlined by red lights on its wings and tail, a tail that seemed to be two or three stories high. The pilot had not shut down the two engines and Kella tried to protect her face from the sand blowing toward her with her right hand. Her left arm was in a cast. The hard soles of the crewman's shoes against the metal of the ramp punctuated the noise of the engines. Steve followed Kella, carrying her suitcase, which with considerable misgivings she had asked Steve to pack for her while she was at the hospital.

Before being hustled out of the plane, Steve, almost shouting to be heard over the noise of the engines, told her, "This is the best thing for you. We're lucky this plane could pick you up. You need to get to a real hospital. Your grandfather the general will take care of you. Call me when you land."

Kella was in pain. She winced as she tried to fit into the uncomfortable seat.

"Take care. You should really leave too. Don't interview al Khalil. Stay away from him. They're killers."

Steve gave her quick kiss on the lips and went back out the loading ramp, which closed quickly behind him.

When the plane reached cruising altitude, the nurse took a look at Kella's temporary cast.

"My name is Viviane," she said. "We're the only passengers. I'm here just to take care of you until we get to Paris. I think that your cast is okay until then. If you're in pain, I can give you a painkiller if you want. It will put you to sleep. This flight doesn't have a movie so you won't miss much."

Kella swallowed the pills that Viviane gave her and slept until they landed at Vélizy-Villacoublay Airport outside of Paris, where an ambulance was waiting to take her to Val de Grâce, a hospital usually reserved for the military. Kella was accorded the luxury of a private room.

★   ★   ★

One evening a week later, during dinner at her grandfather's comfortable apartment on Rue de Longchamp in the upper scale 16th District, Kella's grandfather, General Joulet, asked for a full account of what had happened to her in Timbuktu.

Kella poured coffee for the two of them and recounted her trip and the events that led to the NGO party and the terrorist attack.

"My friend Steve then took me to the Timbuktu Hospital. The doctor was Cuban but he spoke English with a New York accent."

"Yes, Cuba has sent doctors and medical technicians all over the developing world," he said. "During the Cold War, that niche belonged to the Bulgarians."

"But the X-ray machine didn't work, so he thought I should go to Dakar or Abidjan because the bullet fractured the bone. It wasn't a clean break. Doctor Delforge said that I was lucky that the bullet missed the brachial artery. My arm is now held together by a plate and screws. My luck was that you were able to get me on that cargo plane. I am very grateful to you, *Grand-père*."

Pointing to the sitting room, Joulet said, "Let's go sit over there, Kella." And pointing to a sofa, he added, "Take one of those pillows to put under your arm."

After Kella got herself situated in an easy chair, Joulet brought her cup of coffee and put it on a small table to her right.

"Will you be able to return to your studies soon?"

"I've been thinking about that. Forced bed rest does that. I don't know what's happening but in the last few months I've seen my best friend murdered by her father, and I've been shot at and had my arm broken."

"You've been in more danger in the last few weeks than most people in their entire lives. You can stay away from these dangerous people and get back to your main task which is to graduate from the ENA. I've been in touch with the president, a friend from my riding club. He agreed to give you extra time to finish your year's assignments. As soon as you're well, you can go back to school and the slate will be wiped clean. You'll be on the same schedule to graduate as the rest of your classmates, at least those that have made the grade."

"Thanks very much, *Grand-père*, but I don't think that's what I want to do anymore. I've thought a lot about this. What is the connecting thread between these events that have turned my life upside down? Both were connected with the *integristes*, the jihadists. They are struggling and fighting amongst each other and now we, the West, the Christian world, have become targets."

The general smiled and said, "Now you're beginning to sound like my analysts. Except that you're more direct. The only way they know how to write is to start with 'on the one hand,' and then qualify their conclusions with 'but on the other,' so they're never wrong. An American president, Truman I think, said 'Give me one-armed economists.' Anytime you want to leave school, I have a job for you as a counter terrorism analyst."

She laughed at the idea.

"I appreciate the offer, but I don't want to sit in a cubicle, at a computer, all day long. Rather than analyze, I'd rather get the information that someone else can analyze. If your analysts get the wrong information, the end product is not going to be useful, right? But frankly speaking, I'm not sure I'm that kind of person, a collector I mean, who can convince others to steal secrets for me."

"Well, if you prefer after you graduate you can join the diplomatic service and play an important role in this issue, which is the central global issue of your generation—how the radical Muslims are going to fit into the current century, or how they're going to force the rest of us to live in their century. And their clock is no further than the thirteenth century, at most."

"*Grand-père,* I don't think the diplomats have done much. They all gather at the UN, sign meaningless resolutions, and then they go to their next cocktail parties in their chauffeur-driven cars. No, I think intelligence is the place to be in this fight. It's more significant, has more impact. So, can you help me?"

General Joulet spent the rest of the evening trying to dissuade her, but in the end, she said, "I'll be thirty years old soon. I've seen my friend killed, and been attacked by the same ideology. I'm not going to sit back and pretend none of this happened and is not happening to others every day. You said yourself it's the most important issue that my generation will have to deal with. I want to make a difference and this is where I want to do it."

21. Al Khalil's Office

A day after the Salafist attack on the foreign-aid personnel, Hussein brought Karim to al Khalil and, in answer to questions, Karim recounted the operation. Al Khalil sat behind his desk, and Hussein sat in front of it. Karim stood in front of both. He played the role that Steve, whom he knew as Christopher, had outlined for him, although he believed the advice was obvious.

Waving his arms as he talked, Karim nearly shouted, "Dahmane told me this would be easy—convincing foreign crusaders to go home. If you had planned this operation well, you would have known that the party was going to be guarded. Everybody was shooting at us. Dahmane shouldn't have died. I was almost killed. You should have told us that there would be guards. Everybody was shooting. They even had hand-grenades."

"It was Allah's will," Hussein replied. "Dahmane died a *shahid*'s death. May we all be as fortunate," and Karim uttered "*Allahu Akbar*" in automatic response.

Karim exaggerated his account according to Steve's instructions. Also, he wanted to underline that his survival was due to his own skills and that the operation was not the walk in the park that everyone had expected.

Al Khalil picked up a copy of L'Essor.

"This morning's paper reports that, in Canada, France, Switzerland, the United States, and other countries where the NGO's central offices are located, the media have the foreign ministries under siege. I think NGO's will be more careful to keep their people out of our lands in the future."

Hussein drank from a plastic water bottle.

"Timbuktu is now full of diplomats, and newspaper people. The hotels are full."

Al Khalil leaned back in his chair.

"Yes, I know. I already received phone calls and gave a couple of interviews. I'm putting our IMRA work up front, but I'm also explaining how unnatural it is to have missionaries among our believers. We can take care of our own."

Karim walked to the wall on his right, picked up the only other chair in the room, brought it near Hussein and sat.

"What about the police. What do they know?"

"Don't worry. They have no leads. The eyewitnesses were too shocked and busy trying to survive to be able to give the police any useful information or accurate descriptions. Dahmane carried no personal documentation and has not been identified There will be an investigation to satisfy the foreigners but all will go back to normal soon."

"The objective was to chase the missionaries out," al Khalil said.

This was a sign, Karim thought, that al Khalil was closing the books on the attack.

"Some are dead and the rest are leaving. Even some of the NGO people are packing, *al hamdu'llah*. The results are even better than we planned. Next time, Hussein, get more fire power on the target, just to make sure."

22. Hôtel Bouctou

Steve hurried back to his room after getting Kella onto the French military plane, an hour and a half after the terrorist attack. Izem was threatening to burn off the soles of Karim's feet, using the finest interrogation methods he had learned in the Libyan army. So far, Karim, tied to the only chair in the room, had admitted little other than that he was Algerian.

Steve told Izem to go outside and wait. When he left the room, Steve said, in French, "I guess the next step is to call the police. How will you like the salt mines in Taoudenni?"

It worked; Karim looked frightened.

"It wasn't my fault. I was forced to do it," he said.

"Forced to kill innocent people? Who forced you?"

"They are not innocent. They are forcing good Muslims away from Allah. They are saying lies about the Prophet."

"Really? Did you hear anyone at that party say anything at all about the Prophet?"

"They are bad people. They should not be here. They have to leave. This is not their country."

Steve repeated his question: "Who sent you? Who do you work for?"

Karim considered his answer.

"I'm thirsty. I need water."

He glanced toward the bathroom.

Steve leaned down from his chair, pulled out a soda from the small room refrigerator, and handed it to Karim.

"There's an opener on the side of the fridge," he said pointing.

Karim, still tied to the chair, shrugged, "I can't."

Steve grinned and said, "Oh, I forgot. Well, for the time being, you'll have to stay thirsty. Who sent you? It's me or the Malian salt mines."

"I work for IMRA. Either I do what they say or they kill me, so I do it."

"IMRA? The IMRA that does social work among Muslims? Tell me who heads IMRA. Why the killings?"

"I told you, to make the missionaries and the other foreigners leave. We got our orders by Hussein."

"And he is?"

Karim shifted his weight a bit on the chair.

"He's Tariq al Khalil's deputy."

"So, the missionaries and the others were shot because they are foreigners. What about the Malians you killed? And what about you—is this your country? I thought you told my friend that you came from Algeria, right? Why are you here?"

Little by little, Steve pulled Karim's story out. Karim had been a young student in a village outside Oran when the Salafist Group for Preaching and Combat, which later became AQIM, raided it. Karim's teachers, French and Algerians who were deemed too westernized by the Salafists, were among the over two-hundred-thousand people killed over a period of several years.

"One day they came when we were in class," Karim said. "They killed all the teachers. They took nine of us with them. They put us in dirty chicken coops for two days without food or water before taking us out one at a time. We all agreed to become their soldiers. Before we knew it, we were ambushing Algerian patrols.

"I was arrested once and spent six months in jail at Sidi Belabbes. It was difficult; two of my friends died there. But they let me go after a year. Later, I went to the Sudan and I met Lahlou—he's a Moroccan at IMRA—at a training camp. He recruited me for IMRA."

Steve stood up.

"I find your story interesting, but I don't see why I shouldn't just turn you over to the Malian police. You killed some people today, including Malian Muslims. I don't know how your religion works but I don't think that killing other Muslims is the way to heaven, nor is killing Malian citizens the way to live a happy life in Mali."

"I don't want to go to jail. Please, I beg you! Let me go! What do you want?"

"Well, there's nothing you have that I want. You think you can help me? How?"

"I will tell you about IMRA. What do you want to know about IMRA?"

"I'm just a photographer. What makes you think that IMRA is of any interest to me?"

Steve moved to the window and looked out.

"You're an American. I know that al Khalil hates Americans. You are a crusader; otherwise you wouldn't be here, in a Muslim land. I will tell you what al Khalil is doing and planning," Karim said in a rush.

"You're a murderer," Steve said, pointing at him. "I should just turn you over. I don't know. I don't care about your information. But maybe I know someone who is. Maybe I can put you guys together. In the meantime you can talk to me. Let's try it. If your information proves to be good, and you don't lie, then we have a deal. If you're speaking the truth, then I'll say nothing to the police. But in case anything happens to me, I'm giving everything I know about you to a friend in the American Embassy in Bamako. And if something happens to me, the police of the world will be after you. But my friends will get to you first. I guarantee it."

"May Allah, the merciful the beneficent, favor you," he said in Arabic. Reverting back to French, he said, "If Hussein or al Khalil find out, they will kill me on the spot. This is very dangerous. But I will do it."

"I want to see you right here in a week." He looked at his watch. "I want to see you next Thursday at 6:15."

Steve handed Karim the soda on his way out, but before letting him take it, he had him repeat the time of their next meeting.

* * *

Karim showed up. He had thought about it all week and had concluded he had little to lose. He was confident he could meet Steve and have no one the wiser. Rotting in Taoudenni was not an attractive alternative. And if it didn't work out in his favor, Karim thought he could kill the American. He would thus get rid of one person who could identify him, and also get credit with al Khalil for eliminating a crusader who was also a spy, like all Americans in Muslim lands.

In spite of his outward self-confidence, Karim was nervous when he reached the hotel. He rehearsed the story that Steve had given him: *If you're stopped downstairs, say that you're a guide and that I want to hire you, and don't give your real name.*

But there was no one at the desk, so he went straight to Steve's room. Before he knocked, Karim wondered whether the Tuareg who had first brought him to the hotel the week before would be there.

Steve let him in and they first talked about Karim's debriefing following the attack on the missionaries. Karim said, "All is good. Al Khalil and Hussein are happy with me."

"Well, what do you think you know that would be of interest to me?"

"I know many things that are of great value—very important things. IMRA is strong because al Khalil knows Islam and Islam, through the Quran, is the word of Allah as told to the Prophet."

Karim wanted to make a strong impression on the American. He had no clear plan but felt that this could be the opportunity of a lifetime. In weighing the risk of meeting with Steve again, Karim had concluded that he would not be in this situation if Allah had not first willed it.

"So, what is special about IMRA?"

"Al Khalil talks a lot about Hamas in Gaza and about Hizballah in Lebanon. We are just like them. You know, one side helps the poor and the other gives them guns to fight and die for Islam. Like me. One day I will die for Islam and go to paradise."

He smiled in that knowledge. Steve's expression was puzzled.

"Where do IMRA funds come from?"

"I don't know. Only al Khalil knows—and maybe Hussein. I cannot help you. I'm sorry. Wait, maybe I could steal some documents from al Khalil's office."

"No, don't do that. Don't take any papers and don't ask questions that you would not normally ask, for now."

After an hour and a half, Karim had given Steve the names of all of the people he knew in IMRA, the names of IMRA supporters and sympathizers in Timbuktu, and that al Khalil was planning a big meeting in Gao.

"It is time that I go back," he said. "Or maybe someone will ask where I am."

"You're right. Next time, in a week, let's talk about the camp up north."

Karim left without acknowledging he knew what Steve was talking about. On his way back, Karim thought about Steve not knowing if he was a savior to be embraced or a danger to be eliminated.

* * *

Steve moved their next meeting to an abandoned Tuareg camp two miles outside of Timbuktu. He had told Karim it was for his protection. Karim preferred the abandoned camp to the hotel. He was confident but also knew he would be summarily executed, personally, by either al Khalil or Hussein if they learned he was meeting with this American. No cover or pretext would be good enough.

Karim was fifteen-minutes late. To explain his lateness, he told Steve, "You said to come after dark," a directive he had thought to be gratuitous at the time.

"It's important to do things exactly as I tell you. For your safety. It's been dark for an hour. How did you get here and what is your cover for being on away from IMRA?"

"I walked. It's not far. Sometimes, I go see a girl I know."

He smiled at Steve who chuckled back.

They were sitting on the sandy ground of a three-sided corrugated tin shelter when they heard voices and Karim stood up to look toward the source of the sounds. He saw a small fire about thirty yards away. The camp was apparently not totally abandoned.

Steve stood up and motioned to Karim, "We're moving. Come on."

They walked quietly to Steve's car, keeping the shack between themselves and the camp fire. In the car Karim said, "So maybe this was not the safest place?"

Steve did not respond.

They spent the next forty minutes talking in the car while making their way slowly back toward the town. The night sky was bright and Steve, with directions from Karim, could drive without lights. While they saw no other vehicles, there were a few people walking toward Timbuktu. Karim understood that Steve didn't want to give them opportunity to read his license plate.

"Tell me about the camp in the north."

"Oh, yes. I go there sometimes. It is for training. We bring new fighters there."

"Are there any secret storage sheds or underground warehouses?"

"There is an underground room. It's locked. No one except al Khalil and Hussein are allowed there. I think that's where they keep the gold. You know, from the mines?"

"And where do the weapons come from?"

"From many places. Like deserters. A long time ago, several trucks delivered weapons and ammunitions from Libya. But not for a long time. We have many weapons but we always need more ammunition. Al Khalil has contacts. Some Malian officers sell us ammunition from their warehouses. I know that al Khalil's go-between with them is a man who owns a hotel, the Khan Hotel I think."

Steve made sure there was no one on the street and he let Karim out of the car.

* * *

Two weeks later, again meeting in the car at night, Karim handed Steve a typewritten document.

"I was in al Khalil's office this afternoon and he went to the bathroom. I saw a file on his desk and this was in it, the list of all the *imams* in the region who are paying *zakat*, a tithe, to IMRA."

"This is useful Karim. But I told you not to take that kind of risk. What if al Khalil notices and decides you were the only one who could have taken it?"

"Don't worry. He won't notice."

"I worry about you, Karim. By the way, I want to pass on thanks to you personally from John Littlecorn, head of American Intelligence. Some of your information has reached him and he wants you to know that he is appreciative. He wants to know what he can do for you."

Karim didn't read newspapers and did not follow international politics. However, the name John Littlecorn was well known throughout the Middle East. He often accompanied the American president on his trips and had once successfully mediated a dangerous hostage situation—dangerous for the hostages and for the terrorists.

Karim was enormously pleased. Little by little, he had learned to first trust and then to like Steve. That Littlecorn knew of him and was extending compliments and thanks was because of Steve.

"I am honored that he even knows I exist."

"It is important for my country to understand the Muslim world. Otherwise, it will make mistakes. You are now someone who can help us reach that understanding."

Karim listened. He understood that the United States had awesome power, that what the United States did could affect the lives of people all over the world.

"I want to help make things better. I don't ask Mr. Littlecorn for anything."

"Remember when you told me about your family in Oran? What is your little brother's name? Hassan? What do you hope for him, Karim?"

Karim's eyes watered at his brother's name. Hassan would not live this life. He would obtain a proper education. He would become a pharmacist. He remembered that was Hassan's dream, a dream they both knew at the time was just fun to talk about but not any more realizable than, for example, living in their own house.

"Yes, Hassan. I haven't seen him in a long time. He is smart. I want him to go to school, maybe a school in France."

Steve turned left to avoid the more populated part of town.

"Listen to this and tell me if you agree. I want to open a bank account for Hassan. Every month that we work together, I will put money in the account. You can have it whenever you want. By the time Hassan can go to France, you'll have some money to give him, or to your mother if Hassan doesn't want to become a pharmacist anymore."

When he left Steve that night, Karim hoped to be able to work for him for a long time. He was motivated to do whatever Steve asked. At the end of the day, Hassan and his mother would have a better life. He would make it happen. He looked upon Steve as his mentor, as his big brother.

23. Timbuktu

Once Langley was satisfied that Karim was a viable, responsive agent, Steve received further instructions:

    1. We wish to replace SBCALIPH/1'S (the cryptonym, or code name, assigned to al Khalil by the CIA) current satellite phone with one we will provide. He is using a cipher that is taking too long to break in a timely manner. The replacement Trojan Horse will separate and transmit his outgoing and incoming messages to us using an encryption system we prefer.

    2. To that end have SBCALIPH/4 (the cryptonym for Karim) collect the following information regarding SBCALIPH/1'S satellite phone:

    A. Make and serial number

    B. Telephone number

    C. Color and any markings that SBCALIPH/1 might have added, such as his name or the telephone number or any other identifying markings on the instrument

    D. Similarly have him identify any accessories that SBCALIPH/1 uses with the phone such as battery charger, earphones, etc.

    3. Further determine where SBCALIPH/1 keeps his phone in the office, how he carries it, when he travels, whether he ever leaves it and where and when away from his apartment and office

4. Based on the above information please submit operation plan to replace phone and advise soonest
5. Regret that Cos Bamako unavailable to assist in this operation
—*File: SBCALIPH*

Steve had been able to obtain the requested information; al Khalil's satellite phone was a Globalstar, but there had been too little time left before the Gao conference to replace the phone with a CIA Trojan Horse.

Steve liked the idea. He had heard during his short training that the CIA elves were adept and creative technicians. There should be little left to know about IMRA and al Khalil's plans and activities after combining Karim's inside information with intercepts of his satellite phone.

Steve decided he had to go to Gao to try to effect the exchange away from Tariq's home field. He read the last sentence of the message to mean that, given his inexperience, the plan had been for Rod to come and run the switch operation. Steve felt good that Langley had enough confidence in him to go ahead without Rod's assistance.

24. Gao, Mali

On Monday, Steve arrived at the Hôtel Atlantide in this major desert town farther down the Niger and to the east of Timbuktu. Izem met him at the airport. As they walked outside to catch a taxi, Izem said, "The hotel was named after a story of our people. Do you know Atlantis? It was a big city on an island a thousand years ago. Then the desert came, the water went away. The island is now the Hoggar Mountains, over there." He pointed to the northeast. "In the Sahara."

As they got into a taxi and Steve said, "You mean in Algeria? So you could be from the old civilization of Atlantis?"

Izem smiled with pride.

"We are an ancient people."

They stopped in front of the hotel, a one-storey building behind a low decorative barrier on which sat several young Malians. The roof was surrounded by a white balustrade. They walked past the young men who stopped talking and looked at him with what Steve thought were barely repressed urges to assault him with once-in-a-life-time proposals. He guessed Izem's presence was keeping them from trying their luck. In the lobby the overhead fans turned noisily but too slowly to interfere with the squadrons of flies patrolling the super-heated air of their domain.

"How about waiting for me here while I go check out the room?" Steve said. "Then I'll see about renting a car and you can show me around."

By the time he got the car it was mid-afternoon. Nevertheless, they had time to go see Gao's main and only tourist attraction, the Tomb of Askia, identified for preservation by the UNESCO World Heritage organization, an imposing, seventeen-meter-high pyramidal structure dating from the fifteenth century. It was the last resting place of Askia Muhammad, a Songhai emperor who had made Islam the official religion of his empire. Steve also couldn't resist taking photographs of a mosque whose only claim to fame that his photos could bequeath was a minaret in the unmistakable profile of an aroused penis.

Izem snickered when Steve took photos of the phallic symbol.

"Are they like that in America?"

"They're much bigger, especially in Texas."

Steve motioned how big with his arms, causing Izem to do a three-sixty on one foot and laugh while touching his crotch.

Through his camera's lens, Steve noticed the shadows were lengthening and he became concerned about that the light.

"Izem, did you talk to your friends? Can I go visit with them and take pictures?"

"Yes, we can go now if you want."

* * *

The Tuareg camp resembled the one near Lake Faguibine: tents of black leather, tops and sides on sticks and branches planted in the ground, goats and camels off to one side. The young children ran and played games among the tents and the women and the older children gathered firewood, carried water from the well, or cooked dinner over an open fire.

The chief, the *amenokal*, welcomed Steve, as Izem pointed to him and said, "He is my patron, my boss, Monsieur Christophe." The *amenokal* was a couple of inches taller than Steve. His robe hinted at a rather bony body. What Steve could see of his face was all angles and planes when he loosened his *tagoulmoust*—the blue veil and turban that enveloped his head and neck—to eat or drink.

With Izem as translator, Steve said to the chief, "Those are very stylish sunglasses." The *amenokal* took them off and proudly said, "Yes, Italian." Steve could only guess as to their provenance but they undoubtedly added to the *amenokal's* aura of leadership.

Steve spent the rest of the day with Izem's friends, taking pictures and eating the evening meal with them. He was impressed by the Tuaregs' appearance. Their comportment conveyed pride. Since they stayed veiled most of the time, Steve found it difficult to read their expressions. Their eyes were cautious. He found them less forbidding when they lowered the blue cloth that hid the lower part of their face to eat and drink. Their unusual height was accentuated by their *tagoulmousts*. The seven-foot lances and the rest of their medieval weapons, swords, knives, that they still occasionally carried as they did this day, probably at Izem's request, Steve thought, magnified their physical presence.

To show off his knowledge, Izem said, "Christophe, show them the pictures on your computer."

To the delight of audience, Steve then put on a slide show for the *amenokal* and his men from the shots he had taken that afternoon.

Then he gave the *amenokal* a bag and said, "Here are some things that I thought would be useful to you, tubes of antibiotic ointment to treat basic cuts and wounds from infection, and special eye ointment."

He had learned that many of the Tuaregs, especially the children, suffered from conjunctivitis and other eye ailments.

He handed the chief a box and said, "You might also find these walkie-talkie radios useful for communication in the desert."

As the chief opened the gifts, he handed them out. Their examination was a communal experience. Steve asked, "Izem, what are they saying?"

"They say that America should invade Mali," and they laughed.

Steve had another bag for the kids—hard candy and a few inexpensive compasses. On their way to the camp, Izem had told Steve to give the compasses to the kids, not to the chief, because he might be offended.

"He doesn't think he needs a compass, I'm sure of that," he had said. "But somehow the compasses will in the end belong to the adults."

As Steve started to leave, the *amenokal* asked him to wait and in a few minutes someone came to hand him a package wrapped with string.

"You have won many friends today," the chief said. "Izem was kind to bring you. Think of us as your family in the Sahel."

Steve left in the dark as the Tuareg men stood in front of their tents and campfires. He felt deep sympathy for them. The Tuaregs had been important actors of the region's history but they had been bypassed and become victims. It occurred to Steve that instead of giving candies to the kids, he should have given them books.

* * *

The following day, one day before Tariq and Hussein were to arrive, the advance team of Lahlou, Karim, and several additional men who would act as gofers and security guards, arrived in Gao. Steve's first priority was the satellite phone. He only had a few days to come up with a plan and to execute it. While Steve avoided rigid structures and planning, looming deadlines energized him. He already had three-dimensional plans of the fort from CIA Headquarters. He still needed al Khalil's schedule and information on the whereabouts of his satellite phone at any given time.

He was in his room when he heard an urgently furtive knock on the door. He let Karim in and they shook hands.

"I'm picking up mineral water from the hotel so I have very little time," he said.

"Okay. Any word from your mother and from Hassan? Is the family all right?"

Karim smiled.

"I don't hear from them often but I was able to arrange a phone call with Hassan from the Oran Telegraph and Telephone Office. He sounded good."

"I'm glad." Turning to business, he said, "Do you have a list of the attendees to the conference?"

"Not a list, but I know the names."

Steve wrote them down as Karim recited them.

"Is everyone still scheduled to arrive tomorrow?"

When Karim nodded, Steve produced two oversized tacks and said, "These are miniature microphones. What I want you to do is to stick one in al Khalil's room and the other in Salim's room. Out of sight, of course; behind or under a piece of furniture, for example. You explained to me before that Salim is important, maybe the elder statesman of the group, right?"

He didn't explain that each tack contained not only a microphone but also a transmitter and a five-hundred-hour battery.

Karim, gratified Steve took his information and personal comments seriously, smiled his assent.

"Come back when you can. Until you have some sort of schedule, I'll stay pretty close to the hotel. I need to know where everyone will sleep and the schedule for the whole conference. This is going to be the most important thing you have done so far. But also the riskiest so don't take stupid chances."

He had urged caution before but was always concerned that Karim's self-confidence and zeal would make him step over the line and make a fatal mistake. He knew enough by now to realize that, in this business, there were no second chances.

Within two hours, Steve had gained a brief background on all of the expected Salafist chiefs, all on the CIA list of active radical Muslim terrorists.

Karim was able to come late that evening. He told Steve the guards wanted him to get them beer.

"What will al Khalil think about alcohol at the fort?"

"It will be gone by the time he lands," Karim laughed.

With the plan of the fort in his mind, Steve debriefed Karim and quickly determined the use of most of the rooms. Al Khalil had a two-room ground floor apartment in the central tower, originally used by the Fort commander. The only other room in the tower on the ground level was larger than the apartment and had been used as an armory in the past. Now it was used for storage and contained odd pieces of furniture, much of it broken. The rest of the tower was taken up by a stairway to the top, punctuated on several landings by narrow openings in the outside wall designed to be used by armed defenders. He had noted there was a small room on the second landing, but its use then and now was difficult to discern.

* * *

On Wednesday, Steve met Hank, a CIA technician carrying the replacement satellite phone, at the airport. As they got into his car, Hank, in his forties with a light, Irish complexion, didn't beat around the bush.

"I have never run an operation headed up by other than a seasoned case officer. But I'm told you're good, so I trust we can work together."

"I'm glad you're here. I gave the quick-plant mics to Caliphate/4 yesterday. He should have placed them by now."

Hank nodded.

"I'll set up the listening post in my room. From there, the conversations will be transmitted automatically by satellite to CIA Headquarters, translated, and sent back to me via Inmarsat. I'll test the system today. I gather that we don't have much time, which is fine with me. I've been in some godforsaken places but..." he looked out the window at the arid scenery, "this has to be the worst."

"Hank, how long will you need once we get Caliphate/1's phone?"

"Count on one hour. Could be less, could be more; depends. I also want a chance to call headquarters if any special problem comes up."

Hank received the first transcript shortly after he set up his equipment. Since Tariq and Hussein were scheduled to arrive by road later the same day, and Salim wasn't due until the next day, the main purpose of sending a transcript back at all was simply to test the system.

The little audio picked up was clear enough, but the transcript showed how Murphy's Law applied universally. A desk that had been in Salim's room had been moved. Unfortunately, Karim had planted the tack-microphone underneath that desk. It sounded as if it was now located in the room where the Salafist leaders would eat their meals. Rather than have Karim take the risk of moving the tack-microphone, Steve looked on the bright side; the new location might provide interesting conversations among the Salafist guests. He therefore decided to leave well enough alone. Hank agreed.

During their Wednesday meeting, Karim told Steve, "Tariq and Hussein are here. Tariq used his satellite phone almost right away to call Salim. He doesn't get here until tomorrow. The only time when Tariq doesn't carry the phone with him is during prayers. He leaves it in his room, I think."

With a hand-drawn sketch in front of them, Steve told Karim, "Show me the room assignments."

Acting like a zealous pupil, Karim asked, "Do you need to know about locks? There are no locks."

His face brightened as if he was personally responsible for this fact.

"Most rooms have no windows, except high up, like in the room where I sleep with three others."

After trying to understand the sketch for what seemed to Steve like an unusual length of time, Karim pointed to his room triumphantly.

"Is this the tower? Yes, you go in over here," he pointed, "and al Khalil sleeps here. He has a window. It opens on this side. It's a real window."

"Does his window open? Or is it one of the high ones you can't reach?"

"He has a desk in front of the window and he can see the courtyard from his desk."

He smiled and looked very pleased with himself.

Steve smiled in return and gave him a pat on the back.

"That's good Karim."

Together they decided the best time to effect the transfer would be during the Friday prayer. Al Khalil, they hoped, would leave the phone in his room, or he would give it to Karim when he served as his bodyguard, as he sometimes did during that midday period. Karim would take the phone to Steve when everyone else was in the mosque, a room in the fort that al Khalil had so designated. Hank would then make the transfer, and Karim would take the gift from the CIA elves back to the fort.

25. Aéroport de Tombouctou

On Thursday, Hussein went with Karim, the driver, to welcome the Salafist leaders. Hussein saw a tired, rumpled and short-tempered group.

One of the new arrivals looked in the van and, looking toward Hussein and Karim, said with an Egyptian accent, "There was no water on the plane and now you have no water for us. Can things get worse?"

Neither Hussein nor Karim replied.

The promising outline of the Hôtel Atlantide prompted the Egyptian to say, "At last, a place to stretch out and have something to drink."

But Karim continued past the hotel and about a mile out of town to a high-walled structure.

Hussein, who sat on Karim's right up front, turned to the men in back of him and said, "That's where we're staying. Not far from town and very secure. We have it to ourselves."

"I'm sure we do," said Talal Kawar, who had identified himself to Hussein as the Jordanian *Ikhwan* chief. He wore black pants, a blazer and an ascot. His shiny black hair was combed straight back. The scent of his cologne wafted throughout the vehicle.

"It was built and used by the French Foreign Legion," Hussein said. "It was ceded to the Malian Army after independence."

The fort was the same color as the sand that surrounded it. On one side grew several tall palm trees creating shade for a small group of blue-clad Tuaregs sitting on the ground while their camels looked haughtily down at the world. A solid black flag with no design was waving in the intermittent breeze from the top of a crenellated tower rising from an inside courtyard. The tower and its flag dominated the external walls in the style of medieval castles. A massive front gate and a row of vertical slits about halfway up were the only openings in the fifty-foot-high wall.

Karim took the new arrivals to their rooms. These had uniformly high ceilings, with one small barred window about fifteen feet above the floor. The furniture consisted of a cot with a burlap-covered straw mattress, a chair, and a small desk, on top of which was a carafe of water and a plastic glass. Down the narrow corridor were a common toilet and a separate washroom with several large jars of water.

Tariq greeted each of the delegates as they came into the former military fort and, during the rest of the afternoon, visited with them individually. Everyone took note that al Khalil took a brief walk in the courtyard with Ibrahim El Maghrebi, the Algerian AQIM leader, before taking him to his room.

He asked Hussein, "Have somebody bring us some tea. I want to share some of our financial realities with my brother Ibrahim."

* * *

At sunset, they all came together for prayers after which they broke up into informal groups until dinnertime. They prayed again at nightfall. Everyone was awaiting the next day, Friday, when Tariq would give the *khutbah*, or sermon.

Steve and Hank also waited for the *khutbah* that would give Karim his chance to steal the phone. Late in the day, they received a partial transcript from Langley of the take from the tack-mic in the canteen. They were in Hank's room. He sat in the easy chair and Steve sat on the bed. Although Hank had a portable printer, Steve read the transcript on Hank's computer.

VOICE NUMBER ONE: I don't understand why we can't meet in Paris or in Geneva. Next thing we know we'll be whipping ourselves bloody like Shiites.

VOICE NUMBER TWO: [identified as AQIM chief Ibrahim el Maghrebi] Stop whining. In Algeria we're fighting with bullets not with cocktail shakers.

VOICE NUMBER THREE: As long as we settle on positive action, I don't care.

VOICE NUMBER ONE: We all know the problem we have to solve. Not enough funding and not enough progress to show—one leads to the other.

"My guess is that al Khalil was not there," Steve said.

"Is al Khalil the main actor in this play?" Hank asked. "I'm surprised we received this transcript so fast. Once the National Security Agency in Fort Meade receives the signal, it has to find it among millions of messages, process it and get it to the CIA building. In this case, because we're trying to do this as close to real-time as possible, we have a translator working on the Arabic text at CIA. Then it goes to African division where someone has to read it and decide who needs to see it. You should feel lucky. Your operation is getting priority attention."

* * *

On Friday, Tariq made his awaited sermon in the Mosque room.

"Glory to God Most High, full of Grace and Mercy," he began then preached on the remembrance of Allah before launching into the substance of his message.

"You have seen our banner, our black flag flying from the tower. Some of you know that it is a replica of the Prophet's battle flag, may Allah sustain Him. It was the Quraysh tribal banner, the flag the Prophet flew during his military conquests. We will use it to come from the desert as he did and vanquish the apostates, the false leaders of the lands that used to be in the fold of the Caliphate. The lands now outside Islam revere ways that are depraved, trivial, and wanton. Their people revere the false Gods of materialism and technology. They spend more time taking care of their lawns than they do trying to please Allah, the Most Blessed, the Merciful. Satan is their only God, temptation their opiate. Jews are in the positions of power. Their very existence is an insult to Allah, may he favor our ways to please him.

"We are Allah's soldiers, his disciples on earth. Islam will rule all of mankind. Only through *jihad* can we bring about the rule of Islam on earth. *Jihad* is not only the sword; it is also the war to bring about mental and intellectual devotion, most importantly subservience, to Allah.

"Islam is the complete answer. It will bring all people from the darkness and into the light."

The rest of al Khalil's speech was borrowed from the *Ikhwan*'s master plan, couched in dialectical rhetoric reminiscent of the Communist Manifesto. With the final goal of establishing an Islamic State, Tariq struck his familiar themes of temporary cooperation with nationalist groups, the avoidance of unwinnable confrontations, and the support for Jihad across the Muslim world. He also encouraged the use of the Palestinian cause, the use of social, health, and educational institutions to create local Islamic centers of power, and the use of self-criticism and constant scientific evaluation. He reminded the congregation that he would be talking with each and looked forward to their specific recommendations for implementing his plan. He also reminded everyone that the immediate need was for more funds.

* * *

At the Hôtel Atlantide, Steve and Hank waited for Karim to show up.

"Where is your boy?" Hank asked. "He should have been here an hour ago. Either he got caught or he got cold feet. It's going to be no good if I have too little time. I told you an hour."

Steve caught the implication that Hank had lost his trust in him, that he was not a "real" case officer, not one of the elite operations officers from the directorate of operations, the CIA's small but defining segment—what his father Marshall always referred to as "the tip of the spear."

What was he doing in Gao anyway? Maybe he was in way over his head, as Hank seemed to believe.

He left the room and bought cigarettes at the reception. From a non-smoking family, he had smoked somewhat in college, all part of becoming independent, and had smoked in Moldova, but not since then. He walked outside vaguely conscious of the harsh taste of the dark tobacco in his unfiltered Gitane Brune, only thinking of where Karim might be.

I told you a thousand times to be careful, Karim, he thought. You're too macho, trying to prove something. It's not worth it if you get caught.

The air had cooled with the sunset but he was still sweating, and not entirely from the temperature. He wondered if he, too, was trying to prove too much.

He went back inside and found Hank checking the Trojan horse phone. One half of the plastic outer shell was face down on the small table and he was examining the electronics laid bare.

He looked over Hank's shoulder.

"Maybe Tariq's speech was declared a command performance that everyone had to attend."

Hank didn't look up.

"Did you give him a cover, something he could say, in case he got caught with the phone? Did you give him a logical reason? How was he supposed to explain it?"

"There's nothing he could say."

Steve felt guilty he hadn't discussed possible worst-case scenarios with Karim. But there was so little time. Had Karim been caught? Was he, Steve, responsible? Was Karim even alive?

They took turns staying in Steve's room, going to dinner separately. Around 10:30, they gave up.

★ ★ ★

After his Friday sermon, al Khalil met with all of his leaders in the canteen. An unusual discussion took place, reflecting discord in the ranks, bordering on a minor rebellion on the part of Talal Kawar, the Jordanian, and Walid Fahmy, the Egyptian. Since each enjoyed close ties to the Muslim Brotherhood, Tariq listened.

Karim and several other guards and helpers sat on a blanket in a far corner of the sparsely furnished room. Al Khalil and his lieutenants sat at a long wooden table cluttered with cups, plastic bottles of water, tea, coffee and two platters of finger food— dates, peanuts, mango slices, and sugar biscuits on one and slices of dried fish on the other. The one ashtray was overworked for the task at hand since they all smoked, El Maghrebi incessantly. Cigarette butts surrounded the table.

Fahmy was a beefy individual dressed in suit pants and a short-sleeved, Hilton Pyramids Golf Resort polo shirt.

"As you have explained to us in the past, Sheikh al Khalil, the subversion of the Sahelian countries is a worthy objective," Fahmy said. "And it will happen. But to go forward, we need funds and, in spite of our efforts and of blessings from Allah, progress is slow. Our financiers expect results in their lifetime. We need a splashy event that the world will notice. If it happens in Egypt, the population will respond. Egypt must be the core, the focus, of our action. It is the rock on which we can lever the entire Middle East."

Kawar had taken his ascot off and was fanning himself with a magazine.

"Jordan has one of the few remaining kingdoms left in the world. It is ruled by an illegitimate dynasty installed by the British. Over half of the population is Palestinian. We'll have a groundswell of support if we strike in Amman."

Hussein, who usually said little in these strategy sessions, saw an opening to achieve his life goal.

"The Assad family has killed many thousands of our Muslim brothers in Syria, my father among them. What could be more right, more pleasing to Allah, than to strike the Assads?"

El Maghrebi, who had been quiet, pinched his cigarette from his lips.

"You all need to do more than talk. I only hear planning for possible future actions coming from most of you."

He took a long drag on his cigarette.

"You need to start somewhere. Nothing will take place unless you take military action. There is no better time to start than right away. We in AQIM are the only real revolutionaries. You can come to Algeria and I'll show you. But leave your fancy clothes home."

Fahmy and Kawar answered in loud voices speaking at the same time.

"You are so successful that you have to live in the desert and move your camp every day," Kawar said. "In my country, open warfare is not the answer," Fahmy said.

Al Khalil stood up so quickly that his hand brushed his cup from the table. It broke as it crashed against the hard floor.

"I have listened to all of you. We will have a strategy before we leave. The Sahelian initiative must go on. But I agree that it is a long term program that is too subtle for our donors who suffer from strategic myopia."

Salim was at one of the tables but said nothing. He got up to leave with al Khalil.

* * *

Karim knocked on Steve's door at 11:30 p.m.

"Here it is," he said with a nervous smile. "I couldn't get my hands on the phone until after al Khalil went to bed. He always opens his window at night and he keeps it on his desk right under the window. I have to get back right away before anyone notices. I'm the night guard tonight. I'll come back for the phone in a couple of hours, whenever I can. The phone needs to be back in his room before he gets up for morning prayers."

With that he was gone. Steve's questions remained unasked and unanswered.

Hank first looked at all the external aspects of the device to see what he had to do to make the CIA gift identical. He noticed a slight nick on the side of the grey Globalstar 1700 and carefully nicked the new one identically. He plugged al Khalil's satellite phone into his computer and, using CIA-developed software, quickly found al Khalil's password, "1141346." He then transferred all the settings in Tariq's phone to his computer and from his computer to the new phone. He placed the old battery in the new phone as well. He needed no advice from CIA Headquarters, but called his support team in Langley to inform them that he had finished his task. After a few questions to double-check his work, his CIA team signed off. And the waiting resumed.

About an hour and a half before sunrise, Steve was forced to conclude that Karim had run into an obstacle and wasn't coming back to pick up the phone and return it in a way that al Khalil would never know that it had left the fort. If al Khalil noticed that his phone was missing, Karim would immediately be under suspicion.

Steve left the hotel with a bundle under his arm. Before getting in his car, he looked to make sure no one saw him and dressed in the Tuareg robes and sandals that he had found in the package given to him by the Tuareg *amenokal* earlier that week. He made sure that his *tagoulmoust* hid as much of his face as possible. He then headed out for the fort with the CIA phone.

There were no streetlights but his headlights and a star-bright sky provided good visibility. Once out of town, he turned off his lights. Campfires dotting the night landscape helped to keep him on the sandy track and the luminous screen of his GPS kept him on direction. He left his car about a hundred-and-fifty yards from the fort under an ancient and gnarled baobab tree, a symbol of the time when the Sahara was green. Several goats were also under the tree and moved to make room for the car with the utmost reluctance and bleats of complaint.

The front gate of the fort was open. He took a wide turn to his right in order to approach it from the side, where there were no entrances. There were three or four camels near the corner of the side and front walls. Camels were valued property and their owner, probably close by, would not take kindly to having his means of transportation, his source of milk, and his investment threatened or even disturbed. Further, he had learned that camels were as ornery as they were aloof and might complain loudly if they thought he was invading their territory.

He walked toward the front gate staying close to the wall. Voices came from inside the gates as he approached. He moved forward slowly and silently, extremely conscious of the sound his sandals made in the sand. The voices became louder; two men stepped out of the fort through the front gate and continued talking. He was close enough to recognize Karim and waited until he was looking in his direction to loosen his *tagoulmoust*. Hoping for recognition, he then pointed to his right.

Karim apparently understood; he and the other guard started walking slowly along the wall, away from Steve.

He'd had no particular plan when he headed to the fort, except to find Karim somehow and hand him the satellite phone. He now understood Karim could not leave the other guard without a very good reason, and that he would have to return the phone himself.

He looked inside the gate to see if anyone else was in the courtyard and walked in with an air of bravado that he did not actually feel. From Karim's information, he remembered that al Khalil normally kept the phone on a desk inside his room at night. With the layout of the fort in his mind, he headed toward the tower in the middle of the courtyard.

It was still dark. There was no movement in the courtyard. When he made his way into the corridor leading to al Khalil's room, he saw the door was closed.

He placed his hand on the door handle but hesitated and instead went back outside and looked for the window he hoped would be open, substituting for air conditioning. The window was where he thought, and while the bars were close enough together to keep a body from entering they were wide enough for the phone and his arm.

When he got close enough, he used a pencil flashlight to look inside. The bed was near the wall to the right of the window. In the bed, he could see a body turned toward the wall—he assumed al Khalil. Under the window was the desk. He reached inside and put the phone carefully on the desk.

As he withdrew his hand, he heard shoes crunching in sand from the direction of the front gate. He quickly walked around the tower and went into the corridor in order to stay out of sight of anyone in the front part of the courtyard. With pounding heart, he stayed there for about a minute, noting that the sky was getting lighter. It couldn't be long before the morning prayers began, when these corridors would fill with bodies and he would be seen.

The sound of voices growing louder told him people were approaching his location. He felt trapped but retreated farther inside. He guessed someone was supposed to wake up al Khalil.

He went up the stairs to stay out of sight as a man in a *jellaba* entered the corridor. Instead of stopping at al Khalil's door, he kept going toward the stairs. Steve retreated farther up.

At a steady pace, sweating with anxiety, he ascended more stairs until he saw the door to the room that he had earlier noticed on the plans. With his small flashlight he scanned the room for a hiding place seeing only empty ammunition boxes, coils of rope in one corner, and a large piece of black cloth on a table crowded with old candles and booklets yellowed with age.

The black cloth, he realized, was a flag. It occurred to Steve that perhaps that flag was raised every morning. He grabbed a coil of rope and kept going up the stairs, still hoping for a place to hide.

The platform at the top was larger than it looked from outside and could accommodate fifty men firing on attackers below. Steve looped and tied one end of the rope through an iron ring just below the top of the five-foot high wall around the platform then threw the rest of the rope over the wall. It was too dark to see if it reached the ground.

Steve briefly considered waiting in ambush for the guy who would raise the flag; surprise would be on his side and he was confident he could overcome the flagman. But would he have to kill him to keep him quiet?

Instead, he went over the side and held himself steady about ten feet down by wrapping his legs around the rope. He thought he might be able to come back up and escape down the stairs after the flag was up. On the other hand, he might run into someone else in the tower, maybe al Khalil.

He started descending and finally could soon see the ground. His rope was about twenty feet short of the sandy courtyard.

Without any other options, he continued downward, hand over hand.

With just two feet of rope left, he noticed a shooting port below him. He was able to wedge first one leg, then the other into the opening. He let the rope go and was able to grip a ledge immediately above the port. Then he lowered his grip to the opening, got his legs out and dropped his grip to the bottom. From there he swung himself away from the building and dropped.

The noise attracted attention from a man coming into the courtyard. Since Steve was dressed as a Tuareg, the man shouted and rushed toward him threateningly. Until that moment, although his heart had been beating at twice its normal rhythm, Steve had felt in control, unseen, invisible, and almost invulnerable. Now that he was under scrutiny, he went into fight or flight mode.

With a head feint to the right, Steve ran to the left, heading for the open gate. Not used to running in sandals he almost fell but regained his balance and, holding the hem of his ankle-length Tuareg robe in one hand, he headed for the car as fast as he could, knowing this could be a life or death sprint.

By the time he reached the car there was more than one voice yelling behind him but he didn't look back. And ahead, his car was now surrounded by several nomads who, with their goats, were examining it, including one man who was conducting his inspection from inside.

Steve had left the car unlocked with the thought that he might need to leave quickly. Now he wondered if it had been a huge mistake.

As they saw this mad Tuareg moving toward them at flank speed, the goatherds stepped back. Steve threw himself into the car and started it as quickly as he could get the keys in the ignition. His back seat inspector jumped out when they started moving, falling on a bleating goat that had been busy nibbling at the tires.

An SUV came tearing out of the fort and picked up the two men running after Steve. He took off with them in full pursuit. He first headed back toward town but going to his hotel would simply delay the inevitable confrontation. He glanced down at his watch compass. As he drove, he thought his Tuareg costume would minimize the seriousness of the incident in the minds of the Salafists only if his American status was not revealed.

He turned off on a track heading north toward the Tuareg camp he and Izem had visited on Monday. The sun was coming up over the curve of the horizon when he reached the encampment. He sounded his horn as he drove the last fifty yards, stopped the car, and ran toward the tent of the *amenokal*. The chief analyzed the situation in a moment with uncanny precision and called out his warriors, many of whom were already up around their campfires. Several of his men answered his summon armed not with their medieval swords and lances but with guns of various vintages.

The armed Tuaregs surrounded the SUV. Loud words were exchanged. The SUV turned around and headed back to the Fort. In that place and at that moment, the Tuaregs ruled.

26. Gao: A Mosque

The conversation following al Khalil's Friday sermon had been spirited and sometimes acrimonious. Salim had listened but without hearing the details of the conversation. He had heard all this before.

The arguments triggered the memory of similar conversations years ago when he was Said's right hand man, later his deputy and, eventually, his replacement. Then, the mission was to spread the Muslim Brotherhood's organization and concepts throughout Europe. The movement had profited from an unlikely base—Muslim soldiers from the Soviet Red Army captured by the invading Nazi Blitzkrieg in 1941. Mostly from Central Asia, up to a million soldiers agreed to fight for Hitler. At the end of the war, many had been transferred to the Western Front and were captured by the British and American armies, thus saving them from immediate execution by the Soviets. Said, the Brotherhood chief for Europe, accompanied by a young Salim, showed up in a Cadillac and donated a thousand marks when a former SS *imam* announced at a public event that he planned to build a mosque in Munich.

The enemy of my enemy is my friend; the MB was as strongly anti-communist as communism was atheistic.

Following the impromptu meeting in the canteen, Salim and Tariq walked outside in the inner courtyard. The sun had set but it wasn't entirely dark.

"You understand that we need to establish a strong base," Tariq said. "A strong Sunni base. The Shiites are growing in influence. Our Sunni faith is losing its traditional dominance. If democratization catches on, then keep in mind that including Iran, a Shiite country, there are about a billion and a half Shiites in the world. Make no mistake, they're waking up. Sometimes I think that we should first take care of the Shiite apostates even before we focus on the Egyptians, Syrians, and others who call themselves secular. Besides, the Syrians who are run by the Alawite clan are also Shiites. The only alternative operation I would consider would be a major strike against the Zionist entity. That would create great popular support and a way to obtain a nuclear weapon; that would get us the respect we want."

"You have given me much to think about. Let us talk again in the morning," Salim replied

During the night, Salim called David from his room. The next morning, Salim took Tariq for a walk in the courtyard. Salim wanted to continue the trend of thought that Tariq had initiated the night before, which David had found fascinating.

They walked in the courtyard until the mid-morning prayers.

* * *

When Steve received the transcript from the miniature mic in Salim's room, he was at first puzzled. Salim, whom he knew to be the European *Ikhwan* chief and al Khalil's adviser, had called a man named David and given him a summary of the day's discussions at the Fort.

Significantly, Salim had said, "Tariq is thinking of redirecting his focus toward Iran. What do you think?"

David had encouraged that line of thought. At the end of the conversation, Salim said, "I understand. The kind of attack you suggest will please everyone and will do Tariq a lot of good as well."

All Salim had to do now was to convince al Khalil.

27. Langley

Following his return from Gao, Steve had thought he had more than accomplished his mission. Back in his hotel room, he used his steganography system to hide his message in his scenic photographs of the Tuaregs.

Strongly recommend I turn over SBCALIPH/4 to Bamako COS. Return to U.S. and terminate my participation in this operation. Believe that purpose of my mission has been accomplished.

Steve could read Mel's negativism in the reply.

Bamako COS is to depart shortly and we have decided to put SBCALIPH/4 on ice. Pls set up appropriate recontact arrangements in case SB/4 needed at some point in future.

As a result, he soon found himself at headquarters being debriefed again. Steve and his nemesis Mel, the West Africa branch chief—the Queen of Anal, as he thought of her—as well as Philip, the Maghreb branch chief, and Marshall were in the same windowless conference room as before.

Melanie, true to her nature, said. "I don't understand why you recruited SBCALIPH/4 without express authorization from headquarters—from me. Associating with terrorists is not right. You saw him kill people. And that report about the hidden gold," she gave Steve a condescending smile, "We call that RUMINT, intelligence from rumors."

She wore the same dress with broad stripes as before, hardly flattering to her ample figure.

Before Steve could reply, a sudden cannon-shot sound came from an eighteen-inch-square door in the wall that Steve hadn't seen before. He almost dove to the floor, thinking it was gunfire.

"That thing was built around 1961 when the building was constructed," Marshall said. "I don't know why it's still in use. But it does keep most people from dozing during staff meetings."

Just then Thérèse LaFont entered, followed by a bevy of people. She moved to the center of the room and said, "Congratulations, Steve. CALIPH/4 was one of the best recruitments I've seen in my career. You saw an opportunity, you kept your cool, literally under fire, and you made quick, good decisions. We're all proud of what you did. You might think about a career as a full time intelligence officer with this agency. As a result, you not only gave us a view of the target, as we asked, you went above and beyond and actually recruited the source we needed. For that, we're awarding you the Intelligence Commendation Medal."

It was about five inches in diameter and bronze colored. The center design was a four-pointed star. LaFont read the certificate that accompanied the medal: "For performance of especially commendable service for an act or achievement significantly above normal duties which results in an important contribution to the mission of the Agency."

Everyone present, including a tight-lipped Mel, came around to shake Steve's hand.

Following the ceremony, Steve and Hank were joined by Philip, whom Steve had typecast as the little gray man the first time they met. Steve asked him, "I understand from Hank that al

Khalil's satellite phone password was a seven digit number. Did it mean anything?"

"Like his social security number you mean? The number was 1141346. Most likely, those are two dates using the Muslim calendar. The first one, 14 Anno Hegira, or A.D. 732, is when the Muslim armies were defeated at Tours in France. The second number, 1346 A.H., or A.D. 1928, is when al Khalil's grand uncle founded the Muslim Brotherhood."

Philip nodded, smiled an, "Excuse me," and moved away.

Marshall asked, "Are you ready to leave? Maybe we shouldn't have come together, you could have stayed longer. But I'm in no hurry. This is your party."

Steve glanced around the room and took in the animated conversations. How many knew the Salafists first-hand and how many thought of them as an intellectual challenge to slice and dice in think pieces that were steps up the promotion ladder? He thought of Hamad's barely contained rage in the Basilica. He thought of the sounds of the AK-47s and of the bullets hitting the bodies of his friends in the Timbuktu warehouse. He could see the muzzle of the gun barely sticking out the window of the BMW in Morocco. The catalyst who formed and harnessed the ideology behind these actions was Tariq al Khalil, the guy who almost brained the judge at the tennis tournament.

Steve said little until he was in the car with Marshall driving off the CIA campus.

"You know, I don't think that the CIA is fighting the same battle as al Khalil."

28. Paris: DGSE Headquarters

Captain Lucien Roger was in his office at the Direction Générale de la Sécurité Extérieure when his outside line rang. He turned to pick it up, letting his eyes stop for an instant on a large photograph taken when he was still competing after graduating from France's elite equestrian academy at Saumur in the Loire Valley. The horse's head and front legs were already over the obstacle and he, in the uniform of a cavalry lieutenant, was looking straight ahead, holding the reins and a riding crop.

He put the phone to his left ear. The agent on whom the captain was building his career, Tariq al Khalil, said, "We're staying at the fort just outside Gao."

"Isn't it an old Foreign Legion fort?"

"I suppose. It is not as comfortable as a hotel but at least we have total security. Except from thieves but even hotels are not safe from thieves. There were differences of opinion from my Egyptian and Jordanian chiefs. As usual, they want action closer to home. They are like children. They don't understand."

"By the way, how's your friend Salim? Was he at the conference?"

"Yes, he mostly listened."

Al Khalil was still mulling over what he wanted to reveal to Roger.

After he hung up, Roger glanced at the photograph again. He brought his hand up to the right side of his face and felt the frozen muscles under the skin. His fingers felt the rictus-like smile forever painted on the right side of his mouth. The photograph had captured his last triumphant moment. Visitors often commented on it in admiration. What no one knew was that the fall that had caused the right side of his face to become paralyzed had occurred a second after the photo had been taken. His future fame and glory, so certain in that photo, had been destroyed in the next heartbeat. He knew he was ordained to win the next Olympic jumping competition. But life had played a dirty trick on him. He was hell-bent to substitute the life that had been taken from him unfairly with success in other ways. He felt confident that he was owed big time and that he need not play by the same rules. He knew that he was different, that he was gifted, and that laws and regulations were for others.

The army had sent him to study Islam and Arabic, first at the Institut National des Langues et Civilisations Orientales, called by its students Langues O, and then to Tunis where the DGSE had an Arabic language school From the school, he had been recruited by Service Action, the DGSE's special operations branch backed up by the 11th Parachute Regiment of the French Foreign Legion.

As a student of Islam, Roger had managed to meet al Khalil and eventually persuaded him to provide information on radical Muslim movements. In time, al Khalil had grown in stature and was offered participation in alluring financial propositions. Roger often profited personally from these opportunities. Al Khalil had become more than just an agent in Captain Roger's life. In a way, the money he made from these deals made up in small part for the life that had been taken from him.

PART II

It is in the nature of Islam to dominate, not to be dominated, to impose its laws on all nations and to extend its power to the entire planet.
—Hassan al Banna, Founder of the Muslim Brotherhood.

Those who know nothing of Islam pretend that Islam counsels against War. They are witless. Islam says, "Kill the Infidels."
—Ayatollah Khomeini, Qom, 1986

29. Outside Al Khalil's Office

The morning after his telephone call with David, Salim took Tariq for a walk in the courtyard.

"The insights you shared with me last night are worthy of a great leader," Salim said. "You are right that the Shiites are gaining in political significance, thanks in part to the Americans and their 'one-man-one-vote' concept. Taking care of the Shiite problem is major. However, it will follow as night follows day once we take care of the Jew problem. In the meantime, instead of striking against Iran, perhaps we can use its international capabilities to our advantage. Our funders and backers will be happier if we score directly against the Zionist entity. Or against its American parent."

Those had not been David's instructions. On the contrary, David had told Salim to support a strike against Iran. But Salim had turned David's words in his mind for most of the night. It was one thing to give the Americans information of the state of progress of the Sahelian enterprise. It was something else to do their bidding against another Islamic state, even if it was Shiite. The advice he was giving Tariq was his own, not David's.

"What are you suggesting, Salim?"

"That we give Islam a victory against Israel in its own land. Hijacking an El Al plane or attacking an Israeli embassy has become routine, unexciting. A strike in what they call their homeland will renew your mandate as head of Islam's hopes. And I'm not talking about blowing up a pizza parlor."

"Salim, you are inspiring me. But how can we be successful where the Palestinians have failed? Or even against the United States now that their guard is up?"

"Nothing is impossible, Tariq, if Allah is with us, and he is. Now is the time to activate one of the support cells in America. In fact, we could have a two-track strategy. Prepare for both an operation in America and another in Israel. At the right time, we will choose one or the other."

Al Khalil said nothing for several minutes, picking up sand and letting it run through his fingers. Finally he looked at Salim.

"No. We cannot dissipate our resources. We must exert all of our forces on one target, and that target has to be the Zionist presence on our land. Hamas will help us. We have many *Ikhwan* brothers in Hamas."

It was time for mid-morning prayers. They stood up and went to the Mosque room.

30. Paris

Justin, a member of the Paris CIA station, rushed to reach Le Grand Hotel on Rue Scribe, near the Place de l'Opéra. He crossed Rue Auber and was soon in front of the hotel's baroque façade. Before he walked in, he rechecked the picture in his pocket to imprint the target's features firmly in his mind.

He spoke into what appeared to be a cell phone headset but was an encrypted surveillance communications device.

"This is Blue Hunter. I'm in place. I'm about to go inside. Anything new on target location? Over."

Joyce, in the Paris station's communications vault, answered.

"This is Hunter Control. He has not moved. Over."

She was sitting in a room crowded with stacks of communications gear operated by two men busy with their duties.

"I have not heard from Red Hunter or Green Hunter. Are they in place? Over."

"They are on their way. They should check in with you in the next five minutes. Out."

Joyce called Justin to join her in the communications vault.

"Typical Headquarters bugfuck," she said. "They knew this guy was going to have an ops meeting in Paris because they've been monitoring his phone conversations. They also knew from the GPS device in his phone that he was here. There was no need to wait until now to tell us. Now it's a fucking emergency."

She was reading a computer screen.

"Wait a sec. Here, copy down these coordinates: 48.52345N - 2.2250E. Find out where that is."

Justin took the numbers, opened the heavy steel door, and felt the air inside decompress. He went to a wall map of Paris hung in his cubicle that was marked with small colored flags showing safe houses, hot spots where there were more likely than not to have concentrations of police such as banks, embassies and official buildings and the areas where his colleagues had been conducting operations during the week.

He went back to the vault and told Joyce, "It could be the Opera or the Grand Hotel on Rue Scribe."

"Well, the signal has been transmitting from that spot since last night so we'll assume that he spent the night at the hotel and not at the Opera. Headquarters switched the signal to transmit once every thirty seconds instead of once a day when he was in Africa. He, by the way, is CALIPH/1. I'll give you his photo, true name, and basic bio in a minute."

"I'll get ready and we can move out as soon as Larry and Doreen get here. Where the hell are they anyway?" Justin asked.

He looked at his watch. It was 8:30 a.m.

"They were up half the night keeping tabs on FARC visitors from Colombia," Joyce said. "It looks like the French Government is negotiating with the FARC over hostages. CALIPH/1 could start moving any minute, unless he likes to sleep late. I'll tell Larry and Doreen to go directly to the Place de l'Opéra. You can connect with them after they get there. You're Blue Hunter. Larry will be green and Doreen will be red. Go."

Justin walked into the hotel and made a quick recon. When he was with the Marines in Iraq, "recon" meant skulking in the streets of Fallujah fully armed and anticipating hostile fire at any second. This was much better without giving up the feeling of contributing to something greater. His earphone suddenly came to life. He took a quick scan of his immediate surroundings and was satisfied that no one could overhear his conversation.

"This is Green Hunter. We are approaching Place de l'Opéra heading east on Boulevard des Capucines. Over."

"This is Blue Hunter. No sight of him yet. But be aware that the hotel has exits on Rue Scribe, at the corners of Scribe and Capucines, and of Capucines and Auber. There may be another one on the northern side but I haven't had time to check it out. If he takes a taxi, they're on Rue Scribe by the main entrance. Over."

Justin walked through the central part of the ground floor, a vast sitting area lit by an equally large skylight. One dining room was round with balcony-type French windows thirty feet up. Another dining room was flanked by tall cream-colored Greek columns going up toward a Sistine Chapel-like ceiling. Justin searched for an informal breakfast restaurant where he thought his man might be having coffee when he spotted him.

He again looked around before he said, "This is Blue. He is walking toward the Scribe side, probably for a taxi. Pick me up corner of Scribe and Capucines. Over."

"Roger, out."

With Larry driving the ten year old white Renault Clio Hatchback with custom BMW-3 engine installed by CIA technicians to give the little car a dependable source of power, they followed al Khalil's cab down Rue Royale through Place de la Concorde and west along the Seine River until they reached Passy.

"Hunter Control, this is Blue Hunter. Target took a cab to the sixteenth *arrondissement* and went into a building on Rue Chernoviz next to a grammar school. Red is on the street and we are around the corner on Rue Raynouard. Over."

"This is Hunter Control. Determine identity of target's contact," Joyce said. "Out."

An hour later, Justin reported back to Joyce, "Hunter control, this is Blue. Target just exited the building with another male in his late thirties to mid-forties. Right side of his face, I can't describe it exactly but it's unusual. The right of his mouth is up like he's smiling but he's not. Looks like he could star in a horror movie. We'll try to take photos."

Using the cameras in the side-view mirrors, Doreen and Justin were able to take the photos they needed as the two men walked to a neighborhood restaurant. The unknown male eventually broke off from al Khalil. The team followed him to his car and continued to tail him.

As they drove by the Porte de Bagnolet Metro station, Larry said smiling, "I think I know where our friend is going." When their quarry turned left on Boulevard Mortier, he added, "I knew it. This guy is DGSE. I can't believe it! CALIPH/1, a terrorist by any measure, is an agent of French Intelligence!"

*　　*　　*

During their meeting in the safe apartment on Rue Chernoviz, al Khalil had not revealed his major change in direction. Instead, he solicited funds. Captain Roger's reply was "We already give you more money than I can account for with my supervisor. Why do you need more?"

"We are really making progress. You know that unless I gather the extremist *imams* under my tent, someone else will. And French interests will not be safe."

"What about that American professor killed in Paris? We know that was you. You're not living up to your side of the bargain."

"We all know that he was a CIA spy operating in France, so I did you a favor as well. Besides, we never agreed that Americans in France were included under 'French interests.' I'm keeping my jihadists under control. Unless I can pay them and show that we're active, they're going to go elsewhere or go out on their own and your churches and malls and official buildings and metros will be see one firebomb after another. Who do you think has kept suicide bombers away from '*la belle France*'?"

Al Khalil knew Roger well enough to understand that he wanted to continue the relationship. Roger's financial and career advantages were at stake.

★ ★ ★

Commandant Leroux had to do what he most disliked about his job as head of the DGSE's Technical Directorate—ask for assistance from the DGSE's sister service, the DST, the Direction pour la Surveillance du Territoire, France's internal security organization. He made the call from his Boulevard Mortier office.

"We have intercepted a new signal that will be of interest to you. We have been tracking it for several weeks through our intercept site in the Kourou Space Center in French Guyana. It was an encrypted microsecond burst. Unfortunately, there were much higher priorities for the use of our Cray computer here. However, yesterday… no, two nights ago … our center on the Oregeval Plateau at Alluet-le-Roi, in the Périgord, picked up the signal. But now it's more frequent. Instead of once a day, the signal is transmitted once every thirty seconds."

Lacoste interrupted, "Probably a simple locator transmission. If we can't break the encryption, we should be able to find out where it's coming from."

"You may be right. In any case, the source seems to be within our borders and that's why I'm calling."

"Just send me everything you have. It would have been better if we could have had it earlier. It may be too late to make any arrests now. We'll see."

Leroux hung up. He wasn't interested particularly in an arrest.

The DST, part of the Ministry of the Interior, are just cops, he thought. *Promotions are based on collars.*

He shook his head. The better way would be to let the agent run and discover his entire network.

31. DGSE Headquarters

Kella was in her cubicle at her new job in the DGSE building which, so far, was bare of personal items, such as family photos or favorite decorations. Most of her new colleagues were men, about half of whom were in uniform. The atmosphere and the corridor décor were also strongly military. Her feelings about that were fairly agnostic. Her parents had been killed by soldiers but her grandfather was a general. She was the object of considerable curiosity. After all, the boss was her *grand-père*, she was a woman, and she was an ENA graduate.

She had been looking forward to this moment since she learned that her request to be assigned to the Maghreb, or North African, section had been successful. A file marked "CIMETERRE" was on her desk. She opened the red cover of the Tariq al Khalil operation and began to read. Excited, she noted the romantic inference of the name, meaning scimitar, and its invocation of the Muslim conquests that had made this Arab battle-sword notorious.

After her DGSE junior-officer training, she went through a series of interims in each of the five directorates: Strategic, in touch with the users of the information to determine its adequacy, relevance and timeliness; intelligence, the HUMINT collectors; Technical, the intercept operators, France's equivalent to the American National Security Agency; and Operations, or

"Action," the special military groups organized into maritime, air, and ground divisions.

The file was organized chronologically with the most recent reports on top. She flipped to the back and read Captain Roger's version of the recruitment. It read well. Roger had been adept at meeting and developing al Khalil. In time, al Khalil shared information about the leading personalities of terrorist groups in Indonesia, the Jamaat al Islamiya whom he had met in the Afghan training camps. After the Bali bombings, Roger had claimed credit for al Khalil's information that led to the eventual arrest of Abu Bakr Bashir, the Jamaat leader.

Kella was shocked to learn that the DGSE funded al Khalil to the tune of twelve thousand dollars a month. Several assassinations in Northern Mali and in other countries of the Sahel were attributed to al Khalil's group by other sources. However, there was no reporting on those assassinations from Roger. His accounts of IMRA activities in the Sahel focused on social services and health care. It seemed al Khalil was also obtaining funds from the gold and uranium mines of West and Saharan Africa. Some of his military training camps were identified, including the one she and Steve had overflown. She found no mention of his use of Unmanned Air Vehicles or of yellowcake.

She went back over the assassinations reported on by other sources and noted it included Tuaregs. She looked at the bracelet given to her by Thiyya and had mixed feelings. Was she on the wrong side?

"How are you doing Kella?" asked a tallish man in uniform who had stepped into her small space. He wore jump wings and several decorations. She had met him fleetingly during her first day on the job. It was Commandant Jocelin, the Maghreb section chief. She wasn't sure whether to get up but he sat down in a chair beside her desk. His long legs took up the rest of her space.

"Just fine, sir. I'm starting to review the CIMETERRE file. Very interesting."

"Yes. You have to meet Captain Roger. He's the case officer. What do you think of the case so far? CIMETERRE is very knowledgeable and has saved French lives. He's given us information that has helped us prevent several attacks against French targets."

"I'm reading it chronologically and I haven't gotten very far yet. Isn't al Khalil a member of the Muslim Brotherhood, and haven't they been behind several terrorist events?"

"That depends what you mean by terrorism. Besides, al Khalil has agreed not to operate in France."

She wasn't happy with that answer. It was too reminiscent of paying tribute to the Barbary Coast pirates several hundred years before—or of paying off a gang so it wouldn't rob your store. Concerned she might have to reveal what she knew about al Khalil's activities, she decided not to pursue the topic. She knew she shouldn't hold back that she was part of the DGSE. Then again, perhaps the DGSE was better informed than she was, and too many comments from her might suggest she was not a team player, or that she was not sufficiently sophisticated to understand that al Khalil had his uses.

Jocelin stood up.

"Well, keep reading. I'm glad you're with us and I look forward to a major contribution from you. I look forward to your ideas."

After his departure, she did keep reading and noticed the file contained information from other intelligence services, including Israeli and Egyptian intelligence. Typically, the reports showed Khalil unequivocally as a terrorist. However, the word "self-serving" was liberally sprinkled in the margins of these reports by Captain Roger and reflected the view in the DGSE that both the Israelis and the Egyptians had their own reasons to cast aspersions on al Khalil.

The most recent reporting on al Khalil was from his case officer, Captain Lucien Roger, who had met him in a Paris safe house located on the Rue Chernoviz a few weeks before. Al Khalil's Paris visit had involved both the Technical Directorate and the DST.

She read about a signal that was eventually traced to Tariq's satellite telephone. According to the report, Roger was extremely skeptical that the signal, if there was one, originated from anything his agent was carrying or wearing, which, if correct, would infer that something had gone wrong with his case.

Roger's only suggestion was to continue to monitor the signal to determine without doubt where it came from and, if indeed it was related to al Khalil, try to piggyback on it as a check on the location of their agent. However, counterintelligence staff asserted that it had the power to override him and, if there was some sort of beacon in the phone, it indicated that another intelligence organization had gained access to the phone and might have done more than just plant a location device in it.

It was decided to steal the instrument and force al Khalil to buy another one. "Stuff" happened in urban areas, and Paris was no exception; al Khalil would not question such an incident.

* * *

A few days later, Jocelin called to ask Kella to come to his office one floor up. The secretary nodded that she could go in. Jocelin sat behind his desk to the right of the door. On the wall behind him was a map of North Africa and a military unit insignia. A man sitting in front of Jocelin's desk stood up as he said, "Kella I want you to meet Captain Lucien Roger. I'm sure you saw his reports in the CIMETERRE file."

Kella glanced at the captain and her gaze became embarrassingly fixed on the right side of his face, frozen in a permanent grimace. Considering the way the captain had looked her up and down—*the elevator look*, she thought—the grin appeared to her more like a leer.

"Allow me to express my deep pleasure at having you onboard," Roger said. "I heard you graduated from the ENA, whose graduates don't normally end up with us. It is truly an honor. I have to assume that you're being groomed to be our boss in very short order."

The sarcasm was not lost on Kella.

Jocelin's voice allowed her to wrest her eyes from Roger's face.

"I saw you looking at this when you came in," he said, pointing to the insignia on the wall, a blue triangle with the point down, in the middle of which was a flame in the middle of a green and red rectangle. On the left was the number two and on the right was the suggestion of a deployed bird wing.

"It's from my old unit, in Corsica, the Second Airborne Regiment of the Foreign Legion. Great outfit."

"I assume that jumping out of perfectly good airplanes is not a requirement for me," she said with a grin.

Roger, dressed in civilian clothes, said, "It depends on the mission, *Mademoiselle*."

Jocelin shooed them out of his office.

"I have another meeting. But you'll be working together and I assume that Captain Roger has a lot he wants to share with you, Kella."

They moved to Roger's office, on her floor. Sitting across from him, Kella said, "That's a wonderful picture. Is that you? Growing up in Mali, I don't think I ever rode a horse—a camel, yes; a horse, no."

Roger turned away from the photograph without answering and Kella felt uneasy. She went in another direction.

"I was reading the CIMETERRE case, since I'll be doing the operational support work. Al Khalil looks like an interesting person. Do you think he's truly under our control? Also, I was wondering about that signal. What do you think that's all about?"

Roger appeared startled.

"What? You've been on the desk two minutes and you're already questioning me? I recruited him and he's one of the best sources we have."

In the face of his defensive attitude, she clearly had to be more sensitive and diplomatic. But before she could try her new tack, Roger continued in a calmer tone.

"I'm not convinced that the signal is coming from his phone. Those techies have it all wrong. I'm opposed to mounting an operation to steal it. It's a waste of manpower. I could just ask him for it. But the DST boys have their best team on Tariq. They're going to borrow that satellite phone and examine it. It's probably going to create a diplomatic incident."

He shook his head and rolled his eyes.

Roger questioned her about her African background, her studies, and her parents. In a few minutes, Kella felt that she had been wrung dry by an expert.

Finally, he said, "We need to continue this conversation later in a more relaxed atmosphere," which she took to mean that she was dismissed and that he meant to go further than just leer at her.

As she walked out, she noticed another photo on the wall: Roger in a black and gold uniform, spurs and a cocked hat holding a horse by its reins. Unlike Jocelin, proud of his former unit and what it stood for, Roger was very much about himself. And from the way he had reacted, she concluded he was not comfortable in his skin.

★   ★   ★

Maurice, the burly DST team leader, waved to Paul farther down the Rue de Courcelles. They were on al Khalil. Their assigned objective was to separate him from his briefcase, where, they knew from the DGSE, he carried his satellite phone. Al Khalil had come out of the Saudi Arabian Embassy on Avenue Hoche and was proceeding north on Rue de Courcelles. Although Roger had briefed the team that al Khalil usually took taxis in Paris, he seemed headed toward the Courcelles Metro entrance, so Maurice sent two of his men ahead into the Metro station.

The team also knew from tapping his hotel phone that al Khalil was scheduled to make a presentation at the Salle Pleyel that afternoon. The two surveillants preceded al Khalil to the platform that would put him on the Metro heading west toward Charles de Gaulle Etoile.

By the time the subway pulled in to the Courcelles Station, Maurice had maneuvered three men in front of Tariq. He and

Paul were immediately in back of him. As Tariq stepped onto the metro, he was prevented from moving forward by the three men in front of him who, their backs to him, barely gave him room to step onboard. The wagon was fairly crowded and, as the team had hoped, he didn't push forward. Just before the doors to the metro started closing, the two who stayed on the platform acted in unison.

A few minutes before, Maurice had summarized the choreography for his team.

"The first action is to keep him very close to the door. The second action has three movements. That will be you Paul, and me. We don't get on the metro but we'll be immediately behind him as he gets on. You'll be on the left. Movement one, stick him on the left side with this pin to get his attention away from the briefcase; movement two, I tear the briefcase from his hand; movement three, the doors close and the metro takes away us and his briefcase. It's over and we have his phone."

As planned, Paul stuck a needle in al Khalil's left buttock. Al Khalil yelped in pain, turned to his left and looked behind him. As his shoulders started their rotation, Maurice, on Paul's right, seized al Khalil's briefcase with both hands and wrenched it away. The doors of the metro closed within a fraction of a second and the metro pulled away.

"They took my briefcase," Al Khalil shouted. "Stop the train, stop the train!"

People looked at him strangely. The three men in front of him moved away in different directions as if to avoid getting involved with this helpless and indignant foreigner, probably an Arab.

"Served him right," one muttered to no one in particular.

32. Timbuktu: IMRA Building

Hussein saw Karim outside sitting on the sand, his legs crossed in front of him, with a small group of militants in the shade of the building.

"What are you doing?" Hussein asked.

"I'm waiting for the boss. He wants me to drive him to the northern camp."

"Come inside."

Karim got up and followed him past several desks busy with welfare recipients into a far corner where there were two empty chairs away from anyone.

"We don't have enough people at the camp. You have enough experience now to help out with the training. Also talk to Rashid up there. He'll tell you where you're needed most. When you go up there with Tariq, take another driver to bring Tariq back."

Karim was pleased with the increased trust being placed on his shoulders since the attack on the missionaries and the NGO workers. He gave some of the credit for the new mindset to Steve. He had taught him to be less passive, to recognize when he had choices and what they were. Being at the camp meant more responsibility, perhaps more independence, and probably more choices. He came to believe that his meeting with Steve had been meant to take place; Allah had clearly willed it. Such a life-changing event didn't just happen. It had to be part of a greater design.

* * *

At the desert camp, Karim immediately became aware of the almost uninterrupted whining sound of small engines being operated at high speeds. Karim went toward the noise and found the airstrip. He counted five small planes that were flown remotely. Karim was fascinated by them and began to spend as much time as he could around the camouflage netting, under which the unmanned air vehicles, the UAVs, were hangared.

Karim knew that Rashid was in charge of the camp, which also included the obstacle course, the runs in the desert and the other physical training, as well as the weapons familiarization and the firing. Rashid's priority was clearly the UAVs. He left the other activities to others.

* * *

One day after Karim came back from a run with the trainees, Rashid, a Moroccan Berber in his forties with a dark complexion and high forehead, called out to him.

"Karim, I want you to clean the engine of this drone. I'll show you how and then you can finish it. These things weren't made for a desert environment. Unless we can keep the sand out, it's going to destroy the engines."

Rashid spent two hours with him answering Karim's questions on the workings of an internal-combustion engine.

A couple of days later, Karim made a point of sitting with Rashid at dinner.

"Where did you learn about UAVs?" he asked.

"Actually, I'm self-taught, but I attended a technical school near Casablanca, and one day I was given the chance to take an exam for a place in a French aeronautical school near Toulouse. The test was given in Algeria and Tunisia as well as Morocco. The school offered one slot to each country. I went and studied in France for two years."

"Why didn't you stay? I would have stayed," Karim said, splitting the pit of a date out of his mouth.

"After the formal training, all of the French students were offered jobs in the French aircraft industry around Toulouse. The three of us kept getting turned down because we were Arabs."

"The French are pigs," Karim said. "So, what did you do? Go back to Morocco?"

Rashid laughed.

"Well, I felt isolated. The French students didn't let us, the three Arabs, hang with them. One day, for something to do instead, we went to the Mosque. And we went back the following week."

He reached for a piece of chicken in the plate of couscous.

"I don't know what happened to the Tunisian and to the Algerian, but I found that the Salafists liked me. Eventually, I was introduced to Hussein when he was traveling through France, and he brought me to IMRA."

Karim became Rashid's best student and, at Rashid's request, Hussein told Karim to stay at the camp as an assistant. Karim felt he was heading upward. He asked Rashid for manuals, which he pored over, asking a thousand questions about the UAVs. When Rashid taught him to pilot the little planes by remote control, Karim was as happy as he had ever been. Under Rashid's tutelage, Karim became an accomplished UAV pilot.

One day under the camouflage netting, Rashid told Karim, "Our UAVs are not the most recent technology but we don't need the latest technology. Our planes have the capability to carry out multiple functions including real-time or photo surveillance. Next week, I want you to help me experiment with different payloads."

"What kind of payloads?"

"I'm going to adapt them to carry a number of different things since I don't know what the mission is going to be yet. I want to know where to place cameras, sensors, or weapons. Right now, we don't need the specific payload, just their weight and size."

Rashid went and stood by one of his UAVs. He leaned down and touched its wing.

"Are they going to be flying bombs? Like the Americans' smart bombs?" Karim asked.

"Don't know yet."

Karim concluded that Steve would want to know about these little planes and he started to mentally inventory them. Rashid had obtained the first UAV, the Mirsad-1, from the Lebanese Hezbollah.

"This one became famous when the Hezbollah used it against Israel during the 2006 war," Rashid told him.

Rashid had four other UAVs, all obtained, Karim learned, through a retired American officer now in the arms business. Three, an IAI Harpy, an RQ-2, and an RUAG Ranger, had originally been developed in Israel. The Falcon was Jordanian, a joint venture between the King Abdullah Design and Development Bureau and Jordan Aerospace Industries, according to Rashid.

The Ranger was the closest to looking like and being a real airplane. Karim's favorite was the RQ-2, bought and used by the U.S. Navy, which would retrieve it on board with the use of a net. With a wingspan of almost seventeen feet, it was no toy. But Karim found it easy to maneuver, and he loved to fly it around the skies of the Sahara, spotting caravans either in the distance or directly under the craft through its live TV system. Able to fly at an altitude of fifteen-thousand feet, it was unseen and unheard by people on the ground.

Karim made no notes, remembering that Steve told him it was too dangerous, but, since he worked with the planes on a daily basis, he found it easy to remember every detail because one day, Allah would put him back in touch with Steve. In the meantime, he continued to practice his remote flying skills over the Sahara.

33. McLean, Virginia

Steve went back to his West Gate job following his return to the United States and the award ceremony at Langley. His division chief, Charlie Van Diemen, a retired Air Force colonel, walked into Steve's windowless office.

"You did it, Steve! We just received the first payment from the Moroccans for a two-year program to renovate Ben Guerir Air Base for fighter aircraft of the Moroccan Air Force."

"That's great. I discussed that project with the Moroccans but I never had the chance to go down there. Ben Guerir was used to support the Space Shuttle Program for a possible abort landing. I suppose we have other options these days."

Van Diemen pointed to a plaque on the wall of Steve's office addressed to "Boy Genius."

"They were right," he said.

The plaque was from the 51st Fighter Wing at Osan Air Force Base in South Korea, where Steve had worked on Counter Proliferation for two years.

"I really didn't think you could do it," Van Diemen said. "Breaking into a new market already dominated by French companies seemed like a long shot. But you certainly did it. If you can do it there, maybe you can do it in other countries as well. Don't unpack."

Steve knew he was highly thought of by his company. However, now that he was back at work, he was away from the action. He had mulled his options over several times. Joining the CIA fulltime was one. Yet he was extremely reluctant of having to depend on people like Mel. And, there were too many rules. Maybe a large organization had to dumb-down its regulations to protect itself from the lowest denominator. He hadn't yet decided how to keep to his goal to resist the Salafists, al Khalil especially. But he had not dismissed it.

Later, Steve's phone rang. It was "Mel from the office," as she identified herself. That Mel, who didn't think he was a "real" case officer, should call meant there was a serious problem.

"We were wondering if you could come today," she said. "This afternoon would be all right."

He looked at his watch. It was already early afternoon and he had a load of things to do.

"I could come in the morning."

Not wanting to go through the hassle of the security checks and badging, he asked, "How about if you came out to Salona Village? We could have coffee."

They met at the Seven Seas Restaurant, owned by a retired CIA officer and a favorite of Agency employees because it was only five minutes away from headquarters along Dolley Madison Boulevard. When his father was in Northern Virginia on consultation, the restaurant was a favorite venue for his ROMEOs: Retired Old Men Eating Out.

When Steve went in, he immediately spotted Mel, this time in a different tent-dress but, as usual, one of many colors.

Great disguise for a spy, he thought.

Sitting with her was a young man in a dark suit: Josh, a trainee. Mel had told Steve on the phone that he would be with her. He slid onto the red-leatherette-covered bench of the booth across from the two of them, a large poster of tennis pro Pete Sampras.

After the introductions, Mel said, "Thérèse LaFont asked me to talk to you about taking a trip back to Mali, to see CALIPH/4."

Mel and Josh each had already had a cup of coffee and were scanning menus. A waitress poured Steve a cup as soon as he sat down.

"I don't need the menu, thanks," he said. "Go ahead and order if you want. Coffee is all I'll have." He looked at his watch.

It had been three months since Steve had last seen Karim. "How is he?" he asked.

"We had a turnover in Bamako. Rod was reassigned. The new chief of station contacted CALIPH/4 and ran him for two months. First, he said the agent really had not been properly recruited, that he was not fully responsive when he first met him."

Mel's look challenged Steve to rebut her statement. Josh stirred his coffee.

"Not responsive? He stole al Khalil's phone for us! How much more responsive can he be?"

His voice was a bit louder than necessary. He looked around but no one seemed to have noticed.

"Well, Therese thinks you should go over there and try to revive the operation."

"How is the satellite phone I gave to al Khalil working out?" he asked. "I hope you're getting some good info."

"I can't talk about that," Mel said.

"Why not?"

"Well, you're not cleared, not anymore."

Steve became irritated at Mel's narrow view of life and her mindless rigidity. He saw no sense in prolonging the discussion.

"I'll have to talk to my boss. I'll let you know. I have to go back to my office."

They walked out together, Steve giving Mel a wide berth.

"I'll see you back at the office Josh," she said. "I have to run an errand."

She was parked on the left while Steve and Josh walked to the right toward their cars. They reached Josh's car, an Audi convertible.

"How long have you been with the Agency?" Steve asked.

"Three months, sir. I was in classes until last week. This is my first interim assignment. Then I'll have three more months of classes and another interim with another directorate. Then more training."

"How do like it so far?"

He felt sorry that Josh's first job was under the worst manager in the Agency. Josh smiled.

"Not exactly what I expected. But I read the CALIPHATE file. That's how I thought it would be. What you did in Gao was amazing, just like a movie."

Josh took his jacket off and swung it over his shoulder.

"What's your take on CALIPH/4 and this new case officer, then?"

"I haven't met the new Bamako chief—his name is Gregory. But I heard about him, a short man with a tall ego and ambition to match, I gather. He and CALIPH/4 didn't get along. I shouldn't be judging, but it seemed to me he laid some over-the-top requirements on him. When CALIPH/4 couldn't produce, Gregory terminated him."

"What about the money we owed him? We were putting his money aside each month."

"I don't know about that."

"Good luck to you," Steve said abruptly. "Don't let Mel get you down."

"Thanks sir. I'll be on this end answering your mail if you go back out. You can count on me, sir."

Josh opened the door to his car and Steve walked away toward his.

* * *

Steve went to Van Diemen's office as soon as he returned to the West Gate tower.

"I just had coffee with the Agency's West African branch chief," he said. "They want me to go back to Mali."

Van Diemen frowned.

"For how long?"

"I don't know. I'm guessing a week or two."

"The last time, the request for your services came to me from the West Gate CEO. It can't be that important this time. We're going to ignore the request unless the CEO calls. I don't mind helping out but we need you here. Well, actually not here exactly. Sit down."

Steve sat on a sofa and Van Diemen came from behind his desk to sit on an armchair at right angles to the sofa. Like many of the offices at West Gate, Van Diemen's office was decorated by plaques and insignias of Air Force units that more or less outlined the office dweller's career.

"You did well on that Moroccan deal. You'll get a considerable bonus. People like you. You establish trusting relationships easily. That's a definite strength. I'd like you to try some of your magic farther east. We've got a lot of contracts in the Middle East with our own Department of Defense, but so far only with the American military. Well, with the Moroccan exception, thanks to you.

"I'd like you to focus on the mother lode, on Egypt and Israel. U.S. taxpayers are sending more than two billion dollars to Egypt each year in economic and military aid. And a bit more to Israel. Do you think you could go over there and help them figure out how to spend it? I can set up some meetings at the Pentagon for you to get you started. As you can guess, DOD has been working with the Israeli Defense Forces forever and with the Egyptians since the 1979 Camp David Accords, when our government really opened up the purse strings—the reward for making peace with Israel.

"Anyway, some of my contacts over there can give you the lay of the land, and hopefully some names in Tel Aviv and Cairo. I would start with the Egyptians."

Steve listened to Van Diemen's suggestions, all the while thinking about what he had just learned. Not only was Mel incapacitated by a by-the-numbers way of thinking in a profession where wide mental horizons were absolutely necessary, but her field counterpart Gregory also seemed blinded by ego and ambition.

He was arriving at the point where he still wanted to stop al Khalil but didn't think he could do it through the CIA. And, he was angry the commitments made to Karim apparently were not being carried out. He wondered if, somehow, he could help Karim as well as do something to slow al Khalil. But he knew he couldn't do anything from his West Gate office.

"You know me," he told Van Diemen, "anything to get out of the office."

Later, he also wondered if he could manipulate this trip into a visit with Kella.

34. Paris

Kella now had dinner at least once a week at the Joulets on Rue de Longchamp. The general's wife had excused herself knowing that Kella and her husband were about to talk shop. General Joulet had Courvoisier in a large brandy glass.

"I've been through the training," Kella said. "Now I'm on the Maghreb desk, except that we pretty much also run the CIMETERRE case even though it's in Mali—it's so close to the AQIM group, El Maghrebi and his thugs. I've gone on an orientation trip to Algiers. I'm providing operational support to DGSE officers in the field. Yet I don't feel that I'm accomplishing much."

She took her earrings off and held them in one hand.

"To be frank, I'm somewhat disappointed in the people I work with. Most of them are military and they can't wait to get back with the troops. They're not happy in an office environment, that's obvious."

Noticing her grandfather's frown, she added, "Commandant Jocelin is different. He's okay."

She chose not to reveal the growing tension between her and Roger. In spite of their age difference, the captain was showing a strong personal interest in her.

"Keep in mind that you're a junior officer fresh out of training," he said.

As well as a woman and a civilian in a military culture, she thought.

"When I was in Timbuktu," she said, "I learned that al Khalil has UAVs. In fact, I must have told you, one of them shot at our plane. I haven't seen anything like that in our files. I wonder why."

The general blinked in surprise, but she didn't know quite how to interpret his reaction.

Joulet swirled the brandy around in his glass and took a sip of his Courvoisier.

"There have been rumors of UAVs in North Africa, but, as far as I know, no hard information. Did your raise with your supervisor?"

"I did, but he didn't seem surprised."

She didn't want to speak out of school about Roger, but she didn't feel her question had been welcomed. On the contrary, Roger had acted defensively, as if threatened.

When she drove home that evening, she still felt unsatisfied that the DGSE was the warhorse she needed in the fight against the Salafists. She wanted to speak to Steve.

35. Gaza

Najib Salah fell into step with his brother Mahmoud as they walked toward the city's Oriental market along with two Hamas guards. They had run into each other leaving one of the Hamas government buildings and were making their way to Najib's apartment on the other side of the market.

They were both in their late forties, although Mahmoud was a year older. His black hair was graying on the sides and he was stockier than Najib. While Najib, a former teacher, looked every inch the intellectual, Mahmoud had always been more physical. They were both senior members of Hamas. The Muslim Brotherhood's military wing had operated in Gaza since the late sixties and become Hamas in 1987. Since then, it had grown into a hydra with political, social, and military heads.

Najib was with Hamas's social services; Mahmoud was with the military wing, the Izz al-Din al-Qassam and a member of the al Qassam council as well as a respected operational chief. Like many of his colleagues, he had spent time in an Israeli prison. He was picked up after having planned an operation that had killed five Israelis and seven Arabs on a Tel Aviv bus by using a suicide bomber. Hamas had determined that Shin Beth, the Israeli internal security service, had learned of Mahmoud's role through a low-level Hamas militant. He was quickly executed by Mahmoud's men.

Mahmoud had been freed in an Israeli-Palestinian exchange of prisoners. He often joked that his suicide martyrs were smarter bombs than the high tech so-called "smart bombs" of the Jews.

Since the withdrawal of Israeli troops from Gaza, and the January 2005 elections giving the prime minister's post to Hamas, political disagreement between the religious Hamas and the secular Fatah forces had grown into a civil war that had become an all-out war in which Hamas overwhelmed Fatah forces and literally took over Gaza. Mahmoud had been one of the three military leaders, each one in charge of the fight for each of the three Fatah security compounds.

As they walked down the street, while Mahmoud smoked a Camel cigarette, his bodyguard stayed within five yards of the brothers. Najib's bodyguard either followed or led in a looser formation but never farther than 20 yards away. Both had their semiautomatic rifles at the ready, not an unusual sight for a population in constant conflict with Israel and with one another other. All four of them wore wraparound sunglasses.

The street was flanked on each side by six-storey, whitewashed apartment buildings. Colors were provided by the tenants' drying laundry hanging from windows. A multitude of wires and cables, many jerry-rigged by utility customers who preferred not to pay for telephone and electricity, seemed to tether the buildings together.

Mahmoud's eyes constantly shifted, alert to possible threats. From scanning apartment windows, his eyes went skyward looking for an Israeli UAV he knew had to be above them, monitoring Gaza City.

"I am telling you," Najib said, "It's not a desert agriculture experimental station. If it is, it's also a cover for something else.

I've driven by that installation for the last two years many times on my way to Ashdod and I've seen vehicles and people coming in and out. Those people don't look like farmers to me. They could be professors. Some look military. I saw men dressed in civilian clothes but I could also see they were wearing military boots."

"Any guards? Any uniformed military?" asked Mahmoud.

"No," answered Najib. "But remember the hitch-hiker from Nablus I told you about? He had worked as a laborer in this installation. He was telling me about the size of the watermelons. He thought that the place was a front for some sort of Rafael project."

"Rafael? You mean Rafael Arms Development Authority? You didn't tell me that before. Rafael does all of the Jews' secret weapons work. It could be important after all. We definitely would have the world's attention if we destroyed a Rafael site. They built the Jews' nuclear bomb. We could easily get funding for an attack against the Jews' nuclear programs—in fact, against any research site. What led him to think this place is connected to Rafael?"

Najib took off his sunglasses and wiped his face with a handkerchief.

"Well, he's not one-hundred-percent certain. He is sure that it's more than an agricultural station. For example, he's been in some of the buildings and he was surprised how few people were there, compared to the cars parked outside. He saw a lot of people go in, but he saw very few people inside.

"One more thing: It's very close to the Palmachim Air Base, in Yavne, where the Jews have their rockets, and Nahal al Soreq, the nuclear center. So it's logical for them to have this secret base close to these other secret projects."

"The Jews often build their secret laboratories, their essential military offices, underground. That would explain where they all went. We do the same thing; if it wasn't for our tunnels, we couldn't smuggle weapons or people to or from Egypt," Mahmoud said with a chuckle.

"When the Jews started their nuclear center at Dimona, their cover was that it was an observatory, because of the dome shape of the first building. They also floated the story that the other buildings were part of a textile center. So this so-called 'agricultural station' could very well be something else. If we can collect more information, I'll propose a specific operation to our leadership. This could be big. I wouldn't be surprised if the decision is made at Hamas Headquarters in Damascus. The Syrians or the Iranians would help. But I'd rather work with our *Ikhwan* brothers in Cairo—I'm thinking specifically of Walid Fahmy. He's a doer; he's aggressive and he's in touch with Tariq al Khalil. He won't hesitate to help us. The Brotherhood was there at our creation; it will want to take part in what will be a major blow against the Zionists."

Mahmoud dropped his Camel butt and lit a fresh one.

"Isn't the irony delicious? The Jews helped the creation of Hamas, or facilitated our initial existence in Gaza, in the belief that Hamas would weaken the PLO. Now we have actual control of the movement and the PLO is nothing. We own Gaza; we will own the occupied territories of the West Bank; the Jews have outwitted themselves."

Several boys were playing soccer in the street. By accident, the ball was kicked toward the Salah brothers and one boy came running after it. Mahmoud's bodyguard quickly blocked the ball and kicked it back, shouting, "Stupid boy. My trigger finger is very nervous. Don't ever kick a ball toward someone with a gun!"

They reached the market and turned in between stalls loaded on one side with dates in wooden boxes and, on the other, with raisins in flat cardboard containers. The crossed the market and continued their conversation amidst the smells and sights of the temporary stalls. The strong and earthy smells of cumin competed with the lighter but equally fragrant sage and the smoky aroma of paprika. Rusty saffron sat next to vats of green and black olives.

Najib and Mahmoud both believed that, in their own way, they were working so that the people behind these smells and colors could one day have the opportunity to support their families in dignity and under the laws of Islam. To reach that objective, the non-believers in and out of Gaza would have to submit and, with Allah's help, would submit.

They were still a block away from Najib's apartment building when they emerged from the market, one bodyguard now twenty feet ahead and the other in back but much closer. There was only light traffic as they started to cross the street. Suddenly a burst of gunfire erupted and the front bodyguard went down. Another burst quickly followed as both Najib and Mahmoud dove to the ground. People on the near side of the market were all on the ground. Guns appeared in multiple hands. Several single rounds were fired, coming from the market toward invisible targets. The Gaza population had much experience with random acts of violence and weapons were plentiful; the attempted hit soon led to indiscriminate firing.

This assassin had mistimed his hit. If he had waited for the Salah brothers to reach the middle of the street, they would have had no cover. Instead, they had only just emerged from the market and were now crawling quickly back toward the stalls. Najib was bloodied but moving. The rear bodyguard had come from behind and was down on knee looking for his target. He spotted the gunman lining up his own weapon to fire again, steadying his aim and using a metal light pole for cover. Both fired almost at the same time: the hit man at the retreating brothers in a scattered spray that belied his professional preparation, and the bodyguard at the would-be assassin, hitting him in the shoulder, causing him to spin and lose even the slim protection of the pole. The bodyguard then fired again at the now-easy target and cut him down.

Mahmoud leaned down to look at Najib's wound and muttered, "The al Aqsa Brigade. I thought we had killed all those Fatah dogs."

* * *

The next day, Mahmoud went to visit Najib at the Shifa Hospital. From outside, he could see that most of the windows were shattered. Inside, the walls were dirty and too many people waited for medical care by doctors often forced first to take care of those most likely to live. But Najib's and Mahmoud's status as senior Hamas officials guaranteed priority attention.

Najib was sitting in a green plastic chair in a room with ten beds, all of them occupied by patients with more serious problems. His upper body was encased in a cast to keep his shoulder and arm immobile.

"*Al Hamdu'llah,*" Mahmoud said. "You're looking fine brother. If the doctors are done, you're better off coming home. I'll ask for some pain killers and we can go."

He disappeared and came back ten minutes later.

"The doctor said that the hospital is virtually out of supplies. He had four of these pills. He said that each should last about two hours but to make them last as long as possible. He has no more."

As they walked out, Mahmoud said, "Are you okay? Listen to me. This cowardly al Aqsa attack has convinced me to act against that Rafael installation near Ashqelon. By winning the elections, we used the democratic weapon. We won international credibility. But we're not going to get the Jews out through elections. The armed struggle continues to be the key. Look at the increased status of Hezbollah after their month-long fighting with the Zionist army in Lebanon. We can complete our capture of the Palestinian heart and mind with a major victory over the Jews. Your discovery of a Rafael installation is the ticket. I need first to get the political support and then I'll collect the operational information for a plan. I'll get Walid Fahmy or Talal Kawar, or both, the *Ikhwan* chiefs in Egypt and Jordan, to put me in touch with their boss, Tariq al Khalil. My guess is that he wouldn't mind making headlines about now."

Najib walked firmly with Mahmoud out of the front door of the hospital but winced in pain as someone in a great hurry came in and pushed past him. Mahmoud put his hand on his holstered gun but Najib restrained him with his a stern look and a firm, "No."

After they were down the steps and on the street, Najib said, "Military operations are your responsibility, not mine. But my sense is that Hamas is going to let al Khalil fund this operation so you would be wise to get in touch with him soon."

* * *

Mahmoud had called a meeting of the Izz al Din al Qassam Council. They were on the second floor of an apartment building in Gaza City in a one bedroom apartment that belonged to one of the council members. They were all sitting at a wooden table each with either water or tea. As usual, the smoke was thick.

Mahmoud had already given its five members the background of the operation.

"With the help of our brother Arabs who work in Israeli vehicle registration offices and using surveillance as well as the Internet, we have been able to connect vehicles that entered the agricultural compound with personal addresses. From there, using the utmost discretion, we were able to determine that the drivers of these vehicles habitually went from their homes to the Dimona Nuclear Center, to Israeli Defense Forces Headquarters in Tel Aviv, and to major defense-related companies, including Aeronautics Defense Systems Ltd, in Yavne, Elbit Systems in Haifa, and Tadiran Communications in Petach Tiqwa. All of these companies produced high tech items for the IDF, Israeli Defence Forces. None had any connection to agriculture."

He stopped to take a puff on a Camel and gather his thoughts.

"We have concluded therefore that we were right, that the agricultural center is a front for a secret defense installation operated by the Rafael Armament Authority. I request the authority of the council to contact Tariq al Khalil through our Muslim Brotherhood friends to propose he funds and provide the men and materiel for an operation against the secret installation in Ashqelon."

He stopped and took another puff waiting for the council's reaction. Since Mahmoud had already briefed and obtained the support of each individual member of the Council, he expected approval and he was not disappointed.

On his way home, Mahmoud planned how he would exit Gaza without alerting Israeli authorities. He would go out through one of the tunnels under the Egyptian border. The sea was too well patrolled by Israeli gunboats. He would lay out the information to Walid Fahmy first, the *Ikhwan* chief in Cairo.

36. McLean

Steve mulled over his options as he drove to his apartment. As usual the George Washington Memorial Parkway was crowded with commuters. Van Diemen wanted him to prepare for another trip, to Tel Aviv and Cairo. Should he try to fix the operation in Timbuktu?

The car on his right, a silver SUV, pulled even with him although he could have kept moving ahead another twenty feet in the daily driving competition over inches. This unusually laid-back behavior interrupted Steve's thoughts and he looked at the driver, a dark-skinned man with jet-black hair who had been looking at Steve but turned his head back to the front. He was alone.

Steve took note of the car and dropped back to see its license plate. *Probably nothing*, he thought, but he maintained a closer eye on his environment as he drove home. The silver SUV pulled ahead of him and took the Theodore Roosevelt Bridge exit into the District of Columbia, while he stayed on the parkway toward Alexandria.

He parked near his apartment thirty minutes later and wrote down the plate number. He wasn't sure whether to follow-up on the SUV, but his recent experiences in Paris and Morocco didn't allow him to dismiss it. He would keep the number until he decided what to do.

He changed into running shorts and went out, again considering his situation. He was doing well at West Gate. He probably would be offered a higher position and a better salary in the near future. Should he fit a trip to Timbuktu to see Karim on his way to or back from the Middle East? How did West Gate fit into his determination to do something concrete, something that would blunt the ambitious plans of the Salafists and their killing spree? He no longer wanted to put his life in the hands of people like Mel and now this Gregory. If so, it meant his work for the CIA was over. But how could he possibly fight the Salafists single-handedly?

As he closed in on his apartment after a seven-mile run, he saw the silver SUV turn into his street half a block away. He ran past his block and made two rights to circle back. The silver vehicle was nowhere in sight. He nevertheless ran past his street again and came at this apartment from the back by cutting through a neighbor's yard. He wondered if the Salafists, armed with his name and picture from the Paris newspaper, had tracked him down. It would have been easy to do. All they needed was a phone book.

Once upstairs, he called Gordon, an FBI agent he had met at the gym, and left him a message.

He took a quick shower, put on old jeans, and grilled a steak, taking care to season it liberally with garlic. He also prepared a salad and opened a beer. The scent of garlic quickly took over the kitchen, and Steve felt his problems were no longer insurmountable.

Beer in hand, he went to the living room, sat at his computer, and sent Kella an email:

Hi, I'm making plans for a Middle East trip. Any chance we could meet? Paris is not on my itinerary for obvious reasons. If it doesn't threaten to discombobulate your life, how about meeting me in Geneva? We could have some fun and I have an idea that needs the intellect of an ENA graduate. All this on the assumption that you're not yet president!

Then Gordon called back.

"Hey Steve, what's going on?"

"Just one second." He took the steak off the grill and returned to the phone. "I have a favor to ask. Did I tell you I was actually famous, that I appeared in the international press?"

"You mean the Quran project? You didn't say a word about it to me. I know about it anyway. The FBI knows all, sees all."

Steve then related his suspicions about the silver SUV and asked him to trace the plate.

"I can do that. You think they're that organized they would follow you to the end of the earth to get you? Probably not. But I'll do it. In the morning."

Steve went to bed feeling calm.

Gordon called the next day.

"The SUV was a rental," he said. "However, the guy who rented it is on the terrorist watch list: Rafiq Jallad, aka Jabril al Jihad. He's been here two years, from Tunis. Unemployed. Lives in Herndon and frequents a mosque in Herndon that's a center for Muslim activists. He has a bank account and gets money from a bank in Qatar."

"Activist! I love your official euphemisms. Is that a politically correct term to stay under the ACLU's radar?"

"You're welcome. This guy is probably part of a support mechanism responsible for surveillance, renting safe apartments and cars, et cetera. The hit team arrives after all the groundwork is done."

"So, what are you saying—don't worry because the hit team's not here yet? Are you going to arrest him?"

"He didn't do anything illegal. I'll pay him a friendly visit, which should calm him down. In the meantime, maybe you could live somewhere else for a while."

Steve felt hunted. These guys didn't give up. It only reinforced his determination to take the initiative. The next day, he moved into his father's townhouse and decided to speed up his trip to the Middle East and Geneva.

★ ★ ★

Two weeks later, Steve was in Cairo with two days of meetings left on his schedule to try to move the Egyptian military toward West Gate's services. At Van Diemen's recommendation, Steve stayed at the Talisman Hotel de Charme on Talaat Harb Street. It called itself a boutique hotel. Steve assumed Van Diemen had chosen it because it was cheaper than the grandiose Hilton and Marriot where most American businessmen stayed. His main point of contact was an Egyptian armor colonel with a Sandhurst pedigree. Steve concluded that, as a "Yank," he had the wrong accent to be taken seriously by this anglophile officer. He would find someone from the West Gate staff with a British background.

Checking his email after he returned to his room, he found a message from Kella that said in part,

How about meeting in Geneva next week? I can get away from Thursday through Sunday. I have to be

> back at work Monday. I have another message for
> you. Last time I was in T, I met with Mother
> Catherine. She had a message for you from someone
> named Karim who needs to hear from you urgently.
> Who is Karim and why don't I know him?

Steve was nonplussed by mentions of Mother Catherine and Karim and himself all in the same sentence. Perhaps he hadn't been as clandestine as he thought, after all, while he was running Karim.

He replied:
> You caught me in Cairo where, professionally speaking, my progress is under-whelming. But at least no one is trying to kill me. Your message raises a thousand questions on how people in your message are connected – Later.
>
> PS—It's okay to pass my cell number to Karim. Maybe I could stop in Bamako on the way back home but I'd rather not.

Karim called the next day.

"*Monsieur* Christophe. I am so happy we are talking, *grand merci a Dieux*," he began.

Steve picked up on the French equivalent of *Al Hamdu'llah*: "Thanks be to God." He wondered why Karim wasn't using the Arabic, as he had so many times before.

"And I am happy we're talking also. It's been a long time. How is your brother?"

Steve was mindful that, even in urgent situations, family was always the conversational priority.

"Oh my brother, he is dead. He was killed in a firefight between Algerian soldiers and the Salafist rebels, the AQIM. I don't know what happened. He was supposed to travel to France the next day. I wanted him in France working while I earned enough money to send him to America. But *Monsieur* Gregoire, he is not a good man. But that is not why I need to talk with you. I think that something important is going to happen. I remember that you said to never talk about these things on the telephone, so I don't want to. But how else can I tell you? I am flying *avions sans pilotes,* and they will be part of the plan, I think."

Steve was thinking fast, balancing the need to finish his business in Cairo, and his plans to go to Tel Aviv next, against what he was learning from Karim.

"If you have any excuse to go to Europe, I could see you there next week," Steve offered hopefully.

"How did you know? I am traveling to Geneva with Hussein next week. He is taking me with him because I know about these planes without pilots and Rashid is traveling. He wants to buy some more."

"Since you're probably going to be busy during the day, would it be better to meet at night do you think?"

He waited for Karim to answer, but Karim hesitated, so he continued.

"Take this down. I'll be in the bistro section of Le Chat Noir, Rue Vautier, in the Carouge section at 11:00 in the evening on Tuesday. It's a jazz cabaret. Look it up in the tourist information they will have at your hotel. If one of us can't go, then I'll be at the Place du Marché, also in Carouge, not far from Le Chat Noir, the next day at 10:00 in the morning and the day after that. Do you know where you'll be staying?"

"No, *Monsieur* Christophe."

"It's important for you to come to Le Chat Noir—the first meeting. There is a bistro and a nightclub. I'll be in the bistro at 11:00. Do you understand?"

"Yes, of course."

"Okay, I'll see you on Tuesday night."

* * *

Steve arrived in Geneva on Monday morning. In the afternoon he took a cab to the Carouge section and had the cab drop him off at the Place du Marché, about three miles south of the southern tip of the lake. He walked the three blocks to Le Chat Noir and ordered an Orval beer in the Bistro section. He followed a sign down a circular stairway for a visit to the men's room to case the nightclub on the same level.

His waiter seemed in his early twenties, with intelligent eyes and dark hair that was a bit too long to be neat.

"Not too crowded tonight," Steve said, in French.

Tomorrow night is when it's going to be crowded," the waiter replied, in English. "The club usually serves up alternative music. But tomorrow is for local Rock/Pop groups. Who knows if someone will be discovered?"

"Are you a student?"

"Yes. Tell me if you need anything. My name is Luke."

He left to attend to other customers.

Before leaving, Steve paid with his credit card.

* * *

The following night, Steve returned to Le Chat Noir and sat at the same table. But the atmosphere, dominated by the loud rhythms and sounds of people talking and laughing downstairs, was radically different.

At 11:30, on the off chance that Karim had somehow walked past him, or rather improbably arrived early and was in the nightclub area, he went downstairs. The decibel level increased geometrically with each step. It reminded Steve of the increasing water pressure on a diver going deeper.

The loud, funky music came from a trio on a stage lit by a square framework of overhead lights. The rhythmic dissonance of the band moved the profiled bodies on a small dance floor. But only the band was visible. The rest of the room was dark. As he headed back toward the bathrooms, a man with twin lightning bolts on his black muscle shirt, leather wrist bands, and a belt made of three-inch-diameter iron links came downstairs and went by him toward the pulsing pandemonium of the club. Steve went back upstairs.

A few minutes later, the band stopped playing and Steve returned downstairs. The lights were on. He could now see that a car, highlighted by colored spotlights, hung from the ceiling. Underneath sat Karim near the dance floor with an older man, wiry with hard features, who he assumed was Hussein. There were no unoccupied tables near Karim. Steve also assumed Hussein must have seen his picture, so he knew he was taking a chance Hussein would recognize him. About a dozen people were standing, perhaps waiting for a table to clear, and he went to stand near them. He would wait for an opportunity when Karim was alone.

Then Steve saw Luke and intercepted him as he went by.

"Do you think a table might clear soon?"

He quickly considered and dismissed the thought of sending Karim a message through Luke, but too many things could go wrong.

Luke recognized him, smiled, and gave him a victory signal. A few minutes later, Karim summoned Luke to his table and whispered something in his ear while pointing at Hussein. The three of them smiled conspiratorially. Five minutes later, Luke brought their drinks. Hussein tasted his and grinned at the waiter in thanks. Steve was guessing there was more than Coke in that glass. *Maybe it was a Mazout*, he thought, Coke with a shot of scotch, a drink popular in Morocco.

Steve decided to make his move before the lights went out again. He walked near Karim's table but kept in back of Hussein. Karim glanced up and Steve headed toward the men's room, hoping that Karim would follow for a quick meeting, during which they could decide whether and where they could safely meet before Karim left Geneva.

In the men's room, he got busy washing his hands after confirming he was alone. A mop was left leaning in a far corner. A few seconds later, the door opened and Steve looked in the mirror in front of him expecting to see Karim. Instead, a determined-looking Hussein walked in. He began washing his hands next to Steve and said in French. "Haven't I seen you before? You're a famous person. Am I right?"

Steve assumed Hussein was trying to confirm his identity before killing him. "No, I'm not famous."

Hussein, standing between Steve and the door, continued.

"Don't be modest. Yes, I know who you are now. You were in a French newspaper, yes?"

Steve stepped back from the sink and turned to the left to get around Hussein and leave, however, a hunting knife appeared in Hussein's right hand. Hussein blocked his exit.

"You're making a mistake. I'm not the person you think I am."

Steve tried to keep his eyes on the knife and still look around for a weapon. The utility closet was behind Hussein. However, he remembered the mop leaning against wall beyond the stalls. He started backing up. Hussein was in a crouch now with his knife held low, his thumb up and his left arm extended toward Steve.

"You will no longer insult Islam by claiming that the Quran is a fake," Hussein said.

He lunged forward, sending the knife on an upward arc meant to penetrate under Steve's ribcage. Steve jumped back and caught Hussein's wrist in the V of his two open hands with the opposite thumb on each side. He gripped the wrist tightly and kicked Hussein in the crotch then swung Hussein's arm over his head in a three-hundred-sixty-degree turn.

In one motion and with all of his strength, Steve forced the arm up behind Hussein's back. They both heard a crack and Hussein grunted. The knife fell. Steve picked it up and let Hussein go. Hussein was still on his feet and he turned to face Steve holding his right arm with his left hand, his face a grimace of pain. But he made no sound.

At that moment, the man with the twin lightning bolts muscle shirt walked in and stopped at the sight of Hussein and Steve facing each other, the air virtually crackling with tension.

In French he said, "Dirty Arab! These Arabs don't belong here, eh? Let me help." He started taking the chain from around his waist with relish.

"Thanks," Steve replied, also in French, "But I think that's enough. He learned his lesson."

He took his opportunity and left. *The two deserve each other*, he thought. He saw Luke in the hallway and stopped him. Now

that the fight was over, Steve found himself breathing in quick shallow breaths.
"Call the police," he said. "There's a fight in the bathroom."
He stopped a second to take a breath.
"Here, that's for my bill," and handed Luke fifty Swiss francs.
The band was playing again and he couldn't see Karim but headed toward his table. Karim wasn't there. He went back toward the hallway leading to the bathroom and saw him going toward the men's room. He stopped him and brought him to the protection of the dark. He talked quickly, recalling the message he'd planned to give him.
"Your boss just tried to kill me. Where were you? The police are coming so you want to get out of here. Listen, I'll be in the lobby of the Hotel Beau Rivage, Quai du Mont Blanc, tomorrow between 11:00 and 11:30. When I see you, I'll get up and you follow me at a distance. Don't talk to me. If you can't come then, I'll wait for you in the lobby of the Palace Hilton between 5:00 and 5:30, also tomorrow. They're major hotels. You'll find them. Okay? Where are you staying?"
Karim nodded and gave him the name of a small hotel near the Cornavin railroad station. They had been together for less than a minute. Steve left by the back door that opened onto the parking lot after repeating his instructions.
He waved a taxi to the Montbrillant Hotel. He walked to the Cornavin station and took a taxi to his hotel, the Ramada Encore, back in the Carouge district. If the police were looking for him, they would no doubt find him, but not right away. He would have time to meet with Karim and, with any luck, Kella. His hand traced the edge of Hussein's knife under his shirt with both satisfaction and apprehension.

* * *

The next day, as agreed, Steve waited in the atrium of the Beau Rivage Hotel. Behind his *Journal de Genève,* he was inspecting the rose-marble columns and tapestried walls when he saw Karim walk in. He folded his newspaper after he was sure Karim had spotted him and walked out and down toward the river shuttle service. The boats, called *mouettes,* or seagulls, provided convenient conveyances and were part of the city's public-transport system.

As instructed, Karim followed him from a distance, giving Steve a chance to take a position on one of the *mouettes,* from which he could observe the back of the hotel as well as the people boarding. He was looking for anyone paying undue attention to Karim, an obviously young Arab.

As he waited, he wondered if he had made a mistake directing him into an environment where a young Arab man might stand out, especially to the hotel security staff. He hoped Karim would become invisible among the forty-percent foreign-resident population. Swiss hotel security staffs profiled their foreign clientele only out of necessity.

Steve had noticed several Arabs in the atrium wearing the ankle-length *gallabiyya robes* and *kufiyya* head covering. The hotel clearly did not discriminate among its wealthy clients no matter where they came from. But Karim would not fool anyone into believing he was a rich Arab *sheikh* in Geneva on business.

Karim boarded the *mouette* and Steve noticed a well-dressed man who seemed to have his eyes glued to Karim's back. He stayed on the dock until the boat pulled away and began to cross the river. Apparently satisfied that Karim was no longer his problem, the man turned away and headed toward the hotel. His obvious interest in Karim marked him as someone comfortable and secure in his operational environment, not a foreign intelligence officer or agent. Steve pegged him for a retired cop now working for hotel security.

Karim approached him and they leaned over the side of the boat as they talked.

"How much time do you have? What happened last night?"

"Hussein saw you and recognized you. I told him to let me go and kill you. He liked that but said no, he was going to do it, to make sure. There was nothing I could do. He told me not to move. When I went to get him somebody was hitting him with a chain. I stopped him. The police did come but about twenty minutes later. They arrested the guy who was beating up Hussein. He is still in the hospital; broken arm."

Karim smiled.

"The Swiss guy said he hadn't done it, that someone else had been fighting Hussein before he went into the bathroom. I heard him give the police a good description of you, even that you were an American. Did *you* break his arm, *Monsieur* Christophe?"

"I didn't have a choice. What's your schedule?"

Steve could see from Karim's expression that he had gained status by surviving Hussein's assault.

Karim looked questioningly at Steve.

"You could have killed him. That's what he told me."

Steve glanced around at the other passengers to confirm no one was paying attention to them. Then he took Hussein's knife from his jacket inside pocket.

"That's Hussein's favorite thing, his knife!" Karim exclaimed.

Steve held it for a few seconds before throwing it into the water. Karim let out an involuntary gasp.

"What about your schedule?"

"We're leaving tomorrow, I think. I will go get him at the hospital this afternoon."

Karim grinned. "The only thing Hussein asked me to do was to buy him Swiss chocolates."

"How about your brother? Tell me what happened."

"I don't have the details. There was a firefight. He was in the wrong place. He never hurt anyone. He was a good person."

Steve knew how much Karim's brother meant to him. He touched his shoulder.

"I'm so sorry." Seeing that Karim was not going to say anything further about his brother, he asked, "What happened after I left Mali?"

"Your friend *Monsieur* Gregoire didn't like me. He asked me to tell Tariq that an American from the Embassy wanted to talk to him and to bring Tariq to a meeting with him, with *Monsieur* Gregoire. That was like asking for my own execution. He didn't want to talk about how I was supposed to do that and still stay alive. He said I was not worth the money and that you had been too generous. So that money you said was being set aside, is it gone? Did *Monsieur* Gregoire keep it for himself?"

The boat was nearing the Jet d'Eau fountain and tourists moved to their side of the boat to see it up close. Steve overheard someone say the jet of water was over four-hundred-feet high. Steve could see Karim was enthralled and he let him take in the sight.

"No, I don't think he stole it. Don't worry; I'll get that money reinstated. And start thinking of yourself. That money wasn't just for your brother. It was for anything you wanted to use it for—your mother, maybe, yourself?"

Then he turned to business.

"So, tell me about your plans."

He let Karim talk, asking infrequent but targeted questions to keep him on track. But a major piece of the puzzle was missing. Hussein had not divulged what they were getting ready for.

★ ★ ★

They arrived to the other side of the lake and walked up the Quai Gustave Ador to a park on the right where they sat. Small children and their nannies seemed to be in the majority. After five minutes Steve got up, concerned about sticking out. They resumed their walk.

"Hussein has stopped talking about operations in Niger or Mauritania or those places. He and al Khalil have another objective in mind ever since Gao. But I don't know what it is. Hussein talks to me. He trusts me. But he's not talking about the final objective. No one knows anything. Only al Khalil and Hussein, and they're not telling the rest of us. Oh, and he has a new recruit, Habib, a Tunisian who studied in America. He's a scientist. Anyway, Tariq and he have long conversations. I don't know about what.

"Since we've been here in Geneva, Hussein slipped once and told me that I would be taking my UAVs off a beach, close to water. At first I thought the plan was to use the UAVs like smart bombs. But now I don't think so. Rashid, the UAV *patron*, he said the targets would be about twenty-five to thirty-five kilometers away. We're buying more UAVs here in Geneva. The sales agent is an American. I met him with Hussein yesterday. His name is Spaceck. Hussein calls him 'colonel,' which pleases the American, I can tell. The new UAVs are being shipped to Cyprus and from there, I was able to learn that they will be shipped on a second leg, to Alexandria, Egypt, but I don't think that's the final destination."

"Could the target be in Egypt? Where do you think they'll go from there?"

Karim shrugged.

Before they ended their meeting, Karim promised to find a way to send an email to Steve with additional information as soon as he found it.

★   ★   ★

Kella arrived the next day. Before going to meet her at the airport, Steve checked out of the hotel. During the night, he realized he had made a mistake by paying for his first visit at the Le Chat Noir with his credit card, which Luke could easily find if the police asked for it.

He watched her stride toward him. Without wearing heels, she still could see over most of the other passengers coming out toward the luggage area and the exits—beauty in the middle of an otherwise unremarkable gaggle of humanity.

"You don't know how good it is to see you," he told her. She responded with a radiant smile and a kiss.

"There's been a little change in plans," he continued as he led her toward the central part of the airport. "We're going to a village at the base of the Alps, on the other side of the border in France. Do you have any luggage?"

"Of course I have luggage. I thought we were staying in Geneva, in the Carouge district. I was looking forward to it. It's supposed to be an old and eclectic and fun. In other words it's not totally Calvinist."

"That's why I wanted to talk to you."

"You mean to discuss Calvinism? I thought this was going to be a romantic weekend."

"Well, that's certainly not excluded. Sit here a second."

They had reached a restaurant with tables adjacent to the passengers' main route to and from their gates.

"Here's what we're going to do: take a cab to the main bus station and a bus to a village in France. Something has happened. The police are looking for me and I'm not interested in trying to convince the Swiss authorities of my innocence."

"What did you do? Double-park?"

"This is serious. Another Salafist came at me with a knife. It's a long story. I'll tell you everything when we're alone."

"No! Are you all right? Why are you running if someone attacked you?"

She looked at him a second, as if wondering whether to speak her mind.

"If I didn't know you better, I'd say you were living an exciting fantasy life. Tell me, are you still a photojournalist? Or are you into some other 'temporary' profession? Is this some CIA mission?"

"No. but that's sort of what I want to talk to you about—later. Let's get out of here. Too many cops in airports!"

They followed the crowd, retrieved Kella's luggage, and took a cab to the Gare Routière.

"I checked my suitcase in here before going to the airport. While I get it, how about finding out about buses to Saint Genis Pouilly in France? It's probably about fifteen or twenty miles. If I rent a car, the police would find me in a second. From everything I've heard, the Swiss police are a very thorough lot, and the incident was important enough for a paragraph in the *Tribune de Genève*."

"I could rent a car in my name."

"Let's keep it simple. For now, we'll use public transportation. Maybe you can rent a car in France."

★ ★ ★

The bus crossed the border without stopping and, in forty-five minutes, Steve and Kella were in a larger town than Steve had anticipated from his quick Internet search. They quickly settled on the Kyriad Genève Hotel.

"This could be a Holiday Inn," he said.

When they checked in, the lady at the counter asked, "Are you with the CERN? Do you have your discount card?"

"No, *Madame*, we're tourists," Kella replied.

On the way to their room, Steve asked, "CERN? What is it?"

"It's the European Organization for Nuclear Research. A CERN representative spoke to us when I was still at the ENA. This is their headquarters. If you thought there were too many cops at the airport, wait till you see this place. I imagine it's crawling with security."

They had not been able to talk on the bus, so after freshening up, Kella suggested they go for a walk.

"This may be like a Holiday Inn," she said, "but the mountains are pretty."

Once outside, Steve said, "I don't think you ever told me what your job was. Didn't you say a long time ago that it was time for true confessions? Except it wasn't. I think that now, it is. Do you work for your grandfather the general? It's an important question."

They turned up Route de la Faucille walking slowly. She held his hand.

"I'm the one who should be asking questions, don't you think? What was the photojournalist story you told all of us in Mali? Weren't you then working for the CIA?"

It was now late afternoon. A gray cloud cover had turned black. The breeze from the southwest had picked up. Almost imperceptibly, they picked up their pace. A light cream-colored sweater was draped on her shoulders with the sleeves tied loosely around her neck. She stopped to put it on.

As she put her arms through the sleeves of her sweater, Steve said, "Because of my father's connection, the CIA asked me to try to get some basic information on IMRA and al Khalil—because I had met al Khalil before in school. But as things worked out, I didn't have to meet him. Probably a good thing, since the Salafists all think I'm the devil. Then I went back to work for West Gate. And that's what I have been doing. So, your turn. Who pays your salary?"

"I did join the DGSE after graduating. But I would be fired if they knew that I was sharing this information with anyone, especially a foreigner."

The admission opened a floodgate and Kella told Steve about the CIMETERRE file and Captain Roger, al Khalil's DGSE contact.

"The DGSE is paying al Khalil? He's a killer!"

Kella nodded and said, "But not on French soil. That's the deal."

"Bullshit! They killed Ted Coogan in the middle of Paris."

"But he was an American."

Steve was about to explode again when she added, "I'm giving you the DGSE rational."

He had noticed two police cars go by during their half-hour walk. He became self-conscious and they turned off on a street with less traffic.

"I want to stop, or slow down, the Salafists. But I can't function under the myopic rules of the CIA bureaucracy. I gather that you feel the same way about the DGSE. Am I right?"

"Well, I'm not contributing much right now, that's for sure. And the DGSE is not going to do anything against the Salafists. At least not until they attack French interests directly. What's your idea?"

"That we work outside of government rules and constraints. Watching the Salafists is not enough. They killed your friend Faridah in Paris and my friend Ted Coogan. They tried to kill me on ... let me count ... three times. And you told me there had been more murders. Al Khalil has a free pass. And that really pisses me off. It's not right!"

"How can we possibly stop them? By ourselves? We don't have the resources. What do you want to do exactly?"

He stopped and took her arm.

"At least slow them down. To make this workable, we can take small bites. For example, just publicizing al Khalil's activities in Mali would be a start."

"You mean bring public attention to the camp and hope that governments and organizations then take action, having been shamed into it?"

"Right! That would be a start. Let the media do its job, inform the public..."

He looked up at the sky.

"Let's turn around. It looks like those clouds are about to burst open."

He steered her toward the hotel at a brisk pace. It started raining. In a few minutes, it would pour. They were now close to the hotel and ran at an easy pace that Steve thought Kella, who had told him that she hated to jog, could sustain.

* * *

The almost continuous rain and thunder of the night made Kella snuggle closer to Steve under the covers. The weather didn't improve the following day. They stayed close to the hotel and discovered to their dismay that it offered no Internet access. After breakfast in the restaurant, they each brought a cup of coffee to their room.

"You told me about Karim and the satellite phone last night. What about Izem?" Kella said.

"Yes, I think Izem is ready to help. We could use him inside al Kahlil's group. Since Karim seems to be specializing on those UAVs, having Izem help us from the inside of the fighters' group would be good. Do you think you can pull rank as a Tuareg queen? The next time you go to Timbuktu."

"What do we want him to do?"

"He already has military experience and Hussein would love to pick him up, I'm sure. He would get paid whatever al Khalil pays plus, later, I think I could talk somebody in the CIA to reward him. Communications will be a problem. Neither of us lives in Mali. And I doubt that Izem knows about computers. That's something you would have to explore with him. What do you think? Of course, this would be outside of the DGSE as much as it's outside of the CIA. Your Captain Roger can't be witting."

"With Izem inside the fighters' group, we should be able to prevent some of al Khalil's murders. I'll talk to Izem on my next trip."

Steve finished his coffee. "For the first time, I'm beginning to feel that I'm getting some control over events. Until now, we've been like corks on the waves."

"Do you feel like you're creating a new intelligence agency?"

He moved toward the bed. "I'm not that ambitious. But we can't just sit on our hands and watch the CIA and the DGSE simply monitor this movement that is trying to change the world as we know it thinking it's getting direct orders from God."

Kella moved toward the bed from the other side. "Do we know what we're doing?"

Steve reached for her from across the bed. "The biggest mistake intelligence agencies usually make is to not coordinate; to build Chinese walls between each other. Let's work on that."

Lightning lit up the sky. A second later, thunder shook the windows of their room.

37. Brussels: Salim's Apartment

Tariq walked into Salim's stylish place on Avenue Louise, an environment more suited to his tastes than the camps in the African Sahel. He noticed a framed painting on the floor leaning against the wall and picked it up: a crowd of villagers around a horseman in the center and huts on the sides.

"New?" he asked.

Salim took it from him and said, "Brueghel the Elder." He disappeared for a moment in a side bedroom and came back empty handed. He motioned for Tariq to sit.

"We haven't seen each other for far too long my son, since Gao. I hope you are well and that Allah is watching over you."

"He is indeed, my father, he is indeed, *Alhamdu'llah*. I have been traveling more often: Cairo and Amman to examine operational possibilities there more closely with our *Ikhwan* Brothers, and to the Kingdom."

Salim smiled.

"Ah yes, Wahhabist Central. Did they agree to augment our funding?"

"Not enough, but they will after we show that we are the principal players."

"What about Israel? Are you in touch with Hamas? In Gaza?"

"I have sent them a message. We must succeed there. With Allah's help, I will create a firestorm, a final Armageddon, for the Jews."

38. DGSE Headquarters

Despite their age difference, Captain Roger was showing a strong personal interest in Kella. He had taken her to lunch one day from the office. They both sat on a banquette against the wall looking toward the center of the room. *He's sitting closer than necessary*, she thought.

"I knew when I first met you that we were going to be friends," he said. "I love that you were born in North Africa. The Tuaregs, your people, have a great history. To say they were the Lords of the Desert is an understatement. You must be proud. I've worked on and in North Africa for a long time. I know that we're interested in many of the same things. I know the meaning of the tattoo on the back of your hand. I bet that not many people know that you are from noble lineage."

Not sure how to respond, she had asked, "Do you speak Tamasheq?"

"No, but my Arabic is not bad."

He had continued in Arabic.

"I love your eyes. They are beautiful."

Squeezing closer, he enumerated what he liked about her body, growing bolder. Over coffee, he had put his hand on hers and suggested they go to a friend's apartment nearby to which he had the key.

"I want to show you his collection of Tuareg art objects. I'm sure you've never seen anything like them. They are rare and valuable," he smiled.

"I don't think so. Not today, not ever," she had said.

But Captain Roger was not easily discouraged. She wanted to report him to somebody but she knew that, in this French military working milieu, she would only be hurting herself. She also concluded that the captain's relationship with al Khalil was not completely professional. She had noticed, for example, that he owned a rather luxurious new Mercedes SL convertible, a car that a French army captain couldn't normally afford. She had also come across enough clues to conclude that the French oil company, Total, was paying bribes, or tribute, to AQIM through Roger in order to be left alone in Algeria. And Roger, with the acquiescence of Total, was taking five percent off the top. But she had nothing that would stand up in court, so she had held off saying anything to the general.

* * *

Al Khalil was visiting Paris and they were at the Chernoviz safe apartment. The captain was finishing a glass of red wine, and al Khalil held a glass of lemonade in his hand. They were sitting back in easy chairs. The TV was on but the sound was turned low.

"My office is coming up in the world," Roger said. "Somehow we were assigned an ENA graduate. Incredibly, she is knowledgeable about North Africa. In fact she was born in Mali, around Timbuktu."

"I suppose you're lucky to get talented help. I wish I could say the same. But she doesn't sound French. Is she?"

Before answering, Roger stood up and went to the kitchen to pour himself another glass of wine. The weight of each step extracted a squeaking complaint from the pre-war parquet floor.

"That's an interesting question. I guess she could claim a Malian passport, a French passport, and even an American passport."

Roger explained his statement.

"Doesn't the fact that her stepfather is an American diplomat give your security people a problem?"

"He's not only a diplomat, he's also an ambassador. But, on the other side of the scale, her grandfather is head of our organization."

Startled by Kella's background and credentials, al Khalil paid close attention now. This was information he could possibly use.

"Really? And her father, or stepfather, where is he an ambassador?"

"You won't believe this—Israel."

Detecting he was on the cusp of actionable information, Tariq asked, "When she goes to visit, I want to know."

He was aware of his sudden authoritarian tone but didn't bother to disguise it, knowing he didn't need to.

★ ★ ★

A few days later, in her DGSE office, Kella received a CIMETERRE report, a transcript of a telephone conversation between al Khalil and Salim.

AL KHALIL: I am proceeding successfully with our Gaza friends. We'll be on the ground in a week.

Using an Internet bulletin board on vegetarian cooking as prearranged with Steve, she shared the information with him.

He replied:
> As I told you last time we met, the enchilada wannabe wants to transfer his cooking to the East. If we're going to affect the outcome, we need to be in the same kitchen. Could you pay your parents a visit? The date for the ceremony to which I invited you is coming up and I'll be there as I hope you will also. We can discuss that on the phone.

39. On the Road toward Taba, Egypt

Al Khalil confirmed with a glance that two Egyptian police cars still sandwiched his bus. The Egyptians had insisted, explaining it was a routine practice adopted following the killing of tourists near Luxor. He and his thirty men had left the fourteenth century Monastery of St. Catherine, in the Southern Sinai, that morning. They were heading north along the Red Sea coast toward the resort on the Egyptian side of the border with Israel

Al Khalil looked at his men. Some were dozing. Some were praying, fingering their prayer beads. Except that, as part of their disguise, al Khalil, under the Islamic concept of *Taqiyyah*, concealing one's Muslim faith for self-protection, the prayer beads were rosaries and they were all in the garb of Cistercian monks.

Al Khalil, who had spent much of his childhood in Belgium, where the Trappists had several monasteries, seized on the monk disguise because the Cistercians had split from the Benedictines in the belief that life in the abbeys was becoming too comfortable. They had established a reformist Cistercian order, its vows including the observance of nearly complete silence. Another, even stricter, Cistercian order, the Order of Cistercians of the Strict Observance, was created later.

To have his Salafists remain as silent as Cistercians fit al Khalil just fine. In his explanation to his men, he pointed out that they could not be questioned individually at the border. But personally he was just as happy that they remain quiet. Al Khalil, or Father Jerome Benoit, as his current passport read, was the only one in their group permitted to speak in order to facilitate the trip.

As part of their cover, many carried away souvenirs and religious trinkets from St. Catherine. However, the Salafists had considered the visit well within the parameters of their religious beliefs. St. Catherine's Monastery was located at the base of *Jebel Musa*, or Mount Moses, a fourteen-thousand-eight-hundred-foot peak where Moses, one of the prophets accepted by the Quran, was said to have received the Ten Commandments. The Monastery was also built on the site of where Moses was believed to have seen the Burning Bush. Also of interest to the *jihadists* was the Mosque inside the walls of the Monastery. Al Khalil had planned the visit as a means of strengthening their cover, and perhaps also a reconnaissance of a Christian site to be soon reconquered.

While getting his men ready in the Malian desert camp for the coming operation against an Israeli nerve center, al Khalil had told them, quoting from an al Qaeda manual, "The confrontation that we are calling for does not know Socratic debates, Platonic ideals, or Aristotelian diplomacy. But it knows the dialogues of assassination, bombing, and destruction. Islamic governments have never and will never be established through peaceful solutions and cooperative councils. They are established as they always have been, by pen and gun, by word and bullet, by tongue and teeth."

Al Khalil trusted that, even if they couldn't understand the meaning of Socratic debate, they did understand the rest.

* * *

The convoy had to stop for three roadblocks and it was late in the day when they reached Taba, an Egyptian resort where his Hamas contact had told him the control checks were not always as thorough. Rather than try to face the Israeli security gauntlet that night, they stayed at a hotel. They left early the next day and walked across the border, vehicles not being allowed through.

Father Benoit said that they were on a pilgrimage to Jerusalem. He explained their vow of silence, and that they came from six monasteries in Belgium.

"I come from the Monastery of Orval. Maybe you have heard of it."

"Orval beer? How about St. Sixtus beer? Why is it so expensive?" the Israeli guard examining the pile of passports asked, smiling.

Surprised by the guard's question, al Khalil, whose research on his cover had not been sufficiently thorough, replied, "Our Trappist monasteries started making beer in the nineteenth century. Since we don't eat meat, it's a welcome addition to our diet. In those days, it was much safer to drink beer than water. We also make cheese. Beer and cheese give us the income we need to live and to maintain the monastery, a little bit like your *kibbutzes*, I imagine."

"What about St. Sixtus beer? Why so expensive?"

"I suppose the price is simply a reflection of the supply and demand."

The guard looked up at al Khalil speculatively.

"I suppose. It's famous even here. I'm not a *kibbutzim*, but you're right. It sounds very similar. Are you visiting anyone in Israel? You're not importing any beer are you?"

"No, we don't travel with beer bottles. We'll definitely stop to visit our Trappist brothers at Latrun. And, of course, Jerusalem. And, if we have time, other sites with religious significance. But Jerusalem is our first priority of course."

"I notice that your passports are not all Belgian or Dutch. Why?"

Al Khalil again was surprised. Though he did not easily become anxious, he felt a fresh prickle of sweat. This seemed an unusual depth for a screening. The questions, although not hostile, were precise and insistent under the cover of social chit-chat. The guard was obviously trying to lull him into complacency, to lower his guard. But no Jew would ever be smart enough. He found the interrogation offensive, especially considering the source.

His body tightened. He fought to keep his composure. With exaggerated slowness, he said, "Right. The six Belgian and Dutch monasteries sponsoring this trip each has an exchange program with other monasteries all over the world, wherever we have brothers. As you can tell, we have nationals from South America and from Canada, Australia, and so on."

Tariq had carefully asked his Saudi contact to produce passports from non-Muslim countries, in order to keep Israeli security concerns to a minimum.

The Israeli inspector was friendly enough but was obviously following a well-structured set of questions. Unfortunately, the guard knew more about Belgian beers than al Khalil had anticipated.

They were through in two hours, walked out, and saw their Israeli transportation: another bus. One was driven by Hussein, who had arrived earlier by himself through Tel Aviv airport with an alias Sri Lankan passport. His cover was that of an agent to provide transportation, hotel accommodations, and coordinate the group's travel and logistics. They were on the road for forty-five minutes when Hussein alerted Tariq that he thought a car was following them—at a discreet distance, but nevertheless following them.

"If that car is still there before we make the next turn toward Ashdod, let's go toward Jerusalem instead. I don't want to have to abort this early in the game."

Tariq looked at his map and gave Hussein directions.

"We don't have a choice until the main road turns west and becomes Route 25. If we still have a tail by then, continue straight north and stay on number 90. That way, we also avoid going by Dimona. If they have suspicions now, driving by Dimona is not going to help. We'll go to Jerusalem, just as I told the border inspector was our intention. We can spend a day there. I'll have to change the timing with Hamas. They expect to transfer the weapons tonight at the Ashqelon Crusader Castle, where they're hidden. It will delay the final attack by twenty-four or forty-eight hours. You can tell Rashid and Karim in Gaza."

The Israeli follow-on car let them go after they passed the branch—off to Route 25. Al Khalil looked at the desolate landscape of the Dead Sea: a green-blue lake surrounded by tortured salt and limestone formations. The road went through washed out yellowish rocky terrain. He looked to his left, to the West, and saw what must be Masada, now a four-hundred-meter-high publicity icon on which the myth of the Jewish nation had been founded. He turned away in disgust.

40. Herzlia, Israel

"Can I use the car to go to Tel Aviv?" Kella asked. "I need to buy lighter clothes. It's hotter here than I'm used to in Paris. Besides, I should probably buy a new dress for the investiture in Jerusalem. What do you wear to a knighting?"

Alexandria, her stepmother, replied, "There are excellent shops on Dizengoff. But I do need the car this morning. Ezra is coming in about half an hour. He could drop you off in Tel Aviv and maybe we can meet for lunch on Dizengoff."

Kella agreed. She liked Ezra, her stepfather's driver. He had already shown her a photograph of his two daughters, ages eight and eleven, both dark haired with huge smiles. Ezra was an Iraqi Jew, born in Baghdad, who had made *aliya*—emigrated to Israel—with his parents when he was a young child.

"Ezra, you would do me a favor if you spoke to me in Arabic," Kella told him. "I don't want to forget it. Where does your name come from? Why do I think I heard it before?"

Ezra, in his forties with dark hair and always very correct, said in Arabic, "Yes Miss. I am a Babylonian Jew. I was named after 'Ezra the Scribe' from the Torah. My father wanted me to be a rabbi."

Kella sat down to change her shoes. The TV was on and giving the news in English. The broadcast had already started and a reporter was announcing, "apparently for several years. It was transported by truck from Niger under an agreement reached by

A.Q. Khan, the Pakistani scientist who has been under house arrest for several years. The camp belongs to an organization that calls itself IMRA, the International Muslim Relief Agency, a social-welfare group with branches in several African countries bordering the Sahara. Still according to the *Times of India*, Malian authorities have refused to take its calls while the IAEA has responded that it is looking into the story. Our TV station has done some independent research and determined that IMRA was founded by Tariq al Khalil, a Muslim academic who usually lives in Brussels. We have not yet been able to reach him for comment."

Kella jumped up with one shoe on and the other in her hand. She gave a barely suppressed, "Yes!" pumping her fist at the same time. Her initiative had borne fruit. Her friend had been able to place the information that Coulibaly had passed on to her and Steve in the very-respected *Times of India*. She was very pleased.

Alexandra walked in and stared curiously at Kella.

"What is going on? Something good on TV? The media only tell us about conquests, war, famine and death."

"Nothing, really. Just before I left Paris, a friend told me she was trying to place an article and I just heard it on the news."

Kella was ready to go when Ezra arrived.

"On second thought, I'll see you at 12:30 not on Dizengoff—too crowded and touristy—but at the Haviage Restaurant. It's Yemenite; you'll like it, on Yermiyahu Street. I don't know the exact address. Taxi drivers will know."

"*Salaam Alaikum*," Ezra smiled when she got in the back of the black Lincoln Town car.

"*Alaikum salaam*," she responded.

★   ★   ★

The ambassador's residence was located in in a residential neighborhood on the northern side of Herzliya, ten miles from Tel Aviv proper. Surrounded by a security wall, it backed onto a public beach and was less than a hundred yards from the sea. It was conveniently close to the Dan Accadia Hotel, also on the beach, where the ambassador played tennis on weekends, often with the Israeli prime minister. They occasionally included the CIA Chief of Station and Ben Gal, the Mossad director.

The car turned right and made its way toward national Road Number 2, which linked Israeli urban centers from Jaffa, just south of Tel Aviv, to Rosh Haniqra on the Lebanese border.

Kella had visited Jaffa the day before. The visit had evoked a painting in the Louvre by the French painter Gros, titled "Napoleon Visiting Plague Victims During His Egyptian Expedition."

As she stood looking out to sea, Kella thought Napoleon's lightning victory over Egyptian forces had opened a new chapter in world history. It brought home to the Arabs—or it should have—the power of European nations to invade their lands at will. She thought the Muslim religion was still dealing with the trauma of their impotence following a period of imperial dominance. For centuries, Muslims found external causes, the Mongol invasion, and Western colonialism, to explain and rationalize their situation. In a weird way, she thought, the attempt to kill Steve in Morocco, and the attack that had killed people she knew in Timbuktu, were a result of Napoleon's victory over the Egyptians.

"You will be surprised to learn, I think," said Ezra, bringing Kella out of her musings, "that Tel Aviv has what you call a red-light district, and we're about to drive through it. It's called Tel Barbach." He chuckled.

Kella looked around but they were still on the coast road.

"The girls hang around here by the side of the road and take their customers to the right, into the dunes," he was still grinning at Kella's surprised look in the rear-view mirror. "That looks like one down there," he said pointing straight ahead about a hundred yards down the road. "I rarely see any of them in the daytime."

Kella did not think the woman in front of them was acting like a prostitute. She limped and seemed to be crying. As they got closer, they could see her clothes were ripped and her hair was in wild disarray, as if she had been in a fight. It was clear she was motioning for help rather than for a paying client.

"I will call for help," Ezra said as he reached for his walkie-talkie radio. "Marine Guard Post One, this is Mobile One."

Kella leaned forward from the back seat and said, "Stop, Ezra, stop, she's hurt! We can't just drive by and leave her here. Put the radio down and stop!"

They were now very close to the woman, who was standing her ground in the middle of the road, with one hand up imploring the black car to stop and the other hand on her leg, where she was apparently hurt. There was no other car in sight. Kella could see that Ezra was torn. He probably had been told never to stop, but the situation looked dire.

"Stop, look at her, and we'll take her to a hospital."

Kella felt sympathetic, given her own recent experiences.

Ezra stopped the car and Kella immediately got out and ran to the woman. She didn't speak Hebrew, so she called to Ezra who was still behind the wheel, "Come on, help me, she can hardly stand. Let's get her in the car."

Ezra took a quick scan of the surroundings before opening his door. He then stepped out to help Kella. As soon as he was near her, two men stepped out from tall bushes on the side of the road pointing Uzis at Ezra's chest. They were still twenty feet away when he wheeled around toward the car, at the same time reaching down for his ankle holster.

He had his hand on his gun when the bullets hit him and knocked him to the ground. The men were moving quickly toward him and he tried again to reach his gun. But a second burst of machine gunfire ripped into his chest, up his neck, and into his face, blowing out the back of his skull.

Kella was struggling with the woman who, now acting strong and healthy, had her arms around her and held fast.

"No! No! Ezra!" she screamed, tears running down her cheeks, as she saw the men fling Ezra's bloody corpse onto the road. Less than a minute had elapsed from the time she had reached the woman and persuaded Ezra to get out of the car.

Two more men appeared, also armed. They forced Kella toward a car hidden off the road, an old, four-door Fiat. One man drove the Lincoln off the road into an area with bushes and palm trees. He covered it with a tarp and battened it down. Kella was pushed into the back seat of the Fiat and was surrounded by her captors—one on each side of her and two in the front.

41. Church of the Holy Sepulcher

"Whether you believe or not," Steve said, "you feel in your bones that something important has happened here."

He stood with other aspirants and knights of the Order of St John of Jerusalem, Knights of Malta, all in tuxedos, on a small square in front of the church. The Knights wore red capes, each with the white Amalfi cross.

"I thought the church would be bigger. It's a tight squeeze with all these other buildings," he said, sounding surprised. They were waiting for the investiture ceremony that would make Steve a Knight of the Order. The Church of the Holy Sepulcher, the central shrine of Christendom, looked up at the minarets of the mosques on each side of it. The church's reddish-brown stone and brick façade rose from street level, without the usual steps leading to a parvis to enhance the building's profile and status. Half of the double-arched entrance was walled in.

"Getting this ceremony approved by the church authorities has been a hassle, I'll tell you," Marshall said. "The church is managed by six warring orders, running from Franciscan Catholics to Copts, Ethiopians, Greek Orthodox, Armenians and Syrians. Each has jurisdiction over a specific part of the church. The Ethiopians, if I recall, own the roof."

He smiled.

"I'm not making this up. By the way, didn't you tell me that you had invited Kella? Isn't she visiting her parents in Tel Aviv?"

"Yes, I did. I thought she would be impressed, my becoming a knight and all. But she's not here yet. It's not like her to be late. I don't know what could have happened," Steve said.

As they were speaking, a patriarch of the Greek Orthodox Church walked by with full gray beard and tall black hat.

They had a few minutes before the ceremony and Marshall brought Steve inside to descending stairs.

"Look," he said, pointing to the left wall where scores of crosses had been crudely carved. "The Crusaders made those. Some of them were Hospitallers, which is what the Knights of St. John were originally called. In fact, what you see was rebuilt by the Crusaders after the Fatimids, the only Shiite caliphate, systematically destroyed the building."

A Franciscan initiated the investiture ceremony in the Franciscan Church inside the northwest quadrant of the main church. Because of the many nationalities represented, national anthems were dispensed with, although the American, French, Russian, Canadian and British flags were displayed in honor of the countries of those present.

The grand commander, a Canadian, recounted the history of the Knights of Malta. As Hospitallers, they began in 1099 to assist pilgrims to the Holy Land. Recognized by a Papal Bull in A.D. 1113, they quickly took the form of a military order of chivalry and left the Holy Land after fighting and losing the last Crusader foothold at Acre in 1291. They established themselves first in Cyprus, then for over two-hundred years on the Island of Rhodes, and finally on Malta. There they remained until Napoleon forced them out, and they split in several groups with bases in Russia, the Balkans, Northern Europe, Italy, the Americas and in Australia.

Then Steve's moment came. He stepped forward, kneeled and received the light touch of the sword on each shoulder as the grand commander said, "I hereby bestow on you, Stephen Church, the rank of Knight in the Sovereign Order of St. John of Jerusalem, Knights of Malta."

The grand commander hung the white, eight-pointed Amalfi cross around Steve's neck with a red ribbon, and an assistant placed the red cape with the white cross on his shoulders.

As they were standing outside after the ceremony, a knight who had introduced himself to Steve as Chevalier Desandre—"Antoine Desandre," he had specified—walked up to them. Chevalier Desandre was probably in his early fifties and gregarious. His red cape came down almost to his ankles making him appear shorter than he was. His fleshy face was topped by short russet hair.

"One other bit of history you Americans might like to know," he said, "is that the French officers in Rochambeau's army at Yorktown were all Knights of Malta. There's a painting of the surrender ceremony that clearly shows that all of the French officers wore the Amalfi cross."

Steve was only half listening, searching for Kella.

As the group milled around in front of the church, still dressed in their investiture regalia, a monk in a brown robe walked by. The monk was looking down in apparent prayer but his glance strayed to the unusual sight of the knights. Steve glanced at him and, for a millisecond, their eyes met. Steve felt an instant flash of recognition, but dismissed it, his mind on Kella.

Later, in his room at the King David Hotel, Steve checked his email messages and found one from Karim:

Arrived Gaza with my UAV boss Rashid. The father is supposed to arrive in Israel this week with a team from the camp. They will be dressed as monks. I heard that a meeting will take place in Ashqelon before final event.

Steve had given Karim his email address although, at the time, Karim didn't have his own laptop.

He's coming up in the world, he thought, pleased, but even his pleasure with Karim could not push away his disappointment at not hearing from Kella.

He had told Marshall about meeting Karim in Geneva and how al Khalil was adjusting his sights from a long march out of the Sahara to a more instantly gratifying operation somewhere in the Middle East, probably Egypt or Israel. He had not, however, told him that he had decided to go it alone, without the stultifying oversight of the CIA.

He started to tell Marshall about Karim's latest information, when Marshall put his finger to his lips, pulled Steve into the spacious bathroom, turned on the shower, and said quietly, "The Israelis know of my CIA background. You never know," he said pointing at the walls. "Although I hope they've got more important ways to use their time."

"Al Khalil now has a couple of UAV people in Gaza and he and his fighters are somewhere in Israel disguised as monks. I don't know what they're cooking up but it must be important for him to be leading the charge. There's supposed to be a meeting in Ashqelon before the actual operation."

"Monks? UAVs?" Marshall asked. "We can't go to the Israelis with this information. By itself it doesn't mean much. Looks like we should go visit the sights in Ashqelon. We need more information for it to become actionable."

Steve nodded. "This message reminds me of something. Earlier today, I saw a monk walk by—when we were standing outside the church. He looked familiar but I couldn't place him. Now I think it could have been Tariq al Khalil."

"That's his cover to get into the country—'cover for status' it's called. There are thousands of religious tourists in Israel every year, so hiding in plain sight is what he's doing," Marshall replied.

Before they left, a special TV news bulletin announced that a suicide bomber had just blown himself up, killing twenty other people in a restaurant in Netanya, a resort town on the Mediterranean coast north of Tel Aviv. The TV station had live coverage of the tragedy. The area was cordoned off, but organized chaos reigned. Fire trucks, police vans, ambulances, and uniformed men and women worked amid shocked, sobbing, and wounded civilians, some lying in the street, some looking for friends and relatives.

Steve took a drink from a bottle of water on the table. "Another suicide bombing. I don't know how the jihadists convince these people to do it. I assume the seventy-two virgins story is just a product of the Western media."

Marshall took his shirt from the closet and started to put it on.

"Don't be so sure. More than one bomber, who survived for whatever reason, has talked about the seventy-two virgins as a bonus from God. For me, the greater puzzle is in the statements of support from parents. In my opinion, these young people are just handy weapons. They're being used by Hamas, these..."

He hesitated, searching for the right words. "Demagogues of death, who don't volunteer their own bodies to be blown up. They manipulate these frequently impressionable, naïve youths."

Steve threw the empty bottle in the trash.

"I wonder, is suicide the right word? Usually suicide is a very personal act. To me, suicide is the act of taking your life without being told or forced or convinced. Their society glorifies death. In their own way, they're all Manchurian candidates. This is a lot more about power than it is about religion."

"Yes, as others have done before, Hamas and the others are using religion as a front, as a cover for their own ends, to gain and exercise power."

Marshall slipped his tuxedo jacket on and velcroed the red ribbon holding his Amalfi cross near the top button of his shirt in back of his neck.

"Well, let's go down to the dinner, the last official event in your investiture, and the last speeches. Maybe Kella is downstairs looking for you. We'll go to Ashqelon tomorrow and try to get a lead on al Khalil. If he's dressed as a monk and his team is using the same cover, they shouldn't be that hard to find."

As Marshall walked out, Steve said, "I called Kella earlier. I left a message. I'm beginning to worry. I'm going to call again now. Hopefully, she'll tell me she's waiting downstairs. I'll see you down there in a few minutes."

42. Brussels: Mossad Safe House

The apartment windows were cloudy from the soft rain that had been intermittent over the previous few days. The city was dark and glistening. David Ben Tov, Salim's Mossad case officer, his *katsa*, had arrived a half-hour early to do a little housekeeping. He made a mental note to get operational funding for a maid.

The doorbell rang, and David let Salim in.

"We haven't heard very much from you lately. Is anything wrong, Salim?" David asked after giving him a cup of coffee.

"Where is al Khalil?"

"I told you about our conversation in Gao. He wanted to attack Israel. But I followed your suggestion, and I convinced him to focus on Iran instead."

"And what is al Khalil doing now? Where is he?"

"I haven't been in touch with him recently—I don't know. I assume he's probably in Niger or Mali, back to the Sahelian project. I would know if he was in Europe to give a speech."

"Wasn't Israel his real target?" David asked. "Don't you think he's planning something against Israel?"

He tried to look directly in Salim's eyes, but Salim looked at a watercolor on the wall with the hint of a grin. He turned to David and felt the knot on his tie as if to make sure it was perfectly centered.

"I don't know that."

"If he is, tell me. Another conflagration in the Middle East is not going to help anyone, least of all al Khalil and the *Ikhwan*."

* * *

After the meeting, David went his through his surveillance-detection route before returning to his Israeli Embassy office on Avenue de l'Observatoire. There, he sent his report to Mossad headquarters in Tel Aviv.

Salim's evasive manner is troubling. The Gao meeting probably was a watershed. With a man of al Khalil's stature and vision, nothing is out of the question. In the absence of other information, it is best to assume the worst. While we have been fortunate to keep him away until now, his focus may have changed. We need to alert our sources within our borders.

43. Jerusalem: El Wad Street

"*Marhaba*, welcome," said Mahmoud Salah, the Hamas operations chief, to al Khalil and Hussein as they stepped into the apartment on the curved main thoroughfare in the city's Muslim Quarter.

"I have occasion to think of you every time I come here by way of the Jaffa Gate. Did you know that its original name was *Bab al Khalil*? Some people still prefer to use that name."

They were in a well-furnished living room. The man who had opened the door was tall, physically young, but with old eyes that had seen more than their share of violence, injustice, and suffering. Tariq and Hussein, who had changed from monks' robes to less conspicuous slacks and shirt, sat down on a low and long banquette against the wall at Mahmoud's invitation.

"The time to bleed the invader, the occupier of Muslim lands is here, *Alhamdu'llah*. With your help, and with Allah's blessing, peace be on Him, we are going to show the world the righteousness of our cause," al Khalil said.

"*Alhamdu'llah*. I trust your journey was pleasant and safe. We were expecting you earlier."

"Yes, the border control point took longer than I expected. Are you in touch with Rashid and Karim?"

"We have received their equipment. Getting it through the tunnels under the Egyptian border took a month. Your men needed more time to assemble the planes and the ground stations. They are ready now. My entire operation has been devoted to this project. We have been able to do nothing else. When you give the green light, we will help your men to deploy them to the takeoff point. Our commitment is total. The risk is high. But I agree that the stakes are worth it."

"Yes. We could not do it without you. We are in your debt. But we all work for the same goals." He paused and then asked, "What about our hostage?"

"My men captured the American ambassador's daughter. No problem. We can hand her over as planned."

Al Khalil stood up. "His daughter? Did your men know the ambassador would not be in the car? Was the American flag on the car furled or unfurled? If there was no visible flag, then your men should have known that the ambassador was not in the car."

Looking pointedly at Hussein, al Khalil continued. "Hussein, did you explain all this when you helped plan the kidnapping?"

Al Khalil again looked at Hussein and shook his head, deflecting his dissatisfaction toward his own deputy since he needed Mahmoud's assistance.

Mahmoud interrupted. "His daughter may be even better. An ambassador is in the government's service. There is little sympathy for a government employee, a functionary. He is supposed to take his chances. Besides, the American policy is to not negotiate for the safety of its own people. But a young dependent, that's something else. And a young woman, that is even better."

"Are the weapons ready and in place, as you and Hussein planned?" asked al Khalil.

"Yes, they are hidden in the Christian castle. A good idea. No one ever goes there except the occasional tourist. Using the

remains of the Crusader occupation is clever. As is your cover, monks who make beer and cheese,"
He laughed.
"It is ironic. It is right. It is an inspiration from Allah, the Most Blessed, the Merciful."
He grinned in appreciation.
"The Jews are not as smart as they think," replied al Khalil. "Tomorrow night, we will pick up the weapons. We will attack the next morning right after prayers. It will be dawn, enough light for Rashid and Karim to fly their pilotless planes, before the roads get busy, and before the workers show up at the facility. There will only be a night crew. Are your men ready, Mahmoud?"
"Yes, it will be a great victory to the glory of Allah, the Most Blessed, the Merciful."
As they were leaving, al Khalil looked at Mahmoud.
"Islam has two sides. While we submit to Allah's Law, we also have a duty to have others submit as well. And that makes Islam a warrior's faith. It is written, 'It is in the nature of Islam to dominate, not to be dominated, to impose its laws on all nations and to extend its power to the entire planet It's time for the world to see this other side, to feel the sword of our faith."
Hussein, who recognized the statement as one of Tariq's favorite exhortations to his men during training and indoctrination, nodded, and Mahmoud replied automatically, "*Alhamdu'llah.*"

44. On the Road to Ashqelon, Israel

Steve drove a rental car with his father on Route 35 after turning west at Hebron.

"Any news from Kella?" Marshall asked.

"Her cell doesn't answer. I've left several messages. I also called her parents' house, the ambassador's residence, but I haven't been able to get through whoever is answering the phone. Anyway, I left my name and number but she hasn't returned my call. She can't be home, otherwise she would have called."

"Well, I'm sure she's okay. She may have been needed at some 'command performance' event, something important her father said she needed to attend. I knew an ambassador once whose daughter was the hostess for all of her father's official functions. The wife was not interested—too busy having an affair with the chauffeur who was a major in that country's security service."

"You're probably right. But, after we're done in Ashqelon, I'd like to drive up to Tel Aviv and find out what's going on. So, what's the plan? What are we going to do in Ashqelon?" Steve asked.

"Here's the Israeli checkpoint to leave the West Bank into Israel. There's a line. Let's get the Ashqelon map out."

He took it of his bag on the floor between his feet.

"I think we should split up. You keep the car and I'll find a taxi, pretend to be a tourist and have him drive me around. You focus on the Old City and I'll focus on the New City."

As he spoke, he pointed to the old and new cities with his finger.

"We'll divide up the town. You have the best chance of spotting al Khalil if he's given up his monk disguise. We'll meet at the bus terminal at 5:00 p.m. Here," and he again pointed, "If one of us gets lucky, he should call the other. We'll meet and sort out what we've got. We'll have to decide whether to get the information directly to the Israelis or to go through the ambassador, or the local CIA chief of station."

On the way, he added, "Did you know that Ashqelon is one of the oldest urban settlements, about five-thousand years old? It's where Samson and Delilah had their famous barbershop scene. During the Crusades, because the city was the gateway to Egypt to the southwest and Jerusalem to the northeast, it became the scene of several key battles. It changed hands three or four times, was destroyed and rebuilt almost every time, once by Richard the Lion Hearted and another by Salahdin, the Kurd who eventually defeated the Crusaders."

An Israeli soldier walked up to their car and motioned for them to lower the window.

"Passports, please," he said, keeping his Galil rifle loosely pointed at them. He glanced at their American passports and said, "That line on the left." Then he moved on to the next car.

Steve pulled out of the line and got into a shorter one where they were asked to get out and the car was thoroughly searched. Eventually, they were allowed through.

"If you're a Palestinian, you could be here a long time," Steve said. "Working on one side of the line and living on the other must be difficult."

"It's impossible," Marshall agreed.

"Now that I'm a knight, I feel personally involved in the history of the place."

"The Knights Hospitaller fought at Ashqelon, and you can still see the ruins of the Tower of Blood, also called Hospitaller Tower. Now the area around the Crusader Castle is a national park. There are probably campers, young Western tourists, in the park. And there is a Club Mediterranée right next to the Park by the Northern Wall, not far from the Jaffa Gate."

Once they reached the town and went over the map of the city again, they separated and began their search. Steve kept the car and drove south on Hatayasim past the Painted Tomb, made a left toward the Town Hall and parked near the Histadrut Building in the old city. From there he started walking. He knew there was only a slim probability of finding al Khalil but it was their only chance.

While he was looking around, he thought about where Kella might be. Could she possibly still be in Paris, held up by work? But why wouldn't she have alerted him? If she was in Israel, she couldn't be that busy that she would have forgotten. Or maybe they had miscommunicated about the date? That also seemed improbable.

He walked past old buildings containing restaurants, offices, small hotels, smaller apartments and town houses. As he approached the railroad station, he saw a van pull up to a two-storey house. Two people came out to help the driver carry what appeared to be food, dishes and glasses for a lot of people. Steve assumed the van belonged to a caterer. However, the men who came from the building didn't seem to be dressed for a holiday or a celebration. They looked to be in their twenties and fit. Steve noticed they wore combat boots. But in a world where teenage girls often wore combat boots as a fashion statement, Steve didn't think twice about the caterer van and kept walking.

About half-an-hour later, Steve was walking on a quiet street with no vehicular traffic and very few pedestrians. The van he had seen before stopped about ten feet in front of him, pulling up to the curb. He assumed it was making another delivery, even though it wasn't parking in front of a doorway. Two men emerged from the back and two from the cab. As he drew abreast of the van, they seized him and, before he could even try to free himself, he was hustled into the back of the van, where his hands were tied with plastic handcuffs, and he was blindfolded and gagged with duct tape. As the van started moving, the men threw a large duffle bag over him.

The van moved quickly. He felt they had gone only a short distance before stopping. Still in the duffle bag, he was carried out. When they extracted him, they tied him to a chair, still blindfolded.

Steve assumed that although he was looking for al Khalil, clearly the man had found him first. He expected the worst. There was no reason he could think of why his life would be spared. Why hadn't they just killed him in the street? Perhaps his captors thought that their chances of getting away were greater if they killed him in more controlled circumstances? Suddenly he feared for his father. Would they track him down too? They might surveil the car to see who came back to it. He thought of the keys in his pocket, with a tag that provided the license plate number of the rental car.

His more immediate thought was to escape. He wasn't sure if anyone was in the room with him but he thought not. He stayed very still but couldn't detect movement, breathing, or scraping of a shoe on the floor. By peering down, he had a minute window through which he could see his knees and, if he moved his head, a small patch of floor.

He couldn't see his bonds. He tried to loosen his hands tied behind his back but only succeeded in cutting the skin to the point of bleeding. He tried to move his feet as well but to no avail.

Since he couldn't get away, what could he say to improve his situation, assuming he had the opportunity to say anything? He would stick to his tourist cover. He had no brilliant idea. Talking was probably not in his captors' plan. He wondered if al Khalil would question him or if he would leave it to someone else. Would al Khalil know who he was? Or recognize him? Was this still about the Quranic document? After what seemed to Steve to be at least an hour but was probably much less, he heard someone come in the room and walk toward him. Then the tape was ripped off his mouth and blindfold was removed. Tariq al Khalil stood before him and dismissed the two men who were with him.

Al Khalil seemed taller somehow. His gray eyes were laser-like Steve now understood what Kella had meant about his eyes—like a snake hypnotizing its prey, she had said. He stood about three feet from Steve, his arms crossed, dressed in black slacks and a dark blue long sleeve shirt. He noticed that al Khalil's beard, shaven when dressed as a monk, was now starting to grow back. He understood all too well that this was a dangerous man.

"*Marhaba*," Tariq said mock-graciously. "I know you, Steve Church. Do you believe in fate? Is it fate that you keep cropping into my life? Why are you here? I saw you in Jerusalem wearing a costume. Was that a Christian cross, a crusader cross, perhaps? We know that you are all crusaders, wanting to take our lands, you Americans and the Jews. You're the ones who want to go back in time, not us. Or are you still doing research to prove that the Quran is a false document?"

"I know you too. Tying me up like a sausage is a strange welcome. This isn't the Arab hospitality that I've heard about," Steve replied.

Al Khalil's lips compressed into a thin, unfriendly line.

"This will add to your extensive experience with Arabs. I don't have a lot of time to spend on you. Tell me why you are in Ashqelon."

"Do I need a reason? I've never been to Israel before and, since I was here for a ceremony in Jerusalem, I'm trying to see some of the country."

Al Khalil waved his hand dismissively.

"That's not good enough. You seem to turn up wherever I go. I learned that you were in Timbuktu. What in the world does the CIA want in Timbuktu? Yes, I know you're with the CIA. You didn't take a lot of precautions to hide it when you were in Morocco."

Surprised at the accusation, Steve countered, "I recognize the symptom, common in the Third World. It's called CIA Fixation—the CIA is everywhere-and-they're-after-me-syndrome. But speaking of Jerusalem, wasn't that you dressed as a monk in front of the Church of the Holy Sepulcher? When did you convert to Christianity?"

"You must have been dreaming. Unlike your Pope's declaration that Islam acts against reason and therefore against Allah, I am trying to reason with you. Islam is not violent unless forced to be. Tell me what you are doing here."

Now that he could see, Steve reviewed what he knew about his captors. There were at least the four who had snatched him off the street, plus al Khalil and a couple of other men he had heard when being brought up the stairs. Did they have weapons? Al Khalil appeared unarmed.

Steve guessed he was on the second floor. The bedroom had a window. He was thinking that he could probably overpower al Khalil and let himself out the window and down to the street. Whatever he did had to be quiet, though, and it had to be quick to succeed. However, nothing was possible until he was untied.

"Why don't you untie me and show me that Islam is still the faith of the civilized, not of the barbarians."

Al Khalil moved to the back of his chair and undid the handcuffs, but Steve's legs remained tied. He smirked and said, "Maybe you can talk better now that your hands are free. Why are you in Ashqelon? Why did the CIA send you here?"

Steve now sensed his best tactic would be to throw al Khalil off track.

"And you're going to put me to the sword if my answer doesn't make you happy? The same way Islam spread the faith, by the force of arms—the bully of the Mediterranean world? Isn't your theological rationale for violence, your excuse, that Allah is beyond reason? That makes all thoughts of human restraint irrelevant. It gives your armies and thugs the right to do anything at all, including the use of suicide bombers and the mass killing of civilians, in order to bring the rest of us to submit to Islam?"

At first al Khalil's smile had made an effort to resurface. He even appeared mildly amused that Steve would dare to go toe-to-toe with him on the subject of religion. He answered by walking up to him and slapping him with an open hand.

"You, as an unbeliever, cannot use Allah's name without risking your life. You forget that Islam modernized the Western world. Our thinkers, Averroes, Avicennes, Ibn Khaldun, brought the Europeans out of their Dark Age. You're showing your ignorance by looking down on Islam."

Steve tested his ropes by trying to force his legs apart whenever he thought al Khalil was looking away but had no luck.

"All the men you named were rational, or rationalists, *in spite of* Islam. One was Persian and the other two, born in Andalusia, were a product of the mixed Arab-European culture. I wonder what any of them would say about today's Muslim violence and intolerance. When the West complains about Muslim violence and intolerance, what is the Muslim reaction? Its leaders send crowds into the street to destroy and kill, making the West's point. And if Islam has any intention of fitting into the current century, Muslim leaders need to understand that they have to recognize basic rights, such as practicing whatever religion you choose, or none at all."

Al Khalil now paced in front of Steve. He moved his hands from behind his back to point a finger at Steve each time he asked a question or rebutted a comment.

"Hypocrite! You Christians murdered and pillaged our towns during the Crusades. Wasn't that violence? And what about the civilians you killed in Afghanistan, in Iraq?"

"You're right about the Crusades. But that was a thousand years ago. When you kill non-combatants it's by design. When we do, it's unavoidable because your people have this habit of hiding your soldiers and your artillery in schools and hospitals and mosques."

Al Khalil sneered in fury.

"There are no civilians, no non-combatants in the West. You are all guilty. Either you voted for the leaders who do war against us, or you are all in armed forces in one way or another, or you pay taxes for your war machine."

Steve was pleased that al Khalil was no longer focused on the reason for his presence in Ashqelon. He continued.

"We moved on, we progressed, we had a reformation. You didn't. Your theology and your way of life are still locked into the twelfth or thirteenth century. The Quran was probably useful and even progressive a thousand years ago. But it has forced Muslims to stay behind the rest of the world. Am I not right?"

At once, by the look of fury on al Khalil's face, Steve realized he'd gone too far.

"Blasphemer!" His voice was rich with fury. "To call the word of Allah, may He have mercy on us, 'useful'! Dog! If I didn't have a better use for you, you would be dead."

He went to the door and called out, and the kidnappers returned. At al Khalil's orders, they put the handcuffs back on Steve's wrists, in front of him this time, and led him out of the room. Al Khalil personally replaced Steve's blindfold, tightly.

As they moved him down the stairs, a somewhat calmer al Khalil said, "When these houses were built, they all had to include a bomb shelter. Most are made of reinforced concrete with no windows, always under the house. You can reflect in there. Oh, I almost forgot. You'll find someone you know in there as well."

Although he couldn't see him, Steve turned around quickly toward al Khalil on the stairs above him waiting for him to reveal the name of his other prisoner. Could it be possible that al Khalil had also captured his father? He didn't want to ask, afraid to give him more information.

★   ★   ★

That night, al Khalil sent Hussein and four of his men in two vans to the national park on the coast. In the dark, they entered through the central Jerusalem Gate, lifting the barrier to allow the vans through. They turned left at the main parking lot and right toward the water. Another left and they were in a small parking area on the south side near the ancient citadel close to the beach. There, they met two more of their comrades whose cover was that of vacationers at the Club Mediteranée next door to the park.

"Izem," Hussein asked, "are all ten of you at the club?"

"Yes, *Alhamdu'llah*. We are ready. We had no trouble when we arrived at the airport. And the Club Mediteranée bus was there to meet us. *Taqiyyah* is good."

He smiled suggesting that wine and women were sacrifices he was willing to make for Islam. Hussein was not amused. He motioned toward the Club Med to the north.

"Your men should all be here. We brought another van to bring them with us. Tariq wants us all together tonight so we don't waste time assembling in the morning. Go get them while we put the weapons in the van."

Mahmoud, the Hamas military chief, and several of his foot soldiers had been waiting for them in the parking lot.

"The weapons cache is nearby," Mahmoud told Hussein. "We have to walk toward the jetty, on the beach."

* * *

When Steve didn't show up at 5:00, Marshall waited a half-hour then started walking east toward the old city. He was soon in front of the Histadrut House, where he found the rental car, parked and empty. Unfortunately, Steve had the key.

He walked the old city for an hour before returning to the car. It was still there and still locked. He had seen no sign of Steve. He had tried to call him and left several messages, but Steve had not returned them. Knowing Steve was eager to get up to Tel Aviv to check on Kella, Marshall was surprised at his son's disappearance. Could he have been arrested? Hurt in an accident? He tried to find out about hospitals but not enough people spoke English, and getting telephone information was impossible. He found a hotel and rented a room. It was clear they were there for the night.

After dinner, Marshall went out walking again. The car was still there. After about thirty minutes, he knew from the sound of the waves and the salt air that he was close to the sea. It was now dark but he kept walking and looking. He made a left on Hatayasim and saw signs for the Club Mediterranée on the right. He continued past the CLOSED sign at the Jaffa Gate entrance to the national park. He turned right into the main parking lot and went toward the beach.

Not knowing exactly what instinct was leading him, he turned left at the old rampart wall. As he walked he heard men talking in muted voices somewhere in front of him. The language sounded Arabic. He continued to walk toward the sound but he moved more carefully.

The voices came from a small parking lot. There were several vehicles but none had its lights on. The sound of Arabic told him these were not tourists camping in the park, and he was puzzled that they were there at night. He stopped and then retraced his steps to take the stone stairs down to the beach. Now he could see the outlines of several men going down the steps toward what he remembered to be the southern limit of the park, where the ruins of the Hospitaller Tower were located. After the last man in the group had reached the beach and turned left, Marshall advanced, wary of being caught between the men and the steps from the parking lot, in case there were more people coming.

It sounded to Marshall as if the group had stopped and that the men were digging. He started to get closer but he could see no possible hiding places in case they turned around and came back. He stopped and listened. The men were still working. Then he heard them coming back toward him and he backed up. As he passed the steps, another group of men came down and they called out to him in Arabic in low voice. He hurried away past the steps along the beach. The man who had called out to him from the steps stopped once he reached the beach and looked in Marshall's direction, hesitated, then walked away from Marshall toward the digging.

Now Marshall was trying to put some distance between him and the voices. But before he reached the steps to the main parking lot, he heard running steps behind him. He ran up the steps and heard the steps getting closer. He decided that the legs chasing him were younger and faster than his, and he jumped off the stairway, listened, and went back down toward the beach along the rampart.

Supporting beams were jutting out of the old wall and he lowered himself onto one, then another, and then dropped to the beach. He hoped his pursuers would continue into the parking lot and assume he had driven out. However, he realized that another person had stopped and was looking down in his direction. He froze at the base of the wall. He stayed there a minute without hearing any sounds above to indicate his pursuer's intention or direction. He moved to the right, away from the suspicious group and heard one man calling the other above him. They were coming down to look for him.

He first ran farther to the right but knew they would catch him in a footrace, so he headed for the water's edge and entered the shockingly cold Mediterranean. He submerged himself completely and pulled himself along the bottom toward deeper water.

He was about thirty yards out when he heard the popping sound of a small-caliber weapon outfitted with a silencer. He submerged completely and swam for his life toward deeper water. He hadn't heard the bullet's splash and wondered if the shot had been fired at random or at him when he surfaced.

He changed direction and swam parallel to the beach before surfacing again. As soon as he came up, he felt the sting of a bullet hit him in the shoulder, above the left collarbone. He was running out of breath but submerged again and tried to swim a few yards before he was forced to come up for air. His left arm suddenly was useless. There was no more shooting. He looked toward the beach but could see nothing except the black outline of the ramparts. If his pursuer was on the beach, he couldn't see him. Perhaps he was kneeling. He tried to swim again, realized he was going against a light current and turned on his back. He floated with the current toward the area of the digging.

45. Gaza

Rashid visited Karim in his make-do hangar, an old warehouse used by a grocery store chain in the days when the Israeli border was open. For several weeks, they had been assembling the UAVs that Hamas had brought from Egypt through the tunnels.

Rashid's message was simple.

"Karim, I want the planes technically perfect by noon tomorrow and fueled by 4:00. We'll be up most of tomorrow night, and the next morning it will be show time."

The next night, under orders from Hussein not to reveal the final details until the last possible moment, Rashid briefed Karim in the Gaza City apartment where they had been living.

"We have two targets and separate takeoff points. The dispersal will increase our security. Everything has to be ready by 4:00 a.m. tomorrow. This is what we've been working for all these months."

There was knock on the door and a key turned in the lock. Mahmoud Salah walked in. He could see that Rashid had started to brief Karim.

"Go ahead, go on," he said, as he pulled up a chair to the table Rashid and Karim were using. Papers and maps were on the table, as well as cups, a teapot, and a plate of sugar-coated cookies.

Rashid continued, "My target is Palmachim Air Base near Yavne, just thirty-four kilometers away. It is a base for helicopters, UAVs, and the Arrow anti-ballistic missile. Karim, my mission is to support your strike against the actual target, a secret defense installation south of Palmachim and close to the Nahal Soreq Nuclear Center. You will enable al Khalil's fighters to take the objective. They plan their assault as soon as possible after sunrise to give you enough light to see. Tomorrow, sunrise will be at 06:20. I want you to be over your target as soon as possible after sunrise but no later than 06:40. Mahmoud has a sketch of the place."

Mahmoud pulled a hand-drawn sketch from a manila envelope when Karim interrupted him.

"If you have the coordinates, why not look at the Google Earth satellite photo on the computer?"

Mahmoud turned abruptly toward Karim.

"I have better information right here. You can look at your damn computer later. Besides, I bet the Israelis would not allow their sensitive locations to appear on a publicly available system. The official front, the cover, for the installation is that it is an experimental agricultural development center. All this over here," he said, pointing with a pencil, "is fields. They are growing everything from giant watermelons to giant carrots. This is the main road and this is the access road that goes directly to the gate and to the installation. Al Khalil's commando force will be here," and he pointed again. "They are known to show the place to foreign visitors, mostly from Africa, but once they brought Indians from America, to teach them about drip irrigation. Over here are the buildings for farm equipment. Do not waste time and ammunition on them. Here is the main building. Very large.

Looks like a warehouse. Actually, nothing happens here, above the ground anyway. The real classified work takes place in underground spaces. We don't know how many stories there are down there. Tariq and Hussein are going to find out tomorrow."

Turning toward Rashid, Karim asked, "What is your plan, where will your planes be when I come in from the sea?"

"I will attack first because we want the Issies' attention to be elsewhere than at the main location. Also I won't need as much light and I assume Palmachim has security responsibilities for your target. We want them to be very busy when you attack the farm."

Mahmoud, holding a cookie in one hand, said, "At the same time, I have three suicide bombers attacking Israeli checkpoints and two mortars will be set up to fire at the air base just before your attack. It will cause casualties and distract the Israeli response."

He took a bite of the cookie. Sugar stuck to the bottom of his mustache.

Karim picked up Mahmoud's penciled sketch and studied it.

*   *   *

The sun was threatening to appear on the horizon, as Karim prepared to taxi a RUAG Ranger UAV down a field outside Jabaliya, in the Gaza Strip. It reminded him of Colonel Spaceck's words during an early meeting in the El Djazair Hotel in Algiers:

"The advantage of the Ranger over the Predator is first of all the price. Then, it's going to be easier to transport. The Predator has a wingspan of fifty feet, as opposed to nineteen feet for the Ranger. Also the Predator is sold as an entire system of four platforms with a large ground command station. The Predator has a crew of fifty people, more than you can handle!"

Rashid had asked about the craft's armament—missiles.

"Yes, that's a problem," Spaceck acknowledged. "The Ranger's payload is fifty kilos and one Hellfire weighs forty-five kilos."

They had eventually settled on the Ranger. Later, Rashid had customized the UAVs to allow them to carry Hellfire missiles and small bombs.

Karim soon had the Ranger in the air and turned it over to the other two men on his team. He instructed them to "Get it up to five-hundred feet heading directly west, two-seventy degrees." Then he put two additional Rangers up and told their crews, "Fly them west at altitudes of four-hundred and three-hundred feet. One-hundred feet of separation will give us an increased margin of safety when we maneuver them."

A few miles away, Rashid was going through a similar protocol from a beach between the Shati Refugee Camp and the border with Israel to the north.

PART III

And fight them until there is no temptation, and the religion is for Allah.
—Quran 2:193

All our problems come from the Muslim Brotherhood.
—Prince Naif bin Abdul-Aziz Al Saud

06:25 HOURS

Hussein looked at his watch as their small convoy pulled off under trees on a side road. It was 6:15 a.m. They were less than ten minutes from their objective. Hussein thought it would give them at least five minutes more than they needed. His cell phone signaled that it was receiving a text message and he flipped it open: GREEN.

He said to al Khalil, "Rashid's UAVs are up. On time."

"Good."

He looked at the men in back of the covered delivery truck they were using, and told them, "We have twenty-five minutes."

Hussein opened the window, still looking at his watch. He waited. He strained to hear. At 6:25, the faint sound of an explosion came through, and then another.

"The mortars," he said looking at al Khalil.

"Yes and three *shaheed* just reached paradise. I hope they took a lot of Jews with them."

Hussein noticed cars were beginning to appear. He didn't want to stay parked any longer.

"We're right on time," al Khalil said. "Move, go," he commanded the driver.

The men in the back checked their weapons again.

* * *

Following his brief meeting with al Khalil, Steve had been taken to the bomb shelter of the house in Ashqelon. The room was pitch-dark. He knew very well, having gained insights into al

Khalil's operation when he was running Karim, that al Khalil's men were killers. Whatever the purpose for keeping him alive, he doubted al Khalil had any intention to keep him alive longer than necessary.

Although his eyes had become accustomed to the dark, Steve could still see nothing. He assumed there were no windows. His wrists were still bound but he could use his hands to explore by moving along a wall. Then a familiar female voice in the room said something in Arabic.

"Kella? Kella? Is that you?"

"Oh, my God! Steve!"

He moved toward the voice and heard her move, apparently getting up. They touched against each other in the dark.

"What the hell is going on? How long have you been here? Are you okay?"

Kella sobbed briefly. In a quiet voice, she recounted her experience since her capture. She had spent one night in another location. She had not gone through any checkpoint and assumed that she had not left Israel. With one exception, no one had said much to her. She was just a tool, a commodity, to be minimally maintained until she could be used.

"At first, I thought that, as the American ambassador's daughter, they would try to exchange me for Palestinians being held by the Israelis. Now, I'm not so sure. Anyway, no one is saying anything to me or asking me anything. Someone gave me a lecture. I thought I recognized al Khalil's voice. He told me about the crimes Americans were committing every day against Muslims, and about the Jewish occupation of Arab land, and that the Americans and the Jews were the real terrorists. But it wasn't a conversation. Al Khalil wasn't interested in a dialogue. How about you, how did you end up here?"

Fearing that whatever he said was being recorded or somehow being listened to, Steve stuck to the same story he had given al Khalil. He was careful not to mention that his father had come to Ashqelon with him.

They slept little, their handcuffs rubbing their wrists raw. At one point, when he determined Kella was still awake, he tried to raise her spirits.

"Did I ever tell you about the first time I was kidnapped in Israel?"

"This has happened to you before?" she asked in amazement.

"Yeah, I was in high school when my older sister came to stay with us from college for the summer. A friend stayed at my house one night. Around midnight, my older sister woke us up. She had brought an Israeli girlfriend with her. They said they were kidnapping us. I remember that the Israeli girl was doing her military service and hoped to go to some Florida college on a tennis scholarship. They snuck us out of the house—with no resistance from us I should add—and drove us to an orange grove. For a couple of hours we just hung out and drank beer."

"Sounds like quite an adventure," Kella said, sounding a bit cheered. "Given your prior experience, I expect you to get us out of this mess."

★   ★   ★

In the middle of the night, Kella and Steve were walked out of the house and put into the trunk of a Renault. It was a tight fit. Steve protested, "We can't breathe in here. If you want to kill us, just do it. If you want us alive, you have to give us more room. Tell them Kella."

Kella translated in Arabic and one of the men agreed. They left Steve in the trunk and moved Kella to the floor of the back seat, covered with a blanket. Other men talked quietly as they loaded into other vehicles. Steve could hear the occasional metallic sound of weapons hitting against each other, of magazines being loaded, and of breeches chambering the first shell. They were moving for about forty minutes. Then they stopped, apparently waiting for something.

As they were waiting, Abdul, the driver of their car, stepped out and called his wife. Kella could hear enough of Abdul's side of the conversation to make out that the driver seemed to be saying goodbye.

"Tell my father that today I will serve Allah's cause well, that he will be proud of me. Tell our son when he grows up; they will be talking about me. I will be known in our history as one of Allah's warriors."

The trunk opened and Steve felt his blindfold being moved to his forehead. The driver leaned over him and showed him the ravaging effects of forty-five years without dental care. Steve recognized his cell phone in the driver's hand. It had been taken from him shortly after his capture. The driver talked to him in a low voice and held the phone open for Steve to see the text message that he had found. The text read:

31 degrees, 43 minutes N − 34 degrees, 49 minutes E; 31-55-59N − 34-42-26E. 06:30 hours tomorrow.

Steve felt confident Karim's message meant nothing to the driver. The driver's gestures and body language indicated he thought he was doing Steve a favor. Steve assumed that his Good Samaritan was putting some credits in the bank. If the operation failed, he would need a friend on the other side. It also occurred to Steve he might have shown the text message to al Khalil first.

The blindfold was replaced and the trunk closed. They began to move again.

06:40

At 5:34 a.m., Lieutenant Schlomo Gazit had scanned his screen. He had been on duty in the Palmachim Air Base SIGINT center building near the beach for nine hours. He knew from the clock on the wall that he had one hour to go. His mind drifted to Sarah, his young bride, who was at home waiting for him. He would be with her in an hour and a half.

Gazit noted that the call originated from outside Israel to a number not registered in Israel. The key word that triggered the message to surface must have been the coordinates, he reasoned. He had hundreds of other messages to screen and not enough time to research the location. The antennae field and the giant satellite dishes located on the base collected millions of messages, most of which were irrelevant to Israel's security.

Gazit looked at the clock again, then at Sarah's photo on his desk. He went back to the message, and the word "tomorrow" gave him a reason to put it in the queue rather than to forward it for action.

An hour later, as he was going off duty, Gazit's eye caught the text of an Arabic language call from a number originating in Israel but from a phone not registered in Israel. The call was to a Gaza number. Leaving it for his relief to take appropriate action, Gazit walked out to his car and hurried home.

★ ★ ★

At the controls of his first UAV, Rashid looked at the smooth waters of the Mediterranean on his screen. He lowered the Ranger's altitude slightly to better evade detection by Israel's coastal radars. As his drone flew over the beach of the Palmachim Air Base from the sea, he could see the space center to his left. He let it go. Rashid's targets were of a tactical nature, Israel's helicopter fleet, its 200th UAV Squadron, and any aircraft that could be called on to counter al Khalil's ground attack.

He headed straight for the two-thousand-meter runway. As he got closer, he could see hangars on its far side and several AH-64 helicopters parked close together. He knew that, even if the rest of his mission failed, and his UAVs were shot down or crashed, the cost of these three battlefield helicopters meant he was more than even. He fired then circled back and dropped a bomb on another group of the aircraft.

Rashid handed the controls of the first Ranger to someone else to bring back to base and he took command of the second Ranger closing in on the beach. He aimed at HH-65 Short-Range Recovery helicopters parked near a hangar. All five machines were evidently ready to go, because their full fuel tanks exploded and became wicks for thirty-foot-high flames with a rising wall of black smoke.

He then focused on anti-aircraft positions and devoted his last UAV against what looked like the base's headquarters building. He ran out of UAVs before he ran out of targets.

★ ★ ★

A few miles south, Karim brought his Ranger over the beach and, within seconds, he was looking at the experimental farm on his screen. He brought the UAV up a hundred feet for a quick look at the overall target, anxious not to hit the wrong building. He identified the access road and looked for the vans he expected to see there. He didn't see them and assumed they were hidden by vegetation near the road. But he only spent a couple of seconds looking for al Khalil and his fighters. He could see the extent of the fields and quickly located his target.

With Mahmoud's sketch next to him, he identified the large parking lot to the side of the main building. He lowered the Ranger's altitude, swung it around to approach the building from the front, lined up the computer-game-like aiming device on the front entrance, and fired his first Hellfire missile. He saw it strike before he raised the nose of the UAV to fly over and to the right of the building.

He circled until he was facing the front of the building again but found that the dirt and smoke blinded his aim. Kicking himself for not having thought of this foreseeable problem, Karim flew to the left, came around to line up the sidewall of the building, aimed, and fired his second missile. It hit the ground about ten feet in front of the wall. The angle was so shallow the missile didn't explode until its nose contacted the wall.

His bad aim turned out to be a lucky mistake. He then directed his Ranger directly south to get out of the way of the two other Rangers he knew were coming in behind him before heading back out to sea, hugging the waves, hoping to make it more difficult for any Israeli pursuit.

As Karim's second missile exploded, al Khalil's four vehicles drove down the access road toward the gate of the compound. The first van drew near and slowed, a guard came out appearing confused and looking over his shoulder toward the first explosion.

As planned, the driver had his window open and, as he got closer to the guard, who was holding his arm up, he shot him. He fired a burst at the guardhouse just as another guard came out. The driver crashed his vehicle through the bar across the road and headed for the main building.

Al Khalil saw the second Ranger fire its missile against the roof of the main building and he shouted in anger. The missiles were supposed to be aiming for the walls to make entrance easier to his fighters. The third followed quickly but overflew the building.

The driver of the van slowed down and stopped to stay out of collateral damage range. The UAV swung around and came at the building low from the side. Instead of firing its missile, it crashed and exploded against the structure.

People ran out of the building. Several fell, wounded or killed by the air strikes. Some of them were armed and uniformed. A tall man in front seemed to be giving orders. He pointed at the approaching vans and spread his few men in defensive positions hastily. The first van came under fire.

Hussein told the driver, "Pull over, quickly!" He turned toward the back of the van and shouted, "Everybody out!" He jumped out first and began firing at the Israeli security detail.

Hussein spread his men out and told them to move forward. "Don't stop here," he said.

Using the sparse cover, Hussein's men quickly dislodged the outnumbered defenders. They were soon at the front steps of the building. Tariq, Hussein and their men ran up the steps toward the entrance. The Renault was following fifty feet behind the last van but was stopped just beyond the gate by a metal plate that had swung up out of the road, either automatically or activated by an alert guard.

Abdul and the other Hamas soldier jumped out of the Renault. One pushed Kella out and the other pulled Steve out of the trunk. With AK-47 muzzles prodding their backs, Kella and Steve, their blindfolds off but their hands still tied, ran toward the building.

07:20

Rashid, Karim, and their crews were busy flying their UAVs back to their Gaza bases when Mahmoud, who was with Karim to monitor the attack on the primary objective, said, "You have to ditch your drones at sea. You can't return them here. The Israeli Air Force will find them and destroy half of Gaza. You should have used them Kamikaze style against the objectives. Call Rashid and tell him."

"We can't do that. We can use those UAVs again."

"Trust me. The Israelis are taking off right now and they're getting ready to retaliate. Don't worry. What you've done is worth a hundred of your drones. Call Rashid and tell him, now."

Karim beckoned one of his crew and turned away from the controls of the UAV he was flying south.

"What if we land them in Egypt, on the sands of the Sinai? We just fly them a few kilometers farther, past Gaza into the Egyptian desert?"

Mahmoud smiled and said, "That's a political decision—above my head. But in the heat of combat, soldiers have to make difficult choices. I think we can handle the results. The Egyptians won't be happy. They'll confiscate your planes, but it might save Gaza from the usual overreaction of the Jews."

"I'm calling Rashid," Karim said as he grabbed his phone.

Mahmoud stood in front of the crews and told them, "Land all your drones in Egypt."

Karim was pleased that Mahmoud had stopped using the word "toys" to describe his UAVs.

* * *

The fires started by the first Hellfire missile spread quickly. Flames surrounded the front entrance and smoke rose above the roofline. Al Khalil and his men reached the top of the concrete stairs leading from the parking lot to the entrance but were stopped by the fire.

Hussein yelled for his men to follow him around to the side of the building where the Rangers had created entry points. They complied and jogged around the building, finding only light opposing gunfire from the few survivors of the initial skirmish. They entered and spread out into what seemed to be a warehouse with offices at one end. The walls were decorated with agricultural posters, and there were signs over office doors in Hebrew and in English.

They split up and pushed further inside, peering around corridors and office cubicles. The two missile attacks against the roof had, against their initial expectations, caused considerable damage. They found bodies, apparently killed by falling chunks of the roof and walls.

An office door opened and two men ran out drawing bursts of gunfire from Hussein and his men. One of the runners was wounded but kept moving across an open lobby toward a corridor. The Israelis stopped and fired a few shots toward the Salafists to keep them from rushing them. Al Khalil's men rushed their position as soon as the firing stopped. The two men were running down the corridor seeking the temporary safety of the next turn, but the Salafists won the foot race and gunned them down. When the attackers reached them, one was already dead. The other had chest wounds and would not live long.

Hussein told one of his men, "We're going to finish clearing this floor. You stay here and find out where the rest of them are. We're looking for a door that will take us downstairs. Kill him after you're done."

Hussein first made sure there were no other live occupants on the ground floor. Then he told four of his men, "Go back to the front gate and hold off the first responders, whoever they are. They might be firemen or they might be assault troops. It's important that you slow them down. We need time to find out where everyone is, where the real work of this place is done. Then withdraw back here. You have your radio."

Turning to another squad of men, he instructed, "Find defensive positions around the building. Keep me informed."

He instructed the rest to go look for locked doors.

"The most secure-looking door is probably the one we want."

They found two doors with numeric keypads. Al Khalil ordered the wounded man brought to the door and asked him, "Where does this go?"

The bloody employee mumbled, "It's just a closet; nothing in there."

Al Khalil took the Beretta 38 from his holster and shot the man in the left foot. He said, "I'll give you another chance. I don't have time for your heroics. Where is the entrance to the underground? Is there an elevator, stairs?"

The man implored, "The door is behind you and to the right. It's in the back of an office marked 'Director.'"

"Carry him," said al Khalil. "He's coming to the door with us."

They quickly found the director's office. Behind an imposing desk was a door leading to a small private bathroom. In the bathroom was another door with an electronic pad.

"What's the combination?" Tariq asked.

"I don't know. I've never gone down there. I'm not authorized."

He was a tanned, middle-aged man in overalls and ankle-high leather shoes. His fingers were short and thick, his fingernails stained by soil.

"You're staying alive as long as you're willing to help us," Al Khalil said. "If that's all you have to say, you're on your way to your heathen hell."

He raised his pistol.

"Wait! Yoram was allowed to go down there. But he's dead and the combination won't work unless the thumb print is first verified," he pointed to the pad which had a two-by-four-inch black plastic screen beside the numeric box.

Tariq ordered, "Go look into Yoram's pockets. No, bring him here. We'll need his thumb."

In a few minutes, Yoram's body was on the director's desk, the blood from his shirt staining the wooden surface. Yoram had been a thin man, balding, in a white shirt. His dead eyes stared at his killers from under stylish rectangular glasses. One of the fighters handed Tariq an address book, which he looked through. On the last blank page were a series of prices in shekels. They were added and the sum was a six-digit number.

Now they could all hear firing outside. Hussein guessed that the first counterforce had arrived and had tried to come down the main access road.

With the sound of machine gun bursts in the background, al Khalil had one of his men stand the body up so that he could press the dead man's right thumb against the vertical screen. Then he punched the six numbers in the order of the sum derived from the address book. He tried the handle but the door didn't open. He reapplied the corpse's thumb against the screen and tried the series of numbers backward. A green light went on.

"Get the body out of the way, and get ready," Hussein ordered.

He pulled on the handle and stepped back for two of his men to fire into the opening. He had the door open about three feet when a blast from the other side of the door blew it completely open, knocking two men off their feet and killing the man closest to the door.

Hussein said, "Booby-trapped, in case the combination was obtained under torture."

He took charge and went through the doorway first and ran down the stairs to his left. His men followed. Looking for other booby traps, they reached the bottom where Hussein saw another door down a narrow corridor. He told one of his men to fire at the lock, which had little effect. Another one placed Semtex against the hinges and the lock below the handle, and blew the door.

Hussein again rushed through the opening, staying low. His men followed on the run and, with guns raised, spread into the rooms on the right and left. They found twenty-two men and women lying face down in a large room equipped with several rows of computer terminals that faced a twenty-by-thirty-foot electronic map of the Middle East. Tehran and several other locations in Iran, Mecca and Riyadh in Saudi Arabia, and

Damascus in Syria were lit in red, with all the other capitals in green.

* * *

Last to go downstairs after the takeover of the building were Steve and Kella. They were marched first into the large, general-purpose computer center, which reminded Steve of a visit to the Houston Space Center, and then into a small side room that contained the building's fuse boxes, spare computers, and computer boards.

Abdul, their driver and now their guard, who Steve could see wanted to get them out of the way where he could watch them easily, found this room and decided it was the electronic equivalent of a broom and mop closet.

08:30

At 5:30 a.m., Lieutenant Colonel Moshe Avidan and his fifty Shaldag troops had begun their day. They had just completed ten days of joint training with the British Special Air Service, the senior special-operations unit in the world. Avidan was pleased that the SAS had chosen to hone its desert fighting capabilities against his Shaldag troops. Each unit had learned from the other.

Avidan had begun the week with a briefing to the SAS in Building 12, the compound from which the Shaldag worked and trained.

"This base was named for the Palmach, the first Israeli Special Operations unit. In 1974 Palestinian terrorists took over a school in Northern Israel. During the rescue, twenty-one children and four adults died. As a result, the Israel Defense Forces reorganized the special units that had grown as a result of the many terrorist attacks.

"As a part of the reorganization," he continued, "Sayeret Shaldag, also called Unit 5101 or Shaldag, was created and based at Palmachim under the air force and as part of the Southern Command headquartered at Beersheba. We are now the country's primary counterterrorist and hostage-rescue unit, and the only one with its own small helicopter fleet. Our workhorse helicopter is the AH-64, which also fires the Hellfire missile."

Avidan kept to himself that his command was also responsible for long-range patrols outside of Israel, and for marking targets for fighter-bomber-launched, laser-guided bombs. He also did not reveal that his troops had fought the Hezbollah in Southern Lebanon.

Moshe Avidan wanted to pattern his career after former Prime Minister Ehud Barak, Israel's most highly decorated soldier, who famously had led the Sayeret Matkal, Israel's primary special-operations unit during the 1970s.

That morning, Lieutenant Colonel Avidan was leading his men on their daily run. They reached the beach. He always led them where the sand was softer, which required more effort. Today they were running without their equipment because they had been on maneuvers with the SAS until the middle of the preceding night.

Avidan loved this part of the day. He had learned from his girlfriend while at Stanford that the runner's high was not produced by an increased level of endorphins, a seventies idea, but because the body naturally produced a chemical similar to THC, the psychoactive property of marijuana. Whatever the cause, he always looked forward to prolonged physical exercise and imagined bliss-inducing chemicals flowing to his brain.

He and the Shaldag unit were several miles away from Building 12 when a UAV flew over their heads. Seconds later, they heard explosions. Avidan made an immediate U-turn on the beach and they started running back, as fast as they could. At 0700 hours, Avidan called the operations center on his radio but there was no connection.

He sent his second in command with his men back to Building 12 to get ready for action and he headed toward the Ops Center. He first saw the smoke before coming around a block of living quarters and he realized that the building had been a target of the attack.

A firefighting unit had just reached the building and was deploying its hoses. Other unit commanders were arriving at the same time but no one had concrete information. The stories they exchanged ran the gamut from a full attack on Israel by the surrounding Arab states, to one single coordinated attack against the primary air bases, to the assassination of the Israeli Prime Minister, to UAV attacks against the country's nuclear center at Dimona.

At 7:40, Avidan and the other officers who had met outside the destroyed Ops Center learned that the base commander had died in the attack. They all made their way to a crisis center half a mile away. There, the ranking officer took charge. Through the communications at the center, they learned that Palmachim was the only base to have been attacked and that there was no general invasion. However, someone at the Soreq Nuclear Center near Yavne had received a phone call saying that a Rafael center had also been attacked.

Avidan was pulled aside by the acting commander, together with the base's air police chief and Avidan's friend, head of Unit 5707. The unit had been created in 1996 to obtain pre- and post-bombardment intelligence during the continuing war in southern Lebanon, a mission that Unit 5707 took from the Shaldag.

Unit 5707 sometimes trained with the Shaldag, used similar armament, and could be used to supplement the Shaldag unit if necessary. The acting base commander, General Uri Shomron, said, "This attack seems to have come from Egypt. Our aircraft were able to shoot down two or three of the UAVs as they tried to get away but the rest crossed into Egyptian air space. Our pilots asked for hot pursuit authorization but they didn't get it from the national command authority, so far. They are authorized to follow them but not to conduct aggressive operations over the Egyptian border."

A colonel brought him a message, which he read. He then told his men, "Jerusalem is getting in touch with Cairo and with the United Nations. A retaliatory attack against Egypt is not out of the question. Our aircraft are already in the air over international waters waiting for a decision to attack. That's the big picture. Now here's your part."

He turned and looked at Avidan.

"There is a hostage situation developing just south of here at the Agricultural Experimentation Center."

He walked over to a map and pointed to the location.

Avidan, still in his running gear, had obtained a towel which was slung around his neck.

"Is that where I heard the other explosions when I was running on the beach? Is it part of the attack on the base?"

"It looks that way. It all took place at the same time. The ground attack was preceded by UAV strafing and bombing. There were also suicide bombings at the border checkpoints in Gaza, all within a few minutes of each other—well coordinated. As I told you before, we received a few mortar rounds on the base. They hit the runway and the canteen. Ten wounded, four killed. We're looking for the mortars. They were probably fired remotely. In any case, Moshe, I want your unit to get ready for a takedown operation against this location," and he pointed to the agricultural station on the map.

He turned to the Unit 5707 commander.

"Your unit will be in support. Go to your units, I'll get you maps as soon as I can. Now I'd like to see Colonel Avidan alone, please."

When they were alone, the general said, "You need to know that this is not exactly an agricultural station. It's really a Rafael installation. I don't know myself what they do there, but it's related to national security. So you're probably not trying to save farming experts—the hostages are most probably scientists and the like. I know it makes no difference, but I thought that I'd tell you. I'll send the maps over."

"Not to worry, sir. We have maps of all government installations in Israel in Building 12."

"Right, I should have known."

The General smiled and shook Avidan's hand. "Good luck, Moshe."

09:15

Al Khalil had expected to find a secret military project underground, and he was not disappointed. Both his and

Hamas's conclusions were confirmed. He understood that taking the building was one thing. It had been simpler than he had anticipated. But now came the hard part, making the most of what was only an intermediate success.

First, he needed to know what this secret installation was, its importance, and how he was going to use it to his advantage.

He was in a room off the main computer center with a large glass partition allowing him to see inside. He called Habib, his Carnegie-Mellon graduate, and told him, "I want you to start interrogating our prisoners one at a time to find out what this center is for. Start with that one over there. There's something about him that tells me he's different. He doesn't look scared but I think you'll figure out a way to make him talk."

The prisoners sat on the ground with their hands tied in back. One man sat almost by himself on the side of the group, stolid and in his own world. The man combed his brown hair down the middle and wore a tie—unusual by itself.

"As you're doing that, have someone collect all the ID cards, everything that will tell us who they are: their ranks, whether any are related, who they work for, everything. In fact, just have them empty their pockets completely. It will give us an insight into each and probably, from their notes and other pocket litter, what this place does. But *sareeah, sareeah*—speed. There is a whole country out there now that wants to take us down."

He went upstairs to check on Hussein and the imminence of an Israeli attack.

★   ★   ★

In their electronic broom closet, Steve and Kella's wrists were still manacled. The room was narrow but deep and lit by a single overhead light. Another door in the back and on the left provided alternate access.

Steve went to the door and turned his back to it so his hands could reach the handle, but it was locked, as he expected. He searched for some tool he could cut through the plastic with but saw nothing with a cutting edge, only electrical wires and related equipment. He was considering breaking a computer screen to use one of the sharp pieces of glass, when the door opened and Izem entered, closing the door quickly and looking behind him.

"So, you're the hostages! Abdul told me he was guarding a couple of Americans. His description fit you to a T. Why are you here?"

"Izem!" Kella cried. "I never thought I'd see a friendly face in this group of killers!"

Steve was astonished.

"The same question to you. Aren't you on the wrong side? Though I'm glad to see you. Can you help us get out of here? Are there other Tuaregs here with you?"

Izem gave Kella a respectful nod, acknowledging her and her tribal lineage.

"I joined like many others, to make a living. After Steve left Mali, I couldn't just live with my brother; I had to earn some money and my military background was my only *métier*. Then, because I had joined, other Tuaregs followed me. Then it sort of got out of control. I couldn't leave. Unfortunately, my Tuareg brothers have become believers in al Khalil and his cause. I lost any control I had over them."

"And what about Karim, where is he?" Steve asked.

"Hussein sent a team to Gaza that includes Karim, Rashid and a few others. Karim controlled the planes that kicked off the attack. Now his job is done."

Kella turned around to show that her hands were tied.

"Can you get us out of these?"

"I can, but this is not the time. There are still more than thirty of us, and the Israelis are probably getting ready to attack. You don't want to get caught in the crossfire."

Izem quickly cut through both sets of handcuffs with a knife he took from its sheath on his belt.

"You better look like you're still tied. Here, I'll put this wire around your wrists. You can get out of this with little effort, and it will be more comfortable."

He substituted a short electric cord for the handcuffs.

"I better go."

"There will never be a perfect time to break out of here," Steve said, "and we can't wait for the Israelis to come. I'd rather take my chances shooting our way out than to get shot by Israeli commandos or by al Khalil in a final act of revenge. The sooner, the better. Get us weapons Izem. Wait," he added, catching Izem before left.

He looked at Kella.

"Kella wants you to rally your tribesmen. Tell him, Kella."

She spoke quickly. "Yes, tell them who I am, my ancestry, and that I expect them to follow our customs. Tell them that to do otherwise will sully their family names. If they won't listen to you, bring them here to me."

Steve had never heard Kella exercise her tribal leadership before. In fact, she had always downplayed it. But he saw by the look on Izem's face she had struck a chord.

"I will come back as soon as I can," Izem said. "Be ready."

Steve saw Abdul peer in suspiciously when Izem went out the door.

* * *

Back in Building 12, a sergeant found Lieutenant Colonel Avidan in his office putting his combat gear on, handling the phone and reviewing maps.

"Sir, our helicopters were destroyed in the UAV attack. I'm trying to obtain replacement choppers but there's a lot of confusion out there. No one wants to make a decision, to sign off on an authorization."

Avidan looked up from the maps and shouted, "How is that possible? Where the hell was our antiaircraft defense? Our coastal radars? Was everyone sleeping? Were they on leave? Very well, get me Acting Commandant Shomron's office."

"His office was destroyed. I can't reach him."

Leaning forward with one hand on a map and the other pulling a Sig-Sauer pistol from a bag on the floor near his desk, his voice was a bit lower.

"Call the crisis center, then. And get me the squad leaders in here right away."

Avidan laid out other weapons on his desk on top of the maps.

"Crisis center? Yes, sir."

It took Avidan another thirty minutes to obtain authorization to use replacement aircraft. His five squads of eight-to-nine men quickly took their places on the helicopters. Avidan rode to battle with the first squad. As he looked down at the damage, he felt this was his moment. History would remember his name. His men were divided into groups with one of three primary skills: entry, rappelling and climbing, and snipers. They were equipped with older but extremely reliable M4A1 assault rifles with an M203 grenade launcher attached. Their side arms were Sig-Sauer .40 caliber pistols, the long-awaited replacement for the 9-millimeter model. The snipers used the Israeli-made Galil rifle, from the same manufacturers that had created the Uzi.

After sending a reconnaissance UAV over the building to determine the strength and disposition of his enemy, Avidan took his three helicopters at treetop level toward the objective. Flying at close to two-hundred miles an hour, they were quickly on the target. As soon as they landed on a back parking lot, the Shaldag team found firing positions, which they had chosen from the real time images provided by their reconnaissance UAV. Avidan got on his GroupTalk cell phone and said, "This is Gideon One. We just landed. Tell me how the TIBAM team is coming along. I need them here as soon as possible with their laptops and CD blueprints of this building, to include 3D if they have them."

Avidan could see several men in defensive positions around the building. They moved inside when the helicopters landed. He also noticed several armed men making their way toward the main building from the guard gate in order to avoid being cut off. He sent a squad after them.

At first, the Salafists skirted the fence around the property, until they realized the Israeli helicopters covered the back of the complex. Then, using what sparse cover was available, they headed directly for the building. They almost made it. As they were moving toward the entrance point used by the first assault team, Israeli snipers hit two of them. The other two ran for their lives toward their point of access. Neither made it.

★ ★ ★

Down in the underground center, al Khalil, alerted to the arrival of the Israeli troops, grabbed a phone and dialed the American Embassy's number. When the receptionist answered, he said, "Give me the ambassador quickly. This is urgent."

"Who is calling please?" said the poised and friendly female voice.

"Tell the ambassador that I have news of his daughter. This is an urgent call. I repeat, this call is urgent—for her and for him. Now put him on the phone."

His call was transferred upstairs to the chancery and to the ambassador's secretary, who also asked, "Who is calling please? The ambassador is in a meeting. Let me take a message and he'll get back to you."

"I told your other receptionist this call was urgent. It's about the ambassador's daughter."

The next voice, a male, said, "Hello, this is Ambassador Hastings. Who is this?"

"I have your daughter, Kella. If you want her back alive, get in touch with your Jew friends and tell them to stop the attack that is now under way against my position. I am in command of what the Jews call the Desert Agricultural Center near Palmachim Air Base. They will know exactly where when you call them."

There was a moment of silence. Then Hastings said, "How do I know that you have her, that she is alive? Who are you? What do you want?"

"That's too many questions for now. If you don't tell the Jews to stop their attack, they will be responsible for killing your daughter. I'll call back after the attack has stopped. Oh, I almost forgot. I also have one of your CIA officers, Steve Church."

Tariq al Khalil hung up.

While he was on the phone, Hussein assembled his remaining fighters at defensive positions at the ground level. There they waited for the assault.

★   ★   ★

Downstairs, Habib tried to obtain information from the Israeli scientists. One of the men going through the Israelis' pocket litter had interrupted him.

"Look, two of them have the same last name. They're probably married—Shoshanna and Aaron Amitai."

This gave Habib a plan. He would talk to them separately, first on a scientist-to-scientist basis and then ratchet up the pressure and use violence if necessary. Shoshanna was a nuclear physicist and Aaron, who had a Ph.D. after his name, was an expert on lasers. Scanning through the other IDs, Habib noticed that Amitai was the only one claiming a Ph.D., although he assumed that this might mean he was the only one flaunting his doctorate.

Habib was starting to form an idea of what this center was for, but he couldn't believe the conclusion he had reached. He continued to question the Israeli scientists, one by one, but focused most of his time on the Amitais. He spoke to them as their equal, which he was in terms of education and knowledge, and they responded to him but with very general statements that were not helpful.

Nevertheless, he started to put the pieces together. He knew that the laser, invented in the early 1960s and at first considered to be a solution without a problem, showed its military uses in what was termed "precision-engagement" during the first Gulf War. He was also aware that laser weapons had become serious counter weapons to the ballistic-missile threat. The Airborne Laser program had shown that a missile could be shot down at a range of several hundred miles. On a smaller scale, the Zeus, a laser developed by the U.S. Army, was being used in battle to destroy mines from the air. Another laser weapon had destroyed artillery shells and mortar rounds seconds after they were fired during field-trials. A laser beam, with its speed of light, lack of recoil, and long range, was an attractive defensive technology, because ballistic missiles were constructed with lighter metals, as were aircrafts. They could take down a biological, chemical, or nuclear missile before it even left enemy territory.

Habib went to report to al Khalil.

"I've obtained enough information from the scientists to conclude that we're dealing with some sort of laser gun. But I reached a dead end. They refuse to get into the details I need. If we had more time, I could probably get some of them to cooperate willingly. But, since we need the information now, I think we have to use tactics your fighters are better at than I am."

"Right," al Khalil replied. "You should have told me earlier."

He called one of his soldiers and told him to help Habib, who took him into what had become the interrogation room, furnished with computer stations and maps. He had given orders to tie Shoshanna to an office chair before he left the room to seek al Khalil. This was the first signal that Habib was changing tactics.

"Okay," he said, "we tried it the easy way. Unless you start telling me about the specifications of the weapon, its capabilities and controls, we're going to bloody your neat uniform and your spic-and-span laser center."

She looked at him with wide, defiant eyes.

"I knew it. I'm not afraid. My people have survived the Holocaust. You and your kind are doomed to fail, just like the Nazis."

"Well, we will see how well you survive," Habib said then motioned to the guard who produced a bayonet. Under Habib's direction, he took one of Shoshanna's hands, pressed it on the computer table in front of her and made as if to apply the blade to the first phalange of her little finger. She pulled her hand from his grasp in fright. The soldier then forced her hand back to the table and, with a sudden and powerful thrust, plunged the bayonet through the back of her hand and into the wood of the desk. She screamed in shock and pain.

Habib was startled and somewhat unsettled but he told himself that extreme measures were necessary.

"Now, tell me about the controls. There must be some pre-targeting already programmed. Tell me about that. Give me what I need on timing of the laser and on the power settings."

Her only response was to spit in his direction.

The guard said, "I will get her husband."

Habib nodded and the guard came back with Aaron Amitai who, upon seeing his wife's hand nailed to the table, ran to her and tried to pull the bayonet out. The guard hit him on the side of the head with the stock of his AK-47 and sent the Israeli scientist sprawling. His wife called out his name but Amitai stayed on the floor for a few seconds, blood trickling down his face.

"Stand up," the guard prodded him, then tied him to another chair and, with a glance, handed control back to Habib.

"You can stop this," Habib told Amitai. "Your wife doesn't have to go through any more pain. But you must give me the information I want. We will get it, one way or another."

Amitai said, "You are a fascist devil. I don't care that you claim to pray to some god. It's not any god I've ever heard of. Stop what you're doing to my wife."

Habib motioned to the soldier who pulled the bayonet out of Shoshanna's hand—only a small whimper escaped her—and then walked her out of the room. Habib stayed alone with Amitai.

"Let's get serious," he said. "I graduated from Carnegie-Mellon—physics and lasers. Don't think you can bullshit me. Now talk!"

"Who are you? What do you hope to gain? If you have the education you claim, then you know that this can only have one ending. Israel has been fighting back against people like you for a long time. You will not succeed. Give yourself up. Save your life."

Habib realized he was somehow losing control. How did his prisoner now have the initiative? He felt out of his element. He called the guard back into the room and said, "You can talk with me and provide answers to my questions, or I'll let you alone with him, or better, I'll bring your wife back and he can work on her. It's your choice."

Not getting any answer from the Israeli, Habib told the guard, "okay, bring her back."

Just before the guard reached the door, Amitai said, "Wait" in a resigned tone. He took a breath and said, "For us, this all started during Reagan's Space Defense Initiative project. But I took the Israeli part of the project in a different direction. The United States invited several countries to participate in the research and development phase, and Israel was one of them. Israeli scientists worked on the SDI R and D both here in Israel and in the United States. The key obstacles, the real breakthroughs, took place right here."

He stopped, looked at Habib, and said, "I can't do this."

"Yes you can. Here, have some water. I know that Carnegie Mellon received federal funds related to SDI. Go on, but I don't need history so much as practical applications."

"I need to know that my wife is all right. I won't go on unless you release her."

"I promise we'll release her, but not before you answer my questions. Give me the information and I'll get her released. There's no way I can get her out beforehand. She's lucky that she's still alive."

Amitai collapsed in his chair. His shoulders slumped and he would have fallen out if he hadn't been tied to it. He made a slight gurgling sound and tears came down his cheeks.

"Promise you will release her."

"I swear. May Allah cast me in hell if I don't."

Amitai sat up and continued after wiping tears from his face.

"In any case, the idea was to find an effective way to counter the Soviet missile threat. We were looking at, and experimenting with, lasers powered by hydrogen fluoride. The American idea was either to have the laser in a 747 or to establish stations in space that, with the use of mirrors, could shoot a narrow laser beam to pierce the metal skin of the missile. Either the beam hits the fuel tank and the heat causes it to explode, or the beam burns through the electronics and causes a malfunction."

He paused, as his eyes glanced at the bloodstains left by his wife's hand.

"Although we were initially interested in SDI to destroy theater ballistic missiles before they leave enemy airspace, we had a new weapon after we were able to harness the tremendous power we get from nuclear energy. We realized—actually I realized—that we could now attack land targets, especially infantry. We were no longer limited to ballistic missiles."

"I can well understand how a laser beam could easily pierce the thin metal skin of a missile. But directing it at land targets is of a totally different magnitude, Doctor."

"Obviously. A beam still can't destroy a tank or a building, not yet anyway. However, anyone without protection is vulnerable. So the weapon has the potential to destroy armies out in the open and to keep the enemy's physical infrastructure fairly intact. We moved to deuterium fluoride, which has a longer wavelength and therefore allows easier transmission through the atmosphere. But it also requires larger mirrors."

Habib was extremely conscious of the time pressure. He wanted short answers, not lectures.

"Yes, and where did all this take you? Where are you now? Is the beam operational or still in the research phase?"

"Well, eventually, in 1989 actually, after Reagan left the White House, the Cold War was officially over. Someone invented the term 'peace dividend,' and money was no longer available for such martial enterprises. SDI research dried up. But we were very interested in continuing this research here in Israel. So that's what we're doing."

"I don't believe this is all research. Why, then, the maps on the wall? I can bring Shoshanna back in here if you want."

"Shoshanna herself played a big role in thinking of nuclear power in new ways, in ways that the scientific world will one day recognize as historic watersheds. In the mid-nineties, our leadership, Rafael Industries, convinced Jerusalem to make a huge jump. We would power the lasers with nuclear energy. This would allow us to keep the laser gun here, on the ground, and only have to put the mirrors in space. With a lot of expensive and secret work."

Habib nodded and said, "Did you say nuclear? That's impossible. Well, not impossible, but no one has harnessed lasers to nuclear power."

A smug grin crept onto Amitai's face.

"Our Weizmann Institute has always been in the vanguard; not across the board, we're not a superpower. However, on certain technologies that touch on our survival, we've been on the cutting edge. We haven't publicized our advances, and for good reasons."

Although still extremely aware of the need for quick, actionable information, the scientist in Habib couldn't help asking, "So tell me, as a fellow scientist, how you overcame the obstacles that no one else was able to conquer."

Habib read a mixture of despair and pride in Amitai's eyes, as if he knew viscerally that he was not likely to survive, but that this was his only chance to get his story out. Was Amitai hoping for immortality? Was he dreaming of being mentioned in the annals of science that future generations would study?

"Have you ever heard of LAKAM, the scientific intelligence bureau of the IDF?" Amitai asked. "Have you ever heard of Rafi Eban? He's a living legend in Israel. In 1960 he captured Adolph Eichmann, the Nazi, in Argentina. He's now an elected member of the Knesset, the Israeli Parliament. Eban headed LAKAM when it recruited Pollard, the American spy who is still in a federal prison. LAKAM didn't go away when Eban went into politics. LAKAM was able to collect intelligence from the

Russian, American, French, and Japanese consortium committed to a nuclear-fusion reactor project in Cadarache, France, and from the Livermore Laboratory in California. Being small has disadvantages—resources for example—but advantages as well. We can quickly focus on important projects. We set up a small experimental project. At first we used the deuterium-deuterium process to create helium 3. However, we found that the intense heat and pressure necessary were containable only by using the tritium-deuterium method creating helium 4."

Despite the feeling that he was on the cusp of scientific discovery, Habib forced himself to move on.

"That's impressive, Doctor. But even if you use nuclear energy, you're still left with the distance from the space gun to the land target. So, I see two problems that you must have solved: one, the fact that the beam's energy dissipates with distance, and, two, that the beam tends to be scattered by dust and particles in the atmosphere. Brute force can't be the only answer."

"You first test the scatter effect with a test beam, a smaller beam. Then you use the big laser to send a very specifically distorted beam that will be refocused by the dust and water in the air. But the key is the mirror. We needed bigger mirrors than had ever been used. The bigger the mirrors, the more complex they were. In order to distort the beam, we needed not hundreds but thousands of small actuators positioned behind the mirrors to alter the surface of the mirror to compensate, to pre-distort if you will."

"Yes, adaptive optics has been an essential part of the laser magic. But thousands of actuators? How big is the mirror?"

"I designed and built the biggest space-based mirror in the world. It's one-hundred-eighty feet in diameter."

Habib paused before asking his most important question. "Then explain the control room. And how do you trigger the weapon? How do you target it? Is it now targeted against the red-light locations on the board?"

"The map, as you can see, is only of the Middle East, our 'near enemy.' We can target a city within a fraction of a second. Would the entire city be destroyed? No. Very little of the city proper would be affected, unless the beam's heat starts fires. The beam would have to spread out to the size of the city. And the bigger the strike zone of the beam, the more the energy is dissipated. Further, destroying a brick and mortar building is different from piercing the thin metal skin of a missile that is built as lightly as possible. But anyone who was outside and unprotected within a small radius would probably be killed by the heat."

"That's a fantastic achievement!" Habib said. "I guess none of this is in the professional journals? Otherwise I would recognize your name."

"Aaron Amitai, Doctor Aaron Amitai; it will appear eventually, I'm sure."

"Have you actually field tested it?" Habib asked. "Has the laser gun been activated?"

"We built an entire system one-tenth the size of our current system, and the experiments were successful. We've never fired the actual laser gun, of course. It's our last defense. The United Nations and others can make their 'tut-tut' speeches. But we're the ones who will live or die. Anyway, we have to be ready, and we are. We should have fired it to show the world we had it. As a warning. Shoshanna made that recommendation. But she was ignored."

Habib still hadn't gotten the answer he sought.

"I want to know how to target and fire the laser. Show me!" As a reminder of who was in control, Habib motioned the guard closer.

"My expertise was the space mirror. My wife Shoshanna is more knowledgeable on those details."

Habib suspected that Amitai had manipulated him, to deflect his attention away from Shoshanna, the one with the real answers. He felt vindictive but knew he had no choice. He told the guard, "Bring his wife in here. And get him out. Don't let them see each other."

When she came in, Habib behaved as a more serious interrogator.

"Doctor Amitai," he began. He wasn't sure that she had a Ph. D., but it wouldn't hurt to start with a show of respect for whatever academic credentials she had. It had worked with her husband. "Your achievements here are extremely impressive. Once this comes to the attention of scientific community, you will take your place besides Newton and Einstein in science's hall of fame."

He paused a second to judge her reaction, which by the widening of her eyes, he assumed was surprise that one of the terrorists could speak with at least a veneer of education. Then a terse smile replaced her guarded demeanor, accompanied by silence.

Habib continued, "We are actually going to help make that happen. You're going to show the world your achievement by firing your creation. We're going to pick an uninhabited spot, in the Sinai, say. This will better show the world that Israel can and will defend itself. The current policy of keeping this weapon secret until after you're attacked makes no sense. Don't you agree that its main use is as a deterrent to war?"

"Why would you want to do something that would help Israel?" she asked in a tight voice.

"Because it will also help me. Think about it. We are against some of these Arab regimes, and against the Shiite resurgence flowing out of Iran, just as much as you are. I would like you to show me how your creation works. Your husband told me a great deal about the laser, and he said you would give me the rest, which are the operational directions."

She didn't respond, apparently mulling over and answer.

"The use of the weapon will strengthen Israel," he said. "And your name will become a household word in all of academia."

The guard came in holding something in his fingers. He showed it to the Israeli and she gasped. Habib drew closer and saw that it was a finger, freshly cut and still bleeding.

"I knew it. You are butchers!" she cried.

"Be that as it may, that finger is simply a small example of the alternative to your becoming famous. Do we have a deal?"

She nodded solemnly. Her jaw muscles bulged out.

09:30

His arm still throbbing from being shot, Marshall had floated with the current, which had brought him to the jetty. He held on and, hiding behind a pylon, he witnessed Hussein's men unload the cache at the foot of the Tower of the Hospitallers. One man, apparently on a random basis, would open one of the boxes and take out a rifle or a Rocket Propelled Grenade round and examine it briefly before replacing it and allowing the wooden crate to be carried away.

After the men left, Marshall pulled himself painfully toward the beach. His feet touched bottom and he stumbled out of the water. He followed the beach rather than returning through the parking lot, aware that some of the men might still be there. Eventually he reached his hotel room, took off his clothes to let them dry during the night. He bound his wound—the bullet had passed through a muscle—and tried to get some sleep. The next day, after putting his arm in a sling, he rented another car and drove to Tel Aviv, to the American Embassy.

* * *

Following his conversation with al Khalil, Ambassador Hastings immediately called his wife Alexandra to convey the news about Kella. He then asked his secretary to tell Jack Horton to meet him in the acoustic conference room.

Hastings had relatively little experience in the care and feeding of CIA station chiefs. His previous two postings had been as deputy chief of mission and he therefore had not been in the loop; station chiefs normally reported directly to the ambassador. He had heard horror stories of promising diplomatic careers broken by CIA "flaps," operations gone awry. There was a time, he knew, when, starting under President Kennedy, "treaties" were periodically negotiated between the State Department and the CIA. Nevertheless, most ambassadors felt vulnerable to the presence of a U.S. government agency in his domain whose role, by and large, was to carry out activities considered illegal by the host country.

Hastings and his COS, Jack Horton, had a good professional relationship, however. Horton briefed the ambassador once a week in the acoustic conference room, known informally as the ACR, the clear-plastic room-within-a-room, where all classified discussions were supposed to be held—country team meetings in particular.

Within the limits of "need-to-know," Ambassador Hastings was well informed of the CIA station's activities. Horton had told Hastings he would keep him informed at least to the extent of avoiding unpleasant surprises and to give the ambassador a heads-up prior to particularly risky activities with a high potential of political blowback.

Tall, with brown hair and rimless glasses, Jack Horton reached the ACR when Hastings' secretary was opening the door to the vault that enclosed it. He walked in and opened the lever that held the plastic door closed. A minute later, Hastings joined him.

"Do you have an officer missing?" Hastings asked. "Steve Church? Is there something I should know?"

"I have heard of *Marshall* Church. He was a senior clandestine service officer and one of my predecessors here. But, as far as I know, he's retired. I don't know a Steve Church."

"Steve is his son," Hastings replied. "You don't know anything about his visit to Israel? My daughter knows him. She told me he was here, or was coming. But that's what I wanted to talk to you about."

Hastings proceeded to tell the Horton about the phone call.

"Do you want me to talk to Shin Beth?" Horton asked. "Or are you going to have the regional security officer handle this?"

"You better handle it. If I thought it was simply a criminal issue, somebody trying to extort money, I'd give it to the security officer. But I'm sure Kella's kidnapping is politically motivated. Kella would not have been kidnapped if she were not my daughter. She has become the shield against an Israeli takedown. But inform your Shin Beth contact quickly. The caller said there was an attack under way. The Israelis have to know immediately that my daughter is in the hands of the terrorists."

At that moment, Hastings' secretary peered in and said, "Mr. Ambassador, there's a man named Marshall Church here to see you. He said it was important."

"Jack, you better get in touch with Shin Beth immediately. And then come back and join us in my office."

Marshall walked in just as Hastings was hanging up the phone after briefing the Israeli prime minister. Against all probability in this time of crisis, he had been able to get through.

Hastings offered his hand and said, "I have met your son. In fact your name just came up. Is Steve missing?"

He grimaced and said, "Yes he is. We were in Ashqelon yesterday. We split up, and he disappeared. He didn't come to our meeting point, and he didn't return to the rental car. Steve was expecting Kella to attend a ceremony in Jerusalem the day before yesterday, but she didn't come and Steve couldn't reach her on the phone. Do you have any information?"

Hastings briefed Marshall on the phone call he had just received.

"That's Tariq al Khalil," Marshall explained. "Steve thought he recognized him in Jerusalem but wasn't sure. That's why we were in Ashqelon, hoping to spot him. Obviously, he has your daughter, too."

Frowning, Hastings said, "You think that was a good idea, looking for al Khalil yourself?"

Marshall's lips compressed.

"You seriously think anyone, including you, would have taken us seriously? All we had at the time was a suspicion. I don't see the Israelis doing much based on what would have been unverified information."

"Why would al Khalil say your son is a CIA officer?" Hastings snapped back. "Is he?"

"No, but he was mistaken for one in Morocco."

Hastings sighed and noticed Marshall's condition.

"I suggest you stay here until the COS comes back. He's informing Shin Beth about the phone call. In the meantime, can I offer you some coffee? How about if the embassy nurse looks at that wound?"

10:30

"I want covering fire directed at all windows and other possible firing points, now," Avidan ordered. Then he told his intelligence team, "Go!"

Three men ran to the building. One deployed what turned out to be a light ladder that he set up against the wall. The other two threw up grappling hook rope ladders. After two tries, the hooks caught and the two men climbed up to the roof.

The ladder man first drilled several holes in the wall and then inserted listening devices equipped with micro transmitters. The two men on the roof set up heat-seeking sensors that could "see" into the building.

Avidan thought the takedown would be simple. The TIBEAM plans revealed a one-floor interior with offices defined by drywall and cubicle separators, nothing that would provide safe harbor from the firepower of the Shaldag.

★ ★ ★

The Amitais had given Habib a quick tutorial on how to target the laser. The weapon had several preset targeting options that included all of the Arab capitals of the Middle East, plus Tehran. In the presence of the two Israeli scientists, Habib aimed the weapon to a deserted spot south of Cairo, "to show everyone that Israel really has the capability to annihilate any of its enemies without using a nuclear weapon which, depending on the prevailing winds, could also wipe out part of the Israeli population."

After getting the Amitais out of the room, he reset the laser to target the government centers of Tehran and of Algiers, per Tariq's orders. Tariq walked in to check up on progress.

"Why not Cairo?" Habib asked.

"I will capture Egypt through the *threat* of destruction, not by actual destruction," al Khalil said. "Cairo is the most important center of influence for the *Ikhwan* Brotherhood. The brothers will know what to do."

He gave only fleeting thought to his wife and daughter, Malika and Jamila, who were now living in Cairo. He wanted his daughter to grow up in a Muslim environment. In a sea of apostates, they were living in an island of Salafist purity with distant cousins. He had decided that their deaths, if necessary, would be a small price compared with his goals. However, for the moment, sparing Cairo made more sense from a political point of view.

★ ★ ★

Steve couldn't stop his mind from spinning.

"Do you think Izem is really on board? That he's trying to rally his guys to change sides? I don't know how long we should wait. Maybe he's not coming back. Maybe he's already been shot. But we need weapons."

Kella sat on the floor, her back against the wall, her features drawn and tired. She looked up at Steve.

"I think so. But that's easier said than done. What choice do we have?"

He pointed to the rear door.

"Well, we have another door if only we could open it. It's a long shot but I wonder if we could pick the lock."

He walked back to the door and examined it. The pin-and-tumbler lock was about a foot higher than the lever handle, which itself had no lock. This was not a high-security area. The builders had placed their security focus on perimeter devices.

He looked around for a thin piece of metal he could insert into the lock but saw nothing of use, just several computer screens on the floor and an old desk against the back wall. It was dark in the back of their mini bowling alley prison and Steve got down on his knees. He pulled the top drawer open. It was the main residence for a colony of insects. He looked inside a larger and lower drawer. He couldn't quite see anything distinctly and he put his hand inside. He pulled on pliers, a hammer, and several sizes of wrenches, but nothing thin enough to pick the lock.

Now armed with a handful of tools, he sat on the floor, and took the back off one of the computer screens. He pulled wires out where he could see them. With a pair of cutting pliers, he detached a long wire, at the end of which was a stiff and thin piece of metal. He cut it off. He took a pair of long nosed pliers and inserted one end into the bottom of the lock with one hand. With the other, he introduced the metallic pick in the lock and tried to feel the pins inside. He counted four.

Kella came up behind him.

"Do you actually know what you're doing?"

"You pick up very peculiar pieces of trivia growing up in the house of an intelligence officer. So, yes, I'm trying to lift the pins out of the cylinder. The pressure I'm putting on the cylinder with the plier keeps the pins up after I lift them up. When all the pins are up, the cylinder should turn."

The long-nosed plier moved a bit and then all the way. The lock had given up.

"Voilà!"

He put his right hand up in a flourish. Then he pushed the lever handle down slowly and, with Kella peering around him, he opened the door.

* * *

Immediately after leaving Habib, al Khalil went up to the ground floor to check on their situation and see how close the Israeli commandos were getting. He had also gone upstairs to call Salim on his satellite phone. He reached him in Cairo on his way to a meeting of the Brotherhood. He gave him a short version of what was happening.

"I want you to hold a press conference as soon as possible. You're on your way to *Ikhwan* headquarters? Great, schedule it there. But do it within the hour, within the half hour if you can. Say that you have news of the takeover in Israel."

An angry Salim replied, "I'm surprised that you chose a target in the middle of Israel. I didn't know you to have a death wish, to want to die a *shaheed*, a martyr."

"This is the most important blow struck against the Zionists, ever. This is historical!"

Al Khalil quickly brought him up to date on his takedown of the Israeli military installation masquerading as an agricultural research center.

"Salim, this is your hour. Everything depends on our credibility. Alert the brothers to set up security around the press conference. The police may try to shut you down, or worse."

* * *

General Joulet was in his Paris office when an aide walked in with a message, saying, "This is urgent, *mon Générale.*"

The message was an intercepted conversation from al Khalil's phone. He immediately called the Mossad representative in Paris and told him, "We have information concerning an ongoing hostage situation in Israel. Since one of the hostages is my adopted granddaughter, I have a personal interest. The leader of the group responsible is al Khalil. I'm sure you have as much information on him as we do. I don't understand this part about Israeli space lasers that your al Khalil now controls. I'd like you to ask your headquarters and get back to me. I need to brief the Elysée Palace quickly."

Joulet then called his daughter Alexandra, wife of the American ambassador to Israel, angry that he had to learn of Kella's kidnapping from intelligence sources. He then ordered that the entire CIMETERRE case be reviewed by the Inspector General's office, and that the responsible case officer, Captain Lucien Roger, be investigated and punished for incompetence or lack of integrity or even treason.

13:15

Salim stood on a raised platform at one end of a large room lined with forty rows of chairs. The room was half-full but filling quickly. He stood behind a podium with his notes in front of him. When the room was quiet enough to speak, he began.

"I bear witness that there is no God but Allah, and I bear witness that Muhammad is His slave and messenger. Muslim brothers of the world, peace be upon you and the mercy of Allah and His blessings. I bring you an important message from Tariq al Khalil."

After receiving his orders, Salim had tried to reach David Ben Tov but had not succeeded. He was holding his news conference in the Muslim Brotherhood center in Cairo. Not all of the city's media representatives were present; he had given them only forty-five-minutes' warning. However, many Egyptian correspondents were present, especially those of a radical Muslim slant who were more likely to respond to a call from the Brotherhood. Al Jazeera was there, he noted with satisfaction, and would spread Tariq's message worldwide.

"Today is a great day for Islam," Salim continued. "Thanks to the inspiration and guidance of Allah, the Beneficent, the Merciful, Islam has started to re-conquer the lands of the Caliphate. Our son and the right hand of Allah on earth, Tariq al Khalil, may Allah continue to favor him, has taken by force of arms an important military center in the heart of Palestine. On his behalf, I address this message to the chiefs of state who have brought their countries back to the pagan era preceding Allah's revelation to the Prophet, may Allah favor him."

Salim picked up a sheet of paper from the podium. He moved to the forward edge of the platform and raised his voice to mitigate the absence of the microphone.

"'To you, false leaders', Tariq al Khalil says, 'Every day you are insulting Allah, the Merciful, the Almighty. You are blasphemers. You are worshippers of idols. You should be cleansed from the face of this earth. However, I, Tariq al Khalil, am offering you redemption. Instead of sacrificing you immediately on the altar to Allah, as I now have the power to do, thanks to Allah—Exalted is He—I am giving you 24 hours, 24 hours to hand over power to the Ikhwan, or to the Salafists in your countries.

"'To my Ikhwan Brothers, I say, this is the day when we begin the recreation of the Caliphate of old, when we establish Allah's law on earth, Sharia law, to replace the man-made substitutes. This is the day when we begin to retake our land, the land of the Two Holy Places.

"'Who shall rule? Those with the most votes? Those with the most effective and repressive control of the citizens? Or Sharia, Divine Law?

"'I will not talk of the swift punishment that is to befall the enemies of our faith. I will soon exhibit a small sample of the punishment I will mete out to the infidel, corrupt, apostate rulers of our Caliphate lands, from Andalusia to Indonesia, unless they bow to the will of Allah, Lord of the Universe. In His service, my scimitar is sharp and ready for battle.

"'To the brothers in Algeria who now call themselves Al Qaeda in the Islamic Maghreb, the guards of Islam's western garrison, and to the other grandsons of Salahdin, today we are restoring the glory of your forefathers.

"'I repeat: 24 hours. Woe to those who do not take heed. The second strike will be geometrically more powerful. This is as the Battle of Badr was in predicting the success of the Prophet.

"'May Peace be upon you and the Mercy of Allah and His blessings'."

Steve and Kella stepped out of their cell into a dark space. They put their hands out and moved forward carefully. He realized they were in another office in the back of the large map of the Middle East. The door to their closet-cell guarded by Abdul was on the back wall and to the right of the map. He determined they were in an executive area from which the map could be activated and changed. There were two large desks and two doors.

Still in the dark, Steve and Kella explored the corridor onto which the doors opened. To the left, they found stairs heading up to the right. At the top of the stairs was a vaulted door much like the one they had seen at the top of the other stairwell. They went back downstairs.

"This must be another way to come down, and al Khalil must not have found it," Steve said. "Either that or he has a guard on the other side of the door."

They had been out about fifteen minutes when Kella said, "Don't you think we should go back, in case someone comes looking for us?"

"I hope the only one looking for us is Izem. We have a way out, but it's useless without weapons."

* * *

As Salim spoke to the media in Cairo, in Israel, al Khalil gave Habib his orders.

"Can you operate this weapon without the Jew scientists? With or without them, you will target Tehran. I want to strike the buildings that house the Supreme Council and the office of the president, but not the whole city. Then I want a similar strike on the Algerian Government. Our Algerian brothers have been fighting and dying for many years. They have earned this help.

"Algiers and Tehran are lucky. They will receive only a warning shot. The laser should not be on full power this time. But next time, tomorrow, for the leaders who do not heed the warning, their populations will suffer grievously. We're not going to burn Tel Aviv yet. We want to lull them into inactivity. I want them to think that we're only interested in striking Iran and some Arab capitals. If they believe it's our plan, the Jews will leave us alone for a while.

"We're doing what they never had the guts to do. Plus, I'm sure the Americans are telling the Jews not to attack because of the two Americans we're holding. We want to delay an Israeli attack as long as possible so that we can finish our work here. We'll incinerate Tel Aviv later. Go do this now."

★ ★ ★

Izem tried to rally the small group of Tuaregs. There were seven left, not counting him. It was difficult to have private conversations with any of them. Some were upstairs guarding the entry points of the building. Others were downstairs guarding the prisoners, the Israeli scientists and the two Americans.

He rounded up two from a Timbuktu tribe he knew well and brought them to the room where Steve and Kella had been kept.

"This is Kella, the ranking descendant of the leadership of our Udalan clan, which as you know is one of the seven big Tuareg clans. We are all Udalans. We first fought the Arabs when they invaded and made us Muslims; we fought the French who tried to teach us that our ancestors were Gauls. Now we must fight these Salafists, the latest invaders. It is our duty to follow Kella. We owe her allegiance."

The two young Tuaregs looked at Kella and then at Izem with puzzled expressions.

"This is just an American girl, an unbeliever. Al Khalil told us about western girls, all prostitutes. Why do we owe her allegiance?" they asked Izem in their native Tamasheq.

Then Kella spoke up, also in Tamasheq.

"Because I am Tuareg, and this proves my authority."

She showed them the gold bracelet with the geometric-type Tamasheq script, which had been in her family for generations as a symbol of tribal leadership.

Izem told them, "Look closer; see the Tuareg inscriptions?"

The young fighters stepped closer, looking shocked that Kella had understood them and could speak their tribal language. One also attracted the other's attention to the four dots on the back of Kella's hand. By their hushed whispers and looks of awe, Izem could tell that the design had obvious significance to them.

The two men inspected the bracelet as Kella extended her arm. They looked at each other in confusion and indecision. Then one lowered his head and, in Tamasheq, asked, "What is your order, *Amenokal*?" The other likewise bowed in submission.

Izem spoke up. "She wants to speak to all of the Tuaregs in here now. We want all of our tribesmen to act together."

Steve held Izem back. "Izem, you can't keep going back and forth like this. Al Khalil is going to notice. We need weapons, fast!"

"You will have them."

As soon as Izem left, Steve went for the back door.

"Stay here," he told Kella. "I need to find out what's down the other side of that back corridor. Shouldn't take long."

"Be careful," she said.

*   *   *

Steve could go faster this time knowing that Hussein's men had not yet discovered the back corridor. Nevertheless, he assumed that they would find it in time. He made a right turn into the passage, past the back wall of their cell, to another door about thirty feet away.

In the dark, he felt another doorway and carefully groped for the handle. He turned the knob slowly and pushed the door open. He stepped into another dark space, closed the door behind him, and stood for a couple of seconds trying to sense his surroundings before stepping forward.

He found a light switch and flicked it up to find himself faced with an emergency generator and on the left side of the door, cases of water, and canned food. The Israelis, he thought, were ready for a siege. But they had been overly reliant on cover and concealment. Why didn't they have a stronger armed security group to defend their installation?

He turned the light off and went back to the corridor. He again turned to the right. Another twenty feet or so and he found yet another narrow corridor, to the right. He followed it and reached the corridor that originally had led from the front stairwell to the large computer and map room. He turned left and reached a vault door with a pad for digital identification.

A vault within a vault. What could behind this barrier?

Steve turned around and made his way back to the supply room. He was loading a cardboard box when a tremendous explosion suddenly increased the air pressure against his eardrums several fold.

He was immobilized for a second and then grabbed his box, turned out the light, and turned left into the corridor to get back to his cell. He heard footsteps and voices coming toward him in the dark and saw the beam of a flashlight at the far end of the hall.

His one chance was to go forward and slip into the room behind the map. He kept moving quickly in the dark toward the sounds. He entered the office in back of the large electronic wall map just as the light reached the bottom of the stairs. He closed the door behind him and found the back door to his cell.

Kella came up to him and put her arms around him.

"What was that noise?"

Steve put the box down under the back desk. "I think they found the door to the back stairs and blew it open. There goes our escape route."

"Are you all right? What do you have in the box?"

She leaned down to look before Steve could reply.

"Wow! Water! And Spam! Spam?"

"Yes. I found the crisis supply room. There were kosher and non-kosher varieties. You're not Jewish are you? And a couple of flashlights."

Kella pulled out a bottle of water and gave Steve another one.

"Look, Abdul brought these," she said, pointing to two AK-47s lying under the desk.

Steve reached for one of the weapons.

"Abdul?"

"Yes, Izem told him. Abdul has switched sides."

"Or, he's playing both sides."

* * *

The Shaldag team kept firing at the building's openings at random to keep the tension high and prevent the terrorists from getting any rest. While Avidan and his men had access to food and could rest on a rotating basis, Hussein's fighters had to be ready for an attack at any time. They had found fast food and soda machines in the building and were not without sustenance. But they had had not slept the night before. They soon would be fighting their bodies to stay functional, alert, and effective.

The TIBAM team delivered the classified plans of the building to Avidan, who became furious. Speaking to General Shomron on his cell network, he said, "General, you sent me on a mission with bad information. The plans the TIBAM gave me were false, showing a one-level interior. Now I have the classified blueprints showing me that the terrorists are in a subterranean complex with offices, labs, and our country's secret weapon."

"That's because your mission has changed," Shomron answered, "from liberating the hostages and killing the terrorists to disabling the laser."

"What's the difference? I have to go through the terrorists to get at the weapon, right?"

"No. Look at the TIBEAM information. You'll see there's a sliding roof. For the weapon to become operational, the roof has to slide open. When it does, that's your chance to get into the installation. But, keep in mind that, when they open the roof, it means they are ready to fire. We have to hope that, since it's their first time, there will be pauses as they try to figure out the next step."

★ ★ ★

Hussein was busy organizing his few fighters on the ground level and keeping an eye on the Israeli commandos surrounding the building. Not unexpected, they hadn't assaulted his positions yet. Obviously, the Israeli government put a high price on the value of the American hostages, especially the ambassador's daughter. But that didn't totally explain the Israeli forces' relative lack of activity. He left his post to go speak with al Khalil.

They met near the top of the stairs. Al Khalil arrived with an AK-47 in his hand.

"Give me an update. How are the Israelis positioned?"

Hussein leaned on the railing, one hand holding his gun slung around his neck.

"They are firing to keep us busy, but they have not attacked. I don't know what they are waiting for; it must be our hostages. Are you negotiating with them?"

"I am keeping them at bay for the moment. Within hours, we will have the entire Middle East in our hands."

He told Hussein about the laser gun and his plan to fire it as a show of force against Algiers and Tehran. Hussein let go of the railing and looked down at al Khalil a step below.

"This is our chance to finally get rid of the Assad family. This is what I have been waiting for all this time, to revenge my family, my father."

Al Khalil took a step up.

"Don't worry. Damascus will be in the second phase."

In angry outburst, Hussein said, "Damascus! Damascus! That should be our first target. Kill the Assads! Kill those who killed my family."

"I will—we will. Be patient. Do we want an incinerated city? Or do we want the Syrian leaders to hand over the country to our Muslim brothers? Would not that be a greater revenge?"

Hussein felt himself stiffen.

"The Assad family is the greatest obstacle to an Islamic Republic in Syria. The father Hafez, and the son Bashar, have killed thousands of our Muslim brothers. This is our chance. Don't wait. How long do you think the Zionists are going to wait before they attack us?"

"You are right about the Zionists. It's time to remind the American Hastings that we have his daughter here."

* * *

Steve picked up the AK-47 and a flashlight.

"I'm going to try to go out the back way. We can't just wait here for Izem. We don't know what he's doing."

Kella got up and retrieved the other weapon.

"Don't think you're leaving here without me."

"No, you'll be safer here. I'll come back to get you. Have you ever fired a gun, let alone an AK-47?"

"No, I haven't, so you'd better show me."

"Please. Stay here," Steve begged. He didn't want to worry about her, but even in the dim light he could see the determination on her face.

"Give up. I'm going with you."

He sighed, picked up the hammer that was with the other tools in the desk, and nodded.

"All right. Ready? First, about this gun. This is not an accurate weapon. It gets less accurate if you fire long bursts. Try to squeeze the trigger gently, don't jerk it, and then release it quickly. Also, it's going to kick and shoot up and to the right. You have to hold it. And don't point it at anything you don't intend to shoot dead. Ready? Wait for me by the door. Take a flashlight."

When Kella reached the door, Steve smashed all the circuit breakers. He then joined her at the door and they went to the supply room.

"I want to shut down the emergency generator in case it's programmed to go on if the circuit breakers fail."

But the generator was quiet. Steve led Kella back down the corridor now behind the beam of his flashlight. They turned right and took the first few steps when a voice called out behind them, "Ahmed!"

* * *

Hastings' secretary put al Khalil through right away. He was joined by Jack Horton who listened on a second phone.

"Hastings," al Khalil said, "your Jewish friends are on the verge of attacking us. They've been shooting at us and your daughter is lucky to be alive."

Hastings stood up and said with force, "I want to know about my daughter. I understand that you also have another American hostage. How are they both?"

"Right now, they are fine. But if the Jews attack, either they will die from Jewish bullets or from ours. I guarantee that they will not survive a Jewish attack. Talk to your Jew friends. I want their commandos to disappear. Then we can talk about your daughter."

"I heard about you when I was posted to France. Your status as the only intellectual that could establish a dialogue with the West is badly eroded," Hastings said, trying to reason with him. "I can help you regain your standing if you stop what you're doing right now and let all your hostages go. Why are you doing this? I'm sure I could get you out of the country safely."

"Hastings, you are wasting my time with your demands. My next step will be to start killing the hostages. I have not decided who will go first, the Jewish scientists or my American prisoners. Get those commandos to move back!"

Horton, the COS, wrote a quick note and handed it to him. Looking at the note, Hastings said, "I want proof that my daughter is alive."

"You are hardly in a position to give me orders, Hastings. But right now, I can't bring her to the phone. She is in another part of the building. She is well."

Reading from another note, Hastings said, "I want you to take a photograph of her, and of Steve Church, with a cell phone, and I want you to email it to me within the next few minutes. If that happens, I'll have the Israeli commandos back off. Keep in mind that my government is not in charge. Israel is a sovereign country."

He gave al Khalil an email address, which Tariq took grudgingly without agreeing to anything.

★ ★ ★

After al Khalil had put him off by repeating, "Be patient," Hussein walked away frustrated and angry. Al Khalil had been putting off Hussein for years. While his only reason to join Tariq in the first place had been to hit back at the Assad family, Hussein had never been successful in his attempts to influence Tariq into taking action against the Syrian rulers.

Al Khalil's last words to Hussein on the stairs were, "According to the scientists, there is a sliding roof to allow the laser gun to shoot. Get some men up there."

He went back upstairs and walked to one of the window openings being defended by one of his men.

"Ayyub, take some men up to the roof. Part of it opens up. Find it and keep the Israelis off the roof."

Ayyub and three men went up through the damage done by the UAVs. Staying low to avoid being seen by the Israelis, they made their way to the wider part of the roof to the west.

As they moved, Ayyub saw several black boxes. At first, he paid them no attention, not knowing if they were part of the roof construction. Then he stopped and lifted a box, revealing a wire going into the roof. He called one of the other men. They both examined the box.

"I wonder if the Israelis put these up here to listen to us. What else could they be? Bombs? They look new, not weathered like the rest of the roof."

The second man was about to pull the wire, but Ayyub stopped him.

"Not now. It would reveal we are up here," he said.

They resumed their inspection of the western part of the roof.

At that moment a clinking noise was followed by a grappling hook on a nylon rope being pulled back toward the roof's edge. Ayyub crawled closer to the edge and the three others started looking for other places where the Israelis might be trying to climb.

Ayyub and his men waited for the commandoes to show themselves above the edge. Another hook and then a third hit the roof. Three men were on their way up. One climber's head became visible, then the second and the third. It wasn't until the third appeared that Ayyub and his men fired, killing all three instantly, their bodies falling to the ground below.

Ayyub threw a grenade to the base of the wall, assuming there were others down there waiting their turn to climb. He paused a second and then looked over the edge. He barely had time to note with satisfaction the Israeli bodies at the base of the wall before his head exploded from a dum-dum bullet fired by a Shaldag sniper.

Meanwhile, al Khalil sent one of his men to send photos of the American hostages to the ambassador. He remembered that both Kella and Steve had cell phones that had been taken from them.

14:38
Steve and Kella were on the second step of the unlit stairs, plastered against the wall at a right angle from the end of the corridor, listening to the footsteps coming toward them. The reflection from the beam of the man's flashlight pointed at the floor in front of him was illuminating the wall with increasing brightness.

The voice shouted again, "Ahmed!"

Steve and Kella looked to their right up the dark stairs. Steve wondered why the voice thought Ahmed was somewhere in front of him. Or, had he heard their footsteps and assumed that they were those of Ahmed?

Steve's mind was racing, trying to decide how to deal with the company, whether to simply kill him as quietly as possible, or capture him and tie him up. He had concluded they couldn't deal with a prisoner when the man reached the end of the corridor and looked up the stairs.

Steve had the shoulder stock of his AK-47 cocked and ready to smash him when Kella stopped him.

"Wait!"

At the same time, she stepped forward spoke Tamasheq rapidly while pointing her AK-47 at the man whose face was hidden by a Tuareg *tagoulmoust*.

Steve had come within a millisecond of releasing his blow to the man's head. He could see the man's eyes wide with shock and surprise. Taking advantage of the element of surprise, Steve disarmed him and watched the dialogue, only guessing at what both were saying. After several exchanges, the man seemed to ask a question, to which Kella replied by showing him her bracelet and a few seconds later the tattooed design on her hand. The Tuareg paused a second and seemed swayed. Steve recognized Izem's name in Kella next sentence and she appeared to have closed the deal.

She turned to Steve and said, "He's with us but he also wants confirmation from Izem."

"Tell him you want full allegiance now or his family will never live down the shame."

Kella looked at Steve with surprise and translated. The Tuareg looked at both Steve and Kella in turn and replied in Tamasheq. Kella said, "That did it."

"Well, I think I'll keep his weapon for now," Steve said. "Tell him we're going upstairs to save the rest of his Tuareg brothers from annihilation. Ask him how the Salafists are positioned upstairs."

"He said there are about fifteen to twenty left, but some are downstairs watching the prisoners," Kella said. "Upstairs, they're fighting from the windows, and he said some are on the roof, but he doesn't how many."

"Let's go," he said, moving up the stairs first. He stopped suddenly, turned around, and asked, "What's his name?"

"Yubba," said the Tuareg.

Kella and Steve both looked at him in surprise, and Steve led them up the stairs again.

When they reached the door at the top, it was half open and hanging on one hinge, the doorframe a jagged hole.

"Here we go, ready?"

He looked back at Kella. She clutched her AK-47 more tightly to her side. His AK-47 up to his shoulder and finger on the trigger, Steve slipped through the door without having to touch it. Shouting voices erupted in what sounded to Steve like a loud conversation. He motioned Kella to his side.

"What are they saying?"

"They want the lights back on."

Although it was midday, light from the outside didn't penetrate very far beyond the few windows. The three of them had emerged in another office. Yubba motioned to follow him. He opened the door slowly to reveal an external wall on the left. One of Hussein's men was standing on a desk he apparently had placed there and was pointing his gun out a window that was about ten feet off the floor.

While his gun still pointed toward possible targets outside, his eyes followed the door's movement on his left. He quickly tried to move his gun into firing position when he saw Steve appear behind Yubba. But Steve already had his AK-47 pointed toward him. He fired and four 7.62-millimeter caliber bullets penetrated the Salafist's chest. The almost-simultaneous blows hammered him against the wall. He fell off the desk to the floor.

Steve's mind registered that he had killed another human being. But his dominant feeling was that of great danger. The man he had shot could easily have killed them both.

He pulled Kella after him, moving to the right, paralleling the side toward which the Salafist had been pointing his gun. Now the other gunmen were alerted. They would assume a breach by the Israelis.

"Hurry," he said.

They moved out quickly and kneeled at an intersection of two corridors formed by seven-foot-high dividers. He told Kella, "Call to the Tuaregs in Tamasheq. Tell them who we are."

Kella shouted, "Izem and all of you other Udalan fighters. Now is the time to revolt against the Arab master, the poisoners of wells. Kill them now. Do not die for somebody else's cause. Stay with the Arabs and die. Join me and choose freedom. I will get you out of here alive."

They waited in silence. Steve said, "Repeat your message, and then let's move quickly."

Before she could say anything, Yubba shouted it out.

Steve heard footsteps and voices in front of them, so he pulled Kella into the first office cubicle, where they kneeled awkwardly behind a desk. The footsteps drew closer.

They saw Izem go past their hiding place running in a crouch. In a loud whisper, Kella called out in Tamasheq, "Izem, in here." In a few seconds Izem joined them.

Suddenly a loud Arab voice from farther down the corridor shouted, "This is Majid. The hostages escaped. Al Khalil is insane with rage. The hostages are our ticket out of here. They must be up here. Boulos! Gamal! Join me at the top of the stairs and help me find them!"

"Now I know where they are," Izem said. "Stay here. The stairs are very close."

He pointed with the muzzle of his gun. He took the AK-47 from Steve and gave it back to Yubba. He and Yubba headed in Majid's direction.

They heard voices and footsteps. Then gunfire erupted, stopped for a fraction of a second, and erupted again. The sound was badly absorbed and resounded throughout the warehouse building. It also sounded extremely close. Kella looked at Steve. He stood up in a crouch and moved out of the cubicle, with his AK-47 out front.

* * *

Al Khalil was downstairs in his de facto office. He held Abdul, who was kneeling in front of him, by the hair. "How long have you been a CIA spy?"

"Never, never! May Allah curse me if I lie! Izem came to help the hostages. It's the Tuaregs. They are all spies. They are all infidels. They only made believe they are Muslim warriors. Izem liberated the Americans, not me. I could do nothing."

Al Khalil pointed a pistol at Abdul's face.

"You lie. You and Izem worked together, didn't you?"

Abdul held is hands, palms up, toward al Khalil.

"No, no!"

Still holding Abdul by the hair, al Khalil moved the muzzle of the pistol closer and closer to the man's right eye, his finger tightened on the trigger. In desperation, Abdul grabbed the gun. The gun went off as he tried to push it aside. The bullet punched him in the neck. Al Khalil released his hair and Abdul fell forward. He looked at him a second before firing another shot into the back of his head.

* * *

Izem and Yubba appeared in front of Steve. Izem said, "Majid, Boulos, and Gamal are gone to their Paradise."

Then he called his Tuareg brethren in Tamasheq. Within five minutes, after some gunfire, during which Kella kept a firm hold on Steve's arm, three men appeared. They spoke with Izem.

"We just lost one of ours. Hussein and several men are on the roof, and there are the men guarding the scientists, and al Khalil's guards, about fifteen-to-twenty fighters."

There was another conversation among the Tuaregs, which Kella translated for Steve.

"The Israelis have a secret weapon downstairs. With it, al Khalil is going to first threaten the Muslim world with a warning shot against two cities, and then, unless all submit, he plans to obliterate the population of some Arab capitals."

Steve took a deep, steadying breath.

"Let's go downstairs. We have to stop him."

* * *

As the Shaldag and Hussein's men battled for control of the roof on the western side of the building, Habib and the Amitais switched the nuclear power piped in from the Soreq Nuclear Center, from the commercial grid, providing electricity to surrounding towns, to exclusive military use of the center. The energy coursed to three lasers hooked up in series, using a triple-lens system. The system was designed to produce a laser beam with the effective power of a fifty-four-megawatt beam.

The roof was open less than a minute when Habib sent the beam to the satellite. It was received by one giant mirror, fed into the satellite, and shot out through another mirror toward Algiers.

During a full minute, the beam bathed the area from the Place du Gouvernment and its complex of ministry offices on Rue du

Docteur Cherif Saadane, past the railroad line along the coast, to the docks and overlapping onto the sea. Electric power in that part of the city came to a stop. All communications shut down. The explosions of war were absent.

People on the street became instantly aware of increased heat on their exposed skin. Those wearing long sleeves or *jellabas* felt the sensation on their faces and hands. They searched for a cause but saw nothing to explain their quickly rising body temperature. They initially assumed that the heat was the prologue to the sirocco, the wind from the desert. But in seconds they dismissed natural causes. Their skin quickly turned pink and then red. Blisters followed, and the temperature of their blood and other bodily fluids began to climb to dangerous levels.

The lobby of the Es Safir Hotel, located between Place du Gouvernement and the sea, as well as most public buildings in the area, quickly filled up with people looking for air conditioning. The instinct to move inside saved many lives.

Some who lived or worked in apartments or offices on the top floors of buildings died from the superheated air. Fires erupted spontaneously. Any easily combustible material within the half-mile diameter of the laser burst into flames. Some drivers lost control of their vehicles and crashed. In three minutes, within the fifth-of-a-square-mile area, all was quiet. Later, fire trucks from other parts of the city started their sirens and headed for the blighted zone.

Within an hour, a French correspondent in Algiers called his report into his Paris office.

"At 14:30 today, the threat that al Khalil, the Salafist leader whose spokesman in Cairo delivered an ultimatum to the Muslim world to submit to Sharia law, materialized as a death beam from space. Casualties were minimal considering the apparent potential of the weapon—officials initially estimated one-hundred people, but a check of hospital reveals a somewhat lower number. But, as a military strike intended to annihilate the enemy's physical infrastructure, al Khalil's attack was a failure. Physical damage was minimal. We are waiting for an official statement from the Algerian Government. However, judging from the population's reaction, placed in the context of al Khalil's threat communicated at the press conference in Cairo, the death beam has had a psychologically devastating effect. Waiting for the promised 'second strike,' which al Khalil said would be much more lethal, I am Jean Pierre Lemoine reporting from Algiers."

Habib switched the aim of the space mirrors to Tehran and fired.

15:45

Hussein rolled over on his back. He had joined his men on the roof knowing that the entire operation now depended on keeping the roof open so that Habib could fire the laser.

He reached for his walkie-talkie. As his eyes registered the blue sky, still clouded by the smoke rising from the UAV attack, it occurred to him that his life was probably about to end. What had the years brought him? He felt angry and resentful and ashamed that he had not lived up to his commitment. He had bet on the wrong horse. Al Khalil had always had his own agenda and never intended to include Hussein's.

He looked down from the sky and focused on his tactical situation. He reached for his short-range radio.

"Tariq, we can't hold out for your twenty-four-hour ultimatum. I could have told you if I had known what you were planning. I expect the Issies to send another helicopter up. One or two missiles and we are finished. We were lucky to shoot down one of their 'copters. He made a mistake and got too close. This time they will stay out of our range. Ask Salim to correct the time. Make it an hour, two hours at most. Any longer and this operation is over and so are we. Send me more men up to the roof. This is the key point now."

* * *

In Tehran, Gholam Hussein Ejei, the head of intelligence, called Major General Yahya Rahim Safavi from his home in Niavaran, a residential district of choice for the wealthy during the Shah's time.

About a third of its inhabitants had left the country since the 1978-79 revolution, but a new class that thrived in the theocracy of the ayatollahs had replaced them. Ejei shooed away a servant who was offering tea on a silver platter.

Safavi acted as though he was taking over the government following the deaths of both the chairman of the ruling council and of the president. Ejei knew he had to act quickly to support the new power center to survive the inevitable "night of the long knives," a cleaning out of officials with uncertain loyalties.

"General, you must order immediate retaliation against Israel. We have the rockets. We have the aircraft. This is the time. Our population will applaud your courage. You will become the father of the entire Muslim world. They will follow your example and erase Israel from the face of the earth. Everyone will admire you. Now is the time to act."

"I have called for a meeting of our top military and al Quds commanders. I want you to be there—in two hours at my house in Niavaran."

* * *

In Algiers, fighting broke out. The AQIM, led by Ibrahim al Maghrebi, which had never dared attack the government in Algiers proper, took the radio station and broadcast appeals for the army to join the new Islamic Republic of Algeria in response to al Khalil's message from Cairo.

* * *

Al Khalil was in front of a TV in what had become his headquarters, the office with the large window overlooking the computer room with the wall map of the Middle East. The TV was reporting on the reactions to his ultimatum.

The CNN reader said, "Arab governments are speaking out against the Jihadist who allegedly captured the Israeli space laser weapon that caused casualties in both Algiers and Tehran. Tariq al Khalil, through his spokesman in Cairo, has threatened non-compliant countries with devastation from the laser unless they submit to Sharia law. The threatened governments are calling for all-out war against Israel, the source of the death ray. Other Islamists claim that the Israelis are using al Khalil's name as a blind, as cover to attack its Arab neighbors, that al Khalil is not in Israel and that he has been seen in Yemen.

"Saudi Arabia has condemned the loss of life, without criticizing al Khalil directly. The Wahhabist leaders of the kingdom are supporting al Khalil's fervor and, according to reports, are in negotiations with the royal family to take over several ministries to strengthen the enforcement of Sharia law and to allocate more funds to spread the faith globally. Secular countries such as Egypt, Jordan, Tunisia, and Syria are the most strident in their demands for the Arab League, for the United Nations and for the United States to take action against Israel, whom they call the real culprit. A more militant message is dominating the unofficial media, chat rooms, blogs, and YouTube. Tariq al Khalil's prior speeches and presentations are being quoted. 'It is time,' he is quoted as saying, 'for the Muslim world to go back to its roots.'

"Local radical Muslim groups have been emboldened by al Khalil's words and actions. They are attacking police stations and more symbolic, but undefended, representatives of secular power such as ministry buildings. *Imams* and mullahs have taken over churches and other non-Muslim religious edifices. The Secretary General of the United Nations has expressed his hope for more dialogue."

Al Khalil sat back. This was the Western media that he knew to be prejudiced. The real situation must be worse for the Arab powers than he had just heard. CNN was, after all, another arm of the American government. He searched for Al Jazeera's channel.

* * *

In Cairo, Salim, prohibited from holding another news conference, called correspondents.

"Tariq al Khalil has shortened his deadline. You have seen what defying him means. As of this moment, any government in the Middle East that refuses to hand over power to the Muslim Brothers or to Salafist groups will suffer a much more serious fate than Tehran or Algiers. This ultimatum is effective immediately."

* * *

Jack Horton sat in the acoustic conference room with Ambassador Hastings.

"Any news about your daughter?" he asked.

"No. I asked al Khalil for a photo, which he could easily have sent by email, but I have had no contacts with him since then. I don't even know if Kella is alive. What is the CIA reporting on this situation?"

"Since the second release to the press by al Khalil's spokesman, fighting broke out in Damascus and Jakarta. In Cairo itself, the outlawed Muslim Brotherhood activated their penetrations of the army and security services. Several Egyptian army units have made statements in support of an Islamic government. Muslim Brotherhood members are claiming majority power in the Egyptian parliament. Under free elections, they claim, they would have a democratic majority.

"I need to ask you a question—what is your plan in terms of getting our dependents out of here? It's only a matter of time before al Khalil hits Tel Aviv with that laser."

"We can't evacuate our people; it would show a lack of faith, a lack of support for the Israeli government during a crisis."

Horton's voice rose.

"You're talking about perceptions; I'm talking about the lives of our families."

Hastings sat more erect.

"I'm not approving an evacuation. I don't want to send the signal that the U.S. thinks the Israeli government can't handle this situation. Just think of the implications about the bigger issues."

"Well, with all due respect, sir, I'm going to tell my people that those who want to send their families out can. We'll figure out whether they're reimbursed later."

"It may already be too late for Kella," Hastings said. "I'm going to call the prime minister and tell him to start talking with the terrorists. We still don't know what the hell they want. I wonder if their plan went any further than the capture of this laser gun."

"Probably not. As long as they own it, they rule the world."

Hastings hastily got up to leave the ACR, "That's it! The Israelis have to find a way to destroy the gun. I'm calling the prime minister; you contact Israeli intelligence."

Horton left the ACR to inform his staff to evacuate their families in view of the looming threat of a laser attack. Before they assembled in his office, he was thinking perhaps the more timely survival action would be to leave Tel Aviv—there might not be time to get on a flight out of the country.

15:49

In the Israeli Laser Center, Habib was getting ready to fire the laser for the second strike.

Al Khalil walked past the well-armed squad of men that he had posted at the entrance of the Laser Center following Steve and Kella's escape. He took a quick look at the tubes, wires, and machinery that populated the large underground room.

"I was afraid you didn't have power," he said. "We lost all our power on the other side. That devil dog Church destroyed the circuit breakers!"

He glanced around.

Habib pointed toward a corner of the well-lit space.

"The laser has its own emergency generator for lights, air conditioning—which is crucial, because this thing really heats up. But we are hooked up to the Nahal Soreq Nuclear Center to power the actual laser. I will be ready to fire again in about thirty minutes. What are the targets?"

Habib led al Khalil toward a control panel. Al Khalil stopped and Habib turned around to face him. With even more gravity and determination on his face than usual, al Khalil put his hand on Habib's shoulder and, looking up and scanning the electronic map, he said, "Riyadh, Tehran, and Tel Aviv. This time, I want full power."

Habib appeared surprised, "We just hit Tehran."

Al Khalil dropped his hand but his eyes maintained their intensity.

"Iran and Saudi Arabia are the regional centers of power. When both are weak, my governments, my Caliphate, will rule supreme from Cairo. I will replace the al Saud dynasty with my men, people loyal to me and to the true version of our faith, people who will not invite foreign infidels to solve problems."

He paused and stroked his black beard, now starting to grow out again.

"With a strong power center in Cairo, I will establish a borderless region covering the entire Middle East. I will also change that name. 'Middle East' is European terminology. Typical infidel arrogance labeled each region according to its distance from Europe."

16:03

Before Steve went down the dark stairs, he asked Izem, "Can you collect any more of your Tuaregs?"

"There might be one other downstairs guarding the scientists, that's all."

"Let's go then. Do you know where this secret weapon is, exactly?"

When Izem shook his head, Steve said, "We better first liberate the scientists. They can help."

When they reached the door to the large computer room where the prisoners were being held, Steve held up his hand.

"Izem, go in by yourself first. Tell the guards that Hussein wants them upstairs immediately. We'll deal with them when they come out. Say Hussein wants just one guard for the prisoners and the rest to come and help him. And the one who's going to stay to watch the prisoners should be your Tuareg brother."

Izem went in. Steve and Kella positioned themselves on each side of the door, and Steve told the two Tuareg fighters to step back and face the opening.

"Kella, tell them that the idea is to capture them, not to shoot unless we have to."

The door opened and the sound of footsteps signaled people coming through. Steve turned his light on one of Hussein's fighters. Almost as soon, a Tuareg plunged a knife into the man's throat and pulled him to the side. Steve was shocked by the unexpected violence but had no time to philosophize about it. More men were coming through the door into the darkness of the corridor where the Tuaregs knifed and clubbed them into submission.

Then an AK-47 went off, as the finger of a dying man tightened on the trigger, causing an indiscriminate spray of bullets to hit walls, ceilings, and bodies. The light was knocked out of Steve's hand during the general free-for-all.

He tried to use the stock of his weapon as a club, but bodies were too close together, and arms soon grabbed him. He found himself on the ground with his hand closing around a knife then around his opponent's wrist. Blood made his grip slippery and he felt rather than saw the knife coming closer to his face. Suddenly, a flashlight came on, a shot rang out, and his opponent went limp. Kella pulled him up.

"Are you all right?" she asked.

The surprise of the assault in the dark gave the victory to Steve, Izem, and the Tuaregs. The AK-47 bullets had killed one Tuareg; otherwise they escaped with minor wounds. Steve wrapped a shirtsleeve around his hand after Kella, using a borrowed knife, cut the sleeve off.

The small space was now filled with the smell of gunpowder and sweating bodies. Steve's eardrums were still ringing from the painful blow of close-range gunshots. He found his flashlight and gave it to Izem. He motioned toward the computer room.

"Bring them all back in here and tie them up, quickly."

"Kella, untie the prisoners," he said as they got to the computer room, pointing to the Israelis lying on the floor. At the same time, as his ears still subdued the sounds around him, including his own voice, he said, "Listen up! This is almost over. Almost! The terrorists have discovered your secret laser weapon and are about to fire it, maybe at Tel Aviv. I need your help to prevent that from happening. Who's going to help save your country from this weapon?

"We will," said Shoshanna Amitai, holding her bandaged and still-bleeding hand, as she and Aaron stepped forward. "I can show you."

"Izem, have two men guard them," Steve said, pointing at the Salafists. "Bring the rest of your men. This is going to be the final test."

Before he left the computer room, he addressed the freed Israeli hostages.

"If any of you have a way to call outside, tell them what's going on. In the meantime, it's best for you to stay here and help guard the prisoners. There's more fighting to come. Kella, how about staying here?"

Kella glanced at Izem, Steve, and their small band.

"All right, I'll try to find a working phone and call my father at the embassy. The Israelis can try to connect with their government."

Five Israelis came up to him and one said, "We're reservists. If you have guns, we can help."

"There are guns on the floor outside this room. Let's go."

Steve and the two scientists, with Izem, his Tuaregs, and the five army reservists turned left into the corridor, away from the stairs. The beam from Steve's flashlight cut into the darkness.

As they moved, Shoshanna said, "The laser is at the end of this corridor. It's behind a vaulted door and a digital pad. But I can get in."

"Izem, how many fighters do you think are guarding the laser? How many are left?"

"I think five or six. Hussein is still on the roof with maybe five men. So it's Habib, al Khalil's Tunisian scientist, and probably al Khalil himself, plus the fighters."

They soon reached the vaulted door, which Steve recognized from his prior exploration.

"Is this the only entrance?" he asked Shoshanna.

"There is a door in the back, for deliveries of equipment. But I've never been there and I don't have the combination."

"When she gets the door open, I'm sure the Salafists are going to make this a killing zone," he told Izem, "anyone who steps through that door is dead." He asked the other Israelis, "Anyone know how to open the door in the back?"

One of the reservists stepped forward.

"Yes, it's in back of the cargo platform."

"Come and show me. Izem, once this door is open, keep the guys inside busy but don't try to go through. We'll attack from the rear."

Steve took the five Israeli reservists with him, using a corridor he Steve had passed through before. Instead of turning toward the back stairs, they headed for the back of the building and turned again at the end of the corridor. They were on a wide wooden platform the height of a truck bed and running through the whole building. The platform was separated from the outside by two wide, sliding metal shutters. There were two doors that led inside from the platform. One was the width of a three-car garage; the other was another vault door.

The reservist pointed to the large door and said, "That one opens from the inside only. This smaller door opens with a number combination and a thumbprint."

Then they heard to noise of machinery, of gears working, and of metal grinding against inadequately lubricated metal.

The reservist said, "That's the roof opening. That means they're close to firing the laser gun again."

Steve pulled him to the vault door, "Go ahead, we have to get in there to stop them."

The reservist slung his weapon over his shoulder and set to work under Steve's flashlight.

★   ★   ★

Inside, al Khalil said, "Habib, I don't know what is taking you so long. But that is probably all right. It is giving our brothers in Cairo and Damascus time to either force or negotiate their way into power. I am going to talk to Salim. Be ready to fire in a few minutes."

He reached Salim almost right away.

"Salim, what is the reaction to our second ultimatum. We are getting ready to fire again."

"Algeria is won. El Maghrebi was on TV a few minutes ago. He announced the new Islamic Republic of Algeria. There is fighting in a number of other countries."

"What about Saudi Arabia?"

"The al Saud family is negotiating to hang onto power, but the Wahhabists seem to have the upper hand. It is not a done deal. The royal family is buying them off. No need to laser Cairo. I am in talks with the president. He has agreed to speak with you directly."

"Have him step down first, in favor of the *Ikhwan*. You can be the temporary leader until I arrive. Contact the army and prepare an immediate invasion of Israel after I laser Tel Aviv, which will be any minute now."

* * *

Steve and his squad were inside. They carried flashlights that revealed the space to be an office on the side of the spacious, high-ceilinged portion of the warehouse occupied by the laser. Steve still heard firing at the other end of the warehouse. It had to be Izem keeping al Khalil's shooters busy. The reservist motioned to their right as they came out of the office.

"The control room for the laser is three doors down from here," he said.

The sound from the roof stopped.

As Steve and his men emerged, a fighter in front of the door identified by the reservist shouted and shouldered his assault rifle immediately. He went down as two of Steve's men fired at him. Steve ran forward with Izem and the others behind him. He reached the door in back of the dead guard, opened it with one hand with his rifle shouldered. Al Khalil and Steve's eyes locked for an instant. Steve stepped inside firing.

Al Khalil and Steve fired at the same time. Al Khalil's first bullet, fired with the AK-47 held at hip level, crashed into Steve's left side and the rest of al Khalil's burst went off to Steve's left and up. Steve's short burst punched al Khalil back, stitching him from the groin to the chest. Al Khalil fell against a chair, which toppled over as his body fell to the floor. Habib had his hands raised in the air from the moment that Steve rushed into the control room.

Holding his side, Steve moved toward Habib, leveling his AK-47 at him.

"Close the roof. Shut off the laser."

Steve leaned against a desk in excruciating pain.

It wasn't until he heard the roof move back that he realized al Khalil's dream of a new Caliphate was over, that the Salafists' goal of imposing their harsh version of God's law on mankind was also over—for now.

He blacked out.

It was 16:03 hours.

EPILOGUE

Marshall had accepted Ambassador Hastings' invitation to stay at his residence until Steve's medical status became clearer. It was Sunday. Hastings, his wife Alexandra, and Marshall were finishing their lunch at a large dining table. Alexandra Joulet-Hastings took a sip of her Dutcher Crossing Cabernet and said, "I am so relieved this turned out as well as it did. We were so afraid for Kella, and for Steve."

They moved to the living room. Large windows overlooked a patio and pool, and the beach and the Mediterranean below. The inside walls offered a neutral cream backdrop for paintings on loan from the State Department's American Art in Embassies program. Alexandra had chosen a large painting by Bruce Marden, colorful lines on a white background, several smaller works by Marsden Hartley, including one called "Blue Hills," and another modern work by Joan Mitchell.

Marshall put his glass down.

"What's the reporting from Damascus, Jack?"

"The events triggered by al Khalil have given a young set of leaders the momentum to pressure Bashir Assad either to step down or to clean house. We know little about the impact in Iran, since we have no embassy in Tehran. In any case, the gains of the Muslim Brotherhood of the last couple of days have been turned around. But, the previous governments are not back in charge either. New leadership seems to be emerging."

Marshall, who had earlier disclosed to Hastings that he occasionally did work for the agency and therefore still had his clearances, said, "An Iranian counterattack was imminent. The Islamic Revolutionary Guard Corps took over after the laser attack killed the country's top leadership. General Safavi was on the verge of launching his Shahab-3 missiles against Israel. After all, if the attack came from Israel, it was evident to the Iranians that the Israelis were only using al Khalil's name as a cover for their attack on Tehran. That was the Iranian thinking anyway. But cooler heads prevailed."

Marshall adjusted his sling and moved his left arm into a more comfortable position.

"There's more. The Iranian president was killed. He was in an open-top limousine coming back to his office from some sort of public event, a parade I think, when the laser struck Tehran. Apparently the heat of the laser made the car's gas tank explode, probably more due to something about the car than due to the strength of the laser, I'm guessing. Couldn't have happened to a nicer guy!"

A maid brought coffee. As she poured, Jack Horton was let in by a security guard.

"I just had a meeting with Israeli intelligence, and I thought you'd want to hear this, Mister Ambassador."

Hastings invited him to come in and asked Marshall to stay. Alexandra left the room.

"The Israelis have debriefed the Rafael employees and interrogated the terrorists. Each side states the laser attacks could have caused many more casualties. But both the terrorists and the Israeli scientists seem to want credit for the moderation. Habib, al Khalil's Ph.D.—he was educated in the U.S., by the way—is the one who figured out the weapon and fired it. He claims that he thought al Khalil's orders were too inhumane, that he, Habib, had never signed on to commit mass murder. So, although he had no choice but to do as he was told, he said, he dragged his feet to delay the second strike.

"Eventually, as we know, Steve made his escape and stopped the second strike from taking place. We got a similar but not identical story from debriefing the Israeli scientists. One couple in particular—they're husband and wife—said that when they were forced to tell this fellow Habib how the weapon functioned, they intentionally misinformed him about the power settings."

"I'm not surprised," Marshall said. "Human nature at work. Al Khalil's attack has changed the politics of the entire Middle East. We'll be sorting out the positive from the negative for a long time."

Hastings stirred his coffee.

"You're right. This provides a window of opportunity that we need to exploit quickly. Governments from Marrakech to Bangladesh must give their people the hope they now get only from the extremists. Then the Salafists' base, their recruitment pool, will disappear."

Marshall turned toward Hastings.

"You're being an optimist. That is not going to be their first priority; short-term survival, clinging to power, is going to trump your program. The first step the Arab governments will take is to try to do away with the Israeli weapon. They can't do it by force of arms, so they'll want to neutralize it through some sort of international weapons disarmament, or try to make it an illegal weapon, like gas warfare after World War I.

"This is a wakeup call," he added. "I hope al Khalil's attack will have convinced the world that the Salafists are serious and are playing for keeps. These are not people who want to negotiate."

Alexandra returned to the living room and sat down.

"Kella has been through a terrible nightmare. She needs to stay here and decompress for a while. What about Steve, what are his plans?"

Marshall shrugged and said, "I suppose he'll go back to work, but we haven't had a chance to talk yet. I honestly don't know."

★   ★   ★

Kella stepped into Steve's room at the Ichilov Hospital of the Tel Aviv Medical Center and, before she could speak, Steve said, "Hey, look at this. They're talking about my departed schoolmate," pointing at the television suspended over the bed.

The speaker was a historian from the Jaffee Center of Strategic Studies.

"The history of warfare has progressed via a series of epoch-defining developments in weaponry and technology. The stirrup, probably developed by the Chinese sometime during the first few centuries A.D., gave mounted horsemen the stability to wield weapons with longer reach and range, using the horse as the first true weapons platform. Later, the hand crossbow was so lethal that Pope Innocent II forbade its use in 1139 as a machine 'hateful to God and unfit for Christians.'"

Kella sat at the one chair beside the bed. She turned from the TV to Steve and began to speak, but Steve looked at her and raised his index finger to his lips. She sat back and waited for the end of the presentation. Her eyes wandered over the medical equipment beside the bed, which among other things kept tabs on his heartbeat: normal.

Thank God, she thought.

The historian continued about the history of weaponry, some of which Kella found dull, until he moved up to more familiar weapons.

"In the hands of the Japanese in December 1941, the airplane, which had seen only fledgling service in World War I, shifted the balance of naval power across the Pacific in a single week. The submarine, which had first appeared in the last quarter of the eighteenth century, came into its own as a terribly effective weapon of war in World War II.

"'Little Boy' and 'Fat Man,' the first atomic weapons dropped on Hiroshima and Nagasaki in 1945, led to the immediate surrender of the Japanese Empire and the dawn of the nuclear age.

"Military technology stepped into space the day al Khalil used the Israeli laser against his apostate foes."

Kella smoothed the hair away from Steve's forehead.

"How does it feel to have a place in history, to be the guy who stopped al Khalil from sacrificing thousands of people to his ego?"

Steve just shrugged. She imagined it was too much to take in so soon afterward.

"The full story hasn't leaked out yet, how close al Khalil came to firing that second strike. But that's not why I'm here. How are you feeling? Ready to go home?"

"As soon as they let me out. Are you coming with me? To Virginia, I mean."

"Do I look like a nurse? Only when you're fully rehabilitated."

"Well, everything works just fine right now. Lock the door and I'll give you a test run."

She pouted, "If everything 'worked'," and she placed quotations marks in the air in front of her, "your heartbeat should be much faster when I'm in the room."

He laughed and immediately winced, placing his hand against the left side of his chest.

"Come here," he said, and tugged her in for a kiss.

"You are lucky to be alive," she said. "I just spoke to the doctor. He said the bullet hit a rib and was diverted or it could have hit your heart. I brought you some newspapers, by the way."

Steve picked one up and scanned the front page.

"Listen to this. An influential moderate *imam* is calling for a joint international *fatwa* against the radicals. He said Islam is a great religion and must not fear the twenty-first century, and also that a good Muslim need not revert to practices that made sense a thousand years ago."

Kella took the paper and glanced at it.

"Well, it's a start. The Muslim moderates have been the silent majority. If they take charge of their future, the radicals are history."

She paused a second and, with a gleam in her eyes and a smile, said, "Did you ask me about travel plans? I have some loose ends to take care of in Paris, and then I'm on my way to Virginia, ready or not."

ACKNOWLEDGEMENTS

All of the events and characters in this story are imaginary—with one exception; Steve is modeled on our son Christopher, who died in 2002 and to whom this book is dedicated. The settings and backgrounds are factual. I have personally run clandestine operations in most of the countries where the story takes place. Similarly, although I do not claim to be an Islamic scholar, I studied Islam at Johns Hopkins School of International Studies and lived in Islamic countries for many years. While the Islamic content has been double-checked by others with better academic credentials, I take full responsibility for any error.

I have often been urged to write an autobiography. But there are many biographies available, prompted by a variety of motivations, for those who are curious about the life and career of a CIA operations officer. Although it is natural to be proud of one's life accomplishments, and I am no different, my story would not add much to theirs. A novel allows the author to entertain as well as educate. Fictional characters can say and act out their convictions to reflect their worldviews, which can be centuries apart, as they are in this story. For example, while the structures of our international system are still based on the sovereign state concepts of the 1648 Treaty of Westphalia, bolstered by nineteenth century nationalism, many Muslims are working toward a borderless world subservient to the laws of Islam—it is not a subject for negotiation. This story is built around this conflict of views. Presenting the issues in a novel was more fun to write and, I hope, will be more fun to read about than eye-glazing dates and treaties.

I wish to thank all those who encouraged me along the way and for their willingness to spend the time to read part or all of the manuscript, make suggestions, and point out weaknesses: Rita Callahan, Thérèse and Elise, Brittany and Preston, John Panama, Dr. David McCuan, Dr. Barry Goodfield, Denise Constantini, Fred Hill, Philip Giraldi and Philip Gioia. Special thanks to Jeff Cox, successful author in his own right, without whose initial help I probably would not have begun what turned out to be a more challenging project spread over a much longer period than I had anticipated. The book would not have reached publication without the personal interest and generous support of Haggai Carmon, author of the Dan Gordon thriller series. Thanks also to Jordan Rosenfeld, who edited the original manuscript; likewise to Phil Berardelli, publisher of Mountain Lake Press, who produced the updated version of *The Caliphate*.

I'm very grateful to Porter Goss for his attention-grabbing Introduction. Porter, my friend and former CIA colleague, was a member of my Junior Officer Trainee class, a group of dedicated and bright Americans who would have been successful in any career they chose. Our country was lucky they chose the CIA.

Finally, thanks to my live-in editor, my wife Cathy, who experienced the book's several lives and made many helpful suggestions and corrections, big and small.

Made in the USA
Middletown, DE
12 May 2021